MW01135562

Delvers LLC:
Obligations Incurred

Blaise Corvin

Delvers LLC: Obligations Incurred

Copyright ©2017 by Blaise Corvin

All rights reserved.

No part of this work may be used or reproduced in any manner whatsoever without written permission except in the case of brief quotations embodied in critical articles or reviews.

Table of Contents

Dedication

This might be kind of weird, but I want to thank my dog.

Seriously. Hear me out!

I've been through a lot over the last 9 years, and my terrible, grumpy puppy has been with me for every step. Sure, she's antisocial, she hates women (which makes dating problematic), she's mildly special needs, she can be utterly disgusting, and requires a little extra care…

But she's also unfailing loyal and protective.

I love this dog with my whole heart.

She can't read this, and she probably won't be with me much longer, but thank you, Lulu. Thank you for being my best friend. Thank you for being my family. I will always love you. You're like the daughter I will never have.

You left an enormous, positive impact on my life. I will always, always remember you, and hopefully, others will as well thanks to this dedication.

-BC

Foreword

Hello readers! This book is the second of a series that I would classify as a subtle LitRPG Fantasy adventure.

You might be curious what LitRPG is. The acronym literally means, Literary (or Literature) RPG (Role Playing Game). These types of stories have been extremely popular in Russia and other countries. They're just now making an impact in the West!

LitRPG is usually a funky mix of Fantasy and Sci Fi. The types of stories can vary, but what most LitRPG novels have in common is some clear method of progression (like leveling up) as well as a setting that most gamers can immediately relate to.

I really had a lot of fun writing this book. If you'd like to visit my web serial website, the URL is http://blaise-corvin.com/

I also have a writer's note in the back of the book with a whole mess of links as well as a few reading suggestions. If you're on Facebook and would like to join a LitRPG group, the link for the LitRPG Society is here:

https://www.facebook.com/groups/LitRPGsociety/

I hope you enjoy your time on Ludus again with Henry and Jason!

CHAPTER ONE

Mirana Summons

Jason was nervous, even with a longsword riding on his hip. He gaped at the ornate hallways of the Mirana Government Building, which he thought actually resembled a palace. His friend Henry was walking next to him as they both followed their young friend Bezzi-ibbi, his mother Henna-ibbi, and his birth mother Banna-ibbi. Jason had no idea why both of Bezzi-ibbi's mothers had come with them but his father, Hajim-ibbi, had stayed behind.

Mo'hali customs and leadership roles were weird. Every time Jason thought he had the Jaguar Clan figured out, he was proven wrong.

Their whole group was wearing fancy clothing. Since Jason and Henry were adopted members of the Jaguar Clan, they wore the same fine robes of black and green as Bezzi-ibbi and his mothers. They all bore weapons as well. The fact he was allowed his sword had surprised him at first, but then Jason reasoned that, on a world where people could use magic, trying to control bladed weapons would've been fairly silly.

Of course, Mo'hali Heroes could suppress magic in an area if they were near the same strength as a mage or stronger, but Jason was beginning to realize just how rare Heroes were. He snapped himself out of his wandering thoughts and began studying his opulent surroundings again. His group was silent as they followed their guide, a friendly, long-faced Terran woman in her middle years.

Jason absently noted that their guide was wearing the same red uniform as every other Mirana city worker. The black pants, red shirt, and red vest were unchanged with the exception of different badges sewn on the chest. He reasoned the badges noted rank, or position, or both. Their guide's bobbing ponytail was a welcome distraction for Jason to focus on so he could distract himself from thinking about darker, more upsetting things.

The whole group was still reeling from tragedy.

It had been two weeks since Henry had discovered George Jacobs dead, murdered, and the rest of the farming village slaughtered. Since then, Mareen had thrown herself into providing the villagers proper burial, paying off their debts, and hiring investigators to discover who had killed her grandfather and friends.

So far, they'd gotten no new information back. In fact, one

highly recommended investigator had disappeared altogether. He wasn't turning in reports anymore.

Mareen had even called in a favor at the Adventurers Guild, putting out a notice that her grandfather, the late adventurer Thato Jacobs' father, had been murdered. A large number of adventurers had been shocked and tried to help, not least because it had occurred so close to the city. The fact the murder had actually been part of a full-fledged massacre had not been advertised, but some adventurers had found out anyway.

Truth be told, Jason had actually been expecting to be summoned somewhere for questioning. He wasn't entirely sure how law enforcement worked on Ludus or in the country of Tolstey in particular, but a massacre right outside the Mirana city walls definitely had to be of interest to somebody. The night Henry and Mareen had discovered the carnage visited upon Mareen's grandfather and friends, Aodh's nearby family, the O'Breens, had alerted the Guard.

However, while Jason had felt he might get questioned by the Guard, he had not expected to be summoned by Mirana's governor.

Aodh and Mareen both had been invited to the audience as well, attendance optional, but neither of them had chosen to come. Mareen was buried in responsibility, but the way her eyes were puffy every morning made it obvious that she was crying every night. Henry looked haggard too, probably doing his best to comfort his girlfriend while working through his own grief. Jason felt heartbroken, but at least he hadn't seen George's remains.

He could go without that image in his head for the rest of his life. *Thank God for small favors,* he thought.

Aodh hadn't come out of his room much for the past week. The boy was listless. Jason honestly didn't know what to do to raise morale for the members of Delvers LLC, the adventuring company he owned with Henry.

After walking down multiple corridors that all looked the same, they came to heavy, metal-bound double doors flanked by masked, spear-wielding guards. The guards were Mo'hali, both of them rabbit-race, and Jason wondered if at least one was a Hero. He figured if the Jaguar Clan could get pet Heroes, rulers probably could too.

Casta, their guide through the Mirana government building, pushed open the doors and ushered them inside before vanishing down the hall.

The room was not as opulent as the rest of the building, it was actually fairly plain. It reminded Jason of a generic family room on Earth, with the addition of a large desk in the corner and a solid-looking table against one wall. A few cozy couches with sofa tables sat in aesthetically pleasing locations. A few other tables made for handy flat surfaces. Tasteful artwork lined the walls.

Two people in cloaks were sitting on the vintage-looking Earth-style couch to one side. Two Mirana Guards in red uniforms stood at the far end of the room. One, a young Terran man, stood stiffly, eyes darting around. The other Guard, an Areva woman with dusky skin, seemed bored and picked at her fingernails.

The last person in the room, a Terran woman with blonde hair in her late 30s, sat at the head of the table. She had sheaves of paperwork before her and muttered as she flipped through a document. She wore a white halter dress with embroidered red flowers. Her red lacquered fingernails tapped on the table as she read.

It didn't take Jason long to figure out the woman at the table was probably the governor of Mirana. She was thin with pale skin, an upturned nose, low cheekbones, freckles, and a well-defined chin. Her hair was gathered in a bun on top of her head with two thin bronze knives stuck through to keep it in place. An ornate staff leaned against the wall. The fact it was white and decorated with flowers made its owner somewhat obvious.

Jason decided the governor looked like an irritated librarian with a big, solid stick within arm's reach. The thought didn't help his nerves.

Without looking up, the governor said, "Right on time. I appreciate that, especially since nobody in this God-forsaken place has wristwatches. Do you know how hard it is to schedule anything around here when nobody ever knows what time it is?

"The two Mirana Guards are Captain Haili and Lieutenant Boone. They have my full trust, and I believe one of you has met them already."

Henry cleared his throat and waved, "Nice to see you again."

Lieutenant Boone nodded. Captain Haili continued to pick at her fingernails. Jason watched the scene with interest, especially with how Bezzi-ibbi's mothers remained quiet and still. In Mo'hali culture, the guards were acting very rude. This behavior would not be tolerated at the Jaguar Clan House. Jason was fascinated by how the Mo'hali women adapted to the situation. Of course, he realized Mo'hali merchant Families would have to be skilled in multiple social settings or they wouldn't have been so influential and successful.

The next exchange proved Jason still had a lot to learn. The governor briefly glanced up before shaking her head and rolling her eyes. Her voice cracked out, "Henna-ibbi, you put those claws away right now! This is my house, and you are not allowed to go rampaging around because someone hurt your feelings or insulted someone's honor. You want to show honor? Calm down.

"Besides, Captain Haili is probably older than all of us in this room put together, so even by your own standards, she can act however she wants. Plus, I had to beat her at chess on a bet just to get her to come here. You are not allowed to attack her. Besides, she can probably beat you up."

Jason was aghast, but the governor didn't stop there. Her flood of words continued, "You there, boy! Jason, right? Close your mouth or you might catch flies. You just came from Earth? The

US? How much does gas cost now? Actually, never mind, I don't want to know.

"You know, when that charlatan Dolos abducts new people, it actually makes being stuck on Ludus worse. Every time I hear about home, it's like I just got trapped here all over again. But you know the worst part? I had a husband once on this planet, and before he died, it seemed like every other woman around was angry at me. They thought I was selfish, that I was 'hoarding' him for myself. I'm afraid to get married again or I might get run out of office. This world is a hellhole full of crazy people."

Captain Haili sighed and said, "You know, this is one reason I hate coming to these things with you, Maryanne. All you ever do is complain about Ludus like somehow we're not all stuck here too. You moan about missing electricity and 'television' like your primitive, backwards technology can even compare to the Empire I left behind. You should quit whining before I stick my boot up your butt."

"I could have you arrested."

"I'm one of the people that arrests people for you and leads the other people doing the arresting. Good luck with that. Now act like a grownup or I'll douse you with water." Lieutenant Boone looked incredibly uncomfortable as he stood next to his superior.

"I'll call you an elf," the governor threatened. Her nose twitched.

Captain Haili narrowed her eyes. "You. Wouldn't. Dare."

Suddenly, the governor grinned and stood up, putting her work down. "You're right, I wouldn't. I suppose I should introduce myself."

The governor met the gaze of each member of Jason's group, slowly placing her hands on her hips as she faced them. She effortlessly exuded self-confidence and authority. "My name is Governor Maryanne Holtz. For now, you may refer to me as Governor Holtz or 'Madam.'

"I have been the governor, the ruler of Mirana, for over ten years local time. I came to Ludus in my mid-thirties in 1965. I was an art teacher. Now I've probably killed more people than the Boston Strangler.

"You probably noticed I'm looking pretty damn good for an old lady. Well, that's because I'm an orb-Bonded. True, I'm not wearing a mask like the rest of you"—she gestured at the masks Jason, Henry, and Bezzi-ibbi wore—"but you still aren't picking up my name or orb information over your left eye. This is because I know things you don't.

"And this brings us to why I sent for you to come today. You've been conscripted. Congratulations! You just joined the Tolstey Intelligence Agency. I've taken the liberty of submitting a discreet request to the Adventurers Guild and already let them know you took the contract. It's quite lucrative, but unfortunately this means the Guild will not be able to give you any more work or buy any dungeon treasure from you while the contract is active.

I apologize, but you really don't have a choice in this."

Henry managed to get a word in edgewise. "What are you—"

Governor Holtz talked right over him, "Calm down, young man. This will be easier for all of us if you shut up and listen until I'm done.

"Where was I? Ah, yes. You've just been conscripted. While I am the bearer of bad news, I was not the one who came up with this decision. That would be Queen Smrithi, and she—"

"Is that her first name?" asked Henry. Jason mentally facepalmed.

"Yes," Governor Holtz answered slowly, not trying to hide her irritation.

"If she goes by her first name, why did you tell us to call you by your last name? She's your boss, right?"

"Young man, I sincerely hope I'm mistaken, but I have the feeling we might not get along. Your name is Henry, right?" Henry nodded. "Let me make this clear. I am a terribly petty person with a slow, but potent temper. If you interrupt me one more time, bad things will happen to you. Am I making myself clear?" Henry grimaced but nodded, and Jason sincerely hoped his stony-faced friend would shut the hell up.

From the back of the room, Captain Haili chuckled softly but the governor ignored her. She cleared her throat and continued, "Okay, I'm going to skip some of the other things I was planning to say and get right to the heart of the matter since you seem like simple—I mean, blunt folks.

"Tolstey is not a powerful country. In fact, we might be the least powerful country on this whole planet. We have the weakest dungeons, the weakest adventurers, the weakest army, and we just don't have that many people. However, most of the country is run by humans, Terrans, and we have a good relationship with Berber to the north. They're another Terran-run country.

"The mountain range between our countries makes it unlikely they'll ever invade, and we don't have much for them to bother with here anyway. It wouldn't be worth the trouble. The fact Berber keeps nasty groups of monsters from growing out of control and running amok across the whole continent makes us appreciate them staying right where they are, too.

"Recently, someone has been trying to attack our countries from within. We have a suspicion who is responsible, but we don't know for sure. And not knowing things is bad.

"See, Tolstey may possibly be the weakest country on Ludus, but we have an excellent Intelligence network. We know about the war coming between Dolos and his rival. We know all about your exploits and about Delvers LLC, which I think is kind of a stupid name, by the way. Then again, our adventuring group called ourselves, 'Bedrock Stone Age Family.'"

Captain Haili snorted and said, "I still don't understand that reference."

"That's fine, dear, you don't have to. Don't try thinking too hard, I'm sure there will be something for you to break sooner or later." The governor sniffed. "Anyway, the point is that we know most of what happens in Tolstey and on Ludus in general.

"This means we know all about the massacre at Georgetown farm two weeks ago and the murder of George Jacobs, one of our retired Intelligence agents."

Jason was shocked. George had been a spy? If that was the case, what had he been doing out in the middle of nowhere when they'd met him? Then again, the revelation explained the man's uncommon knack for learning languages and writing everything down. Mareen had all of George's old books. Maybe they could find some more clues about the man's past life in them later on.

Governor Holtz rolled her eyes. "I can already see what you're all thinking. You obviously didn't hear me say, 'retired.' George served faithfully and was no longer activated; in fact, he quit when his son was murdered and he began caring for his granddaughter. However, we keep tabs on our past operatives. They tend to retire with secrets, and we want to keep it that way. You know, he actually sent me a note endorsing Delvers LLC, which was why I largely left you alone until now.

"However, things change. George was murdered, and we have reason to believe it's linked to the bandits you wiped out, the warehouse you burned down, and a few other things that have happened in Mirana and the capital of Tolstey, Taretha.

"Your exploits have proved that you're fairly capable. Mor

importantly, you have history with these insurgents now. Our friend from Berber," she said, gesturing to the larger cloaked figure sitting on the couch, "has asked for reinforcements. Berber has its own problems.

"In fact, all of this is happening at the worst possible time. There are three continents on Ludus, which is about half the size of Earth. Right now, our continent is experiencing a huge surge in monster activity, especially within Berber. Another continent is at war, and the third and most dangerous continent we barely hear anything from. Now we have a war of the gods in a few years to prepare for, and on top of all that, we have this new problem.

"See, at first glance, all the assassination attempts, organized crime, manufacturing of gunpowder, all these things seemed like ham-handed attempts by a country across the ocean to weaken us. However, we may have bigger problems on our hands.

"Some of our best people have been gathering information on the insurgents for a while. Quite a few of them have disappeared. However, we learned something disturbing recently. Some of the people they'd been tracking were holding dark, religious ceremonies, some even involving human sacrifice.

"We think they might be a cult worshipping a dark god. What's more, we're not yet sure why they're doing what they're doing, but they could be trying to involve their god as a third player into Dolos's pissing contest.

Henna-ibbi's fur bristled. "Dark magic." She growled, the

sound so low it made Jason's eyeballs vibrate. "Which god? What does it look like?"

Captain Haili answered, "Asag. A really nasty one. His symbol is a diagram-looking thing with crosses up top and circles on the bottom. So far, we just have confessions, though. There's nothing to actually verify that we're dealing with cultists and not seditionists."

"Captain Haili is correct," Governor Holtz said, nodding. "But Asag's symbol was drawn on the wall of George's house in blood. We still don't have anything to tie the Georgetown massacre to any of the other occurrences, but the symbol showing up at all is concerning."

Suddenly, Henry stepped forward and placed a large coin on the governor's desk. When she saw it, she gasped. "It looks like you have verification now," grated Henry. "I found this on the body of a man we killed while escaping the gunpowder warehouse. If these are the people who killed George, just tell me where they are and get out of my way."

Delvers LLC: Obligations Incurred

CHAPTER TWO

Magic Tech

Jason wasn't quite as surprised as the others when Henry stepped forward with the coin. He'd known Henry still had it, and he'd recognized the mark on the wall in George's house after all the carnage was removed. However, he was curious what the governor would say.

"Not so fast, young man," the governor said, as she quickly recovered from her surprise and shook her head reprovingly. "You know, I understand the anger, I understand wanting to avenge your friend, but you really have no idea what I'm about to tell you. If you want to survive on Ludus, you need to keep a clear head."

"I dunno, we've done pretty good so far," Henry grated.

Governor Holtz shook her head. "No, you've gotten incredibly lucky. Even if I told you exactly where to go, even if you took your entire posse with you, including your very impressive bronze tank, you'd still be destroyed. You know nothing about this world. In fact, perhaps I can ask our guest to explain it to you." She gestured at the larger of the robed figures on the couch.

As they focused on him, the man threw his cowl back. Henry hissed and whispered, "I'm sensing a shit ton of magic from that guy." Jason nodded.

The man had dark hair, dark eyes, slightly tan skin, a triangular face, and a hooked nose. He was clean shaven, kept his hair short, and stood average height for a Terran. He cocked an eyebrow at Henry and flatly pronounced, "You got lucky." Then he shrugged.

The governor rolled her eyes, "Can you please elaborate, Gonzo? Maybe introduce yourself, even speculate on this coin Henry showed us? You were the one that delivered this request from your country in the first place."

"Alright, no problem. My name is Ryan Gonzolez, but everyone calls me Gonzo. I'm originally from Earth, and I came to Ludus about ten years ago. My background on Earth is as a US Air Force med lab tech. After I got out of the military, I was a sheriff for a few years until I found myself on Ludus. Now I'm a Berber Intelligence Officer. You are going to be working with me and travelling to Berber, the country to the north."

Jason wasn't sure what to think at this point. The conversation wasn't going as he'd expected. *What did he just say?*

Gonzo gestured at the other person on the couch, "This is my apprentice, Vitaliya." The smaller cloaked figure threw her hood back to reveal a pretty redhead girl in her late teens or early 20s. Jason mentally shook his head. No, this was Ludus, so she could have been any age. He had a feeling he was correct, though. He also had a feeling she was an orb-Bonded or a mage too. He glanced at Henry, and his friend gave a tiny nod, affirming Jason's suspicion that she had some kind of magic mojo.

After Vitaliya nodded to everyone in the room, Gonzo continued, "A demonstration of how little you know might help. Henry, why don't you spar with Captain Haili over there?"

Henry was silent a moment before replying, "No."

Jason inwardly smiled as Gonzo sputtered for a moment. The man had obviously not been expecting a refusal. A lot of people assumed that Henry was simple for some reason, but that was not the case. Not at all.

"Why not?"

Henry's answer was delivered evenly. "Because I'm not a fucking idiot. You wouldn't be telling me to fight her if you didn't think she would beat me. This is obviously to prove a point, especially since she's so cute and tiny. What's more, I caught the governor saying the captain is older than all of us, and I'm automatically wary of anyone the leader of this entire city seems to respect. Last but not least, if something went wrong and you misjudged her ability to beat me, this is a tiny room. I don't want to sling magic around near so many people, especially people I definitely don't want to piss off."

Captain Haili laughed, the sound like bells falling on concrete. "Maryanne, you may not like this kid, but I'm taking a shine to him. This group seems to be full of innovative survivors with brains. Perhaps the future isn't so bleak after all."

The governor ignored her.

Gonzo blinked, but to his credit, he readjusted quickly. "Fine. Be that way. We still need a demonstration, though. I'm going to ask again, could you please attack the captain?"

Henry gave the man a deadpan look and turned his attention to Captain Haili. "Really?" he asked.

"It might not be a bad idea to see this with your own eyes. I was planning on kicking you through the doorway if you actually attacked me, but luckily, you're not a moron. I hear you can shoot projectiles. Just do that."

"At you?"

"Yes."

"Fine."

Jason's raw nerves grew more frayed as Henry unslung his rifle from his shoulder. Over the last week, Henry had tinkered with all his inventions, probably as part of his own way to deal with grief over George's death. One result of his efforts was that his rifle now featured a pump action mechanism. Henry practiced with it—a lot.

Henry shouldered the rifle and hesitated, but Captain Haili made a beckoning motion. Henry shrugged, muttered, "Fuck it," and the air-splitting crack of a sonic boom rattled the entire room. The air in front of Captain Haili grew opaque as Henry's projectile slammed into a barrier surrounding the dark Areva woman. After the impact, pieces of the gold projectile were directed to the side, embedding into the wall. However, Henry didn't stop there. He pumped through his entire magazine, sending slug after slug screaming towards his target at hypersonic speeds.

While Henry was firing, after a brief moment of confusion, Gonzo and Vitaliya plugged their ears but didn't react much other than that. Meanwhile, Lieutenant Boon fell to the floor and scampered away from Captain Haili as fast as he could. Governor Holtz's reaction was most interesting. Her eyes widened and her entire form exploded into dust, hanging in the air before it moved to one corner of the room and re-solidified into the form of the governor, her white dress unmarred.

Everyone in the Delvers LLC group was accustomed to Henry's inventions by now and simply covered their ears.

After Henry was out of ammo, he slapped another magazine into place and shouldered his weapon again, but Captain Haili held up a forestalling hand. "I think that's enough. You get the point, and I think a few more shots would actually take my shield down. Let's not go that far. However, I should probably show you —"

The door to the chamber burst open and the Mo'hali guards rushed in, spears at the ready. Jason began feeling a strange tingle in the back of his head, almost like his magic was writhing around. It seemed he was right that at least one of the guards outside had been a Hero. The governor's voice cracked out like a whip, "Get out of here at this instant! I ordered you not to disturb us regardless of any noise!"

The pressure on the back of Jason's mind eased and the guards immediately left the room with sheepish expressions, closing the door behind them.

Captain Haili shook her head and said, "That was exciting. Now watch, please." She held her wrist up and several small beads detached from a bracelet, hung in the air for a second, then zipped forward, embedding into the stone wall to one side of the room. After that, she drew her sword and cut in one smooth motion, the blade generating a thin wave of air that rushed forward to cut the wall over 20 feet away. "I think you get the point now."

Henry nodded and Jason was fascinated. Now that he was looking for it, he noticed that Captain Haili was covered in jewelry and various straps or buckles that could all be magic devices. Jason scratched his head and asked, "How many people have items like you do, Captain Haili?"

The Areva woman grimaced and replied, "You can call me Naloo when we're in private. I get tired of hearing my title all the time." She glanced sternly at Lieutenant Boone. "I'm still 'Captain' to you, though, understand?" The other Guard nodded.

Captain Haili continued, "Fewer people than you might think

own gear like this, actually. See, every magic item, whether a burning sword or a ring that creates shields, is considered a magic item, and on Ludus, enchanted items can only have a certain number of owners."

Jason nodded; he'd already heard about this. "Three, right?"

"Correct. So if you see a magic item for sale, it can accept at least one more owner. However, if someone is using one and you take it or they give it to you, it could crumble to dust depending on how many owners it's had.

"The rarity of enchanted items, plus their average costs, makes it hard for most people to have many. But like Maryanne said, I'm fairly old. I could probably get older if I bonded with an orb. However, I hate Dolos and I want nothing to do with that, what do you say? *Rat bastard.*" She said the last portion in accented English.

"English?" Henry asked.

The governor said in English as well, "Yes, I taught her some years ago. I guess I can't completely forget the teacher in me." She spoke with a Welsh accent. The powerful woman looked wistful for a moment before switching back to Ludan, saying, "This is another reason I hate running into people from Earth. It reminds me of my Cardiff…" Her voice trailed off into silence.

Henry spoke up, his voice terse, "That was really impressive and all, but what the hell does it prove?"

"It proves you don't know much about this world," Captain

Haili said, shrugging. "I've heard about all your adventures so far. You've done a great job surviving, but you've only fought small fry. We don't even know the highest rank of Bonded on Ludus. There are entire strike teams of highly trained soldiers like me out there with weapons like mine. They could be Areva, warriors who can literally train over a hundred years to master combat styles effective on Ludus.

"There are other countries with entire armies...well, small armies of Bonded that train together for war! Despite how Maryanne speaks of me, I'm just a Mirana Guard with a few handy gadgets. Yet I could still be a threat to you, if not kill you both. What's more, enchanted tools aren't affected as strongly by Mo'hali Heroes as Bonded are. Trust me when I say I would not go down easy in a fight.

"And on that note, you probably still think of every conflict as a slugging match or throwing power around. Ludus doesn't work that way.

"You saw what Maryanne just did. I wouldn't bring this up if you hadn't already seen her power, but imagine a sandstorm approaching you and sand filling your lungs. How would you fight that? Not with a rifle," she said, pointing at Henry's weapon. "Although that is such a fine weapon I kind of want to marry this boy right now so I can touch all his inventions." She licked her lips.

What in the hell is it with Henry attracting all these scary older women? Jason thought, bemused. Henry looked uncomfortable.

Governor Holtz clapped her hands and announced, "That's enough! I'm going to end this now before my Guard Captain starts preying on confused, defenseless boys who haven't even been on Ludus for a year. Seriously, Naloo, do you have any shame?"

Captain Haili shrugged. "Nope, don't think so. And he did say I was small and cute." She made some kind of sound, almost a purr. Jason wasn't sure who looked more uncomfortable, Henry or Lieutenant Boone.

"Fuck me…" muttered Henry.

"That's the idea." The woman's eyes sparkled.

The governor cleared her throat and announced, "That is quite enough. I'm very busy and I have another meeting soon. Henry, Jason, you have your orders.

"I want to congratulate for joining the Tolstey Intelligence Corps! You are technically in the Guard for the duration of your mission as well. Your direct superior is Agent Gonzo. Your contacts from this point forward in the Mirana Guard are Lieutenant Boone and Captain Haili. Do you have any questions?"

Henry shook his head, asking, "Why us? And this whole thing sounds important. Why not give us a choice? In fact, why not send a hundred, no, a thousand people on this mission?"

The governor tapped her chin and shook her head. "When you

get to be as old as I am, you prefer forcing people to do things instead of asking for volunteers. I like predictable results. I don't care for being disappointed. I understand your confusion, but I have a lifetime of experience at this. For everything else, Agent Gonzo can explain. Now shoo."

The guards and the spies started walking towards the door. Jason quickly asked, "So you're giving us money?"

Governor Holz looked at Jason like he was an idiot. "I am sending you on a mission to possibly stop a war before it starts and prevent utter catastrophe. Your mission involves evil magic and cults. Of course you get a bloody budget! What, did you think I was going to send you on a critical quest with no help or money? That would be stupid."

"Well, yeah, I guess." Jason had a lifetime of expectations from video games, so the governor's willingness to fund their mission surprised him. The audience wasn't going exactly as he had feared, and he had to admit he was relieved. It sucked that he and Henry were being conscripted, but arguing about it now would obviously not be a smart move.

"Just follow Gonzo's directions," the governor said, rolling her eyes. "Dismissed."

* * *

In the hallway, Gonzo bowed to Bezzi-ibbi. Then he bowed to Bezzi-ibbi's mother Banna-ibbi and his *rekke*, non-birth mother, Henna-ibbi. "I apologize for being rude in the room out of necessity. I greet the Jaguar Clan."

"At least you have some manners," Henna-ibbi grunted.

"Sister, leave it. You should get back to the Clan house and eat." Banna-ibbi gently took her arm.

Henna-ibbi crossed her arms. "Yes, fine. Let's go. Jason-ibbi, Henry-ibbi, please come see us when you are done. The governor made this a Clan matter by inviting us here." She turned to Bezzi-ibbi, saying, "Since this one is a *Hero*"—she snarled the word —"he may go where he will."

The two Jaguar Clan women left at a stately pace, following a servant that materialized out of nowhere to guide them.

When they were far out of earshot, Henry muttered, "I'm glad she's not my mom, *rekke* or anything else." Jason could only silently agree.

Off to the side, the two Berber agents stood silently. Jason approached and asked, "Ryan, er—Mr. Gonzalez, could you please tell me what the hell is going on?"

The man smiled and Jason sensed some legitimate compassion from him. "Please, call me Gonzo. I know this is probably a lot to take in, and I promise you that I'll explain everything, including how you got conscripted into this. However, I think first you need to have a conversation with the Jaguar Clan. I will meet you tomorrow morning for our first meeting.

"That said, I have seen your Battlewagon and I am very impressed. First, I should probably explain something. I used to play a few games when I was a kid, and I recognize some of the similarities between games on Earth and life on Ludus. So here is some knowledge for you: if Ludus were an RPG world, Tolstey would be the starting zone."

"The starting zone?" Every near-death experience Jason had had since his arrival on Ludus suddenly flashed through his mind. "Seriously?"

"Yes." Gonzo's expression was somber. "You see, there is much more advanced technology and magical devices in Berber than here in Tolstey. There are also barely any people in Tolstey... but we can talk about all that tomorrow. For now, I need to give you some instructions and ask you for a trade."

"We're listening." Henry's voice was short, but Jason appreciated his friend trying to be polite.

"Your instruction for now is that you need to talk to Captain Haili and the lieutenant over there for your budget from the city. Actually, it's money the Tolstey queen earmarked for this mission, so they don't have a choice." He chuckled, the sound surprisingly warm. Jason hadn't been expecting a legit spy to be so likable!

"And the favor?" Henry urged.

"Yes, as I said, Berber has many things that Tolstey doesn't have. However, most Magi-artisans, mages that craft magic tools, usually only create machines for important work or public transport. There are weapons and vehicles for war, too, but those belong to the military. Your Battlewagon is somewhat unique."

"Spit it out." Henry was beginning to sound less patient.

"Okay, okay." Gonzo held his hands up. "I want a motorcycle."

"A what?" Henry frowned.

Well, that came out of left field. Jason felt bemused watching his friend and the spy continue their bizarre conversation.

"Yes, you see, back on Earth, I used to love riding my dirt bike for fun." Gonzo's eyes positively gleamed as he continued, "I think you can probably make a vehicle smaller than your Battlewagon while using the same tech, right?"

Henry seemed to think about it for a while before replying, "You seem very well informed, but I guess I should expect this from a spy. Maybe. What's in it for us?"

Gonzo grinned and pulled a folded piece of paper out of his trouser pocket. "You must have noticed by now that I am hiding my Holder status from casual detection. This is a note explaining how Holders or Heros can do it."

Henry's eyes widened. "Casual detection…you mean like the info scrolling over people's eye?"

"Exactly."

Gonzo definitely had Jason's attention. Out the corner of his eye, he caught Bezzi-ibbi focusing on the conversation as well. Every member of Delvers LLC was used to wearing their distinctive masks, but it'd be nice if they could take them off if they wanted to. Plus, a few other adventuring companies had already begun copying them. The look wasn't as unique as it had been before.

Jason spoke up, "That won't be cheap. Henry uses up a lot of materials."

Gonzo shrugged. "After you talk to Captain Haili, I doubt you will have any money problems. What do you say?"

"Just one bike?" asked Henry.

"Two, if possible. One for me and one for my apprentice." Gonzo gestured towards the red-haired girl. She slightly narrowed her eyes, showing no other reaction.

Jason asked, "How long do we have until we leave?"

"You mean if you decide not to run away?" Gonzo smiled knowingly. "I was thinking we could head out in about two weeks. It will be a long journey, and we need to leave as soon as possible, but we don't want to be stupid about it. Preparations are important."

"Okay...done." Henry held his hand out for the paper.

Gonzo placed the note in Henry's hand, but before he let go, his entire demeanor changed. His jaw tensed, his eyes grew flat, and Jason thought the man suddenly looked very dangerous. Gonzo quietly said, "I suggest you destroy this after you read it. If you share this information with anyone outside of your company, I'll be forced to kill you and hunt down anyone you told. Information this powerful is guarded jealously. Please don't test my resolve. You're not just dealing with me right now; I'm acting as an emissary for my country."

Over his time on Ludus so far, Jason had begun listening to his instincts about approaching danger. They were currently screaming at him to take this man seriously.

"Alright," Henry said, pocketing the note.

"Good, good." Gonzo was smiling again. "I'll see you at your house tomorrow morning if you haven't run away. Please don't run away. I will find you, and it won't be pleasant. Goodbye," he said. With that, he began walking away, his apprentice following him. No government worker or servant came to lead them. For the first time, Jason noticed that the passing servants didn't look at Gonzo at all. They all seemed nervous.

How did I not notice that before? Jason wondered.

* * *

Jason, Henry, and Bezzi-ibbi headed to the Jaguar Clan House from the government building. On their way out, they took a letter of credit from Captain Haili, who said she'd be in touch. Before he'd left, Lieutenant Boone had sighed and instructed them to tell him if they needed anything else. He'd cautioned that they wouldn't get any more money or value than what was promised in the letter, though.

The letter of credit was riding in Jason's pocket. He still didn't really understand Tolstey currency and didn't really want to. He was planning to give the note to Mareen and be done with it. He knew that eventually he'd have to learn about Ludus currency, but it was terribly dry. He wished that everything matched up with Earth currency in multiples of ten like in fantasy books in games, but unfortunately, conversions on Ludus were nowhere near that simple.

As he walked, their group got some attention. He realized they had to appear like two men in opulent robes, armed to the teeth, traveling with a Jaguar Clan boy, all wearing masks. It was probably a bit of a sight. Jason ignored the murmurs and the finger pointing.

He hoped that Henry had his super senses turned up to notice any potential danger, but he knew better than to ask. Henry still felt their capture and imprisonment in the storage building when they'd arrived in Mirana had been partially his fault, and Jason agreed with him. He'd never say so out loud, though.

"Hey," he said, tapping Henry on the shoulder. "Are you going to grab Mareen and Aodh?" Mareen, Henry's girlfriend and their company's treasurer, lived with Henry in his room. Aodh, the Delvers LLC explosive triggerman, a 16-year-old mediocre fire mage, usually stayed in the garage. Through a cruel twist of fate, he looked almost entirely Fideli despite actually being mostly Terran. The nonhuman physical traits he'd inherited could be useful as an adventurer, but they had also made him an outcast for most of his life.

Bezzi-ibbi suddenly spoke in broken English, "Rark-han too, please." Jason's eyebrows went up. The kid was getting better at

English, which was fantastic since he refused to speak Luda like everyone else did.

Jason agreed with Bezzi-ibbi, they should get Rark-han. The one-armed wolf-race Mo'hali man followed Bezzi-ibbi as some sort of religious servant. He had simple quarters in the small home Bezzi-ibbi rented near Henry and Jason's house. Jason still wasn't sure he completely trusted the lupine man yet, but he was a part of their company.

Plus, Jason knew their new conscription affected them all. Every member of Delvers LLC deserved to be involved in the meeting. There was no use getting upset about it yet, but they were all pretty much over a barrel. Jason had felt the jaws of inevitability closing in on them ever since they'd gotten the summons to see the governor. He was disappointed that the feeling had been accurate.

Sure, they could have tried running away, but the reality was they had no other friends, no powerbase, and if they were wanted by the entire country, much less two countries, that would be a terrible choice to make in their very first year on Ludus.

"Yeah, I'll go," Henry replied. "Meet you there."

At the next street, Henry took a turn and Jason went the other way with Bezzi-ibbi. Jason knew Bezzi-ibbi was intelligent and could display a startling amount of wisdom, but he didn't want to burden the boy with more problems. Bezzi-ibbi was apparently lost in his own thoughts as well.

The rest of the walk to the Jaguar Clan House was quiet, and Jason wondered how the meeting would unfold.

CHAPTER THREE

Stepped on Tails

Henry had a lot on his mind as he approached the rental house he shared with Jason. The garage they'd built in the alley next to the house was locked up tight. It made Henry uncomfortable that they still had so much wealth in there, but burying it all under a few tons of bronze had helped make it more secure. The fact the buried loot was in a hole beneath their large, parked armored vehicle also made it unlikely that a casual thief would be able to steal anything.

Not that a casual thief would have escaped the attention of Rark-han. The big wolf man was constantly checking on the garage from the house Bezzi-ibbi rented across the street. Henry still felt it was a little strange the boy had had to rent his own house, but with Mareen living with Henry, Jason in his own room, and Aodh sleeping in the garage, their little house was already getting kind of crowded.

Henry wondered what would happen with Jason and Uluula. It seemed it had taken Uluula a long time to decide whether she was going to make their relationship official, but once she made up her mind, she didn't pussyfoot around. Jason never really had a chance.

Henry suddenly got a dark premonition as he picked up female voices. He was using his enhanced hearing and caught snippets of a conversation inside his house. He was still developing a habit of alternating between enhancing his various senses in waves. It was hard to control, especially his hearing, but he was finding the ability could come in handy.

He could tell the voices in the house belonged to Uluula and Mareen. That fact in itself made him nervous. He wasn't entirely sure why, but ever since Mareen and Uluula had begun forging a friendship, Henry had felt something looming over him, like someone had stepped on his grave.

He waved Rark-han over from where the Mo'hali man would probably be watching through the blinds across the street and slowed his pace. He wondered what the women were talking about. However, all he could catch was a muffled word or two. It sounded like they were speaking softly behind multiple closed doors. Henry's nervousness increased, although he didn't know why.

He loved Mareen, a fact he wasn't shy to acknowledge. She

was smart, brave, and had already accomplished a lot in her life despite living on a hellhole, monster-filled planet. The dark-skinned farmer turned adventurer showed flashes of wisdom and cunning at times that floored him. He had shittons of respect and admiration for her. In fact, Henry sometimes forgot how young she really was…which was a problem for him. He still felt vaguely creepy for dating a 19-year-old when he was about to turn 30.

He knew he shouldn't feel odd, that love didn't have an age, and pairings with far greater age differences were common on Ludus. In fact, he knew people sometimes got married at 13, at least in Tolstey, same as people used to on Earth in the last hundred or two hundred years. In fact, Mo'hali had really, really strange marriage customs. Intellectually, he knew that 10 years wouldn't even be that much age difference on Earth. And to top it all off, he and Mareen were capable of living a few hundred years due to their orbs.

Henry had no reason to feel the way he did, but he couldn't deny it was still something he was working through.

He thought it was funny how Jason was freaked out about the possibility of multiple wives, but his friend had no problem with the fact that his girlfriend was a different species and over a decade older than him. Meanwhile, Henry didn't mind the theoretical idea of polygamy, as long as it was Mareen's idea, but felt a flash of guilt at Mareen's age.

They were still adjusting to Ludus, that was for sure. Maybe Mareen had been right and he and Jason really were idiots. *Nah.*

Henry glanced over at Rark-han, who was jogging toward him from Bezzi-ibbi's house. He shrugged and gave up trying to eavesdrop on the girls. If he had actually managed to hear them, it would be kind of a dick move anyway. He just couldn't help feeling like something bad was coming.

He sighed and raised a hand to knock on the door. It was his house, but Henry tried to be polite and avoid barging in on people. He never wanted to walk in on people taking a bath together again. He sniggered at the memory.

That poor bastard. He really never had a chance.

* * *

Aodh walked down the busy Mirana street with Henry, Rark-han, Mareen, and Uluula. Hawkers behind carts lined the street, and a few shops generated inviting smells. He would have loved to browse the vendors' wares, but he had to focus.

He knew they were heading towards the Jaguar Clan House, and he was busy trying to convince himself he was as unconcerned about this fact as his companion. It wasn't working.

Aodh surreptitiously glanced at Henry before he realized what he was doing and jerked his eyes forward again. He hadn't meant to overhear Uluula and Mareen talking. He really hadn't. He couldn't help that they had been in the next room and he had exceptional hearing due to his Fideli genes…Of course, his Fideli genes hadn't forced him to put his ear to the wall…

He wished he hadn't heard anything. Poor Henry, he had no idea what was coming.

Well, it'd probably be good for him. Aodh still didn't know Henry or Jason very well, but he had a decent grasp of their personalities. For all he knew, Mareen and Uluula were right to plan an ambush.

He shrugged. It wasn't his problem, but he couldn't help but worry a bit. Luckily, he'd been getting better at controlling his worrying nature, a necessity while carrying gunpowder bombs around all the time. After thinking about them, Aodh consciously felt the bronze, tubular "grenades" on his belt that swayed and hit his legs while he walked. He shuddered. It was time to think of something else.

Aodh tried his best not to dwell on topics that would upset him, like the explosives attached to his body, screaming hordes of ork warriors, or his psychotic cousin. In fact, thank the Christian God he hadn't seen her for a while. No matter what happened while working for Delvers LLC, he took comfort in the fact he'd never have to coexist with his cousin again. The remainder of the walk to the Jaguar Clan House, Aodh took simple pleasure in the fact that he wasn't exploring a dungeon kitchen full of burned bodies.

* * *

The Jaguar Clan House was huge. Aodh nervously crossed the

threshold with the rest of his group and envied their self-confidence. Of course, they were all impressive people, so the source of their assurance was obvious.

Mareen was in mourning, so she wore an orange dress, the same color as the smoke from funeral pyres after adding dried polleena flowers to the flames. Mareen didn't have her massive bronze hammer, but as usual now she wore the machete recovered at the site of her grandfather's murder. Aodh thought it was a little macabre, but nobody really talked about the machete. He thought it might be a revenge thing.

Mareen was as pretty as always. Her dusky skin, big eyes, delicate features, and shiny hair made her look like a noblewoman. Aodh still could hardly believe she was the daughter of his childhood hero and had grown up on a farm.

While Mareen was dark and curvy, Uluula was pale and petite. The tiny Areva woman's white hair flowed down just past her shoulders. Her high cheekbones, pointed ears, and subtly inhuman blue eyes gave her an exotic air. She was wearing crude grey cargo pants manufactured in Mirana and a small jacket of the same material over a white shirt. In a show of support for her friend, she wore an orange mourning armband. As always, she carried her bronze, leaf-bladed spear.

Rark-han was a huge, brute of a wolf-race Mo'hali. As usual, he wore leather pants, laced sandals, and a leather vest. He carried a big, heavy bronze axe on one hip. Where another axe would have hung in the past, his belt was empty. His amputated arm sported a bronze prosthetic made by Henry.

Rark-han's wide face was mostly humanoid with a few canine features, including a rough nose, fangs, shaggy hair, and fur on the side of his face. His hair was dark, and his large, upright ears began where a human's would have but were obviously inhuman in size and shape.

Henry walked with his usual confident swagger, one hand resting on the pommel of the bronze short sword he had on a baldric. He was wearing fine green-and-black Jaguar Clan robes, probably because Mareen had forced him to for his earlier audience. His freshly trimmed his goatee and combed hair were simple concessions to his appearance that made him look dashing.

Even his mask looked like a fashion statement. While Aodh looked stupid and awkward wearing his mask, Henry's made him seem he was heading to a ball. Henry's mask covered most of his Asian features, but he was still dark and striking. Aodh knew Henry was an important man, and he wondered why he didn't put effort into his appearance more often. What Henry usually wore still suited him—serviceable old leather and thick linen clothing—but when he actually tried to look nice, he literally stopped traffic.

He just had that sort of effect. It drove Aodh crazy how Henry had no clue about his effect on people. In fact, he had no idea where the man actually got his self-confidence from. He knew Henry's obliviousness irritated Jason, too, but Jason was likewise clueless. Both men were idiots. At least Mareen seemed to actually know she was pretty.

Meanwhile, Aodh knew he was nothing special. He hadn't done anything interesting in life; he was only sixteen. He wasn't very tall or muscular, and he looked Fideli. He hated the white forelock in his dark hair, his sharp canines, pointed ears, tiny pupils, and second eyelids. His whole life he'd been mocked and even beaten up for how he looked. It wasn't until he'd joined Delvers LLC that he had felt like he belonged anywhere.

And yet, while he felt like a real adventurer now, he still didn't feel like he was important enough to be walking into the Jaguar Clan House. Meetings were for people who mattered. He was just a farm boy that could make things explode.

He was trailing the rest of the group, thinking about turning around and making a run for it, when Bezzi-ibbi appeared out of nowhere next to him. The other boy put his hand on Aodh's shoulder and said in halting English, "Come, I will help you find good chair."

Aodh smiled despite himself. He knew Bezzi-ibbi was younger than he was, but the Mo'hali boy had already accomplished so much in his life. He was even heir to the Jaguar Clan in Mirana. Bezzi-ibbi was wild, and Aodh wasn't always sure what the other boy would do next, but he couldn't deny that the merchant prince had a calming effect on him.

He stopped planning to make a break for it and headed deeper into the Clan building.

* * *

Bezzi-ibbi sighed internally. Aodh—or Tony, as everyone called him—was perplexing. He was older than Bezzi-ibbi by several years, he'd been free his own life, he had incredible destructive power, and yet he always acted like a mouse in a den of cobras. Bezzi-ibbi had seen what those "grenades" could do, weapons that Aodh was currently carrying with him!

Bezzi thought it was a little overkill to bring weapons of war to a meeting. Aodh could blow the entire house up if he wanted to, but the other boy still acted afraid. It made no sense.

Bezzi-ibbi quickly led Aodh to the meeting hall and sat him near where Henry and Jason would be seated. Then he tried to decide where he should sit.

His standing in the Clan was complex at the moment. On one hand, while he was an acting Hero, he had no Clan obligations and would be treated as an adult. However, his *rekke* Henna-ibbi was angry at him for his choice. In fact, several other Clan members were ignoring him and twitching their tails as well. His sister Yillo-ibbi, one year his junior, was actually bristling at him while she looked the other way. Bezzi-ibbi felt hurt.

Yillo-ibbi was one of other Jaguar Clan children closest to Bezzi-ibbi's age, and even though he'd never gotten along very well with her birth mother Henna-ibbi, he loved his sister. Bezzi-ibbi gave his *rekke* respect for creating his favorite sister and

41

passing on her best qualities, like leadership and intellect. However, apparently now he and Yillo-ibbi were not talking. Bezzi-ibbi's whiskers and tail drooped.

He didn't regret his decision to put on the ring and become a Hero, but he really hoped he could maintain friendship with Yillo-ibbi during his adventuring years. He felt a flash of frustration with Henna-ibbi, but he knew she was doing what she felt was right. His *rekke* was a woman of great integrity, even if she wasn't very warm or social.

Bezzi-ibbi almost sat down but hesitated. It was important that he accurately gauge his standing or others would think him arrogant or stupid; he could afford neither.

He tried to dispassionately observe his personal situation. He was not technically part of the Jaguar Clan at the moment, but he was still the heir of the Clan in Mirana. His birthright would not change as long as he was still alive and didn't reject it. He was a member of a successful adventuring company, he'd just attended a meeting with the governor of Mirana by invitation, and most importantly, he was a Hero.

It was rubbing his back fur the wrong way to admit it, but his standing had actually increased. It felt wrong to do so, but he took a seat at a higher position than he ever had before. He carefully observed the reactions around him and saw some ears laid flat, but most Clan members just pretended indifference. Among Mo'hali, this usually meant deep thought or keen observation. It seemed he had chosen wisely. His tail twitched in satisfaction, and he immediately stilled it as soon as he realized what he was doing.

He couldn't act like a cub anymore. Bezzi-ibbi had fought for his adulthood, even risking his life for it. He had to act worthy of his new role or dishonor himself.

Bezzi-ibbi greeted his uncle, Yanno-ibbi, held hands with his birth mother, and settled in to wait for the meeting. He perked his ears up but swished his tail, signaling that he wished to be left alone. He had no patience for Family members that might offer phony, yowled compliments to him as a Hero. Many Family members had supported Henna-ibbi's policy to keep Bezzi-ibbi cooped up in the Jaguar Clan House, and now pretended they never had.

Deep down, Bezzi-ibbi had to admit they'd been right to protect him, especially after he had been captured and held captive. He'd never admit it to them, though. Plus, right or not, the attitude of some Family members grated on him. They felt Henna-ibbi should have birthed the heir, not his birth mother Banna-ibbi.

Bezzi-ibbi would not tolerate people speaking ill of his birth mother. She wasn't the smartest woman on Ludus, true, and she didn't have a great memory, but she had a huge heart and Bezzi-ibbi loved her dearly. He understood why his father had gently suggested to his *rekke* to give her a chance. Bezzi-ibbi was glad that Henna-ibbi and his mother had become friends, because otherwise he wouldn't have been born.

With a start, he realized the meeting was about to begin. Everyone was gathering. Bezzi-ibbi was interested in the fact that Kinwe-na-ibbi, Bezzi-ibbi's *uma*, his non-dominant, non-birth mother, showed Jason, Henry, and their first mates Uluula and Mareen where to sit. Since Henry and Jason were adopted into the Family, both women were seated in front of them as a sign of respect for their possible future marriage.

The Terrans all looked confused. Bezzi-ibbi sighed. He really needed to become fluent in English so he could explain to his stupid brothers how to act in civilized company. Of course, Bezzi-ibbi had to acknowledge his own pride was the only thing preventing him from speaking Luda, but he would not go back on his promise. It was easier to learn a new language than it would be to deal with the shame.

He noticed Rark-han walk in, and the big Mo'hali immediately fulfilled his duty by unseating the Family member behind Bezzi-ibbi to take that seat as an honor guard. Bezzi-ibbi was still not sure if he'd made the right decision by sparing the man's life. Perhaps he should have just killed him like the rest of the Family thought he should have, but so far he believed he had made the right choice. Death was easy; duty was hard.

He knew that part of his Family's disapproval with his decision was because Rark-han was low-wolf race. If he were high-wolf race, they'd have been more understanding. Bezzi-ibbi snarled. He loved his family, but their obsession over birth station was not something he shared.

Once everyone was seated, the meeting began. Henna-ibbi stood and opened the gathering. After she formally made the meeting announcement, she sat, and Hajim-ibbi, Bezzi-ibbi's father, introduced himself. Next, he sat back down behind Henna-ibbi, formally displaying his confidence in his wife's leadership.

The meeting really began when Henna-ibbi stood again and gave a quick synopsis of their meeting with Governor Holtz. There were low hisses and growls around the room, signs that the usually stoic Mo'hali were incredibly agitated. Bezzi-ibbi couldn't blame them. Dark gods were serious business. Every Mo'hali in the Jaguar Clan studied the histories and knew how dire the situation could be.

All of the proceedings eventually led to the part of the meeting Bezzi-ibbi really wanted to hear. He already had a good idea of what would happen, but he wanted to witness it play out. It would affect the rest of his life, after all.

Henna-ibbi still stood at the front of the room, her posture and the angle of her tail conveying her dominant position. She paused to let everyone calm themselves before saying, "I think we can all agree that this is Clan business. Based on Governor Holtz inviting Jaguar Clan leadership to the meeting today, there are several things we can assume."

She nodded to guards stationed near the doors and said in Panum, the Mo'hali language, "Secure the House and secure the room." The guards bowed, displaying the backs of their necks and shut the doors behind them. Then Henna-ibbi bowed to Bezzi-ibbi, her posture rigid but polite, asking, "Would the Hero please help us secure the room?"

Bezzi-ibbi had known this part had probably been coming and dreaded it. It meant he had to speak Luda. He said in Luda, "I stand as Bezzi-ibbi, Hero, future heir of the Jaguar Clan. I will honor your request." He glanced at the other members of Delvers LLC and said in English, "Do not be alarmed." Bezzi-ibbi sincerely hoped Mareen, Jason, and especially Henry would stay calm. He released his Hero suppression power. The feeling was strange, almost like flexing his brain.

He got a surprise when he felt Jason and Henry resisting. After Bezzi-ibbi extended his suppression field as far as it would go, which was barely to the edges of the room, he could tell that neither Henry nor Jason was completely suppressed. However, the fact he could suppress them at all now that they'd grown meant he'd grown too.

He trusted his brothers. He was glad they were able to retain a portion of their power while Bezzi-ibbi did his duty.

Every person in the room felt the unique sensation of a Mo'hali Hero using suppression power, the feeling almost like small insects walking on their skin. There was no need for Bezzi-ibbi to announce it was done, so he sat back down.

Henna-ibbi briefly turned a hand over, displaying her wrist in appreciation. Then she said, "This room is as secure as we can make it now. Every attendee that is not a full member of the Clan is either vouched for on pain of death or neutralized." She looked meaningfully at Rark-han.

Bezzi-ibbi still disagreed with the Clan for requiring Rark-han's tongue to be cut out, but the big wolf man hadn't seemed too concerned about it, so Bezzi-ibbi tried not to let it bother him either.

Henna-ibbi continued, "There are matters of secrecy to the Clan that must be discussed, facts that Henry-ibbi and Jason-ibbi are not aware of.

"First off, since you are actually sitting here and don't seem flustered, I assume you already know you can't run from this mission you were given?"

Henry just shrugged. Jason said, "It is fairly obvious, yes. If we couldn't trust the governor, you would have already said so. Since the queen of Tolstey wants us to play ball, there really isn't much we can do about it other than leave the country…which is what she wants us to do anyway."

"Play ball?"

"Uhhh…" Jason thought for a moment before responding, "Obey instructions."

"Yes, you have the right of it." Henna-ibbi grinned, tight-lipped and ears forward. "What you don't know is that we have been in secret discussions with the governor for years. She is the most influential governor under the queen. What she told you about Tolstey being weak is true, but the aristocracy of this country are not pleased with the current state of affairs. In particular, Tolstey receives no real trade in technology. Our country is technologically backwards compared to the rest of Ludus.

"Plus, the way the governor described Berber having no interest in Tolstey is not entirely true. While it's true this country isn't teeming with natural resources or much infrastructure, we do have some of the safest land on Ludus."

"This country is safe?" Henry asked, aghast.

"Compared to the rest of the world, yes. We also have the only known trade route to Teteth. If Tolstey had more military strength and more ships to trade with Teteth across the Ocean of Tears, we could be the wealthiest country on Ludus."

Bezzi-ibbi watched carefully. He knew his brothers probably had no idea what his *rekke* was talking about, but they should understand the gist; nothing was necessarily as it seemed.

"Right now, some of the High Tribes of Jallen, other powerful merchant families, are controlling trade in Berber. Our goal is to replace them, or at least join them. We want to set up a trading branch in Berber, and this goal is supported by the Tolstey government."

"Wait, didn't you have enemies that were going to destroy you here in Mirana before we came along and basically saved your asses?" Henry asked. Bezzi-ibbi hid a grimace. The question was fair, but Henry had a way of cutting to the spine of a subject. There were already members of the clan whispering that he was a Truth-Hisser.

Henry had already unknowingly weakened Henna-ibbi's position of authority before, and her dislike was obvious to Bezzi-ibbi when she answered, "Yes, but they have since been dealt with. The rabbit-race Tatir Clan was planning to expand from energy sales to general trading by destroying our Clan. We discovered evidence they were communicating with the bandits you destroyed.

"We attacked and dissolved their Clan and distributed their business among our Clan and our allies over a week ago."

Uluula stood and formally announced, "I stand as Uluula b' Anami b' Pairose of the Blue, daughter of Amani b' Pairose b' Heseth of the Blue. I speak as courted of Jason-ibbi and I wish to add my words in the day."

Henna-ibbi graciously turned both wrists and replied, "We recognize you, Uluula b' Anami b' Pairose of the Blue. Continue." Bezzi-ibbi mentally applauded. At least someone had been listening when he'd tried to give etiquette lessons. He winced when he saw Henry roll his eyes. Was his brother trying to start a fight with Henna-ibbi? It was already common knowledge that she had tried to kill him on their first meeting. The fact he still lived weakened her position enough, but any disrespect was even worse.

The end of his *rekke's* tail twitched, and Bezzi-ibbi knew he was not the only person watching warily. Uluula was obviously clueless how close Henna-ibbi was to jumping past her to attack Henry. The Areva woman said, "We didn't know any of this. It seems you're about to ask my beloved to do something dangerous again, and he would be able to better prepare if we were kept informed. Also, how were the Guard not involved?" The Areva woman sat back down.

Areva made Mo'hali nervous anyway, and the way Uluula had just questioned the chain of command increased the volatile atmosphere in the room. The white-haired woman seemed somewhat aware of what was going on, but all the Terrans were clueless.

Henna-ibbi answered, "Who said the Guard wasn't involved? That which benefits the city not to be investigated, will not be investigated. Not every Clan member is told of every matter, and you are not even Clan. An empty mind cannot feed lazy lips."

Suddenly, a big hand landed on Henna-ibbi's shoulder. She looked back, startled before slowly sitting down. Hajim-ibbi uncharacteristically stood, announcing, "I stand again as Hajim-ibbi, interceding for one I love and for the good of the Clan. I will finish this meeting." Bezzi-ibbi's eyebrows rose. He'd never heard of his father interceding for his *rekke* before.

Hajim-ibbi cleared his throat and said, "I have spent much time around Terrans. I believe I can say what must be said in a way that will avoid wasted time or stepped-on tails. The situation is simple. We want to get a trading foothold in Berber.

"To do this, we need to find a way over or around the mountains between our countries, which presents many problems right now. We are asking you to do this because you are Family. Also, Delvers LLC has already established a reputation for being unique as well as employing talented people. We believe you can find a way. Obviously, having this Clan backing you is already a benefit, but if you increase the reach of the Jaguar Clan's power, you will be increasing your own as well."

"Okay, that makes sense," said Jason. "But still, why us? Why is Berber working through Tolstey to force us to travel there? The whole thing seems overly complex."

"I have no idea. You'll have to talk to your Berber contact, the spies. However, to help you with our interests in this matter, we are sending Yanno-ibbi, my brother, to travel with you. He can also help educate you on Ludus trade and Mo'hali culture on your journey."

Figures, thought Bezzi-ibbi. *They don't trust me right now, and Henry-ibbi and Jason-ibbi are not fully trusted either. At least it's Uncle Yanno-ibbi going with us, though.*

"Understood. I'm assuming the Clan will help fund our expedition, then?" Jason asked.

"Yes, as much as we can. We still haven't replenished our coffers, and won't for some time. However, if my informants in the government are right, you should have received plenty from the Tolstey government. You should have plenty of money to build or buy whatever you need already, so what we can give you should offer even more flexibility."

The rest of the meeting was fairly straightforward. All the important information had already been given. Bezzi-ibbi stopped paying close attention and began waiting for his chance to ask about what was really on his mind.

* * *

After the meeting disbanded, Bezzi-ibbi caught up with Henry and Jason as they left the Clan House.

"Oh, hi, Bezzi-ibbi," greeted Henry.

Bezzi-ibbi gave a Terran nod in return. Then in English, he said, "Important thing forgetting. Paper."

"Oh, that's right!" exclaimed Henry. He reached into his back pocket and flashed the note he'd gotten from Gonzo at Jason. "We still have this! The thing to make the masks unnecessary for me, you, Mareen, and Bezzi-ibbi, remember?"

Uluula and Mareen gave each other a look. Mareen began to say something, but Uluula gave a slight shake of her head. The two women folded their arms and watched. *That's right, they weren't at the government building*, thought Bezzi-ibbi.

There were a few moments of silence while Henry and Jason studied the note. Suddenly, Henry whispered, "No fucking way."

"What?" Jason's voice was confused. "I don't get it. This part doesn't make any sense."

"Don't you remember when we first got to Ludus? Like the first few hours?"

Jason studied the note for a moment longer before saying, "Now that you mention it, yeah…" A slow look of horrified comprehension crossed his face. "You've got to be kidding me."

Delvers LLC: Obligations Incurred

CHAPTER FOUR

Bush with Death

Henry woke before dawn. The shirt he'd thrown over his alarm clock the night before kept it muted enough so Mareen could keep sleeping. Dolos wouldn't let anyone on Ludus use electricity for some dickhead reason, but at least there were plenty of mechanical inventions recreated from Earth's history. Alarm clocks weren't exactly cheap in Mirana, but they weren't rare, either.

As Henry got dressed, he shook his head. It'd been another long night. Mareen was holding up better in public now, but she was still a raw bundle of nerves in private. Henry wasn't very good at comforting people, or with emotions in general, but he tried to do his best to be available for Mareen. Her entire world had been turned upside down.

Henry hissed as he stubbed his toe. He really wished he had a lamp, but magic lights were expensive, candles took a while to get going and could be stinky, and electricity was forbidden.

When Henry had first begun building machines using magic power, he had briefly thought about experimenting to get around the ban on electric technology. He wasn't an expert, but he knew how simple things like lightbulbs worked. However, after he'd seen multiple warnings about the types of technology Dolos outlawed on Ludus, and well as verifying that, yes, he was dead-ass serious about enforcing it, Henry had decided it would probably be a bad idea.

Dolosbots were known for wiping entire villages from the map, and a single 'bot could easily take out multiple orb-Bonded. Henry wondered what kind of technology the Dolosbots used. He was convinced they didn't run on the same principles of magic that people on Ludus were stuck with. The longer he was on Ludus, the more convinced Henry was that Dolos was more of an alien on a power trip than a god.

Either way, he was a piece of shit. Henry had to play by his rules because Dolos had cured his mother of cancer. It didn't mean he had to like the situation, though.

Henry padded out into the little rental house and knocked on Jason's bedroom door. Uluula wasn't in the room, she'd gone home the night before, which was good because he had to knock for a while to wake Jason up.

Henry went outside to wait for his friend, mask in place, and eventually Jason joined him, wearing a pack and muttering groggily under his breath under his own mask. Jason was not a morning person.

Without another word, they began walking at a brisk pace. Neither man said anything, which was probably for the best before Jason fully woke up. When they got to one of the gates to the city, Henry nodded in a friendly manner to the Guards on duty. They nodded back; most of them knew Henry by now.

It doesn't matter what city or world you're in, it always pays to be on good terms with the police, Henry thought smugly to himself. They walked for another few minutes until they neared the first evidence of farmland outside of Mirana. Jason turned off the road and Henry followed.

Eventually, Jason stopped and said, "This should be good. We can talk here."

Henry rolled his eyes. "I really don't understand why we needed to come all the way out to BFE just to have a chat."

"This is super serious and you know it. Plus, we have literal spies involved in whatever it is we're doing now, and we need to have a private conversation."

"Yeah, I suppose we do." Henry was aware that other than George's murder, they'd hardly talked about business or anything serious. Everyone's life and goals had been thrown in disarray. "Okay, let's start with the obvious. What the hell is going on?"

Jason took his pack off and set it to the side near a handy rock. He sat down and faced Henry, saying, "First, we both agree that I will be leaving after this meeting, right?" He gestured at his pack. "I'm ready to go, but that means you'll need to tank the meeting with Gonzo later today."

Henry groaned, but he had already known he'd need to run point on the meeting. He really didn't want to, but he agreed with Jason that his friend should go, though. "Yeah, but that's why we're having this convo in the first place, right?"

"Yes. Okay, first things first. We got the secret note from Gonzo explaining the method to remove the left eye data feed, the LEDF, from occurring if we have our faces uncovered. Also, I still think this is a stupid acronym and we shouldn't use it."

"Well, everyone else disagrees with you. Plus, it's a good way to talk about these sorts of things all sneaky-like. Not many people on Ludus use acronyms at all."

"Whatever. Anyway, the tea the note explained how to make, that we would need to drink to get rid of LEDF, uses material that is ridiculously expensive and hard to come by on the market. It comes from an extremely rare monster."

"Yup, and we already ran into one." Henry shivered at the memory. Their first day on Ludus, Henry had seen a bush with pretty pink flowers and gotten a weird feeling about it. They now knew it was actually the top of a blind ambush monster called a "flowertop popper." Most of its body stayed buried in the ground until prey got close enough. They were native to Tolstey and only lived in remote areas, feeding on animals or people that got too close.

Henry had almost died even before fighting the goblins. The thought chilled him. Thank God for instincts. When he'd seen the bush, it had made him nervous, so they'd gone around it.

Jason said, "Yes, we did. You saved our lives. Thank you, by the way. I don't think I've been able to say that since we found out how close we came to dying that time."

Henry felt a little uncomfortable. He hadn't done anything all that special, just paid attention to a hunch. "Yeah, whatever. Don't worry about it. Anyway, how are we sure that fucking note Gonzo gave us is legit?"

"We don't, but I think it's worth it to find out, especially since we know where a flowertop monster is. Plus, I've never tried this before, but I can move really fast by teleporting through the air. I should be gone a day or two max, and being a second rank Bonded now means one ambush monster shouldn't be too much of a threat."

Henry frowned and asked, "Speaking of which, didn't we also have this meeting to talk about the orbs and your level up?" He started looking around for his own rock to sit on.

"Yes. To be honest, it was one of the main reasons I wanted to keep this conversation semi-private. I'm beginning to realize that secrecy about what our orbs do is part of how the orb-Bonded culture works. It makes sense, too. Someone will have a lot harder time killing you or planning for your abilities if they don't know what you can do."

"It's cold, but I agree," said Henry. He couldn't find another rock big enough to sit on and remained standing. "Okay, so you never told me what you used your upgrade points for after you hit second rank. So spill. What did the purple cartoon cat give you, other than some morning soreness and a little shame?"

Jason frowned, and Henry had to work hard to keep a straight face. He knew he was being a dick, but making fun of Jason was really fun sometimes. His friend had about zero ability at hiding his emotions.

"Fine," Jason grated. "But first, let me tell you why I did what I did. I gave it all a lot of thought." Henry nodded and Jason continued, "We keep getting surprised, and we still don't know much about the world. Plus, the fact we discovered the orks were intelligent enough to have their own written language in Yanbei Cavern kind of floored me.

"I started thinking about George's notes and Bezzi-ibbi's ability to learn languages. I think we did really well to survive so far, but we need to start planning our endgame. I took some support skills."

"What do you mean? I took that dungeon finding skill before and it hasn't been too useful."

"That doesn't mean it won't come in handy more in the future." Jason thought for a minute before he said, "Second rank for us is 12 points, as you know. I took Magic Power (Rank 2, 2 points), Speed (Rank 1, 1 point), Magic Control (Consciousness/Space Rank 2, 3 points), Mind Strengthening (Rank 1, 1 point), and…Monster Lore, which was 1 point."

"Monster Lore?" Henry hadn't been expecting that. He did the addition in his head and gave Jason a flat look. "You probably already know what questions I'm going to ask, so just keep talking."

"Okay, that works. Basically, I realized we've been acting reactionary and making choices without a lot of information. In the past, it was a necessity, but it's not anymore. The writing and ork journals I found in Yanbei Cavern made me realize we know nothing, but we're surrounded by data if we can just recognize and understand it.

"I took a point in mind augmentation because we learn too slowly. Bezzi-ibbi basically learned another language in less than a month. Uluula can learn new things and actually retain them ridiculously fast. You and I both know part of that is because of the Areva hardware in her head, but that's irrelevant. I'm not dumb, but I wanted an advantage.

"So far, that one point skill has been amazing. I learn things quicker, I remember things easier, and I even understand my magic better.

"The other part you're probably wondering about is the four points I didn't use for my upgrades. This is one of the things we need to talk about most. I spent a lot of time talking to my orb—

yes, the cartoon cat. It was hard to nail him down on any specific answers, but I figured out how to ask questions he couldn't evade. I learned some really, really interesting things."

Henry's full attention was on what his friend was saying now. He had to admit that he had never really tried getting too much information out of his orb's manifestation. Henry's orb appeared as a childhood hero, and the disrespect made him angry every time every time he met with the thing. He still told Jason that his orb appeared as a bikini model, though. His friend's reaction was always hilarious. "Okay, I'm listening."

"Basically, what we see in our upgrade menu when we are in the orb dream is not complete. There are skills and abilities we can unlock."

"Unlock?" Henry asked.

"Yes, it's a pretty standard game mechanic, and we know Dolos is modeling at least some of this world after an alien role-playing game. Basically, it's hard to pin my orb's interface down on anything, but I think we can get new schools of magic by choosing to add another, basic school of magic. This will cost five points for the magic school and require at least five or six levels of magic focus between two schools or subschools. Well, I think."

"What?" Henry wasn't following too well. He'd played games before, but was not a real gamer like Jason. Plus, the whole abstract way the orbs and their rankings worked seemed strange to him.

Jason paused for a moment before answering. "It costs five points to add another magic school and subschool, or do what you did with Metal and actually reverse it so your subschool affinity is stronger. If we have our original magic plus another set, I think it will open up even more types that are hidden right now.

"In fact, I think we just saw evidence of this. Remember how Governor Holtz turned into sand?"

Henry's eyes widened as he remembered the feat. He hadn't really thought of it since. "Yeah, now that you mention it, that's not really anything I could do with Earth magic. In fact, from what I understand, it shouldn't be possible."

"Exactly. I have a theory that Governor Holtz's orb confers two types of magic in a specialized way. You and I have orbs that are harder to optimize, but we have a lot more versatility. Basically, I'm playing a hunch that when I get to my next rank, by purchasing a new school of magic, I'll be able to see some unlocked abilities. I want to save some points for that."

"Okay, that makes sense."

"Okay," said Jason, "that covers the upgrade stuff I wanted to talk about. I suggest you take some extra time with your bikini model orb to figure out what direction you want to go with future upgrades. I don't think I need to hold your hand. Even though this isn't your thing, you've made relatively intelligent decisions so far."

"Thanks, I think." Henry wasn't sure if Jason was being

insulting or not. He decided to take everything said as a compliment. Life was easier that way.

Jason continued, "So anyway, I took Monster Lore and I'm glad I did. It's ridiculously overpowered for only one point. Dolos would fail as a game designer. Well, never mind. We don't know how any of this works. He might not be calling the shots with the points.

"Anyway, Monster Lore gave me some background on monster information, general classifications, and several languages...all for a single point. I've been able to read the journals we found in Yanbei Caverns. This is what I really dragged you out here for.

"Dolos was playing those orks. He found them on the planet they were on previously, played to their religion so they'd do what he said, brought them here, and only took males so they couldn't breed. He also didn't warn them that their iron and steel would rot. Henry, those orks had their own technology back on their own world."

"What?"

"Yeah, it explains why Uluula hates them so much. She doesn't really want to talk about it, but I was wondering how creatures with stone clubs could bother a space-faring race like the Areva. Anyway, the orks are simple, but they're not nearly as stupid as I first assumed. Their leader—the closest translation I can find for his name is 'Smartstrong'—was convinced that Dolos was a friend or messenger for their god, Tartooth.

"Dolos is straight-up lying to intelligent, if violent creatures, bringing them here, and making us all fight like a child throwing bugs together in a jar."

"That motherfucker." Henry thought he should have felt more surprised than he did, but nothing really floored him anymore. Ludus had that kind of effect.

Jason continued, "And the assumption we had about Dolos testing us and making life harder on purpose was probably true anyway, but I'm even more convinced after reading the ork leader's journal. I think learning more about monsters, maybe even talking to them, might be a key to understanding this planet better. The more we understand, the better chances we have for keeping ourselves and everyone else alive."

Henry nodded and said, "This is all good stuff to keep in mind, but we have a few other things to talk about and you need to go soon."

"Yeah, like about what to do with our leftover loot."

"We don't have much left of it, which is good since the fucking governor tied up the Adventurers Guild for us. Now they won't buy any more of our shit."

"Yes, and what we have left is pretty pricey." Jason pulled a note out of his pocket. "I actually had Uluula write a quick list for us."

Henry took the list and read through it, but everything was as he'd expected. "The list says we have a few enchanted items that we couldn't sell right away, three in fact. Nobody knows what they do, us or the Guild. Pretty much all the weapons and metal we recovered was sold. We only kept the material from the bronze doors.

"We kept a good amount of magic stones to power the Battlewagon. The one spirit stone we found you already used." Henry scanned the list again. "The only other thing worth mentioning is the Dolos orb. Are you sure Uluula doesn't want it? It seems weird to have a Dolos orb just kicking around."

Jason nodded. "She doesn't want to be orb-Bonded. I think she thinks it will interfere with whatever she really wants to achieve, and since she will live to be a few hundred years old anyway, she isn't in a rush. I haven't had a chance to really talk to her about it, I keep forgetting. That said, after I told her about Captain Haili, she wants to look into magic tech. She's going to buy some books on the subject before we leave Mirana and maybe pick up some gear."

"So we're going to leave for sure, huh?"

"Yes. There's really no way we can get out of this, Henry. I've looked at it from multiple angles. Plus, if we're going to do what Dolos obligated us to do, we can't just be low-level, safe adventurers in Mirana forever. We have to take over the world or something, remember? In fact, if we tried to keep a low profile, Dolos would probably make our lives even harder.

"I did some asking around and found out the highest-rank orb-Bonded anyone heard of before is like rank eight. That's nuts. They could probably destroy us."

Henry nodded. "I just wonder what level of orb-Bonded could actually go toe to toe with a Dolosbot. There really is a lot of stuff we don't know. But speaking of us leaving soon…you know Uluula is going to be mad as hell that you're taking off. Especially without saying goodbye to her first."

"Yes, but it's necessary."

"Yeah, and it prolongs the inevitable a little," said Henry. "You know those girls are gonna want us to marry them soon. This is not Earth. Plus, you and Uluula have started fucking, right?"

"Do you have to be so crude?" Jason asked, wincing. "You know, you don't always have to phrase things in such an abrasive way, especially when you're not even speaking English."

Henry rolled his eyes. Not this again. "Whatever. I have to be in this shitty world, I have to work for shitty Dolos, I am damn sure not changing who I am to do it. But that doesn't answer the question. You're pretty sure Uluula is going to push marriage, right?" Henry couldn't believe his friend was so uptight. In the past, he'd thought Jason needed to get laid or something, but now he had a girlfriend and was still acting like he had a stick up his butt.

"Yes," replied Jason.

"Me too. And the other day when I was walking to the house,

the girls were talking and being all sneaky-like. I couldn't hear what they were saying even with my hearing cranked up."

"Probably because they know you keep spying on everyone."

"Yeah, but Tony was also acting really squirrely after that and wouldn't look at me."

"Hmmm. They probably will bring it up soon, then. However, more importantly, how are you noticing all this stuff? You used to be the densest person on the face of the planet."

"Well, after I spent a few weeks with a hot chick wanting to jump me every day and not even noticing, I decided it was time to stop being so retarded. It's not rocket science, it's just a matter of paying attention." It seemed obvious to Henry. He didn't like being surprised by things, so he'd simply adjusted his thinking. It was past time he got over his divorce and stopped acting like a weakling.

"Well, on that subject, I've been doing some research," said Jason. "You know I'm a little wigged out by the whole multiple wives thing. It's not that I don't want to marry Uluula or that I'm not willing to adapt, I just...need more time."

Henry had a sudden flash of insight. Without thinking before speaking, he said, "I think you're full of shit. You are a dude. I think what probably really bothers you is that you might like having multiple wives or you think it might cheapen what you have with Uluula."

Jason paused before answering. "You are being kind of a dick, but yes, the thought has occurred to me. I really care about Uluula. I know this is all her idea, but I also know that she is still a person with feelings and I don't want to hurt them. I also don't know if I could go through with it and not feel guilty or feel like I'm a cheater."

Jason waved a hand and shook his head. "But on the other hand, with Ludan and Areva culture, we should have married both our girlfriends a while ago. And in the rest of the universe, women are looked down on if they have a husband and no sister wives. Hell, I might hurt Uluula's feelings if I don't go through with all of this. You heard what the governor said. I bet women from Earth that come to Ludus are either outcasts, unhappy, have to adapt, or just endure a lot of gossip like Governor Holtz did."

Henry replied, "Well, it sounds like you're getting ready to adapt, but I'm also guessing you have a plan. You sound like you have a plan, anyway."

"Yes. We're not going to wait for them to bring it up. We're going to propose to them, which as males is unusual for Areva and Ludan culture, probably because Terrans on this planet picked up a lot of mannerisms from Areva. Anyway, whoever does the asking has more control over when the actual marriage takes place.

"We can get engaged, then tell them we will get married after this mission is over. It's a reasonable request, and should give me more time to adjust. Plus, if more than one woman is engaged to a man and get married at the same time, the roles in the household are a little more murky. Usually the first wife has more control of the household than the second wife, and so on and so forth.

"There are exceptions, but usually if a woman is engaged, she doesn't try as hard to find a sister wife until she's married, because it'll mess up the pecking order."

"Okay, that could work." Henry wasn't as worried about Mareen going off and trying to find a bajillion other women to fill his house like Jason seemed afraid Uluula would do. Henry was just not in a big hurry to get married again. "I do think it's kind of funny that you seem to be growing balls, though. I thought you were going to just roll over and do whatever your elf girl wanted you to do."

"Don't call her an elf." Jason glared at him. "And fuck you. I'll be back as soon as I can. Try to handle that meeting later today with Gonzo without me."

"Okay, before you leave, what should we do about outfitting for the trip?"

"Well, all our money isn't much good if we're dead. Since we're going to be traveling anyway, as far as I'm concerned, we can use almost all of it as long as we keep a little extra on the side. Make sure everyone in the company is going to stay with us, and if they are, let's gear everyone up. It may not be the best for business, but we always knew that Delvers LLC was just the first step towards our endgame."

"I'm assuming you already told Uluula all this stuff too, about the gear?"

"Yes. Okay I need to go now, the sun is starting to come up." Without warning, Jason took off, teleporting with a sharp crack of filling vacuum. Henry saw his friend reappear in the distance up in the sky.

Wow, he's a lot more powerful now. Henry shook his head and started walking back to the city. It was almost time to wake up Mareen. For the first time since they'd gotten to Ludus, he wished he had Jason's magic instead of his own. If he could teleport, he could be going monster hunting instead of dealing with meetings. And shopping.

Henry shuddered. He'd much rather be fighting monsters.

Delvers LLC: Obligations Incurred

CHAPTER FIVE

Ignoble Nobility

Henry had time to tinker in the garage before the meeting with Gonzo. Luckily, as long as he made an effort to keep his work quiet, he knew he wouldn't wake Aodh in the corner. The kid slept like the dead.

Uluula arrived before Mareen got up for the day. The Areva woman almost always arrived early to scheduled meetings. She was carrying her spear around as usual. When she saw Henry by himself, her eyes tightened but she didn't say anything.

It was obvious she had figured out what happened, that Jason had gone out alone. The woman was quick-witted. Jason was so screwed.

Oh well, better him than me.

As usual, Henry and Uluula didn't really have much to say to each other. What do you talk to a space elf about? He didn't dislike Uluula, not anymore, and he was glad Jason was happy, but he still had nothing in common with her. At least she didn't feel the need to make things awkward by trying to be friendly. He did like that no-nonsense side of her. He respected her, she respected him, and that was good enough.

Mareen left Henry's room a while later, her hair wet from a shower. Mirana city amenities sucked, but at least they had running water and flushing toilets. There wasn't much in the way of temperature control, though. Mareen looked gorgeous. Her dark skin glowed and she wore a light blue, short-sleeved dress. The only thing marring her casual appearance was her baldric with Henry's old blessed steel machete. Well, he supposed it was her machete now. Henry couldn't see it, but he knew she probably had the dagger Jeth had used to torture her somewhere too, maybe on the back of her baldric.

Henry agreed with being prepared; it was the reason he wore weapons despite not really needing them anymore. He didn't want to be helpless if a Mo'hali Hero ever suppressed his magic. In theory, he also supported revenge, especially if it involved killing the fuckers that had murdered George. However, he thought Mareen might have been taking it a little too far. That sort of darkness could eat a person up.

But what right did he have to say anything? Henry Sato was many things, but he refused to be a hypocrite. The best he could do was just be there for her and try to keep her from flying apart.

She did a good job hiding her grief around other people, but everyone needed someone to lean on.

As soon as Mareen showed up, the normally stoic Uluula smiled and both women went off to talk in a corner. Henry briefly wondered what they were chatting about, probably stupid shit like clothes and shoes...then again, maybe not. Henry had to mentally amend that Mareen was becoming increasingly interested in cutty-stabby things, and Uluula was wound so goddamn tight she could double as a pointy-eared spring.

Weapons. They were probably talking about weapons. Henry approved.

The next to show up for the meeting was Bezzi-ibbi. The boy wore his usual showy, fancy clothing, and Rark-han followed the little Hero like a shadow. Bezzi-ibbi nodded at Henry, flashing a quick grin before he found a seat. Not for the first time, Henry wondered if a grinning Mo'hali kid meant the same as a grinning human kid. He doubted it.

He felt a little guilty again for letting a kid be an adventurer, but Bezzi-ibbi was an adult now by Mo'hali law. He could do what he wanted, and what he wanted was to travel with Delvers LLC, apparently.

Henry had already talked to the crazy little bastard about it, but Bezzi-ibbi's mind was made up.

With the group there, Henry cleared his throat to make an announcement. All eyes turned to him and he decided to be blunt, to just say what was on his mind. "Look, everyone, me and Jason are pretty much screwed here. I have no idea where all this is headed or how dangerous it's going to be.

"I appreciate all of you, and right now we all have had a good haul from Yanbei Cavern. None of us are really hurting for money. I want to make it clear that nobody is being forced to come with us when we go with Gonzo. Bezzi-ibbi, I'm not sure if you have much choice, Hero or not." Bezzi-ibbi nodded and Henry continued, "But anyone else can choose to stay behind, to leave the company.

"Past this point, everyone is a volunteer. If you want to leave, this is probably your best, last opportunity."

Everyone stared at him like he was an idiot. After a second or two, the rest of the Delvers went back to what they'd been doing before. *Well, that was interesting.* Henry had already figured that nobody would leave the company, but he'd wanted to make sure. He had a feeling the next few months would be intense.

Gonzo and Vitaliya arrived without much fuss. After the knock on the front door, Henry answered and the meeting started almost immediately. The Delvers stood in the house's small living room in a half circle. Henry knew Gonzo must have noticed Jason wasn't present, but the spy didn't show any reaction at all. *This guy is hard to read.*

After a few polite greetings, Gonzo said, "Good, obviously none of you have run away. I actually would have had questions about that right now with one of you missing, but my informants updated me this morning." He gave Henry a meaningful look.

Wow, Jason was right. Henry made a note to figure out a way to have private conversations easier in the future. Walking for several miles was inconvenient.

"Most of you have met me already. My name is Ryan Gonzolez, but I go by Gonzo for those who know me. You know me now, so you can call me Gonzo. I'm going to quickly update everyone in this group. Unfortunately, security in Mirana isn't great, so our best bet is to just get this conversation over quickly. Bezzi-ibbi, would you mind securing the room from magic?"

Bezzi-ibbi nodded, and Henry felt the weird, itchy feeling of the kid using his Hero power. He also felt his own magic get suppressed like at the Jaguar Clan House when Bezzi-ibbi had used his mojo there. It wasn't a pleasant sensation.

Gonzo nodded briskly and got back to business. "Our mission is both simple and complex. We are going to be traveling to Berber, the country to the north and the central country of this continent. It is primarily settled by Terrans with a strong Areva presence in the ruling class, most of them nobles from Hanana to the northwest.

"We'll be crossing through the Tolstey mountains by way of the Stem River. This will lead us to Rose Lake. We have a party that will be waiting for us there to bolster our strength for the last leg of the journey.

"We'll be following the shortest route to Mensk, the capital city of Berber. Our route will take us up the Berber Army road near the Berber Mountains, heading into the Fertile Valley where most of the farmland is. We'll be resupplying in Tauris and then heading north to Mensk.

"Vitaliya and I," he said, gesturing at the redhead girl, "came here on a flying ship that travels between Tolstey and Mensk once a year. The ship already left, so we have to travel on foot, or via magic-powered vehicles.

"Your individual assignments and cover stories will vary. Your mission specifics are being left up to your group to decide. Our overall mission is to discover and expose terrorist and/or cultist activity and capture a leader alive for interrogation. Your secondary mission is to prevent any more loss of innocent life.

"You were chosen for this mission because you have a reputation for results in circles that matter, you are all unknown in Berber, and a number of you are Bonded, mages, and Heroes. This assignment will require infiltration of the Berber aristocracy, where we have reason to believe at least some funding for terrorist activity is originating.

"The only nonnegotiable guidance I have is that at least one person must attend the Mensk Officer Academy, which is really just a magic and etiquette school for children of the aristocracy to play soldier at. This will be our primary means of infiltrating the ruling class.

"My government and the Tolstey government have several plans in motion to protect its interests. Your group is just one of them."

There was a few moments of silence before Mareen asked, "But why us, or at least, why Henry and Jason?"

"Yeah, aren't we a little old to be going back to school?" asked Henry.

"There are several answers to that question," replied Gonzo, looking at Mareen. "The first is that Dolos orbs are uncommon and incredibly expensive. They're usually very rare to come across. Meanwhile, your little group seems to be finding them practically under every rock.

"While it's true that more orbs are on the market now than ever since Dolos made his planet-wide announcement, the added danger of acquiring them has actually made the average price rise. Spirit stones can't even be found. Since most aristocrats from notable Families are either powerful mages by ancestry or orb-Bonded through wealth, it makes agent placement difficult.

"So what you're saying is that normal people won't work?" asked Mareen.

"Correct," answered Gonzo. He continued, "The fact that you are legitimately unknown is important. Agents from Berber always run the risk of being recognized or identified. Our only hope of infiltrating the aristocracy is to basically invent a new Family. This is only usually possible through a rapid rise in power from a new transplant. We can't just create a Family out of nothing, and it can't be fake. This approach would be too easy to disprove. For a successful cover story, we will be legitimately creating noble Houses."

"We're going to be nobles now?" Henry asked. He couldn't believe what he was hearing. As a younger man, the idea would have excited him, but now it sounded like a huge pain in the ass.

"Effectively, yes. The Berber Crown has given me deeds to land and other documentation to make everything legitimate."

"This doesn't make much sense. Can't you just buy information from informants you already have?" Uluula sounded extremely skeptical.

"We have already tried and our efforts have not been successful. Meanwhile, people continue to die or go missing in our larger cities. Many of them are children." Gonzo's expression was serious. "This is not a game. I wouldn't call the situation desperate yet, but the possibilities we shared with Governor Holtz are terrifying. My country's ruler directly approached the queen of Tolstey and came to an agreement."

Uluula said, "So basically, you couldn't buy informants, so you're creating them."

"Exactly. Berber called in a favor. If some of you, probably Henry and Jason, are Berber nobles, it will obviously actually make you citizens of Berber. To be honest, this is a play between the queens, too. The Tolstey queen is giving up resources to maintain security and prevent a possible cult uprising.

"As for your question about age," Gonzo said, looking Henry in the eye, "aristocrats don't really have anything to do. It's not uncommon for noble sons and daughters to attend school later in life, especially while looking for marriage prospects. Additionally, and more importantly, you are Bonded now. You will live for at least a few hundred years unless someone or something kills you.

"You need to stop thinking like an Earthling. You are on Ludus now. Age matters a lot less—"

Gonzo was interrupted by a shriek.

Henry quickly spun, his adrenaline spiking, but calmed when he saw Tony in the doorway to the garage, shaking and pointing an unsteady finger. Henry absently thought, *Huh, I forgot the kid was in there. He must have just woken up. My bad.*

Tony sputtered for a couple seconds before uncharacteristically cursing, "What the hell is she doing here?"

"Nice to see you too, cousin Aodh." Vitaliya smiled warmly. Henry felt a chill run down his spine.

I got a bad feeling about this.

* * *

Jason flew through the air, eventually pulling his new goggles out of a pocket and putting them on to protect his eyes. The goggles weren't that great. When he'd commissioned them a week before, he'd gotten what he had asked for, not what he wanted. They were made of glass and rubber, and weren't easy to see out of. The glass was kind of smoky. It still beat freezing his eyeballs, though.

Jason had been flying for several hours. He was following the meandering trail that he had traveled months before with the Georgetown village. The trail was hard to see sometimes through the trees, and he had to backtrack occasionally. He was still making excellent time, though.

He judged he was travelling over 100 miles an hour since he spent so long in freefall between teleports. His travel was hard to control, but from high in the air, following a path through the forest, he could manage it.

He was really impressed by his endurance now that he was second rank orb-Bonded. There was no way he could have hoped to travel so far as first rank. Second rank not only gave him more power, it also helped with his control. Jason calibrated each teleport vector to make the most of his speed, getting the greatest distance possible.

He would shoot forward at a 45-degree angle, eventually plummeting back towards the ground, and as soon as he thought he hit terminal velocity, he would repeat the process as far away as he could teleport, converting his freefall into flight of sorts.

Jason was glad he didn't get motion sickness, or he'd have been miserable.

He figured it was going to take most of the day to reach his destination. What he was most concerned about was where he would spend the night. Security was definitely an issue. He'd cross that bridge when he came to it.

The trip was boring after a while. Other than the handful of times he couldn't see the old road anymore and had to search for it, the travel itself was fairly simple. He'd found a groove. It gave him time to think.

He wasn't entirely sure what to do for the near future. He was obviously going to travel to Berber with Henry and help root out the cult-based conspiracy, but it felt small to him. It was important, but if he and Henry ever wanted to get home, they had to unite the world. Hell, they probably needed to do something significant just to survive. He was starting to think of the task Dolos had given them as their "main quest."

War was coming.

Jason pondered the favor that Dolos still owed him. He wondered what he should do with it. In fact, he wondered how he could even call it in. Keeja was supposed to be their liaison with Dolos, but she'd been gone for weeks.

Jason wasn't sure what to think about the main quest, but at least he was doing something productive now. He considered his current mission a side quest. Having a task and a clear goal was refreshing.

It was especially handy that he could travel so fast. Jason had been doing some reading about magic, at least what he could. The Air school of magic was common, so there was a good deal of information on it.

When air mages flew, the amount of effort sounded similar to the null-time shields he could create. Jason didn't even want to imagine creating null-time shields all day. Plus, flying required a constant effort, whereas Jason's teleport travel was just brief bursts of magic between gliding and free falling.

If he thought about it critically, he was really a lot faster than he had any right to be. For an air mage to replicate his speed and range, they'd probably have to be at least a 6th rank orb-Bonded. He wasn't even sure if natural mages of such power existed on Ludus. He should find out.

When Jason finally reached the abandoned little farming village where he'd spent his first night on Ludus, he was overcome by nostalgia. He took a break on top of a roof, resting his freezing, aching joints. Even with his endurance skill, the trip had been grueling.

It was obvious that monsters, probably goblins, had visited. Shutters were hacked to pieces, furniture had been pulled out of buildings and torn apart...The villagers had been wise to leave when they did.

The village itself was already being overgrown by the forest. A small tree was growing right outside George's old front door.

Jason sat down with his chin in his hand and just rested. He knew he only had a few hours of daylight left, but he was suddenly emotionally exhausted. This was where it had all begun. This little village out in the middle of nowhere…if they hadn't come to this place, he might not have even been alive today to feel so melancholy about the place.

It was a sobering thought. Not for the first time since coming to Ludus, Jason felt incredibly lucky. However, with his new suspicions about Dolos, he wondered how much of their good fortune was actually luck. Just how far did the manipulation go? If there even had been manipulation. They had no proof.

Jason sighed. He couldn't sit around feeling melancholy all day. He had a job to do. He teleported into the air, and a few minutes later, he found the clearing he'd first seen Mareen and George in. The trail remained; there were probably goblins nearby.

As Jason started walking through the forest towards his destination, he realized the flowertop demon probably survived off of goblins.

When he had spotted his objective, he stopped. About 50 yards ahead of him, Jason spotted the bush with pink flowers. It looked interesting, like something he'd walk up to just to study. That was probably the point.

He drew his sword *Breeze* and advanced slowly. He wasn't too worried. If the monster did anything too surprising, he was just going to teleport away.

About 25 yards away from the creature, Jason realized he was being an idiot, an arrogant idiot. He sheathed his sword. *Why fight if you don't have to?*

He teleported to the top of a tree near his target. Even so close, the monster just looked like a bush with pretty flowers. However, when he threw a throwing knife to the ground, the whole ground erupted a split second after it landed.

Tentacles lifted from soil in an explosion of dirt and leaves, grasping blindly as the creature lifted itself from its hole. Jason was sickly fascinated. The bush seemed to actually be growing from a depression in the monster's head. The rest of it was blocky, with thick, leathery skin. It almost looked like a worm with its mouth in the wrong place, on the side of its body.

Tentacles whipped around, coiling around trees, poking into the foliage, searching everywhere for food. The tentacles all had thick hairs at the end that Jason figured were for sensing prey. The monster itself was obviously blind.

As Jason observed the creature, he was glad he'd been smart enough not to deal with the chaos on the ground. He didn't think he would have been in real danger, since he'd known that he would have been ambushed, but the tentacles looked strong and the creature's mouth was huge and full of sharp teeth. *Discretion is the better part of valor.* He decided to use a new skill to kill the monster.

Jason held up a throwing knife and concentrated, causing the blade's edge to shimmer with null-time. His target was currently at the farthest range that Jason could maintain null-time fields attached to objects after throwing them.

It would be enough.

Delvers LLC: Obligations Incurred

CHAPTER SIX

Enchantment Emporyum

Uluula had a pocket full of money and wasn't quite sure what to do with it yet. After the meeting with Ryan Gonzolez had ended, all the Delvers had gone their separate ways to begin preparing for the mission. Mareen had gone looking for Henry to accompany them while shopping, but somehow the man seemed to have vanished into thin air. Eventually, Uluula and Mareen had left together while Mareen grumbled about, "That man."

Uluula thought about what Henry had said in the meeting, that people could choose not to go on the mission if they didn't want to. The truth was, even if she had not been romantically involved with Jason, she would have still volunteered. The entire operation sounded incredibly interesting.

Uluula hadn't been to Berber yet. At some point, Uluula had wanted to visit. Berber was also a border country with the Areva nation Hanana to its northwest.

However, she definitely had to improve her armor and weapons before going anywhere more dangerous, and she didn't know the first thing about enchanted items. She also had to consider cost. The Mirana government had given Delvers LLC a small fortune as an advance, true, but most of that had to be kept for Henry's projects before they left.

Maren had graciously donated what was left of her money to Uluula. Mareen hadn't really needed any more gear, and if she did need anything, Henry could just make it for her. Still, Uluula was grateful.

Uluula held a sizable amount of money, enough that it made her uncomfortable.

The first thing she did was visit a weapons shop and learn the basics about magic items. Basically, magic items came in two types. The first could be operated by anyone and didn't require any other equipment to use. These were usually simple items like elemental weapons or cups that created water. They had a switch, button, or some other physical means to activate them.

The second type was more complex and could be activated with a thought. Uluula believed most, if not all of Captain Haili's items were this type. Complex enchanted items required the user to wear a focus crystal in order to sync with the item. These types of items were useless if their owner was not wearing the paired focus crystal, but they were more valuable because a random person couldn't just pick one up and be the new owner after a random amount of time.

Pairing the enchanted object with a new focus crystal established new ownership.

Uluula discovered that rings were the most popular and most expensive types of focus crystals, and she didn't understand why. She bought a necklace instead. She figured if she lost a hand she could still be fighting, but if she lost her head, she probably wouldn't need the focus crystal anymore.

She chose a choker necklace, the choice being partially influenced by how Mareen usually dressed. Uluula was used to Mareen wearing a lace choker to help hide the line around her throat for her servitude contract. Uluula reasoned she could do something similar to hide her new focus crystal necklace.

It didn't hurt to be careful.

Still, all these decisions were fairly simple. Actually deciding what enchanted items to buy was another matter entirely.

There were weapons, shields, projectiles, utility items, even clothing. All of it was expensive, even ridiculously so. Uluula kept thinking about how the enchanted items in other parts of the world were reportedly stronger, too. She had to keep in mind how important an item was and how easily it might be replaced if she found a more powerful item of that type in the future.

She wished Jason were with her. Mareen was good company and she was sharp as a *vibrade*, but Jason would have been much better to discuss strategy with. *I wonder if I should wait for Jason to get back?* The thought was tempting, but she rejected it. A warrior never knew when she'd be called upon to defend her life or the lives of others. Even a day or two was unacceptable, since she already knew what her course of action had to be.

Plus, she didn't know when Jason was getting back. She dispelled the thought before it could ruin her mood, but her demeanor must have changed. The old shopkeeper she had been talking to wrung her hands and backed away nervously. Of course, Uluula and Mareen both wearing Delvers LLC masks probably didn't help matters. Rumors were being spreading about people wearing metal masks. Uluula thought the whole situation was ridiculous.

The shopkeeper kept slowly backing away and Uluula sighed. She didn't want to be too rude, but she was done at this store anyway. She jerked her head at Mareen and her friend followed her out into the street.

There was only one more notable store in Mirana that sold enchanted gear. In fact, it was the largest. Uluula had been avoiding it since it was also the most expensive. *Oh well, no other option now.* She and Mareen had visited almost a dozen shops already and hadn't seen any gear that caught Uluula's eye. Most of the items they'd seen so far were simple enchanted weapons.

Uluula had her spear with her, as usual. She trusted the spear, but she knew she needed an upgrade, preferably another spear. She preferred spears or halberds, and on Ludus, where everyone and everything seemed to be taller than she was, she wasn't in a hurry to shorten her reach.

If she had to kill monsters, she wanted to keep the things at a distance while skewering them.

Mareen chatted idly with her as they walked. Uluula wasn't very interested in inane conversation, but she knew it helped Mareen. Her friend had a lot on her mind and seemed to think she was required to present a strong front. Terrans were truly bizarre. Uluula wondered if the reasons Terrans always tried to act as if nothing was wrong was so other Terrans would not take advantage of their weakness.

Earth must truly be a hellish planet. She wondered how Jason was able to stay kind despite coming from such an evil planet full of violence and brutality. If anyone ever tried to change Jason, Uluula was going to carve their heart out with her spear while they still lived, and let them watch.

She would raze their homeworld to the ground. Nobody had better change her gentle giant. Well, gentle when he wasn't teleporting behind people and stabbing them, but she liked that side of him, too.

They reached *Enchantment Emporyum,* the largest enchanted item shop in Mirana, while Uluula was still thinking dark thoughts about revenge genocide and Mareen was prattling on about tasty pies. The white-haired Areva woman shook her head; it was time to focus, time to get serious.

Even shopping could be a battle.

Inside, the shop was decorated very tastefully, the aesthetics pleasing to the eye. Nice colors, not too overdone, but with an undercurrent of wealth. It immediately set her on edge.

These merchants at this shop were probably very skilled negotiators. They'd be dangerous. Uluula would much rather have dealt with bumbling, stupid shopkeepers. The people running the Enchantment Emporyum were probably predators, skilled hunters.

The portly Terran who stepped forward to greet them had every appearance of a kindly old man. His eyes twinkled, and his smiled seemed genuine. He wore clothes more after the Ludan style: dark robes with a vest. Uluula didn't trust his smile for a second.

"Hello, and welcome to Enchantment Emporyum! Based on the masks, I'm assuming you ladies might be part of Delvers LLC?"

Uluula could not believe the salesman had so brazenly tipped his hand. He'd just demonstrated how well informed he was, only possible if he kept close tabs on potential targets. Uluula increased her mental armor even further. Salespeople were all crooked.

Mareen began to speak, but Uluula cut her off. Her friend had already demonstrated earlier that she didn't know what a pack of scavengers all these salespeople were. "Just tell us where everything is and leave until I get you," Uluula demanded.

She spoke so abruptly, she almost expected the man to respond in kind. However, all he said was, "Very well. Utility items are on this floor. Armor, weapons, and higher-end utility items are grouped accordingly on the second floor." Then he bowed and left them alone.

Uluula was so suspicious her skin began to crawl. A salesman who listened to her and even walked away...and a Terran, too? If she bought anything from these pirates, she was going to haggle them into the ground.

Into. The. Ground.

Mareen gave her a questioning look, but Uluula ignored it and stomped up the stairs. Anything she would want would be expensive. Unfortunately, that was just how the world worked. Her only recourse was to treat every sale like a fight to the death. She would not lose.

She studied and dismissed the decorations on the second floor, namely stuffed demon heads on the wall and paintings of dungeons, all of which were tacky. The exception was the decoration in the center of the room.

The centerpiece of the room, a giant crystal carved in the likeness of an Areva woman holding aloft a blazing sword, was lovely. The figure's crystal sword used Ludus tech to glow and help light the room. Uluula recognized the artistic skills of her people in the piece, so of course it was nice. She nodded in satisfaction as she passed the beautiful sculpture.

From the center of the room, she glanced around. The shop's reputation was well earned. She conceded it had the largest and most varied selection of magic equipment in all of Mirana.

Uluula noticed a couple guards out in the open, both of them Mo'hali. Both wore masks. She wondered if either of them was a Hero, but she doubted it; the masks were shoddy and didn't look fitted to either guard.

She had a feeling that most shops employed Mo'hali guards whether they had a Hero or not, since the mere threat of one would probably deter most mages or Bonded. She had a feeling there were other, unseen eyes around the store as well, though.

She went to check out the utility section first, completely ignoring another salesperson and a few customers walking around. Despite herself, Uluula was impressed by some of the items and descriptions she saw. As with all the other shops they had visited in Mirana, each device was behind glass so customers couldn't accidentally take ownership of anything. Uluula reflected it was a necessary precaution. Enchanted gear could only recognize three users before dissolving, after all.

Uluula examined a number of items, some of which had truly remarkable functions. A cloak that helped make its wearer harder to see, a necklace that changed the user's voice, a hat that kept the user from being rained on, even in a thunderstorm, a belt that allowed someone to stay underwater on one breath for over an hour…

The item selection was extensive. There were even a few blessed steel items mixed in the merchandise such as cups, cutlery, and random bits of metal like hinges.

In the utility section, there was a staggering number of rings. There were rings that created light, rings that lowered light, rings that tested for poison, rings that could create a loud siren noise, even a ring that purified water.

Uluula moved on to the armor section of the Enchantment Emporyum and found more merchandise than in the utility section.

The Emporyum seemed to classify anything that created protection or was created from armor as "armor." Uluula thought it would have been more accurate to call it the protection section.

The most common types of items in this section were rings and bracelets that created magic shields. Most shields created would be about the size and shape of a standard round shield, just made of force, or air, or some other element. Uluula began to realize that the items Captain Haili had demonstrated were probably individually more powerful than anything available in the shop.

In addition to all the items that generated magic shields, there was a surprising number of normal-looking armor pieces with resistances to various elements or attacks. Mareen pointed out a helm that was resistant to fire and gauntlets that were resistant to wind. Uluula agreed they were interesting, but she believed they were limited in value. Unless she had her whole body covered by a single elemental resistance, a single piece didn't seem that useful to her.

What was far more practical was a leather chestpiece she noticed that offered puncture and slashing resistance, effectively making it the same grade of protection as steel armor. Uluula was interested until she saw the price and almost gagged. What the shop was demanding was obscene!

Robbery, just robbery. She continued to list every item, its description, and its price in her neuralcomp, the Areva hardware in her head. She'd been doing so all day at each store they went to. It paid to be informed. So far, she was surprised the Enchantment Emporyum actually didn't have much more expensive list prices than the other stores in Mirana, but she was still suspicious. "Deals" were all relative, too, since all the merchants were thieves.

She'd sold enchanted items on behalf of Delvers LLC. She could make a guess on what kind of markup the Emporyum was making, and it almost made her sick again.

Robbery!

She noticed some armor that truly caught her interest when she was almost done browsing the protection section. They were a set of light bracers, nothing really amazing to look at. However, the description made her eyes open wide in interest. She also did a double take when she saw at the price. So cheap!

Then again, thinking about it more carefully, it made sense that movement items would be less popular among other, larger races.

They would probably be painful, if not impossible to use for larger people. There weren't many Areva in Mirana; if there were, Uluula was sure the bracers wouldn't have still been around, especially at their current price. She smiled and put a mark next to the bracers on her mental list.

Lastly, she perused the weapons section, the larger portion of the shop. Mareen visibly brightened up. This was the section she'd told Uluula she wanted to see.

As Mareen hummed to herself and moved over to examine the heaviest, largest weapons, Uluula idly continued adding entries to the database in her neuralcom as she made her way to the spear section.

There was a staggering amount of diversity in weapons. Rings that could produce sustained jets of flame, daggers that left infected wounds, bracelets that caused metal weapons held in the hand to glow, swords with elemental damage, even an axe that could almost effortlessly cut through stone. The enchanted weapons themselves were made of a variety of materials: bronze, copper, tin, blessed steel, even metals Uluula couldn't identify.

When she got to the spear section, she almost immediately found two things she wanted. One was a ring that could create a spear of fog twice a day. The description stated the spear could be held and used as a weapon for a few minutes, or shot from the hand as a projectile.

The other weapon took her breath away. It was a *jaalba*,

plasma halberd...or at least looked like one. Uluula had no idea why an enchanted item had been created that so closely resembled the traditional Areva melee weapon of war, but it called to her.

She read the description and saw it even had a plasma-enhanced cutting edge. It included modifications to reduce its encumbrance to the user, too.

Due to its energy output, it required magic stones for power. The description stated it used them up rather quickly, which was probably the only reason it was even in Uluula's price range.

Uluula was in love, but the weapon would still come in second place to Jason, though. Nothing at this point could replace her tall, messy-haired Terran. Thinking of him made her bring up a viscap she stored of him in her neuralcomp. She especially liked how, after gently making love with her, always so gently, he'd kiss her nose and...

She shook her head. *Neither the time nor the place for thoughts like that.* She walked over to stand by Mareen, but only half paid attention to her friend. It was crazy that a year ago she hadn't even known for sure that Terrans existed. She'd never thought she'd have a Terran friend, much less a Terran lover.

Then there was Henry. She didn't hate Henry, but she had no idea why Jason and Mareen cared about him so deeply. She admitted that he had a kind of efficient pragmatism and a number of talents. Deep, deep down, she had to admit that in some ways he reminded her of herself. So yes, she didn't hate him, but if he ever got himself killed, she wasn't planning on wearing mourning clothes.

No use in being insincere.

The truth was she still didn't like Terrans very much in general. The mere thought of them didn't terrify her like they once had, but she was still suspicious of Terrans, and Terran salesclerks in particular. She loved Mareen as a sister, bonding over their shared awkwardness, and she was going to marry Jason. In fact, she had to hurry her marrying of the fool man so she could start growing his household.

She knew he wasn't entirely comfortable with the idea, and she didn't want to push him, but she agreed with Mareen that neither Henry nor Jason knew how important establishing their families would be on Ludus.

No, Uluula truly didn't want to make Jason uncomfortable, but with the type of political snake den they could be walking into, he needed all the support he could get. She refused to lose him. It had taken her over 40 years to find the man, so she would not allow him to get himself killed because he had worried nerves about marrying her and another woman or two.

It still stung her why he felt that way, that he focused on the carnal aspect of it. Did he not trust she'd pick worthy suitors? Not for the first time, she had to remind herself that he was from a different culture. A stupid culture. An incredibly stupid culture if people really got married to one person "for life," only to get divorced and make the same vows again to other people.

It was madness.

*It is common sense that with more than one wife in a household...*Uluula's thoughts trailed off. She stopped thinking about bizarre Terran customs and made her decision about the magic items.

"Mareen, I think I'm ready to try buying what I want."

"Oh?" answered the darker-skinned woman. "You finally found something you like?"

"Actually a number of things."

"How much will everything cost?"

"About three times more than I have with the money you lent me."

Mareen arched one eyebrow at her. "You want to haggle, don't you?"

"Yes."

"Don't you ever get tired of spending all day trying to wring every coin you can from a deal? I mean, if you can get the price down to a third of what they're asking, I'll be impressed, but why do you think it's even possible?"

"Because I saw Henry's old axe he sold. Remember the *"Badaxe"*? It was very distinct-looking. I know what we sold it for to the Guild, and I know what they're selling it for here, so I can guess at the general markup in the store."

"I see." Mareen sighed. "What all are you trying to get?"

Uluula's smile was predatory. "You will have to wait and see. I have to fight this battle first." She stalked down the stairs of the Enchantment Emporyum to find the old snake that had first greeted them. The war had begun!

* * *

Two hours later, Uluula and Mareen were walking back to Henry and Jason's house. Uluula admired Mareen's fearlessness to live with Henry so quickly. The thought of living with a man still made her nervous, even though she had activated her sexual bridge and was having…relations with Jason.

"I wish I had the nerve you do," she said.

"What do you mean?" asked Mareen.

"The way you live with Henry. We talked about this before."

Mareen shook her head. "You make no sense at all. You can kill monsters five times your size, you rarely ever show any fear about anything, but you're still afraid to live with a man you're already sleeping with? Seriously?

"Uluula, you just bargained in a shop for hours and even shouted at that poor old man. I think he let you have everything you wanted just to get you out of the store. The fact you are so nervous about natural things just makes no sense. Have you talked to Jason about it?"

"Yes, he said I can move in with him whenever I want, that he loves me," she answered uncomfortably. Well, at least Mareen was right about how she'd gotten everything she wanted at the

Enchantment Emporyum. She had to admit she felt a little smug. The plasma halberd, the mist spear ring, the movement bracers, a shield ring, and the concealment cloak had all been purchased for slightly less than all the money she'd had.

She'd spent a small fortune, but she knew she had stretched every coin.

Still, she reflected again on how lucky she was there were so few Areva in Mirana. With more small-statured people frequenting the Emporyum, she didn't think she would have been so lucky. For instance, her shield ring was marketed as a "large shield." Full-body shields in the shop were priced more than triple what the standard shield devices were. If the people running the stop had realized that the dimensions of a "large shield" would completely cover her body, they probably would have marked up the price.

Uluula thought for a second before slowly saying, "Jason being comfortable with it doesn't mean I am. You wouldn't understand. Cohabitation is a big deal in my culture, more so than sex or even having children. Some married people don't even live together."

"That...doesn't make any sense. Not only that, aren't we basically planning to push Henry and Jason to deal with this thing that makes them uncomfortable? Isn't your resistance kind of hypocritical?"

"No, because my hang-up isn't going to put my life in danger," Uluula replied with a raised eyebrow.

"Well, I guess you have a point. I just don't like being devious like this. It feels wrong.

"But I have a change of topic. I've been meaning to ask you for a while...why are you buying all this enchanted gear? Why didn't you just take an orb? I know we don't know what kind it is since Keeja's been gone, but wouldn't the orb have solved all your gear problems?"

Uluula missed a step but kept walking. She'd known this question would come, and would probably come up again, too. Unfortunately, she couldn't tell her friend the truth. She hadn't given up on her dream completely yet, what she'd been aiming for ever since her sister had been killed. Uluula knew she may never be an admiral now since she was stuck on Ludus, but that didn't mean she had no chance of ever attaining an Artifice in her lifetime.

Of course, she had to get off this planet first and take Jason with her, but it was her dream, her passion, to earn an Artifice.

Still, it was more than passing odd that she never heard anyone mention Artifices on Ludus. Nobody ever discussed how Dolos was obviously trying to mimic Artifices with the Dolos orbs.

She was almost certain that Keeja was a high-grade Artifice Holder, too.

Uluula was raised to always watch her words, to always observe the world around her. Until she understood why nobody on this planet so far talked about Artifices, even people who should have known of their existence, she was keeping her mouth shut.

"I have my reasons," was all she said.

"There you go being mysterious again." Mareen sighed. "Fine. Have it your way. But I'm bored and I don't really have anything to do. Later today, want to test out all your new enchanted gear?"

Uluula gave a genuine smile. "I'd like nothing better."

CHAPTER SEVEN

Fancy Nuptials

Rark-han crossed the street to join the meeting at Henry-ibbi and Jason-ibbi's house. He agreed with Bezzi-ibbi about meetings —less was more. He sighed.

As the air exited his mouth, he felt the stub of his tongue and winced. This in turn made him think of his missing arm and he winced again. Rark-han was maimed. He was a shadow of himself. The world was unjust; he hadn't deserved to be banished from his Clan, but the incredible shame and debt he'd acquired by standing by and doing nothing while bandits tormented innocents…there was no way to atone for it in a lifetime.

His only hope was to follow the wisdom of the Hero, and in turn follow the leaders of Delvers LLC as his liege did. Rark-han knew his very soul was on the line. There was no room for error.

Such a man as he had no right to complain about anything

anyway. A missing arm and tongue were nothing compared to the evil he'd witnessed while he had frozen in indecision, questioning whether he should break his promise to Bandit Thod. He'd agonized over his honor until he'd realized he had none left. He'd never be that foolish again.

He'd follow Bezzi-ibbi into the bowels of giant Fenrir himself now. His own desires were no longer relevant. However, possibly rooting out the *scorra* that had funded the bandits and other insurgent groups in Tolstey was a mission he believed in.

Not for the first time, Rark-han was humbled and appreciative for his chance to atone. He was a disgusting, fallen Mo'hali. But as long as he served his Hero faithfully, he had at least a small hope at redemption for his soul. It was too late for him in this life, but he was desperately fighting for his eternal future.

Enough of that. He couldn't effectively serve his liege if he moped about all day, dwelling on his missing tongue and arm. He had a prosthetic for his arm, and he never really spoke that much to begin with. Of course, that in itself had been a problem, hadn't it? Perhaps if he'd spoken up, spoken for himself, he wouldn't have been banished from his Clan.

If he was patient, he knew his chance to rend and tear the enemies of his liege Hero would come again. Perhaps one day, his liege would even right the wrongs that had caused Rark-han to be rejected from his Clan.

He donned his usual neutral expression as he opened the door to the Masters' house and shut it behind him. As usual, the unpleasant odor of Terran occupation hit him, especially as he passed the bedrooms, but he endured. He couldn't help twitching his nose, though.

The rest of the Delvers were in the garage. Some of them were actually on the monstrous contraption Henry-ibbi had named the Battlewagon. Rark-han's ears laid back when he saw it. Unnatural and far too powerful to be a battle tool of such a small group, he kept wondering if the gods or the ancestors would come down from on high to punish them.

Then again, until recently they'd been travelling with Keeja, a demigod, a demigod that had sexually harassed Henry-ibbi. Every time Henry-ibbi had cursed at Keeja, Rark-han had wondered if they would all die. It hurt his head to think about it.

Henry-ibbi was an idiot. Then again, so was Jason-ibbi, which was why they were having this meeting in the first place. Jason-ibbi had gone off on a mission by himself and come back.

Rark-han slightly bared his teeth before he stilled his face again. The casual arrogance and irresponsibility of those with such earth-shaking power was something he would never understand.

"Okay, everyone's here," said Henry. The man's goatee and hair were newly trimmed. Rark-han figured Mareen had done it. Henry himself seemed only peripherally aware of anything around him these days other than his inventions. He had just started working on the "motorcycles" for Spy Gonzolez. However, against the far wall, Rark-han could see the outlines of four new contraptions, not two.

Henry-ibbi was obviously building a couple extra magic machines. Why, Rark-han didn't know. He just hoped it didn't involve him.

The big wolf man glanced around the room. There wasn't a lot of space in the garage now, especially with extra people. Henry, Mareen, and Jason were on the Battlewagon. Uluula was at her desk. Aodh stood in the corner where he usually slept, glaring at Spy Vitaliya and unsuccessfully trying to hide it. Spy Vitaliya herself stood on the other side of the room, pointedly ignoring Aodh for the time being.

Rark-han stood by Bezzi-ibbi and the boy's uncle from the Jaguar Clan, Yanno-ibbi, near the door to the house. Spy Gonzolez remained by himself.

Henry cleared his throat and said, "As you can all see, it's been a couple days, but Jason is back. Jason, could you update everyone on what you were doing while you were gone and what we did this morning? Also, something I forgot to ask earlier is where you slept by yourself. I knew you'd figure something out, but I'm curious what you did for security."

Jason took a half step forward and rested his arms on the wall of the Battlewagon's cargo area. "What I did was fairly simple. I traveled a long distance to obtain materials for the neutralization of our LEDF. This means we won't have to wear masks anymore."

"LEDF?" Aodh asked.

"The Left Eye Data Feed that Dolos initiated."

Henry looked smug. "I knew that acronym would come in handy."

Not for the first time, Rark-han had to admit he didn't understand Terrans at all. The company masters were openly disrespectful to each other, they backed down and acted weak at times, showing the backs of their necks, but Rark-han had seen them fight. He'd even seen them lay waste to hundreds of other warriors like it was nothing. Rark-han shook his head. It was not for him to understand the strange Terrans. Bezzi-ibbi counted them as brothers; he could deal with them. Rark-han just had to follow.

Jason ignored Henry and continued, "What I needed was inside a rare and dangerous monster. We were pressed for time, so I went myself. It was actually more dangerous than I was expecting, but I was able to kill it with a new ability I've been practicing." Jason smiled.

Rark-han felt a chill. Jason was already an incredibly dangerous man. He couldn't imagine what deadly, terrifying new abilities he was perfecting, especially if it made him smile like that. Terrans scared Rark-han on principle, probably even more than Areva. However, the fact that Uluula was softly growling from her desk in the corner was straining Rark-han's normal hierarchy of caution. He really wished she would stop making that noise.

"To answer Henry's question about security..." Jason turned to his friend and said, "I camped by finding small caves. I used null-time on my blade to collapse the entrance before sleeping. Then I would teleport outside to continue travelling. Coming back took me longer because I was tired and had to find safe-looking caves to rest in from time to time."

Henry chuckled. "That was smart. Now that I think about it, I probably could have done the same thing and just blown all the rocks out with magic when I needed to leave my cave. Good to know."

"Indeed. Anyway, I found seven of the items we need to make tinctures that will remove the LEDF. This morning, Henry, myself, Bezzi-ibbi, and Mareen already took a dose. We haven't tested the effectiveness yet, but I don't think we will need to wear masks anymore." He leveled a meaningful look at Spy Gonzolez.

Rark-han winced inwardly. If Jason and Henry were going to get involved in politics, they really needed to learn to better control their body language.

Spy Gonzolez said, "I'm impressed. That was fast. However, I'm not sure why you invited Vitaliya and myself here to tell us this. I realize I may be more cynical than the average person, but you're freely telling us about extra resources you haven't used. You're speaking of real wealth and power, especially in this world."

Jason rolled his eyes. "Oh, come on. Somebody or somebodies

are going through a lot of effort to get us to Berber. If you sold us out for some monster parts, you'd not only be stupid, you'd probably also be dead. I don't think your government would take kindly to such a thing. Plus, you're basically turning us into nobles in actuality, since faking it won't work. Pissing us off would be incredibly shortsighted, especially for a rational person like you appear to be.

"We invited you here since we will be travelling together for a while. Everyone in our company stays on the same page at all times so we don't have misunderstandings."

Maybe they're wiser than I thought. Rark-han truly didn't understand these Terrans, but occasionally they seemed to make surprisingly intelligent decisions.

"Thanks, Jason," said Henry. "We have two other things to talk about. First, we're leaving in about a week. We should have the bikes done by then and all our gear ready to go. Everyone plan on leaving Mirana in seven days. Actually, why the fuck is a week on Ludus still seven days?"

"Probably because the people populating Ludus are from other planets," said Jason.

"Bezzi-ibbi, do you know if a week is seven days long on your homeworld? What about you, Uluula?" Henry absently patted his leg as he glanced around.

Bezzi-ibbi just shrugged, but Uluula replied, "Yes, a week has always been seven days for me. However, didn't you just say you had something else to announce as well?" Her voice wasn't unfriendly, but to Rark-han she sounded terse.

"Henry, stop getting sidetracked. Just say what you need to say." Mareen was scowling, but her voice was warm. Rark-han didn't understand why Terrans never seemed to just say what they meant. Mareen tried to present a prickly front, but her body language and what he could understand of her Terran musk practically howled that she was deeply in love.

"Well, I actually have two more things to say, not just one." Henry looked hesitantly as Jason, who nodded. "Okay, first is that we're giving our extra Dolos orb to Tony if he wants it."

"What!?" Aodh was so shocked he almost fell on his butt. He leaned against the wall instead and opened and closed his mouth like a fish. Rark-han thought it looked rather comical.

"Yeah. We don't actually know what it does because it didn't come with a note, and Keeja hasn't been back. On the other hand, all these fucking things always have the exact same instructions. To be safe, think about a specific type of magic all day and before you go to bed, in case it's a modular-type orb. It it's not, it will just do whatever it's supposed to do after you swallow it before bed.

"Anyway, Tony, if you want the orb, we also have a tincture for you to take with it so you'll never have to worry about the fucking left eye whatsit."

"LEDF," muttered Jason.

"Yeah, that." While Aodh continued to sputter, Henry's

posture changed and he looked unsure of himself. Jason nodded again and Henry swallowed. He turned his whole body, staring into Mareen's eyes as he asked, "Will you marry me, Mareen ni'Haniyya Jacobs?"

Absolute silence rang in the garage. Rark-han felt his ears going back, but he couldn't help it. He was not equipped to deal with how quickly the scents and body language in the small space suddenly shifted. He was nervous, surrounded by emotionally unstable people who could break him in half without much effort. He was never sure what they'd do next.

Before anyone could speak, Jason formally said, "Uluula b' Anami b' Pairose of the Blue, will you marry me?"

Nobody spoke. Rark-han's skin prickled. When he glanced at Bezzi-ibbi and saw his liege's wide, feral grin, it didn't help settle his nerves at all.

Uluula replied first. "Jason James Booth, I accept. However, I would like to know when you actually want the ceremony to take place?"

"Henry Mirai Sata, I accept and I have the same question." Mareen's voice wavered and she had tears in her eyes. She trembled, and her body language screamed she wanted to throw herself at the man that had just proposed to her. She was holding back, and Rark-han was not sure why.

What on Ludus is going on? Why are these men proposing, and both at the same time?

Jason spoke, his words smooth like he'd practiced them before. He said, "I would love to marry you as soon as possible; however, it takes two weeks to prepare a marriage ceremony in Mirana, and we are leaving in a week. Unfortunately, I believe we will need to be engaged for some time."

"Why can't we just move our departure date back by a week or two?" asked Mareen.

"We can't. I already spoke to Gonzo about it and we have to leave as soon as possible, right, Gonzo?" Spy Gonzolez nodded. He looked as confused as Rark-han felt. "See? It's regrettable, but it will be some time before we can formally get married," Jason replied.

"It's really too bad," muttered Henry.

Then a curious thing happened. Uluula and Mareen smiled, their expressions predatory. "So now that I've accepted your proposal, you would get married to me as quickly as you could if the situation were different?" Uluula asked.

"Definitely," responded Jason.

"You know I love you, Mareen," said Henry. "The timing is just not right."

The women smiled wider and Rark-han almost whimpered; the strong emotions and smells in the garage were overpowering.

Uluula crossed her arms, her expression turning satisfied. "This is actually quite a coincidence. I've been inviting Yanno-ibbi to spend time in the garage for the last couple days, teaching us Jaguar Clan history. Imagine our luck that Yanno-ibbi happened to be here to witness this conversation today. Yanno-ibbi, you are officially empowered to officiate marriages, correct?"

The older Mo'hali man frowned, but the twinkle in his eye gave him away. "I am, yes. This is correct."

"I see. And in Mirana, Mo'hali are not required to file the same paperwork as other residents for marriage, nor book a temple, which takes about two weeks, yes?" Uluula sounded a little smug.

"This is also correct."

"In fact, in your capacity as a recognized Mo'hali elder, what do you actually need in order to legally marry people?"

"Well, they need to be Mo'hali, or at least one person does. I also need to witness the proposal or a declaration of love."

"So would the proposals you just witnessed satisfy the requirement?"

"Wait a fucking minute!" Henry slightly raised his voice. "We aren't Mo'hali!"

"Oh, but legally you can be, Henry-ibbi," Mareen said, stressing his Jaguar Clan honorific. Tears were running freely down her face in happiness, but she still had a predatory grin.

Jason just looked at Yanno-ibbi and blinked stupidly.

"So," Uluula continued, "Henry-ibbi and Jason-ibbi are of the Jaguar Clan, they proposed to Mareen and I, and we accepted. In your capacity as a Jaguar Clan elder, what does this mean?"

Bezzi-ibbi began laughing softly, covering his mouth with both hands.

Yanno-ibbi coughed several times, trying not to laugh as well. "It means," he choked out and stopped talking until he got control of himself again. "It means I have the pleasure of pronouncing Mareen Jacobs and Henry-ibbi married as of this moment, standing in the light of the day. It means I pronounce Uluula of the Blue and Jason-ibbi married as of this moment, standing in the light of the day. This pronouncement has been witnessed by three other souls and is legally binding by Mo'hali and Tolstey law as soon as I turn in the paperwork tomorrow morning. Congratulations, and continue to stand in the day, to embrace the joy of being honest and guarding your family from enemies."

"Fuck me," whispered Henry before he was tackled by a crying, affectionate Mareen. Uluula walked over to the Battlewagon and climbed aboard. She grabbed Jason's collar and yanked him down into a kiss. To Rark-han, it almost sounded like she was purring.

Do these people do anything the normal way? They're all insane! Rark-han couldn't wait to leave the confusing language and overwhelming smells in the Delvers garage. Bezzi-ibbi was still chuckling as they left, and Rark-han longed for a good fight. At least violence made sense, unlike his Terran and Areva companions.

* * *

Just over a week later, the Delvers plus two spies and Yanno-ibbi had been travelling on the southwest road from Mirana all day. They had left early in the morning and made great time, so they were already outside the relatively safe, cultivated land near the city. The plan was to travel to Pilk before heading due west to the Stem River. Then they'd follow the river north through the Tolstey Mountains.

That evening, they found a decent campsite off the road and made camp before dusk. The Battlewagon made carrying equipment easy, so full-sized tents went up in no time at all. Before long, the four *magicycles*—the name Henry had coined for the hovering motorcycles he had built—were parked by the Battlewagon. The fire was roaring, and food was cooking.

Unfortunately, nobody in their group was a very good cook other than Mareen, but she didn't want to cook every day. That night, it was Yanno-ibbi's turn to try destroying their food as little as possible. It was a valiant effort.

Eventually, after the group fell asleep, Jason sat with Henry near their campfire. It was Jason's turn at watch, and he woke Henry so they could have a chat. Due to their endurance abilities, they could go without much sleep anyway, so the night watch was the perfect time to talk.

The flurry of activity before they'd left Mirana, including officially moving out of their house and spending one full day with their new wives, hadn't left them any time to privately talk.

"So, we're married now." Jason poked at the fire with a stick.

"Yeah. Your little plan kind of backfired in a big fucking way. Turns out your wife is smarter than you."

"Yes," Jason said, smiling. "I guess she is."

"Oh well, it's not all bad. I guess I was being kind a pussy anyway. I talked to Mareen about it. She said she knew I was going to drag my feet, and she didn't want to risk dying as an unmarried woman. This gig is dangerous, so I guess I kind of think she had a point. On the other hand, I know she's chomping at the friggin' bit to try 'growing our house,' which apparently means finding other chicks she thinks are good enough to play house with us.

"If I ever have to experience my own newlywed wife trying to play matchmaker for me, I'm going to feel awkward as fuck."

Jason nodded. "I got similar logic from Uluula. She also gave me a few specifics on how she put the trap together. I don't know whether to be frustrated with her or impressed. I think deep down I'm irritated I'm so happy right now, which proves she was right all along.

"She actually apologized for treating me like a mission objective, but she said she would have done the same thing again. Once again, I can't really be angry at her. I mean, I did propose. It was my choice." Jason looked wistfully into the fire, one side of his mouth quirked up into a smile.

"Whoa, dude, don't go getting all mushy on me. Get a hold of yourself."

Jason sighed. "You're such a dick, Henry. Fine, whatever. The real reason I called you out here…Actually, you know what? You're so polite and thoughtful, you can find out for yourself." Jason stood and brushed himself off before gesturing for his friend to follow.

Henry grumbled but got up and followed Jason through the sparse forest composed mostly of scraggly pine trees. Jason knew that for all his blustering, Henry was probably holding power from the earth and using his enhanced senses to scan for any danger.

Jason continued leading the mumbling Henry away from the camp, heading for the road. After they were a decent distance away from the camp, probably at least 200 yards, Jason finally said, "Here is fine." He was enjoying the look of frustration and impatience on his friend's face.

Henry squared his shoulders impatiently. "So what are we doing out here now? Are you sure you're not going gay on me? I know I'm sexy as hell, but you just got married, and Uluula will have your balls if you go after a dude. Areva really don't like gay people, you know. Did you know your wife is homophobic?"

Jason closed his eyes and prayed for patience. Even with his eyes shut, he could sense Henry's grin. He breathed slowly out his nose and opened his eyes again. *I suddenly feel even less bad for doing this to Henry.*

"So what is this about, huh? You just going to stand there all night with your eyes closed? I could be sleeping right now."

Jason grinned. "Okay, fine. I'll show you." And with that, Jason looked the opposite direction from their camp, turned to the sky, and yelled, "Keeja, come talk to us!"

"What the hell are you yelling about, dude? Keeja has been gone for weeks." The slight edge of nervousness in Henry's voice could only have been picked up by someone who knew him really, really well.

Jason smiled. He'd heard the quaver.

After a few moments, Henry began grumbling again, but Jason just waited. He knew his reasoning was sound. He'd been thinking about Keeja all week, wondering where she'd gone off to, and then realized the answer was staring him in the face the whole time.

She couldn't have left indefinitely. He and Henry were indirectly working for Dolos, and more importantly, Dolos still owed Jason a favor.

Jason had a hunch the favor he was owed was at least one reason Keeja hadn't shown herself for a while. At the same time, every old story or bit of lore he'd ever heard stated that gods and powerful supernatural beings had to keep their word. He was betting on the fact that Dolos had the same requirements.

Suddenly, as if she were summoned, Keeja appeared directly before them. Tall for an Areva, as usual she wore Earth clothing: short jean shorts, a black, baggy t-shirt with a rock band logo, and a stylish hat. It was dark, but Jason was pretty sure she was wearing expensive ankle boots too. The golden necklace of her office glittered in the starlight, and the markings on her face gave her a devilish appearance in the dark.

"Took you long enough," the priestess growled. "What do you want?"

Jason smiled. "Dolos owes me a favor. I'd like to talk to him."

Keeja frowned and said, "What, like right now? It will take me a little bit to contact him. It'll be at least a day, maybe two before he shows up after that, too."

"That's fine, please get him here as soon as possible." Jason noticed Henry's discomfort. "I also would like to formally invite you to travel with us again. I don't know why you've been away, but there's no reason not to be a part of the group."

"Well, it's true that you've been doing some interesting things. I had to run an errand right after you killed all those orks. Since then I've been...busy."

"Yeah, sure you have," said Jason. "If you're not still...busy, you're free to join us. And one more thing."

"Hmmm?" The ancient, rowdy priestess cocked her head to the side in challenge.

"Henry has been talking about you nonstop." Keeja turned her head, regarding Henry with a smile. Jason snickered as Henry coughed, hiding his sudden choking.

Jason loved having the last laugh, at least on occasion.

Delvers LLC: Obligations Incurred

CHAPTER EIGHT

Purple Triangles

Aodh trudged along behind Henry and Jason, rubbing the spot on his back that had been leaning against the inside wall of the Battlewagon. Aodh was already tired of traveling, but it'd been less than a week. He'd never known sitting around doing nothing all day while watching the countryside pass could actually make him anxious and sore.

The trip to Yanbei Cavern and back had been similar, but the battles had added an element of terror that had been distracting, to say the least. The last few days on the other hand had just been... boring.

Aodh felt ridiculous for mentally complaining of boredom when the other option was fear of impending death, but he couldn't help it. The only bright side was that Vitaliya rode a magicycle with Gonzo, Bezzi-ibbi, and Rark-han. This meant she stayed either in front or behind the Battlewagon while they traveled, so Aodh didn't have to see her very often. He stayed away as far as possible, but he knew it was only a matter of time before she started her old ways again.

Just the other day, she had made a point of crossing the camp to remind him to brush his teeth. To brush his teeth! He was a grown man! What's more, when he scowled at her, she just gave a grin like a dead hare and walked away.

What in under fuck was she doing working as a spy, anyway? How had that even happened? Did their family know? She hadn't said anything about their family so far. Aodh was dying to ask whether they knew about her profession, but he didn't want any unnecessary contact with his cousin. The fact she was even here, traveling with him while he was heading to a foreign country, was further proof of his terrible luck.

At least something had gone his way lately, though. A couple days ago, he'd found a bronze dagger buried in the dirt under where he placed his bedroll. Henry had been able to clean it up in less than five minutes, and it had actually turned out to be really beautiful.

The dagger had a wavy blade and a nicely detailed horse head handle. After making a quick sheath for it out of some spare leather, Aodh wore it at his back now.

However, finding the dagger was more than offset by the worst bit of bad luck he'd ever had. The absolute proof the universe had it out for him, the thing he couldn't stop thinking about as he helped Henry and Jason gather firewood, was how his orb didn't do anything. He was supposed to be orb-Bonded now, but he didn't feel any different than he had before.

He'd been incredibly excited, completely awed to receive an orb, something he'd never thought would be possible in his life. He would finally be strong on his own and Vitaliya would stop trying to mother him all the time. He would be a true adventurer, one of the best!

Instead, the next day after he had taken his orb, he hadn't felt anything different. There'd been no change at all. He'd spent hours trying to make different powers happen that he'd read about as a child. He had even asked Mareen what it was like when she became orb-Bonded. She had said she just woke up knowing what she could do.

Aodh was truly the unluckiest person on Ludus.

He couldn't even verify that he was actually even Bonded because he'd taken the potion Jason had made to hide his status if he had one! Nobody would see anything different about him whether he'd changed or not. He couldn't be sure if his orb just didn't work at all or if he'd just swallowed a marble.

Aodh was so lost in thought, he wasn't paying attention to what Henry and Jason were talking about. He just continued to pick up dry sticks behind them. He didn't even notice when they stopped and he almost ran into them.

Then, while still looking at the ground, he heard a deep, booming voice. "Unfortunately, we meet again, lower lifeforms. I'm busy so let's make this quick." The voice had an accent he'd never heard before and was speaking in English.

Aodh slowly raised his eyes...and saw Dolos for the first time.

The god floated in the air, slowly coming down to the ground. He stood at least seven feet tall and wore clothing that seemed to represent every color of the rainbow. He was bald, his face incredibly handsome in a dispassionate sort of way. He wore a stone crown, stone sandals, and flashes of tools could be glimpsed through some of his clothing as he moved. Aodh immediately recognized who the man was, who he had to be, and felt too shocked to even think.

"These Terrans...No respect, no sense of propriety. So cheeky and coarse, telling my High Priestess to summon me like I am some common servant and not the Great God Dolos. Ridiculous."

"Nice to see you too," Henry said drily.

"Oh, and these small, repugnant, ignorant Terrans have the gall to talk to me in a familiar manner. I can't believe that I must tolerate this. It's simply dreadful. Well, at least they aren't trying to use their pitiful powers this time."

Aodh's brain caught up to his eyes and he fell prostrate as quickly as he could. He was terrified. Dolos, THE Dolos was right in front of him...and talking to Henry. Oh no.

"Ah, the smaller mortal rubs its nose in the dirt. See, this is how mortals are supposed to act, and Terrans in particular. On the ground, terrified. I find this appropriate," said Dolos smugly. "These other miscreants should take note."

Suddenly, Aodh felt hands on his shoulders. Fear tightened his whole body, but the gentle hands kept pulling him upright until he was standing again, albeit with a hunch. With a start, he realized it was Henry who'd picked him up, his eyes flat. He shook his head.

Jason said, "Okay, Dolos, I know you don't want to be here long. Let's make this quick. You owe me a favor."

Dolos frowned. "I find you suspiciously rational. Terrans are never friendly or even respectful. They push and they push until you destroy their toys and then they cry about it."

"I find it suspicious that your High Priestess is not here," said Jason.

"Yes, well, the lowest of lifeforms find many aspects of the world confusing and frightening. I'm surprised you are not mucking about in a swamp somewhere, eviscerating some helpless animals to try divining the future."

"I can't help but notice that bug over there." Jason pointed to an insect in the distance that was moving unnaturally slowly through the air. "This is some kind of time dilation bubble again. However, I wonder why you put one up. Why don't you want people to see you? Was it to keep from meeting with Keeja?"

Dolos rolled his eyes. "Terrans think they're so clever. Seeing plots where there are none, making accusations to the Great God

Dolos as if they had any right. How has the world come to this? It seems the pitiful, mewling Terran can't seem the grasp the idea of stretching time to get more done.

"Then again, at least they truly aren't trying to use their trifling powers this time. I can avoid that disrespect, at least."

"Look, dude," said Henry. "Me and Jason already talked about it, and there isn't any point in trying to use magic when you're around. You'll just shut down our abilities and then get all bitchy about it."

Dolos narrowed his eyes and began to float again ,but before he said anything, Henry waved a hand and said, "Yeah, yeah. I'm trying your patience. You'll destroy us. Blah blah blah, Great God Dolos, blah blah blah. If you were going to kill us, we'd be dead by now, like months ago. Plus, we're not stupid; we know you've been making our lives on Ludus even harder than it has to be, asshole. It's not like you haven't already tried to kill us indirectly a few times.

"We're not as ignorant as we were before. We have a better idea now of what all this is about. It means we also know we've been extremely good little guinea pigs."

Jason quickly interrupted, "Look, Lord Dolos." His voice was placating. "You kidnapped us to this world, you've obviously tried to indirectly kill us several times. You've told us to do something impossible and even asked us to work on your behalf against a rival. I get that you don't like our entire species, and trust me, we wish we'd never met you. But you owe me a favor. Can we stop the blustering and just talk?"

Dolos continued to float, his expression twisted like he'd just eaten something rotten. "The universe is going to hell," he grumbled. "Insignificant little Terrans not knowing their place." He said more loudly, "What do you want? I am losing patience quickly."

The scene was so surreal, Aodh couldn't wrap his head around it. Dolos, the Great God Dolos, was physically standing before him and arguing with Aodh's employers. To be more specific, Henry was arguing with Dolos. Henry Sato. And he'd called Dolos "dude."

Jason said, "I want the ability to call you directly once a week, and I want you to be willing to answer questions."

Absolute silence rang for several moments other than the rustle of Henry crossing his arms. Dolos didn't move during that time, his body and face both inhumanly still.

Suddenly, with no warning, Dolos turned and gestured up. A large swath of trees was violently ripped out of the ground, roots scattering rocks and dirt. Dolos hollered in rage, punching forward with one fist. Every uprooted tree erupted into tiny pieces. The trees were torn asunder, a huge cloud of sawdust erupting outward from the origin of the explosion. Dolos kept yelling and hissing for a few seconds before he abruptly stopped.

The cloud of debris caused by the sudden display of power

seemed to hang in the air, settling down in slow motion once they were outside the time dilation field. The display was oddly beautiful despite the terrifying destruction.

When Dolos turned around, his normal expression and sardonic grin were back in place. Aodh hit the ground again, forehead to the dirt. This time, Henry let him stay there, but Aodh cautiously glanced up to see what was going on.

Jason audibly swallowed at the display of Dolos's temper, but he didn't change his relaxed posture. He asked, "So, what will it be? You said when you first promised me a request that I could make a case for whatever I ask of you. The reason for my request is simple. You have effectively asked us to help save your world. Furthermore, now we're tasked on a mission, again without any choice, to find Asag worshippers or something. Our success will positively affect you.

"And here's the kicker. I don't think this is the end of the complications we'll come across over the next few years. What I'm proposing is not unreasonable considering the task you've given us."

Dolos's face was unreadable. He said, "Once a week is far too often to visit with stinky, immoral Terrans. It's bad enough I have to meet with such useless, repugnant creatures as often as I already do. It's even worse that these upright animals would dare attempt to take advantage of an all-powerful god. I refuse. I would rather destroy this world than adhere to such insulting terms."

Henry grimaced and said, "Listen, dude, we don't like you either. But you were the one that brought us here against our will. You did me a solid with my mom, so I'm going to hold up my side of our deal. But what we know of the situation on this planet keeps getting worse. We want to get home, and it sounds like a bunch of divine jerkoffs are trying to muscle in on your territory. Your hands are tied in some way you won't explain to us. We need information if we are going to work for you."

Jason glared at Henry before he turned his gaze to Dolos. "If what I'm asking is too much, let me know what could work better. I wouldn't say it the same way as Henry, but you really have asked us to work for you."

Dolos got a strange look in his eyes. "So you freely admit you are working for me?"

"Yes, I think that's rather obvious."

Dolos put his chin in his hand. He said to himself, "Hmmm. I really don't want simple Terrans getting uppity ideas, but these ones do seem to be rather resistant to dying…Perhaps they can continue giving me good data." Dolos floated higher as he thought. Eventually, he came back down to his earlier position again. "Once a week is far too often. I will not be at the beck and call of lower lifeforms."

Jason glanced at Henry before replying, "Okay, how about this? You give me the ability to call you once a month. You are obligated to show up within an hour. If I call you again earlier than that by the Ludus month, I will owe you a favor."

Dolos regarded Jason with interest, his eyes narrowed. "Two hours. Not one."

"Done. And when you show up, you have to list at least three things that my company or myself would find interesting."

"Agreed, but if you want any more information about anything I tell you, you will be agreeing to me giving the same information to a rival group or persona of my choice, and giving them similar information of the same importance. For instance, if you ask where a rival group is, I will have the option of telling the rival group where you are."

Jason thought for a moment before responding, "Okay, and you have to answer any other questions we have as long as you are not restricted by whatever rules govern your conduct that you can't or won't tell us about."

Dolos coldly crossed his arms. "If so, the same rules will apply for any and all answers I give. I will have the option of sharing the information with another group."

Henry butted in, "You also need to stop sending random packs of monsters to attack us."

Dolos eyed Henry with disdain but didn't reply directly. He asked Jason, "Does this one speak for you?"

Jason sighed, "Yes."

"These ridiculous, disrespectful mortals feel empowered to haggle with a god. They obviously don't know the power of the

Great God Dolos." Dolos glared at Jason and spat, "Agreed. Do you agree to our terms, mortal?"

Aodh couldn't believe what he was witnessing. He wanted to warn Jason, he wanted desperately to tell him not to make a deal with Dolos, but he was too scared to move. His tongue felt five sizes too large and he couldn't stop sweating. *No, don't make a deal with him!*

"Yes, I agree," Jason said slowly.

Dolos gave them all a look full of malice. "Was there anything else?"

Jason coughed. "No, I think that will do it."

"I see. So we have an agreement to solidify our relationship, that you two work for me?"

"Yes," said Jason.

"Yes," Henry sighed.

"Done!" cried Dolos, his entire demeanor changing. "You get your first three facts immediately. First is that there is a music player rigged to run on magic stones in a nearby dungeon. It is full of Earth songs. Second is that you are being hunted. Third is that I recently transported four new Terrans from your world to this area and they are all in danger."

Aodh choked out a gasp. *No, don't make it worse.* He willed Henry and Jason not to ask questions, or at least to carefully think them through.

Jason frowned. "Where are the people from Earth?"

Dolos smiled; the expression was predatory. "You did not specify a number, so I will choose to tell you where two are. One is several miles due east. One is northwest about twenty miles, as you Terrans from your primitive country illogically measure distance."

Henry's eyes widened. "You have got to be fucking kidding me."

Dolos chuckled, clearly enjoying Henry's realization of how he'd taken advantage of their agreement. "And our pact is in effect. One question has been answered."

Jason closed his eyes. Henry angrily gestured as he said, "I can't believe this. Well, if you won't play straight with the answers, at least tell us whether Aodh has a working orb or not."

"Yes..." Dolos hissed, not even trying to hide his mirth anymore. "He does. One more question answered."

Jason's eyes snapped open. "Hey, wait a minute. I didn't even ask that question."

Dolos chuckled softly. "Oh, but part of our agreement was that you can ask any questions you like. Plus, you said earlier that your friend speaks for you." He suddenly snapped his head to the side, intent on something none of the humans could see. "Our time grows short," he spat. "A pact is a pact."

Aodh despaired. He felt incredibly guilty for just hugging the ground and doing nothing. His employers were brave, but they were also deeply ignorant. Even a child should have known better than to make a deal like the one they had just agreed to. Aodh might have doomed them by not being braver, for not speaking up.

Dolos held out a hand and a glowing white ball manifested above it, slowly growing brighter until it shot at Jason, penetrating his chest.

"Ow, that stings!" Jason yelled.

"Are you okay?" asked Henry.

"Yeah, it didn't go very deep." He glared at Dolos. "What did you—"

Henry quickly clapped a hand over Jason's mouth. "Be careful, dude. Questions."

Dolos chuckled again, the booming sound seemed to make the remaining trees sway. "And one more thing: Three times freely given, three times witnessed. Thank you for your loyalty. Thank you for 'working for me.'"

Dolos gestured and the clothing on Henry and Jason's left arms just fell off. A searing burst of light flashed; both men yelped in pain. After the light faded, a glowing purple triangle was revealed on the skin of their shoulders.

"What the fuck is this?" yelled Henry.

"I will give you this one for free. That is my mark. As you both have said you work for me, and you confirmed it three times, that mark proves your patronage to the Great God Dolos. Please be good little Terrans and don't get killed. I may need your services for some small task in the future."

With that, Dolos rose into the air, laughing uproariously. He ascended straight up into the sky, his velocity rising so quickly he was almost immediately out of sight, breaking the sound barrier in his wake. After the thunderous crash of the sonic boom faded, the time dilation bubble that followed Dolos dropped and the cacophony from the trees exploding washed over the land as well.

Suddenly, Keeja arrived in a flash of movement and a breeze of displaced air. "What just happened? That was him, wasn't it? That had to be Dolos...I can't believe he's avoiding me..." Her gaze landed on Jason and Henry's shoulders. "What happened?" she breathed.

Aodh felt a tear in his eye. He mumbled, "They made a deal."

"Why didn't you stop them!?" Keeja yelled.

"Hey," Henry growled. "Take it easy on the kid. We just secured a way to get intel for the rest of the time we're on this fucking shithole of a planet."

"But at what cost? Do I even want to know?" Keeja's eyes flashed, "Even a mentally retarded *yukka* should have known better than to make a deal with Dolos."

Henry put his hands on his hips. "Well, you haven't exactly been very helpful, lady. How were we supposed to know? Why do you suddenly care about what we're doing or whether we even live or die all of the sudden?"

"He's got a point," murmured Jason.

"My mission changed, and now I have a reason to care

whether you idiots live or die. So in the spirit of sharing, what else under the rotting sun did you do?" She pointed to the triangles on their shoulders. "You let Dolos give you the D?"

In a deadpan voice, Henry asked, "What?"

"The D. He gave you the D." Keeja lifted up her sleeve and showed them her smaller, identical mark. "Welcome to the family, I guess. May the Creator have mercy on your souls. It looks like you just allowed yourself to become priests of Dolos."

Several heartbeats of silence were followed by Henry breathing, "Fuck me. Oh, fuck me sideways with a shovel. Now I'm a priest for a god I hate? I really hate this planet."

Jason facepalmed. He muttered, "Well, this idea didn't work out as planned."

Delvers LLC: Obligations Incurred

CHAPTER NINE

Crouching Keeja, Little Aodh

Vitaliya was mildly entertained as she stood next to Gonzo, listening to Jason and Henry relate their meeting with Dolos. The various levels of shock, disbelief, and anger in the group amused her. Of course, she was a member of Berber Intelligence, born in another country, trained for years in state secrets. She had already been debriefed on Dolos, his High Priestesses, and every other god and monster that had visited Ludus for the last three thousand years.

As a result, she was wary of Keeja, but she knew exactly how helpless she'd be to stop the demigod from doing whatever she wanted. As such, it wasn't worth worrying about. As for Dolos, it amused Vitaliya that even after hearing Dolos speaking in everyone's mind earlier that year, many people on Ludus were still having a religious crisis.

As usual, Gonzo seemed entirely unperturbed by the new events, but the Delvers' reactions were all over the place. Yanno-ibbi was by far the most shocked. On the other hand, the rest of the group seemed more angry at Jason and Henry than upset about Dolos visiting.

"Why didn't you tell us what you were going to do?" Mareen appeared the most frustrated. The newlywed woman shook her head violently. "You really don't understand how dangerous Dolos is. Have you ever even read any of the myths or history books I said you should?"

"No, but we've talked to him, what…three times now? Yeah, something like that." Henry didn't seem concerned. Mareen started fuming again and Henry put an arm around her, saying, "Look, I'm sorry I didn't tell you. Next time I want to talk to the self-absorbed, floating asshole, I'll let you know first."

"And I'll come," said Mareen.

"The hell you will! You all saw what he did to the fucking forest, right? That was a temper tantrum. I love your spirit, hon, I really do, but Dolos would probably kill you for it."

"You have got to be kidding me, Henry Sato. You are telling *me* that *I* am too hotheaded?"

"Yes, because I can get away with being a moron. If Dolos kills me or Jason, he'll be making a ton of work for himself and it'll also make him look stupid. Ask her," Henry said, pointing at Keeja. Keeja glanced up long enough to nod before furrowing her brow again, deep in thought.

"Plus, he's even less likely to kill us now because of these." Henry pointed to the purple triangle on his upper arm.

"You don't even understand what that means!" yelled Mareen.

"Yeah, you're right. But we have an entire journey to figure it out while in the meantime everyone yells at us and thinks we're crazy. *Then* we can probably feel bad about it. But right now, we should go looking for these transported people that may, you know, die if we continue sitting around with our thumbs in our asses."

"As much as it pains me to say this, I agree with Henry," Jason sighed. "Now is the time for action. We have to—"

"Wait a moment." Keeja held up a hand to interrupt. "I need to explain something. Shut up and listen."

Henry grumbled but the group quieted. Vitaliya was curious what the High Priestess had to say. She hadn't figured out what her angle was yet; neither had Gonzo.

She glanced over at Aodh to make sure he was doing okay. He looked terrified, but seemed to be holding up. He looked a little dirty, though. Vitaliya wondered if he was bathing enough. He also looked too skinny. It was getting harder and harder for her to give him space. She knew he'd get upset, but he truly needed someone to oversee his care.

All the other children had been so cruel to Aodh back on the farm, sometimes Vitaliya had had to go out after dark to teach them a lesson. A few singed eyebrows, some burned arms, no problem. Little Aodh...poor little Aodh.

After Vitaliya had left to start her active duty tour as an Intelligence agent, she hadn't thought she'd see Aodh for at least another year. She had known he'd wanted to be an adventurer, but she'd been sure nobody would hire such a frail, frightened boy.

The fact they had met up again in such coincidental circumstances was truly the gods' way of reuniting her with her troubled cousin. He needed her help, and he wanted her help. The confused boy just didn't know he did, didn't know what was best for him, probably due to his Fideli blood. Poor thing.

Vitaliya began paying attention to the conversation again.

Keeja said, "My role has changed. When I first met you, I was only meant to give a piece or two of information within certain limitations. I really didn't want to be involved. However...things are different now."

The High Priestess breathed deeply. "Dolos is so happy with the data he is getting from Bonded hunting each other and a few preparing for the attack on this world...Actually, it's more accurate to say he's happy with the data he is getting from the growing chaos in general.

"He has offered a two-hundred-year vacation to any High Priestess that sufficiently impresses him in some way, including shepherding one of the teams in play. What this actually means, I'm not sure. However, Dolos does not lie. I'm not entirely certain how to go about this. I still have all the same limitations I had before. I can't just tell you things. In fact, I have reasons that I can't tell you why I can't tell you things. On the other hand, now I am much more motivated to find loopholes.

"However, Dolos also does not play fair. At all. Ever. I've been asking for a music playback device for over six hundred years. The other Priestesses have too. Dolos telling you about the music gadget was for my benefit.

"If I act, if I get this music device for myself, it will mean I will not be able to interfere in your affair for a long time afterwards except in self-defense. I'll also be a target for others that will want it, too. However, I can't pass up this opportunity, and Dolos knows it."

"Excuse me, but I am not sure what you're talking about," said Jason.

Keeja smiled sadly. "This is a story thousands of years in the making. We don't have time for it right now, nor do you have the context to understand. I'm not sure I want to pry open old memories anyway. The point is, I'm a more willing participant in helping you now, but I still have to abide by strict rules."

Jason nodded thoughtfully. "Like not being around until we figured out you were there, probably for some reason you can't tell us."

"Precisely."

Henry frowned and said, "Okay, enough Kumbaya bullshit.

There are people out there who still need a hand while we stand around gabbing. It sounds like we need three teams, one of them being Keeja, and—"

"I'm taking Jason," Keeja said.

"You're what?" asked Uluula. The diminutive woman was calm, but Vitaliya noticed she tightened her grip on the strange spear she held.

Keeja rolled her eyes. "Oh, simmer down, little girl. I'm not taking your Terran toy. Besides, this one is much more my type." She took a quick step forward and squeezed Henry's upper arm before he stumbled back with a yelp. Keeja chuckled. "I just said I am more willing to help now. Take this on faith. Also, here." Keeja pulled a map out of thin air and handed it to the dubious Henry.

"What's this for?" he asked.

"You can find dungeons on a map, yes? You have the skill?"

"Oh, yeah. Hold on a sec."

"Also, Dolos said the dungeon was 'nearby,' yes?" Keeja asked.

"Yeah."

"That means nearby for him, not you. Henry, what dungeons do you see up to about 300 miles away?"

"What makes three hundred miles so special—"

"Just do it, Terran." Keeja let iron command bleed into her voice.

As Henry grumbled about "Terran-this" and "PMSing hobbits," Vitaliya watched with interest. This side of Keeja was a lot closer to myth and legend. Keeja the Ravager, the selfish general. Vitaliya thought it was fascinating to observe the creation of new legends in her lifetime.

She watched Aodh out the corner of her eye and clucked her tongue. The poor thing was still so scared. He was so small and defenseless. She wanted to walk over and give him a hug. He truly didn't seem to know what was good for him sometimes, and she might have to persuade him to cooperate, but it was truly for his own good.

She wasn't looking forward to telling little Aodh that their entire family for the most part had been working as Intelligence officers for generations. In fact, it kind of amazed her that he'd never wondered how his Da had ever been able to meet Aodh's beautiful, half-Fideli Ma while abroad if he were just a simple farmer. Oh well, at least his lack of curiosity had been convenient. Plus, they were travelling together for a while now, so their family's secret was a moot point for now. Vitaliya had to think carefully how to break the news when the time came, though.

Aodh was probably going to be upset. He always was when he found out she hadn't told him something, but Vitaliya knew what was best for him. That terrible man, Henry, might have been making things worse lately. She frowned while she thought about it. He even called little Aodh "Tony" and had given him weapons!

The entire grouped treated Aodh like he was a real adventurer! It was incredibly irresponsible.

But now that Vitaliya was here with him, it was fine. She could watch over him and make sure he was safe as could be and taken care of. Of course, her job had to come first, but she was very good at multitasking. She would always take care of little Aodh.

Henry listed off the dungeon locations he was seeing, and Keeja thought for a moment before she said, "I think I know which of these that old snake hid my music player in. It's probably the one about two hundred twenty miles away, one hundred fifty Ludan turns, or about three hundred fifty kilometers. What measurements would you like me to use?"

"Around us, use miles," Henry growled. "So you're going with Jason to this dungeon in the middle of nowhere to get your magic Walkman or whatever, then you'll become even more useless than usual?"

Vitaliya was accustomed to Keeja's presence, but she still cringed on the inside when Henry talked so familiarly. She spared a glance at Gonzo, but he still hadn't reacted at all. He was probably in observation mode, just storing away data.

Uluula bristled and asked, "Jason doesn't have to fight, does he?"

"Of course not." Keeja scowled. "Really? That was your question. You think I'll need your Terran husband's help? Your second rank orb-Bonded husband? Really? Have the Baglan Blue gone senile?"

Uluula looked embarrassed, but Vitaliya had no idea what the exchange meant. She decided it might have had something to do with homeworld Areva politics, so she needed to include it in her daily report. When she eventually turned all of her reports in, they might find it valuable.

She kept a separate report on her cousin Aodh. She still needed to jot down everything she had seen him eat that day. She also had to make sure he never found her notes. He wouldn't understand.

"Okay, enough grab-assing." When Keeja's eyes lit up and she opened her mouth to respond, Henry growled at her and the woman just smiled. Henry continued, "This is how the op is going to play out.

"Jason and Keeja are going to..." He consulted his map. "They're going to the Halls of Grief. Dolos apparently tells the truth, according to Keeja, which doesn't make any sense to me since he lied to us in the first ten fucking minutes we met him, but I already know I'm overruled on this one."

Keeja looked amused. "What I meant was he doesn't lie within the realm of a deal or a bargain being struck."

"Yeah, whatever. I don't care. Losing Jason stretches us thin. It also grounds the Battlewagon. Are you sure you're going with her, Jason?"

Jason looked at Keeja for a couple seconds before replying,

"Yeah, I think I'm going to chance it, man."

Henry grumped, "Fine. I'm going northwest with Gonzo and Vitaliya on magicycles. They've been riding them and I invented the things. We'll make great time.

"The rest of you will go east to see what you can find. It's close by. If anyone runs into trouble, fall back here to the Battlewagon."

Vitaliya was curious. "Why don't you have someone else pilot the Battlewagon so you can operate its guns?"

Henry sighed. "Because this is a rescue, not a combat op. I have enhanced senses and the Mo'hali do too. We need to actually find these people in order to help them. I still don't really know what you and Gonzo do, but I doubt you'll just tell me."

Gonzo finally spoke, "In this situation, sharing information would be ideal."

"Oh," said Henry. "I thought you wouldn't care about stranded people from Earth."

Gonzo smiled grimly. "I may be a spy, but I'm still originally from Earth, too. Plus, one directive of Berber Intelligence is to make contact with new refugees to Ludus whenever possible."

"I'm sure finding new orbs wouldn't hurt either, right?" Uluula sounded skeptical.

Gonzo ignored her. To Henry, he said, "I am a water and life mage. I specialize in ice. Vitaliya is a fire mage."

Vitaliya noticed how much information Gonzo held back and

approved on principle. She really had gotten lucky to be paired with Gonzolez as her first partner.

"And do either of you have tracking abilities?" asked Henry.

"No," Gonzo lied.

Once again, Vitaliya approved.

"Okay, fine, my decision stands. Everyone saddle up and go. If these Earth people really exist and Dolos isn't just playing games, who knows what we'll find. Remember, if you run into trouble you can't handle, head back to the Battlewagon and send an MMB to the other group. Each team has a mage, and at these distances, an MMB will take no time. Don't bother sending anything to Jason or Keeja, though. They're doing whatever it is Keeja wants to do."

"Damn right," the demigoddess purred.

Henry didn't respond to her. He just ordered, "Okay, let's go!"

Vitaliya noticed how Henry had placed Gonzo and herself in his team, probably to keep an eye on them. He'd even found a way to ask them what their abilities were in a way they couldn't refuse to answer without ruining goodwill. Vitaliya actually thought it was fairly well done, even if a little ham-fisted. It worried her. Aodh was spending a lot of time with Henry, almost like a surrogate older brother. Vitaliya would have to be careful around the man.

Henry seemed to be a lot smarter than she'd originally believed. That could be a problem both for Aodh's safety and her future plans.

* * *

Jason flew through the air in teleporting hops as fast as he could while using a reasonable amount of magic power, but Keeja easily kept pace, scowling at him and motioning him to go faster. The most disturbing thing was after each teleport, she was almost instantly near his side again. *Just how fast can this chick fly?* Jason felt a chill.

He had not forgotten the display of power Keeja had given within the first few days of him meeting her. He remembered the awesome beam of energy. Jason had a very, very bad feeling about what was to come. On the other hand, he also strangely believed Keeja that it would be in his best interest to come with her.

Suddenly, he felt himself slowing down until he eventually stopped, floating in midair. Keeja hovered into view and said, "You can't hear me when you're darting all over the place like a minnow. You are going way too slow, and it's boring me.

"Keep your goggles on and don't teleport. I'm going to gradually speed up for a while before slowing down. After that, give me a thumbs-up when you're ready to go fast again. You won't be able to breathe when we are accelerated. Just focus on breathing when we slow down and holding your breath when we go fast again."

"Wait, what are you—"

Jason began accelerating forward at a terrifying rate, so he quickly gulped some air and held his breath. *What the hell did I get myself into this time?*

Delvers LLC: Obligations Incurred

CHAPTER TEN

Powerleveled

Jason was freaked out at first as Keeja towed him behind her, rocketing forward at incredible speed. Luckily, he was wearing his goggles, so he could still see, but the High Priestess had been correct that he wouldn't be able to breathe while moving so fast.

He briefly thought of teleporting away, but he somehow knew that it would be a bad idea. He was not sure how he knew, he just sensed it.

He settled in to wait and merely held his breath between rests as Keeja had instructed. Eventually he got the hang of it and it wasn't too bad. He judged they were moving at least a few hundred miles per hour every time Keeja got up to speed. An ugly suspicion formed in the back of his mind that the experience might have killed him prior to becoming orb-Bonded. Then again, perhaps Keeja was doing something to protect him.

Jason got the feeling Keeja could move much faster if she wanted and was limiting herself for his sake. It was a scary realization.

He couldn't really do anything else while they traveled, so Jason had time to think. He wasn't very happy about where his thoughts led him.

He had to admit that he'd been fairly stupid with how he'd approached Dolos and what had resulted from it. His first clue it was a bad idea should have been that he and Henry had been trying to hide it from the others.

He still didn't think it would have been a good idea to meet Dolos as a group. It could have been disastrous. He and Henry had some immunity against Dolos's temper, but that didn't mean anyone else in the company enjoyed the same protection.

On the other hand, Jason really had no excuse for being so stupid. He was the gamer of the group, the guy who had been playing roleplaying games his entire life. He should have known there would be issues, and at the very least he should have caught on when Dolos began playing word games. Jason kept kicking himself. *Stupid, stupid Jason!*

The only reason he could think of that he'd acted so dumb was how he was getting used to life on Ludus. The more normal his average day felt, the less he analyzed everything that happened around him. He was starting to see everything less as a challenge, as survival. Getting married hadn't helped. He was glad he was married, and he loved Uluula to pieces, but sometimes it was hard to spend time thinking about how the planet would gladly kill him or trick him when he was so happy all the time. When he cuddled with Uluula at night, murderous monsters were the last things on his mind.

As he was pulled through the air by unknown means, travelling as fast as an airplane by a woman who claimed to be several millennia old, Jason realized his threshold for weirdness had been permanently altered, if not forever destroyed. This might have been another reason he'd screwed up so badly with Dolos.

Oh well, there wasn't anything he could do about it now other than try to make the best of the situation. However, one way or another, he vowed that Dolos would not get the best of him again.

While Jason was still trying to figure out what to do about Dolos, Keeja began to reduce their speed. They were approaching a mountain. In the distance, Jason could see an enormous doorway set in the side of a cliff, but Keeja wasn't heading that direction. She set them down on a hillside instead.

The High Priestess stared at the mountain for a moment before glancing at Jason. She frowned and levitated a couple feet off the ground. "Do you know how irritating it is to look up at you all the time? Why must Terrans grow so tall?"

Jason decided not to say anything. Keeja seemed to be growing more grumpy, and he'd already been conned by a god. He didn't want to piss off a demigoddess on the same day.

Keeja grumbled under her breath for a while before ordering, "Be ready to move. I'm extremely irritated with Dolos right now, and I don't like feeling manipulated, so I'm taking advantage of a loophole to help you out. However, you're the only member of your group that could survive this and you are still going to be in great danger. Just try not get hurt too badly. I'm not very good at healing."

"What do you mean? Aren't we still in Tolstcy? I thought we just took out one of the most dangerous dungeons in the area."

Keeja rolled her eyes. "Tolstens really don't know as much as they think they do. Most of them live in their capital city, Taretha, and most Tolsten adventurers farm dungeons and monsters to the south. They avoid places like this because it's just instant death for most of them. Elite dungeons were not the best challenges Dolos ever introduced. They're very poorly balanced for the areas they're in."

"Elite dungeons?" The term was familiar to Jason. In gaming culture, it meant battles that were harder, sometimes exponentially harder than regular challenges for players, but usually offering better loot.

"Yes, it's how I knew this would be the place. Dolos is obviously trying to set me up. He wouldn't have put a music device anywhere that your group could handle on its own, or you could have just teleported in to get it for me. He was trying to force my hand.

"Plus, I believe this dungeon was just reworked a few years ago. It means I wouldn't be able to give you any meaningful data. As far as I know, no adventurers have bested this place for over a thousand years.

"Most adventurers would die before even getting to the front door of this place."

Jason shook his head. "What—"

"That's enough. I'm not sure what this location's new defenses are. Try to be as quiet as you can."

Jason whispered, "Can't you just...do something from here? You have that beam you showed me before."

"Really?" Keeja blinked. "I want an item inside and you can benefit from what we find as well. What would I be accomplishing by probably destroying everything, including the items we seek?"

"Uh, yeah. That makes sense," Jason responded lamely.

"Fine, follow me closely. Pay attention." Keeja floated to the ground and began slowly walking toward the mountain.

Jason cautiously followed. He had no idea what to expect, and kept a hand on his sword hilt. He also mentally prepared to throw up a null-time shield. He still wasn't entirely sure how powerful Keeja really was, or how dangerous this dungeon could be, but he wasn't taking any chances.

Suddenly, the Areva woman held out a hand. "Stop here. Actually, wait a moment." Keeja took a couple steps towards Jason, reached up, and slapped him on the side of the head.

"Oww, what was that for?" Jason was tired of being confused and getting such cryptic information from the ancient little woman. The side of his face stung too. "Why the hell did you just hit me?"

"Now you'll be able to hear my voice if I need to talk to you. Teleport back as far as you can while still seeing me so I can keep an eye on you in turn. I'm not sure what other dangers are around here. I'll let you know when to meet up with me again."

Jason scowled, but he had no way to test the accuracy of what she had just said. Either way, it wasn't like he could do anything about it. He sucked up his pride and did as the High Priestess had instructed, teleporting about half a mile back to a handy outcropping of rock he'd seen.

As he stood staring at Keeja in the distance, he decided to try one of his new abilities he'd been practicing. With a small flex of his magic, he bypassed the distance to Keeja so he could watch her as if he were only twenty feet away. He didn't use this technique very often because it could be so disconcerting to see two perspectives at once. The effect was not at all like using a telescope. It seemed as if he were actually there near Keeja, but also seeing his normal view from where he was standing. It took concentration to maintain the effect and not get a headache.

He figured he should probably just trust Keeja. She was acting like something big was going to happen any minute, so Jason also slowed down his perception of time. He hadn't felt any danger yet, but he knew from his time on Ludus that shit could go sideways at the drop of a hat.

With no warning, the dungeon itself seemed to attack Keeja.

In a split second, shimmering shields of energy appeared around the demigoddess, her hand held out before her. The shields barely formed in time to turn aside the barrage of destruction from several origin points on the mountain, the projectiles slamming into the barriers and glancing off to drive deep, smoking furrows into the ground. Keeja seemed to glide to the side and her other hand flicked out, sparks dancing from her fingers and shooting out in several directions, resulting in muted explosions on the mountainside.

As Jason watched Keeja using her power, he began hearing music in his head just like he had when she'd shot a beam into the sky over a month before.

Another barrage of fire lanced out, but was stopped by Keeja's shields. She flicked her hand and more explosive sparks lashed out. Torn ground extended in two long furrows to either side of the Areva demigoddess; a small clump of grass had caught on fire. Trees were shattered, their entire trunks reduced to splinters.

On the mountainside, the explosion from one of Keeja's attacks started a landslide that Jason could feel through his feet. The violence that the High Priestess had casually unleashed in a few seconds was astounding. Without warning, Jason heard Keeja's voice say, <*Yes, I know you've never seen anything like that before, but try to pay attention. Now that I've destroyed the automated defenses, there will probably be something else out here with us.>*

It sounded like Keeja was talking softly, directly into his ears. The sensation was weird, but he had to admit the communication method was handy. He mentally nodded and snapped his vision back to normal. His perception of time was still slowed down, though. He figured it was better to be safe than sorry.

Jason was still watching Keeja when the mountain attacked. He would have entirely missed the danger if he hadn't been watching with his altered perception of time. Jason saw movement out of the corner of his eye and didn't waste time turning his head for a better look. He immediately teleported away. From the new hillside he stood on, he glanced back and gasped. A huge fist was buried into the ground where he'd just been standing. A giant rock man climbed straight out of the stony outcropping.

The creature seemed entirely made of stone. Its mouth and eyes were just dark pits. Its form was rough, like a child's block drawing of a person. It only had two fingers and a thumb.

"What in the hell...elementals?" The creature jogged Jason's memory of games he'd played in the past.

<Sort of, but close enough,> Keeja's voice whispered. *<You don't need to worry about destroying any of them. I'll take care of it. Just keep yourself alive.>*

Keeja could obviously hear him, so Jason acknowledged her

out loud. "Okay." He bounced on his toes, ready for anything. He wondered what the High Priestess would do. Elementals in games were usually more easily destroyed using an opposing element that varied per game. Like in some games, earth was super effective versus air, while in other games it was completely ineffective.

Keeja obviously didn't care either way. She just used brute force. She came flying up to the giant rock monster and obliterated it in a single punch. The explosive force of the strike blew the elemental into pieces. As before, every time Jason looked at her, he could hear the unfamiliar music in his head.

Keeja reached sideways and her hand disappeared before pulling a huge halberd out of thin air. Jason watched curiously as she put the weapon away back wherever it had come from, brushed her hands off, and pulled it out again. She looked directly at Jason the last time she withdrew it.

What the hell is she doing? Jason asked himself. He kept an eye out for more elementals while he pondered Keeja's strange behavior, and eventually deduced his answer. She was probably trying to show him something. *Pocket dimensions…no way!* Jason felt a flash of insight. This was probably one reason Keeja had brought him along.

She couldn't teach him any magic. She probably couldn't even tell him certain abilities were possible. But if she actually needed to fight and he happened to see her do something that he might be able to replicate with his magic…

With Jason's enhanced perception of time, only a few seconds actually passed while he furiously thought about pocket dimensions and ways to twist space. So it actually wasn't very long before the very forest itself seemed to come alive.

Multiple trees slammed together, branches twisting, trunks cracking and opening in facsimiles of gaping mouths. Branches ending in wicked points formed hands with too many fingers. Most of the trees in the forest were uprooting themselves. They seemed to be moving to tear the two trespassers apart.

More rock elementals began pulling themselves out of the surrounding boulders and cliffs. Jason felt the ground below him move, so he teleported straight up into the air. The elementals began throwing things at him. He moved around randomly, teleporting from place to place. Boulders and needle-sharp spears of wood flew through the space he'd just been occupying each time he changed position. *Gotta keep moving.*

From high in the sky, Jason got a bird's eye view of Keeja unleashing her power. In a flicker of motion, she moved from elemental to elemental, cutting them in half with mighty swings of her polearm. Her weapon began to glow green, and the wooden monsters burst into flame. She moved so fast, Jason would not have been able to see her strikes without having slowed down his perception of time.

She was a tiny engine of destruction. Jason watched in astonishment as she zipped from monster to monster, utterly annihilating each target with only a single strike. She wasn't even breathing hard. She pointed her halberd at another of the rock monsters and cut it in half from crotch to head with a beam of energy from the tip of her weapon.

The elemental enemies were a mass of grasping hands and thrown projectiles, but Keeja moved around them like they were in slow motion. A boulder got in the way of one of her dashes, so she simply smashed it aside with a tiny fist.

Jason felt a chill. If Keeja wanted to, she could wipe out him and all of his friends at once with ease. Even if all the Delvers tried to prepare for her to attack, it would be useless. The High Priestess was on another level entirely. It was humbling.

But Jason was getting seriously tired of dodging missiles thrown from elemental monsters. It was time to contribute to the fight. He needed to practice some of his new attacks anyway.

He wasn't exactly safe while constantly dodging deadly projectiles, anyway.

Jason teleported, adjusting his vector to arc him behind a rock monster. He drew two bronze throwing knives and waited for the right moment. He needed to be fairly close for this new attack to work, the same attack he'd used to kill the flowertop popper demon. *Henry is right about one thing, some of these monster names are silly.*

He concentrated briefly, making the edge of a throwing knife flicker with a thin line of null-time, forming a vorpal edge. Then he concentrated again to anchor it. It was still difficult, but he was getting faster, and it wasn't as difficult as it had been the first time he'd discovered the ability. He watched the back of the stone elemental flash by in slow motion, his slowed perception of time allowing him to perfectly time his throw.

His hand flashed forward, index finger on the handle of his throwing knife, executing a perfect no-spin throw. The distance was short enough that the attached null-time enhancement on the blade held, allowing the knife to punch through the monster like paper.

This would be a lot easier if I could teleport null-time knives, Jason idly thought has he watched the knife pass through the monster.

Luckily, he was paying attention when the creature's arm flashed back, its hand open to crush him to death. Jason teleported away and frowned in irritation.

<Didn't I tell you to try not to get killed?> Keeja's thrown voice sounded irritated. *<These things have a core somewhere centrally, but the location is different every time.>*

Jason said out loud, "Why don't you just blow them all apart with whatever you did to the perimeter defenses?"

<I can't use too much power here. I have to limit my output, or I could be more easily sensed by people you really, really don't want to randomly show up.>

She truly is limiting her power right now? With stunned

fascination, Jason wondered what Keeja would be like if she went HAM, all out. He decided he didn't want to know. If he was being honest with himself, he was already intimidated enough as it was.

Keeja's voice came to Jason's ears again. Her tone was odd, like she was trying to call his attention to what she was saying. *<I'm going to continue destroying them like this. You should watch me deal with them.>*

Jason obeyed Keeja and observed as she dashed from elemental to elemental, more or less splitting them in half. A single tree monster managed to touch Keeja, and with an irritated wave of her hand, she generated destructive force that destroyed several of them at once. The shockwave of the attack buffeted Jason as he continued to juke around in the sky.

After the explosion cleared her some space again, Keeja went back to cutting the monsters up with her ridiculously oversized weapon. With a flash of insight, Jason realized that this was part of his training too. There was no real reason for Keeja to continue using her halberd to destroy the monsters when she could blow them apart so easily.

Jason could only think of one logical explanation. *I'm being powerleveled.* Powerleveling was a term Jason had used in his gaming days. The term described when a low-level player's ability was quickly and unfairly increased by following around a much higher level player. Jason wasn't entirely sure what to think of this new development, but he decided to make the most of it.

He wondered what other new things Keeja would try to sneakily teach him before they eventually left. They hadn't even entered the distant dungeon yet. Apparently, Dolos wasn't the only underhanded being on Ludus. Jason got the feeling Keeja was exploiting a number of loopholes. *Keeja is a rules lawyer*, Jason thought with amusement.

He closely watched Keeja, trying to glean as many new insights and techniques as he could. Strange music rang through his mind as he watched her effortlessly destroy monsters that would all be enormous threats by themselves to him and his group.

I'm sure glad she's on our side. Well, I hope she's on our side. Keeja's casual demonstration of power was a wake-up call. Jason had a long way to go to protect himself and the people he cared about. He needed to get stronger.

He had a long journey ahead of him if he ever wanted to get home, especially to bring his wife with him. Whether he really wanted to return to Earth anymore was something he would have to think about later when Ludus wasn't actively trying to kill him, at least for a moment.

CHAPTER ELEVEN

Not Kansas Anymore

Henry took point as he, Gonzo, and Vitaliya sped through the forest on magicycles. Every once in a while he had to dodge rotten logs, hanging creepers, or low branches. If someone forced him to be honest, he'd have to admit he'd based a lot of the magicycles' design on speeder bikes from one of his favorite movies of all time. As he maneuvered through the forest, he could almost imagine he was on Endor.

It wasn't like Henry was ignorant of all nerdy things.

Building the magicycles had been surprisingly easy. Henry still wasn't sure exactly how he was making them work, powered by magic stones. When he'd started tinkering, he had just known what would work and how to convince the metal to function with power running through it. When he'd asked other Earth mages in Mirana about the process, they had had no idea what he was talking about. Henry was beginning to suspect it had something to do with who he was as much as his orb powers. Plus, the fact that his primary magic school was Metal might have had something to do with it.

He kept a careful eye on Vitaliya and Gonzo as they traveled. He still didn't really trust them, especially Vitaliya. From what he understood, Tony had lived with her for years, being raised as de facto brother and sister, yet her job as a spy had been a shock to the young man.

Henry wasn't sure why, but it bothered him.

He was also irritated by how badly he and Jason had fucked up with Dolos. The grinning dickhead had them over a barrel. Henry definitely needed to talk to Jason later about it. He wasn't blaming his friend for what had happened, especially since he'd have a better chance than Henry at finding a silver lining somewhere in the situation.

The symbol on Henry's shoulder itched when he thought about it.

Suddenly, Henry heard screaming in the distance and he focused entirely on the present. He could sense Gonzo and Vitaliya speeding up behind him, too. They burst into a clearing with a few large trees in the middle.

In the branches of the largest tree, Henry could barely spot a woman. Arranged around the tree was a pack of horned demon wolves. *Fuck, these fucking things are everywhere!*

Then Henry looked closer and noticed these ones looked different than the kind he'd seen before. They had some kind of scales on their body in various places instead of fur. "Armored demon wolves," Gonzo shouted behind him. "Stay alert. Their hide is tough."

Great, it's always something on this planet. Henry sighed in frustration and nerves. As he got nearer, he noticed that the monsters had been chewing on the trunk of the tree. It would only be a matter of time before they brought it down.

Henry jumped off his magicycle and ran forward, noticing Gonzo and Vitaliya do the same out of his peripheral vision. He knew Gonzo was orb-Bonded, so he was sure the spy would be fine. Vitaliya, on the other hand, was just a mage. Henry was a little worried about her safety.

He really didn't want to be responsible for getting Tony's cousin killed. Natural mages all seemed to be fairly weak on Ludus, after all. Well, he suspected with the exception of Kinwe-na-ibbi.

Suddenly, Henry felt a bloom of heat, making his whole side uncomfortably hot. Vitaliya had wreathed her entire body in fire. She darted forward, scorching one of the armored demon wolves with a jet of flame from the blaze covering her body.

To Henry's other side, Gonzo gestured up, and a huge spear of ice grew from the ground before them, impaling another lupine monster. Henry blinked as he raised his strength from the earth and slapped an exogun onto his forearm. He'd thought he would have to do most of the fighting, but it turned out he wasn't even really needed. It was a strange feeling.

The rest of the fight was sort of anticlimactic. Between Henry's exoguns, Gonzo's ice spears, and Vitaliya's jets of flame, the monsters never even had a chance. In fact, they didn't even get close. Henry's sword was never even used the entire fight.

As he stood there, surrounded by bodies of dead monsters while the two Berber spies ensured each monster was truly dead, Henry felt a strange hollow sensation mixed with relief. On one hand, he did like a challenge. On the other hand, there was no such thing as a good fight, but he was pragmatic enough to prefer a quick victory with minimal risk.

* * *

Henry inwardly groaned. Nobody had gotten hurt killing the handful of armored demon wolves. Their steaming, ruined bodies littered the clearing where they'd fought.

However, traveling back to the Battlewagon wasn't pleasant. The woman who'd been in the tree was still in hysterics. All they'd gotten out of her was that her name was Emilia and she was from Chile. She seemed to only speak Spanish, but Gonzo was fluent.

Gonzo trying to talk to her wasn't doing much good since she wouldn't stop crying and screaming, though. She also refused to get on a magicycle, which was proving to be an enormous inconvenience. Gonzo walked with Emilia as she sobbed and stumbled forward. Henry and Vitaliya kept pace on magicycles. Once they got back, one of them would have to double up and take someone back to pick up the magicycle that Gonzo had left behind.

Emilia seemed to be in her mid-twenties. She was pretty, with short, curly hair, olive skin, big eyes, and a curvy body. She wore a torn, dirty black dress and carried her pumps in her hand as she gingerly picked her steps through the forest. Her pantyhose were a mess, with sticks and leaves stuck in them.

She stared at the ground, her eyes wild, sobbing and holding herself tightly like she would otherwise fly apart. Every time she glanced up and saw a magicycle, she'd shudder and wail, her sobbing getting harder.

Henry felt bad for her, but there were very few sounds he hated more than a crying woman. The noise was cutting right through his spine and making his nerves raw.

When they got back to the Battlewagon, Jason and Keeja hadn't returned yet, but the rest of the group was standing in the distance. Bezzi-ibbi was the first to notice their arrival and ran out to greet them. Henry thought the kid looked relieved, which was strange. As soon as Emilia saw the Mo'hali boy, she completely lost her composure again. She went into hysterics, screaming bloody murder. Gonzo tried to calm her down, but wasn't having much success.

Henry didn't speak much Spanish, but he heard "Diablo" and several other interesting words. *Great. This should be wonderful.*

Gonzo led the traumatized woman away, speaking quickly and quietly. Henry gestured the very confused-looking Bezzi-ibbi closer and said softly, "Hey, kid, do me a favor. Go with Vitaliya and pick up the magicycle we left behind."

Bezzi-ibbi nodded and got behind Vitaliya on the back of her magicycle. The red-haired woman seemed to be dividing her attention between Gonzo, and trying to see on the other side of the Battlewagon. Henry assumed she was probably looking for Tony. A flash of annoyance crossed her face, but as soon as Bezzi-ibbi was settled, she gunned the throttle and headed back so Bezzi-ibbi could fetch Gonzo's vehicle.

Henry rounded the Battlewagon and saw most of the group standing off to one side, staring at a tall, black woman in a dark, sequined dress. She wore a little black backpack. Henry noticed that she was really tall, maybe even a little taller than Jason. She had fantastic legs.

Then she turned around, smiling. Henry smiled back and thought, *That is definitely a drag queen.* He remembered how he had been looking at her legs and shrugged. *Shit happens.*

The tall queen was wearing purple lipstick and eyeshadow with white highlights. Her hair, probably a wig, was straightened and fanned out around her, an artistic fake flower woven into one strand. She said, "Oh, another one. Are you gonna give me the cold shoulder too? All these other people keep staring at me. It's like they'd never seen such a fierce bitch before.

"I mean, I realize I'm on another world. You'd think that with animal people and shit walking around, people would have more interesting things to look at than li'l ol' me."

Henry quickly adapted to the situation. "It's okay, girl, it must be hard to be so fabulous."

"Oh, it most definitely is. It figures that I'd get zapped to a place like this on my way home from the club. And now here I am, stuck on some busta ass planet, but the Scooby Gang that saved me is acting all goofy."

"What did they save you from?"

"I was feeling hungry. I was thinking about eating some berries. It turns out they're poisonous. Silly me!" The tall queen giggled. "My name is Thirsty. Thirsty Zha Zha."

"Henry."

"Nice to meet you! Someone will finally talk to me!"

"Yeah, no problem."

"So can you tell me what the hell happens now?" Thirsty adjusted her backpack's straps.

Henry really did have to admit that in his opinion, she was a pretty good drag queen. He found it humorous that he actually knew something about drag queens and had reason to call on that knowledge on an alien planet.

He'd gotten bored in the past after his divorce and watched

some Drag Race on TV. When he was younger, there would have been no way he would have watched a show about drag on TV. But some of the friendships he'd made over the course of his life had opened his eyes.

Ever since he was close friends with his gay battle buddy Benjamin in the Army, he'd felt comfortable around gay people and with gay TV programming in the US. After discovering drag culture, Henry was actually surprised to realize it interested him. He himself would never be an artist, but he could recognize real art in others.

Being able to actually act on creativity was one of the things that Henry most envied about Jason, in fact. From coding, to drawing, to singing, it seemed like Jason could express himself any way he wanted. Henry knew he sang like a stepped-on frog. It was awful. He hated even hearing recordings of his regular speaking voice.

He said, "Calm down, girl. Let me go talk to my people."

"Okay, honey, I'll be right here. It's not like I'm going anywhere else."

Henry walked over to the rest of the conspicuous group, who mostly looked freaked out and uncomfortable. He nudged Mareen and whispered, "Babe, why are you all just standing around and staring at Thirsty?"

Mareen put her mouth right in Henry's ear and whispered, "Henry, I don't think that woman is really a woman."

"No shit. That's a guy in drag."

"You mean a...a homosexual?" Mareen sounded like she couldn't believe it.

Uluula drifted over and must have heard Mareen. "That is a man? Why is he wearing women's clothing? Why did you call him 'girl' in English?"

That's right, most everyone can speak English now. "He is what's called a drag queen. While he's in drag, calling him female pronouns is appropriate. Most drag queens are gay, but Thirsty definitely is."

"But why?" Uluula asked, frowning and staring at Thirsty.

"It's a type of performance, a type of art. And stop staring. It's rude."

"Henry Sato, I am not staring." Uluula's voice was curt.

Henry sighed and gave his attention back to Mareen. "So you saved her from some berries or something?"

"Yes," Mareen said, trying to watch Thirsty without staring. "He had a whole pile of poisonous berries and he was going to eat them. If we had gotten there a few minutes later, he would have been dead."

"Well, good thing you got there in time, but while he's in drag, you should probably call him, 'she.'"

Mareen ignored Henry's correction. "Dying might have been for the best." She didn't meet his eyes.

"What the fuck does that mean?" Henry was aghast. He knew

Uluula was homophobic, but that was apparently a normal Areva thing. Mareen was a big-hearted human girl. What the hell?

"Henry, this planet is not the planet you come from. People don't like...gay...men here. Women outnumber men three to one. If a homosexual man...partners...he will leave six more women to be absorbed into other families or left adrift."

Henry got the math, but he shook his head and asked, "What docs that matter? There are still gay people, right? What about women?"

Mareen looked uncomfortable. "Women who...prefer the company of women are usually absorbed into families, often with a sister or some other family member. But even if they aren't, they live and let live. It isn't uncommon for them to have a long-term partner."

"So only gay men are discriminated against?"

Uluula spoke up, her voice a deadpan. "In most Areva-controlled territories, they are sent away to colonize new worlds or work in space stations."

"So they're segregated." Henry blinked rapidly. He glanced around at the others. Even Yanno-ibbi seemed extremely uncomfortable and wouldn't look at Thirsty.

I can't fucking believe this. I'm the most tolerant person here? Seriously? Me? Henry walked back to Thirsty Zha Zha. He had a feeling the situation was going to get progressively more awkward.

178

* * *

Jason was almost finished being towed back to camp by Keeja. Running through a dungeon with the High Priestess was one of the strangest things he'd done on Ludus so far. He had felt like he was walking following around a high-level player in a game using a God mode cheat. It was utterly ridiculous how easily Keeja had wrecked the whole dungeon, demolishing every challenge. Jason even got a very impressive amount of loot to bring back. Keeja had only taken the music player from the treasure room.

Jason had also been able to witness a number of abilities he might be able to replicate with his magic. He was happy that he had so much research to do, but he thought the whole experience of being powerleveled in real life on an alien planet was so bizarre, his dreams might be confused for week.

However, then he got back to the Battlewagon and noticed Henry chatting with a tall drag queen while Gonzo had a strange, sniffling woman off to one side, talking softly. The rest of the group was standing some distance away, staring at Henry and the drag queen while trying to hide it with various degrees of success.

What in the hell is this? As Keeja flew in for a landing, she finally released control of Jason and he teleported down to the ground. As soon as the woman Gonzo was comforting saw them, she started screaming at the top of her lungs, tearing at her hair.

*What the eff...*Jason was stunned to immobility.

In the next few minutes, Jason met with Henry and stepped

away from the others to discuss all the new developments. The entire time they had their quick conversation, Emilia continued to wail and the majority of the group maintained their strange standoff with Thirsty Zha Zha. Thirsty took a mirror out of her backpack and played with her hair.

Jason felt a headache developing, especially when Henry relayed the depths of the bigotry against gay men on Ludus and apparently the rest of the universe. *What the hell are we going to do about this?* Jason was absently disappointed with people in general and Uluula in particular.

One thing he knew for sure: They were going to help other people from Earth, period. If he was honest with himself, Thirsty made him a little nervous, a little uncomfortable too. He didn't hate gay people or anything, but he wasn't like Henry. He couldn't just meet random new people everywhere he went and make friends at the drop of a hat. Jason could be socially awkward even around people he actually related to.

But Thirsty was from Canada and said he used to visit NYC a lot. Not only was he, she, whatever from Earth, he was even from the same continent as Jason. They were going to help him. Jason just wished that for once on Ludus there would be a problem that wasn't complicated by culture clashes.

Jason walked towards to Gonzo and gestured him over. Emilia tried to grab at the spy, attempting to make him stay, but he gently removed her hands. As soon as he disentangled himself, the woman just seemed to deflate, sitting on the ground.

"How is it going?" Jason asked.

Gonzo frowned. "I've tried to tell her that she isn't dreaming, that this is real and it isn't Hell, but she's hysterical. She didn't meet Dolos or get an orb. She just appeared in the middle of the forest with a note in Spanish about settling Ludus and warning her to beware of monsters. Then she stumbled around for a long time until the demon wolves almost got her. She's been in a tree for half a day. Best I can tell, she hadn't eaten or drank anything for 36 hours or so."

"Wow. That...really sucks. You gave her food and water, right?"

"Of course," Gonzo replied. "She's just really badly shaken. If anything, I think she's just a normal person and reacting to this world like a normal person would."

Keeja walked over, joining them. "What about the homosexual. Is he hurt?"

Jason frowned. "That's kind of rude, and Henry didn't tell me..."

Keeja shouted towards the tall drag queen, "Hey, homosexual!"

Thirsty Zha Zha slowly lowered her mirror and said, "I know you are not talking to me with that rude-ass tone of voice, little sister. You best come correct before we have issues."

"Shut up and answer a question. Are you hurt?"

"No, but if you think—"

"Did you swallow an orb?"

"I've swallowed a lot of things, but do you mean that silver pill thing in the box? Hell yeah, it sounded cool. Nothing happened, though."

"Didn't the directions say to take the orb before bed?"

"Yes, but why does a—"

Thirsty didn't get a chance to utter another word. Keeja dashed forward, jumping up to touch the queen's forehead. Thirsty immediately collapsed in a boneless heap.

Keeja dusted her hands. "I hope I got here fast enough. The fool was courting death or worse. Always follow directions when dealing with magical weapons."

Jason internally groaned. Things had been difficult enough, but the group had begun to settle into a routine. However, he could tell everything was just going to get vastly more complicated. At the very least, the group dynamics were going to change.

The rest of the day was a blur. The group didn't start to travel again, they all just made camp in place. Jason tried to make sure everyone had a place to sleep as well as necessary basic gear. Finally, night fell and nobody stayed up late. The whole group awkwardly went to sleep, minus the first Mo'hali on watch.

The next morning, Gonzo woke to find Emilia dead in her blankets. She'd found a knife and slashed her wrists. She looked peaceful, but Jason felt his heart grow cold. Ludus had claimed yet another victim. They would never even know her story.

He wondered if her family would ever know what had happened to her. Probably not. The thought made him feel desperately lonely. He went to find Uluula and buried his face in her hair, hugging her tightly.

Thank God he had his fierce little anchor in the world, an anchor on reality. Uluula patted his arm and whispered, "What?"

Jason just hugged her tighter.

Delvers LLC: Obligations Incurred

CHAPTER TWELVE

Culture Club

As the group prepared for the day, the atmosphere was somber and quiet. News of Emilia's death had spread instantly after Gonzo's shout. Practical as always, Henry had gone off into the woods to give the dead girl's body a proper burial. Nobody else had felt led to go with him; death on Ludus wasn't exactly a shock to anyone. Gonzo did say a prayer over the body before Henry left, though.

Bezzi-ibbi felt guilty. His whiskers drooped and his tail dragged. He knew Yanno-ibbi and Rark-han both felt the same way. They'd all been on guard shifts, and none of them had noticed the smell of blood until Emilia was found dead.

If they'd been paying attention, she might still have been alive.

Bezzi-ibbi knew he could make excuses for himself. He had been focused on scanning for monsters, exterior dangers. He had been patrolling the perimeter. He'd been tired. But he also knew that he could have noticed something was wrong, too. His sense of smell wasn't at the same level as an animal's, or even other races of Mo'hali, but it was better than a Terran's. He should have caught the smell of blood.

Bezzi-ibbi's tutors hadn't always had an easy time with him in the past. He had preferred running through the alleys of Mirana, learning to play musical instruments and singing; studying was not his favorite activity. However, when he did sit down to study, he'd tried to take it seriously. One lesson that had stuck with him was how to objectively frame a situation, how to see the truth of a matter, even if was unpleasant.

Bezzi-ibbi had failed the group. Nobody knew when Emilia had committed suicide, and Henry wouldn't tell them how long she'd been dead for, a fact he could determine from his EMT experience. However, the fact was Bezzi-ibbi had had the last watch. Even if she'd already taken her own life, he should have at least noticed.

He felt ashamed. He hadn't liked Emilia. She had acted hysterical and hadn't been adapting to the reality of her situation. She had been weak. Bezzi-ibbi knew and respected Terrans like Jason, and Henry, and Mareen. They were tough and smart. They didn't show the back of their neck to any situation. In comparison, Emilia had been so scared she couldn't talk, couldn't function.

Bezzi-ibbi's first reaction when he'd heard Emilia was dead

had been one of relief. He'd tried to convince himself he was happy that she had found peace, but the reality was he was just glad he wouldn't have to hear her wailing anymore.

This attitude was unacceptable; logical, but unacceptable. For Bezzi-ibbi to be a good Clan chief, much less a proper Jaguar Troubadour, he needed to understand and empathize with others. He could still be firm; he didn't have to agree with everyone else. He could even disagree with a blade. But to feel so little about the death of an innocent person bothered him.

Was he truly really becoming so callous, before even reaching adulthood? He knew he was a little unbalanced from Thirsty Zha Zha being around too, but that was even less of an excuse for so deeply failing at his duty.

Bezzi-ibbi felt the Great Creator had a plan for him. He even thought he had a good idea what his destiny was, and letting his heart harden would be spitting on the gift he'd been given. It made him want to hide his eyes from the light of the day. No more, though. He was going to correct the situation. What better way to soften his heart than to sincerely get to know someone who made him uncomfortable? Just like Henna-ibbi always said, the best way to grow stronger was to face the whip directly and cover your fangs.

Bezzi-ibbi walked through the camp as everyone else prepared to leave for the day. With Henry gone, Mareen was doing the majority of the heavy lifting. She could carry their thick tents with little effort. Aodh helped her break down the equipment.

Rark-han and Yanno-ibbi worked to hide any trace that the camp had existed. Towards that end, before they left, Henry would cover the camp's male and female slit trenches, too. It only took him a minute to do so using magic.

Gonzo and Vitaliya had accompanied Uluula to the nearby river to fill their purifying, chilling water containers. Henry called them "water zappers." Bezzi-ibbi didn't know how the containers worked, just what they did. After being filled with water, if a magic stone was pressed to the power-point for a few seconds, they'd create clean, cool water for the day.

Bezzi-ibbi had no idea where Keeja was. She still hadn't shown up yet for the day. However, Thirsty Zha Zha had headed down to the river earlier. Bezzi-ibbi's sharp ears had caught her saying something about "taking her face off." He had no idea what it meant. He began heading to the river and noticed Jason ahead of him.

Bezzi-ibbi jogged forward to catch up to his friend. He said, "River?"

Jason replied, "Yeah. I want to check on Thirsty. I think she'd rather talk to Henry but he's…busy." Jason's eyes looked haunted. Bezzi-ibbi knew the whole camp was sad, but Jason seemed to be taking Emilia's death hardest. After Gonzo had found her corpse, Jason had walked off to be by himself for a while. Bezzi-ibbi had to remind himself that Terrans from their homeworld had strange morals about protecting women.

He thought it was odd. Females didn't need protection, the most obvious reason being that they were largely expendable. In fact, most often on Ludus, males of any importance were kept secure and protected. Women were most often police, soldiers, even adventurers. It was a shame if a woman died violently, but it impacted the community less than if a man perished.

Bezzi-ibbi wondered what would transpire in the future if someone tried to put Henry and Jason in civilized captivity, tried to keep them protected. He grinned, the thought banishing some of his depression from earlier.

His brothers were like forces of nature. He wasn't sure it would be possible to cage them. At the moment, his brother Jason-ibbi wasn't looking very sure of himself, though.

When they got near the river, Gonzo, Vitaliya, and Uluula came into view. Jason headed that direction and Bezzi-ibbi followed. Uluula kept working as they arrived. The two Berber spies looked bored.

"Does anyone know where Thirsty went?" asked Jason. "Is anyone keeping an eye on her?"

Uluula smiled at him and said, "I am busy and have not been scanning my surrounding." True to her words, Uluula kept filling water containers, purifying the water, and stacking the water zappers neatly on the riverbank for the group to pick up with the Battlewagon before leaving the area.

Vitaliya didn't say anything, just kept acting as a guard. The role was necessary in case an aquatic monster tried to ambush them. However, Gonzo relied, "How should I know? Does it matter?"

Jason paused for a moment before asking, "Do you have a problem?"

Gonzo rolled his eyes and said, "I've heard about how Earth is now. I know what the US is like. Gay is cool now, that's fine, I don't care. But look, I'm Catholic, and I just had to deal with the corpse of a nice, normal girl who was sent to a strange world against her will and dumped into a situation with monsters, animal people, and mages running around.

"If you are asking if I'd rather the freak was dead instead of her, yes."

Bezzi-ibbi needed to pause a moment in order to remember what "Catholic" meant. He recalled that it was a subset of Christianity on Terra, one of the major religions. Religion had never interested Bezzi-ibbi much. The Great Creator created the universe and was the universe. The night was Her gift of rest, the day was His blessing to all thinking people. One should try to be kind and avoid or destroy evil. These things were not complicated. The other races made everything far too complex.

Jason replied, "That's harsh."

Gonzo crossed his arms. "Yes, it is. And yes, I know that it's not very Christian of me. I know that Jesus traveled with undesirables and whores. But I have no reason to avoid the issue, and I am not a very nice person, Jason Booth. I have done many things on Ludus that have left me soiled. I am a spy. I've had to murder in cold blood. Judging some silly man for wearing a dress is the least of my sins.

"If this were any other kind of mission, I'd tell you what I thought you wanted to hear, or what my cover persona would be thinking...but this is a very unique situation. You are basically my peer. You've been drafted into my organization. I am just accompanying you to Berber, so I can truly speak my mind. I thought long and hard about this, and I think it'd be better for our future working relationship if I'm straightforward with you, both good and bad.

"I don't hate Thirsty or have any ill will towards him, but I couldn't really give a shit what Mr. Diva is doing right now."

"I see," said Jason. "There's obviously no point in arguing about it. So do you know where Thirsty went or not?"

"He, she, it—whatever—they went that way." Gonzo gestured upriver and pointedly turned the other direction.

Without another word, Jason began walking towards where Gonzo had indicated. Bezzi-ibbi followed and decided it was a good time to practice his English. He asked, "Can you explain what that was about?"

Jason sighed. "It's really difficult to explain because it's a cultural thing. Well, actually, you know how some races look down on Mo'hali, and you know how apparently the whole universe looks down on gay, or homosexual men? Basically, in my culture, where I come from, fairly recently a lot of people have recognized that it's wrong to treat people badly or hate them for being different.

"This is really hard to explain and I know I'm being vague, but some people still don't like others for their differences, even though they believe it's morally wrong to feel that way. I think Gonzo is like this. I think he knows he's wrong, but he's not willing to change his mind."

Bezzi-ibbi thought about it and replied, "But Areva and other races send away homosexual men because they compete for resources—males. Most don't hate homosexual men, they just make other people uncomfortable. Some people fear they'll sway men to being homosexual. Do Terrans hate homosexual men?"

"Well, I'd be lying if I said everyone doesn't. However, people can be very complex. Some people dislike groups but are often friends of individuals from that group. Different cultures on Earth are vastly different, too. Like in my country back home, gay people can have positions of power and influence, but in other countries, they can be killed for being homosexual. I mean, either way, Gonzo is acting homophobic."

Bezzi-ibbi screwed up his nose; the gesture let him feel the point of one of his fangs. He asked, "Phobia means fear, yes? So the word means to be afraid of something? Gonzo doesn't seem afraid to me."

Jason eyed him for a moment and said, "You know, you're really too smart for your own good sometimes. You're making this even more difficult for me to explain. On Earth, whenever there are two sides to any opinion, there are different degrees of agreeing or disagreeing. This goes for pretty much everything.

"Homosexuals have been fighting for civil rights for a long time now. I don't know exactly when, but in the past, people who were anti-gay were called homophobic, the idea being that they were just afraid of gay people or weren't used to them and that was why they didn't agree with homosexuality. Of course, this wasn't always true, but the word stuck and now people use it as a general term to mean anti-gay, at least most people do."

Bezzi-ibbi asked, "Again, gay means homosexual, right?" Jason nodded and Bezzi-ibbi asked, "So are all Catholics anti-gay?"

Jason sighed. "No, not even close. Well, some are. The thought is that since the Bible has passages against gay people, if Christians support gay people, they're supporting sin. We all sin, but some think that if someone knowingly embraces the sin in their life, they're rebelling against God.

It's kind of complex, and more than I can go over in just one conversation. But Catholicism is a major religion. Any large religion has many different schools of thought, and even within smaller sects, there can be individuals with differing beliefs.

"Now, in the past, things were different, but these days, there are differing opinions all over the place, about pretty much everything. The same is true for Christianity. In fact, some churches even allow for gay ministers and preachers now. If you ask ten different Christians what they think about this, you may get ten different answers."

"Then why did Gonzo say he was Catholic before?"

"You know, Bezzi-ibbi, I've never had to explain this before, it's a difficult subject," muttered Jason, his frustration bleeding into his voice. "Maybe you should talk to someone else who knows more about it, like maybe Henry.

"You know, speaking of that, if I hadn't just run through a crazy dungeon with Keeja yesterday, or just visited with my nonhuman wife while she was using magic to clean water a few minutes ago, I'd say that fantasy-football-player-Henry knowing about drag culture was too weird to be real."

Jason coughed into his hand and continued, "Anyway, to answer your question, a lot of humans either feel a certain way about a group either because of religion, or they use religion as an excuse to feel that way. A person's religious beliefs are very real to them. Most people in the world, in my opinion, are trying to be decent people and do what's right. Unfortunately, belonging to a group, for Humans, can make us dislike other groups and even act violently towards them.

"In fact, there are still some countries on Earth where different types of people can be killed in groups, or legally treated terribly. It even still happens to Christians in some places. In other words, you can be killed for being the wrong religion. Hell, wars have been fought over religion. It's not the most fun subject to talk about, especially since I consider myself a Christian; Assembly of God, actually."

"So Christians hate 'gay' people?" The word seemed strange to Bezzi-ibbi. He'd thought gay meant happy. Why would Terrans call a group of people "happy" just to hate them? It made no sense.

Jason's expression looked pained. "You basically just asked me the same question as you did before. The answer is not necessarily. I sure don't, although I'd be lying if I said Thirsty doesn't confuse me. The actual teachings of Christianity are to love everyone, that only God has the right to judge any other person. You know, Catholics are a sect of Christianity, that is why Gonzo said some of the things he said earlier. Christianity, Islam, Hinduism, Judaism, these are all huge religions. Each religion has a large spread of beliefs and differing morality among even billions of people. Different sects can interpret their holy books in different ways. Wars have been fought over this, too.

"In fact, in some of the same countries that gay people can be killed for no reason other than being gay, Christians can be too."

Bezzi-ibbi was trying hard to understand Jason-ibbi's words. "Catholicism is a sect of Christianity, and has its own sects...with people who may disagree with the sect they're in?" Bezzi-ibbi was baffled. Terrans were truly insane. "So if both groups of people, gays and Christians or other religious people, can be bullied, even bullied together by some other group, why do they dislike each other? Or are people mistreated all over your world depending on where they are and what group they're in?"

Jason pressed his palms into his eyes before answering, "This is a very depressing conversation. Probably the latter. Some places on my world are bad to be a certain race. There's probably at least one place somewhere on Earth where any person would be in danger if they visited. Some countries or areas discriminate on skin color, religion, family, wealth, sexual orientation, age, or even gender."

Bezzi-ibbi's eyes grew wide. "Gender? You mean men are even mistreated for being men?"

"Well, some might agree with you, but I was actually talking about women. Throughout human history, females haven't always been treated very well."

After hearing what Jason said, Bezzi-ibbi's first reaction was disbelief. His second was to scoff and feel superior. He'd heard stories of Terrans his whole life, how they were brutal, and primitive. Jason's words seemed to reinforce that.

However, the Jaguar Clan heir took a mental step back and thought critically. If he was brutally honest with himself, Mo'hali weren't that different. There was definitely a hierarchy of sorts.

When the Jaguar Clan had applicants to become an indentured Hero, putting their life on the line for a job, knowing they would probably die in the process, it was never a Jaguar Clan member doing so.

The applicant was usually a lesser race Mo'hali from a poor family, sometimes even *idril*, adrift, Clan-less.

Bezzi-ibbi though about how to say what was on his mind in English. Then he slowly pronounced, "On Ludus, mouse Mo'hali are usually lower than other Clans. Jaguar Clan is higher ranked than Rabbit Clan."

"Ah, so you might understand, then," said Jason.

"No, because most Mo'hali Clans on Ludus are new, only Clans by decision." Bezzi-ibbi paused again to remember some of his lesser-used English vocabulary. "What is the word? Planet. Before Ludus, most Mo'hali stayed on their own planet. The Jaguar race had many clans on a world. So few of us are on Ludus, and our power is so weak, that we organized Clans by sub race."

"And some Clans are looked down on or considered more worthy than others?" Jason's eyes widened and he said, "Yet you probably grew up loving and respecting your mother, Kinwe-na-ibbi. I bet you've had confrontations with other Mo'hali."

"Yes," said Bezzi-ibbi. He felt uncomfortable. Even thinking about others talking badly about his mother, Kinwe-na-ibbi, made him feel angry and ashamed all at once. He didn't want to elaborate.

The topic hadn't really ever come up before; he hadn't had to explain it. Mo'hali just all knew and understood the politics on Ludus. "Feline Mo'hali and canine races are above most other races. Which Clans are at the top changes, but the Tiger Clan and Leopard Clan are strongest right now. The Tiger Clan deals with mercenaries and weapons. Leopard Clan is known for magic vehicles and tools.

"These are high Mo'hali. Low Mo'hali are lower. Dog, Mouse, and Fox Clans are lower."

Jason looked confused. "High, low, what do you mean?"

Bezzi-izzi was exasperated. How could he explain such a thing to a Terran? "Breeding is important. Long ago, to survive on Ludus, more civilized, smarter Mo'hali had ownership of the main branch Clans. The shaggy Mo'hali, people closer to the ancestor animals, they got their own Clans too, and they are below the main Clans."

Jason asked, "So Mo'hali have their own issues too, huh? So what about the Heroes that volunteer to work for the larger Clans like yours? Are they all from poor families or less affluent Mo'hali Clans?"

Bezzi-ibbi had been dreading that question, but he'd known it was probably coming. He opened his mouth to respond, but then they rounded a bend in the river, went over a hill, and saw Thirsty.

Almost immediately, Bezzi-ibbi saw text scroll over his left eye:

Dashawn David Givens, Terran, Canadian

Dolos Orb, Enchanting, Elemental Focus

First Rank

Jason had obviously gotten the, what did he call it? He'd gotten the LEDF. The tall, sandy-haired Terran man muttered, "Now that is interesting."

* * *

Jason marveled at how much Thirsty Zha Zha's appearance had changed. Before, he'd been a drag queen with long hair, distinct makeup, and glamorous fashion. Now he was a tall, dark-skinned man with short hair and big, calm eyes. The long hair had apparently been a wig.

Thirsty wore dark-colored skinny jeans, yellow sneakers, a cream-colored t-shirt, and a yellow handkerchief around his neck. The t-shirt had a recognizable half-white, half-red ball and the text "Balling" underneath. He wasn't in drag anymore, but Jason thought Thirsty might still have been wearing light makeup, maybe mascara.

Jason didn't know what to say, and he felt awkward as Bezzi-ibbi stared at Thirsty, while Thirsty stared right back at the Jaguar Clan heir. Neither the tall man nor the boy seemed upset, but Jason felt like they were playing a game to see which of them could make Jason more uncomfortable...and they were both winning.

He wanted to fill the silence somehow or he was going to just teleport away on nerves. He said, "So you had another outfit, huh?"

Thirsty answered, "Yes, I always keep a change of clothes in case I end up crashing somewhere after a show. It's a lucky thing, too, since I sure as hell wouldn't wanna be walking around a freaky wilderness in heels. I am really not enjoying this new change in my life. I think I liked puberty more than this.

"I'm used to being the freakiest thing around, honey. This is not my scene."

Jason wasn't sure how to respond to that. The little group started heading back to camp. After a brief silence, Jason asked, "So your name is Dashawn, right?"

Thirsty abruptly stopped and Jason came to a halt too. After a few breaths, Thirsty began walking again. "Look, I know you're all elves or wizards or whatever the fuck, and I've accepted that. However, I am not cool with you reading my mind. Get out of my head. Stop that shit. Bzzzz!"

"Wait, what?" Jason stammered. "No, I am...I didn't..."

"Also, you do know that there's a little cat-looking boy here with us, right? He's kind of cute in a weird, freaky way. I'm not just imagining him, am I? Every time I think he's real, I notice again how well dressed he is and how adorable he looks. There is no way any kid, human or otherwise, can exist on this ratchet-ass world and still have fashion sense that good.

"I'll admit, I've done acid before exactly once in my life, but the last twenty-four hours have that experience beat hands down. Still, I gotta admit that I wanna ask this figment of my imagination who his tailor is. That is one fierce-ass outfit."

Bezzi-ibbi rolled his eyes and said, "Everyone can see your name. You are orb-Bonded."

Thirsty missed a step. "The little animal boy just talked. Did you see the little bastard talk? Do you think he'd tell me where he got that vest? Also, is his hand covered in metal? It's very Michael of him; you should tell him that if he's real."

Bezzi-ibbi sighed and muttered, "Terrans." Then he gave a sidelong wink at Jason before smiling broadly at Thirsty, his grin putting his entire mouth full of sharp teeth and prominent fangs on display. Thirsty gulped, and Bezzi-ibbi chuckled. The boy said, "We will talk again soon." Bezzi-ibbi grinned again, less widely this time, and jogged ahead.

As the Jaguar Clan heir rapidly left them behind, Jason had no idea what had just happened. *Mo'hali sure can be strange*, he thought.

He cleared his throat and said, "Look, I think you have the wrong idea. First off, what should I call you, Dashawn or Thirsty?"

The tall, black man looked off into the distance for a moment. "Call me Thirsty. I usually don't go by my stage name unless I'm performing, but now that I think about it, most of my friends call me Thirsty. I think I'm happier when I'm in drag or people are talking to me like I'm in drag. If I'm gonna be living a whacked-out situation like this, I may as well do some experimenting to see what makes me most happy. There's no time like the present to reinvent myself...again."

"That's a strange thing to say," said Jason. "I mean, I'm kind of surprised you're taking everything so calmly."

"Well, did you freak the fuck out when you got here?" Jason shook his head and Thirsty said, "Well, then, why should I? Just because I can wear a dress and look fishy as hell doesn't mean I break down at the drop of a hat. Trust me, honey, getting a tuck done right can be scarier than any crazy-ass monsters or whatever."

"Have you actually seen a monster yet?" asked Jason.

"Touché. Anyway, we all saw what happened with the pretty Latina girl this morning. Losing my mind or flipping out won't help me or anyone else at all. I haven't had the most awesome life so far, but it's made me tough. I don't plan to give up, I'm too fabulous for that. Way too goddamn sexy."

Jason nodded thoughtfully. "On that note, I should probably tell you about the planet we're on. It's called Ludus. I also need to tell you about a dickhead named Dolos. In fact, I should probably fill you in on Mo'hali, magic, everything."

"Magic...real magic, huh? I woke up today knowing I had powers. So I wasn't having delusions? I've imagined some pretty crazy shit after a bender. Once I thought I was a love child of Adele and Beyoncé. It was the best night of my life until the hangover and reality both beat the shit out of me."

"Nope, no delusion." Jason chuckled softly. "You're orb-Bonded, which means you're going to live a very, very long time and you have magic powers now. However, people are going to want to kill you for it, though."

"What? Baby, you did not just say what I think you did. Tell me you didn't."

"Like I said, I have a lot to fill you in on. We're going to have to decide what to do about weapons and armor for you, too."

"Look, honey, I'm a lover, not a fighter."

Jason grimly said, "That's what I used to think about myself, too. Trust me, this world will change you."

The next few minutes as they walked back to camp, Jason gave Thirsty a quick rundown of Ludus just like George had done for him and Henry months before. Thinking of George made Jason sad.

It felt like years ago that he'd arrived on Ludus with Henry. In fact, his first Ludan winter seemed to be creeping up quickly. Sometimes Jason forgot it was currently fall since so many of the broad-leafed trees on Ludus didn't shed their leaves.

Winter was coming. Times would probably get tougher. Their journey to Berber had really just begun. There was a lot to do and a lot to think about, but Jason was sure of his moral obligation to help keep Thirsty survive.

Emilia was dead, and probably untold others from Earth who had been transported to Ludus over the years. The other two people from Earth that Dolos had mentioned might be dead too, but he had no way to be sure. At least Thirsty was here; he was alive, and he was someone they could actually save.

The fact he was gay and liked to cross-dress or whatever was largely irrelevant. He was from Earth, he was a human being, and he needed help, just like Jason and Henry had in the past.

In that moment, he decided that Thirsty was going to survive. Period. Jason wouldn't tolerate any more preventable deaths, and everyone else just needed to get with the program.

After they got back to camp, Jason knew the first thing he was going to do. He planned to give Thirsty the second-to-last tincture to hide his orb-Bonded alert, his LEDF. He wished Henry would just get with the program and adopt the term. The first step of effective communication was using the same acronyms. Well, that was what all the project managers in IT used to say.

As Jason trudged along, he thought about project managers, and how much more unpleasant his stay on Ludus would have been if one of those people were along for the ride.

He shivered.

CHAPTER THIRTEEN

Change of Plans

It had been the better part of a week since Thirsty had become part of the group, and Aodh liked him a lot.

When he had first joined the group, Thirsty had seemed most fascinated by Bezzi-ibbi. Since Aodh and the Jaguar boy were friends, they all chatted together fairly often. At first, Aodh could tell the dark man was taken aback by his appearance, but Aodh was used to that. Unfortunately, he looked Fideli. Terrans from Earth thought Fideli looked strange, even frightening, and others feared them by reputation.

But Aodh didn't have a stereotypical Fideli temperament at all. He didn't want to hurt anyone. It hadn't even occurred to him in the past that he would have to actually kill things while being an adventurer. Sure, he'd known that being an adventurer was violent and dangerous, but his idea of what that would be like had differed from reality. In his mind, he would perhaps thump monsters and bandits into submission, being praised while his enemies groaned on the ground.

He had not expected to be throwing terrifyingly powerful bombs that reduced monsters to bits of bone, ropy innards, and other unidentifiable pieces.

Luckily, Thirsty seemed to accept how Aodh looked rather quickly and they began having normal conversations. At first, Aodh hadn't been sure about the strange, tall man, but as the days passed, he discovered an unexpected kinship.

They were both outcasts—Aodh for looking Fideli, and Thirsty for being a ponce.

Thirsty described growing up in a place called Ottawa and being sad in school. He had never felt accepted, and others had even been cruel to him. Then Thirsty described how he had discovered "drag" in New York, and eventually moved to a large city named Toronto. Toronto was where a lot of Thirsty's friends lived now. He'd been happy there for a while, but said he had been starting to get sad again. Money was a problem, or rather, a lack of it.

Aodh didn't understand why anyone would want to wear women's clothing. He also didn't understand how a man could be attracted to other men. However, he did understand being desperately unhappy and wanting to do something different, anything to reinvent his life.

Aodh had become an adventurer. Thirsty liked to wear pretty makeup, sing songs, and dance for other people. They were different people and they'd taken very different paths, but Aodh could understand why Thirsty felt secure in his new life and liked who he was.

The young adventurer felt like his realization about Thirsty meant he was growing up a bit. He was proud of himself. After he understood how they were similar, he didn't feel uncomfortable around Thirsty at all anymore, even when the man put on light makeup or asked Bezzi-ibbi about Ludus fashion.

Aodh ignored Thirsty if he tried asking about men back in his old village, though.

In many ways, Thirsty stuck out and didn't fit in on Ludus, but at the same time, he was acclimating and becoming useful to the group faster than Aodh ever had. Thirsty was orb-Bonded and had started to learn how to use his magic. Aodh didn't even know what his own power was. He still didn't feel any different, and he couldn't use any magic other than the Fire school magic he was born with.

He watched Thirsty work with a few twinges of envy. Occasionally, when their group would stop to relieve themselves or eat, Henry would make a new ring or bracelet for Thirsty to enchant while they traveled.

The flamboyant man was getting good at it. Aodh watched him work on his newest project, some sort of rod made of bronze cones. Thirsty was chatting with Aodh; Bezzi-ibbi was out on a magicycle. Uluula and Mareen were in the back of the Battlewagon too, but they were speaking quietly among themselves. They still didn't talk to Thirsty much.

The tall, dark man was carefully rolling the pieces of bronze around in his hands. "It's weird, you know," he said. "How to do this stuff just pops into my head like an info bubble, but I can't actually be any good at it unless I practice. It's a good thing Henry's been able to break down all the shitty stuff I've made so I could try again. He's a sweetheart."

Aodh nodded and continued to watch him work with the bronze. "Why are you rolling it around like that?"

"It's like...I'm getting to know it. Now I kind of know what Henry meant before when he said building all the vehicles was like having a conversation. Like, I have an idea of what I want to do, and the more I play with the material, the more clearly I see the picture in my head of how to make it happen."

"So what are you making now?"

"Well, everyone keeps tellin' me I need to have weapons and gear. If I gotta be stuck on this lame-ass planet, I can at least make my gear look fabulous. I don't have any cute dresses right now, and I don't wanna chance messing up the only formal dress I have, but I can still work on accessories. I'm gonna be serving up some hardcore magic warrior girl realness, believe it. Yessiree."

Aodh had no idea what any of that meant and wondered if he

was misunderstanding Thirsty's English. Thirsty could speak Luda now after being orb-Bonded, but he still spoke English most of the time, and Aodh didn't mind. It was good practice.

Thirsty pointed to a smaller piece of bronze, shaped like a cone. "I'm stacking these up on top of each other and using metal magic to hold them all together with Earth. My four main schools, Earth, Air, Fire, and Water, are strongest. I can't really mess with subschools yet. Anyway, I'm using air magic between each cone, storing power to shoot them when it's triggered. Aiming is kinda hard, though."

"Did Henry help you with it?"

"Yessiree! He also taught me about magic. Jason has helped a little, too, but his lady...friend has been demanding lately." Thirsty gave a significant look out the corner of his eye at Uluula. "I don't think everyone here is happy about little ol' me being around."

Aodh wanted to deny it, but Thirsty was right. The majority of their group still had not warmed to him. Luckily, Henry had never seemed to care, although Mareen was annoyed with his attitude over it. Aodh had heard them yelling at each other in the distance during a rest stop the previous day. Ever since then, Mareen had been irritable and short with everyone, especially Henry.

Uluula had been acting distant. Yanno-ibbi had been keeping a physical distance. The spies, Gonzo and Vitaliya, always kept to themselves, but they seemed more withdrawn than usual since

Thirsty Zha Zha had arrived. Aodh was thankful for that. Even if he hadn't liked Thirsty, he would have stayed near the man since it kept his cousin away. Still, he knew it was only a matter of time before she started acting like herself again. He could see the madness in her eyes when she thought nobody else was watching.

"It's really my own fault," Thirsty sighed. "When I first came to this planet, I was so fucking fabulous and beautiful that the goddess RuPaul herself would have approved."

"What?" asked Aodh. He'd never heard of a goddess named RuPaul before. Buddha, Jesus, Mohammed, Zeus, God, and other names he recognized. RuPaul was definitely new. "Who is RuPaul?"

"RuPaul is the goddess of drag, honey. Everyone knows this. Like, if I could meet Ru in person one day, I would die a happy queen."

"Uh, okay," muttered Aodh. As usual now, whenever Thirsty said something he didn't understand, he changed the subject. "Okay, so I know what the rod is now, and most other things you've worked on before got melted down again, but what about your bracelets?" Aodh pointed at the handful of bronze and copper bracelets on Thirsty's wrists.

Thirsty began to answer, but Keeja dropped out of the sky with no warning, landed gently next to Aodh, and answered for him. "They are shields," she said. "I've been watching Thirsty make them." She turned to address the tall man directly. "You are most interested in defense, protection, yes? That would explain why you didn't do anything except craft shield bracelets during the first few days you learned to use your power."

Aodh swallowed. He didn't pass out anymore when Keeja was around, but he didn't feel comfortable, either. He trusted Henry and Jason; he'd made a conscious decision to follow them. However, he didn't think they realized how dangerous and unpredictable Keeja the Ravager was in all the legends.

Unfortunately, when Keeja was around, Thirsty gave Aodh even more anxiety than Henry and Jason did. Aodh hadn't even known it was possible. Thirsty took irreverence to a new level, almost like he was perfecting an art form.

The drag queen rolled his eyes, huffed at Keeja, and said, "Where the hell have you been, you little super-elf, crazy-ass, wannabe midget cowgirl? You are about a thousand years too late to be a Dallas Girl, girl." He pointed at her cowboy boots and said, "You should really dump those hideous boots."

Aodh mildly wondered if it was possible to die of fright. He hoped not; he had so much more to do. Perishing with a life full of regrets was not how he wanted to go. At the very least, he really wanted to get married before he died, or at least date. In fact, he'd settle for just losing his virginity.

Keeja cocked an eyebrow at Thirsty and drawled, "I've been flying, because, you know, I can do that. But I'm surprised that this crazy is coming out of your mouth. I mean, all this sass is coming from a random queen with some raggedy-ass budget wig and skinny jeans from inside a backpack? Don't tell me, I already know. You were so broke on your planet, you had to use actual chalk instead of makeup, and that's why you looked like someone dragged you through a cornfield dusted with cocaine. From now on, whenever I see anyone look that busted, I'm going to say they look 'Thirsty.' You have your own look now, congratulations."

Thirsty blinked and exchanged a smile with Keeja, all teeth. The tension shattered when Thirsty burst out laughing. He chortled, "Oh shit, I just got read, didn't I, you little mighty mouse-lookin' elf bitch? That was fierce. Have you been practicing?"

Keeja just sniffed and gave a slight shrug. Aodh had no idea what the exchange meant, he was just glad the unpredictable demigoddess hadn't killed them all.

Keeja held out a hand and ordered, "Tony, give me your dagger."

Aodh immediately complied, grabbing his dagger where he kept it behind his back, and slowing down in panic when he realized Keeja might think he was attacking her. Her amused smile at his nervousness made him flush down to his neck in embarrassment. He presented the dagger on the palms of both hands and noticed Uluula and Mareen watching them with interest out the corner of his eye. "Lady Priestess, my dagger," he said formally.

Keeja plucked the blade out of his hands and examined it. Aodh had seen the dagger many times and he loved it. He'd been incredibly fortunate to find it randomly in the middle of nowhere. The weapon's blade was wavy, like a snake. The handle was all one piece, made with the same metal as the bronze blade, and the pommel was fashioned after the head of a horse.

Keeja held the weapon towards Thirsty and said, "Work on this. You should be able to imbue a dagger with several powers at once. This will allow you to train your abilities much faster than making the same types of items over and over again."

Thirsty accepted the dagger and slowly nodded. "I don't know how, but I can sense you're right. I have something for you, too." Thirsty took one of the bracelets off his wrist and bounced it on his palm, his expression hesitant. Eventually, he held it out to Keeja and said, "I want you to have this. It's not very good and you probably don't need it, but when you knocked me the fuck out the first time we met, you probably saved my life."

Aodh's breath caught in his throat. Thirsty was trying to give Keeja, High Priestess Keeja, a bronze bracelet? Aodh braced himself for an explosion of anger or force, but nothing happened. Keeja just cocked her head and continued to listen.

"I don't have much on this whack-ass planet," explained Thirsty. "All I have is what I've been given through charity, and what I've been able to create with it. Well, I have my phone, too, but I dropped it in a puddle when I first got transported and fell on my ass. I haven't been able to turn it on."

Keeja had been slowly reaching out to accept the bracelet, but her head snapped up. She snatched the bracelet, put it on her wrist, and said, "Give me your phone, you fool. You truly do have a death wish."

Thirsty frowned, but didn't argue. He dug in his backpack and produced a square object the likes of which Aodh had never seen. Keeja picked it up gingerly between two fingers. She said, "I might need to give this to Jason or Henry. You're lucky you never turned this on, or you would have been framing your death. I need to think about what to do with this."

Thirsty grunted and said, "And now people are stealing my cellphone like it ain't no thang. Fine, take everything. Do you want the panties from my backpack, too?"

Keeja smiled like she was going to say something, but glanced at the bracelet on her wrist and just shook her head. After a brief pause she said, "It's for your own good, you silly homosexual." She chuckled and floated upwards. "I'm going to fly again, because I can do that."

As Keeja floated away, Thirsty frowned and growled, "Yeah, you better get your cheerleader wannabe, Oompa Loompa ass out of here! That's right, I see you running off, bitch. I know what's up."

Keeja didn't even turn around, just chuckled more, and Aodh began having second thoughts about his friendship with Thirsty.

If Thirsty couldn't keep his…sass under control, he might truly get them all killed.

After Keeja was gone, Aodh began to ponder again about how he really didn't want to die without ever having a girlfriend. He was wondering if there were even any girls out there who wouldn't be disgusted by his Fideli appearance when he noticed the caravan slowing down. This usually meant it was time for another rest stop.

Aodh looked forward to rest stops. The novelty of traveling quickly and smoothly over long stretches of land had worn off long ago. Now Aodh couldn't wait to take breaks and stretch. He usually most looked forward to training with his staff or practicing other adventuring skills.

This break, after the caravan was ready to get going again, Jason called a meeting. The group gathered facing one side of the Battlewagon. Jason stood in front of everyone while Henry sat on the side of the turret keeping watch, his rifle slung over his shoulder.

"Okay, folks," said Jason. "I know this is sudden, but Henry and I have been talking about our route. I've been thinking about it, and now that I've made up my mind, there's no point in continuing this direction."

Aodh wasn't sure what Jason was talking about. He looked around quickly and noticed the rest of the group looked as confused as he felt. Jason held up a hand to keep anyone else from speaking yet. "Look, I know this is sudden. Please hear me out until you start asking questions. Give me a chance to explain myself, okay?

"Basically, we've been making terrible time. We keep going around entire wooded areas because the Battlewagon is so big. Driving through the wilderness should have been quicker to get to the Stem River than any roads because there's a lot less distance to cover.

"Instead, not only is it slower, we've been dealing with an increasing number of monster attacks, too. We can bypass most monsters while travelling, but clearing them out in the evening before we camp is starting to take its toll on our resources.

"Which is the last point: we need to restock. We're running low on supplies that we'll need later. Plus, winter is coming soon, so we need to get some warmer clothing. Well, that's what Mareen said, and I have no reason to doubt her."

"What does this mean?" asked Yanno-ibbi. "We are still heading to Berber, correct?"

"I am curious as well," stated Gonzo.

From above them, Keeja startled most of the group when she spoke. She mused, "He's talking about heading back to the road between Mirana and Taretha. If you travel the longer, safer route, you'll be able to resupply more often, travel faster, and avoid monsters."

Jason nodded up at Keeja and said, "Precisely."

A few members of the group asked Jason more questions. Henry looked extra grumpy, frowning everywhere. Thirsty seemed to start getting bored. The tall, black man began noisily complaining about bugs and "dirty-ass shoes."

Aodh just shrugged and accepted the decision. There was no point in arguing even if he disagreed, which he didn't. The decision had been made.

He was secretly happy that the caravan was setting a new course. He had been getting really tired of trail rations and eating vegetables in the wilderness. Henry was right about how they tasted. There was a reason farmers grew crops. Edible, wild Ludan plants were all over the place, but Aodh would be happy to never eat them again in his life.

He decided in that moment that he wanted to be rich one day just to avoid eating wild vegetables ever again. With a big house and guards, maybe he could also keep Vitaliya from bothering him. He could give his aunt and his uncle some money for taking care of him after his parents died, too. If he were rich, maybe a girl would give him a chance despite his appearance and be willing to learn who he was as a person. He wasn't scary or mean like a Fideli, just awkward.

Aodh daydreamed as Thirsty began imbuing magic power into the wavy-bladed dagger, the countryside flashing by again as the group headed back towards the road.

* * *

Liangyu held out a hand to accept the note from Raquel, the leader of her four mercenaries. The average-looking woman would not have made an impression on most, but Liangyu noticed the sharp glint of ambition in the other woman's eyes. *I must be careful around this one*, she thought.

She opened up the note, skimmed it, and grunted. "Where did you find this?" she demanded. The look in Raquel's eyes was replaced by fear when their met gazes. *Good*, thought Liangyu.

"My lady, a priestess of Dolos delivered it to me and said it was for you."

"Just a priestess, not a High Priestess like Biivan?"

"Yes, my lady."

"Was she anyone notable, any name I would recognize?"

"No, my lady. I believe she was a lower-level official," replied Raquel.

Liangyu frowned and tapped her chin. She ordered, "Go find Ghinsja and bring her to me. See if you can find Biivan, too."

"Yes my lady."

After Raquel scampered off, Liangyu settled in to wait. She was good at waiting; it came more naturally the older she got, too.

She decided it probably wouldn't be very long before her second-in-command and the High Priestess were found. Despite keeping a low profile in Tolstey's capital, Taretha, most of Liangyu's team would probably be nearby. Old habits died hard, and she managed her group like an adventuring company, just like she'd led long ago.

Of course, these days they hunted people, not monsters.

She smiled ruefully through her veil, the fabric obscuring her face enough to keep strangers from identifying her as orb-Bonded. For her, the mask was a necessity. Luckily, the mewling cattle of Taretha had no idea how serious the struggle between orb-Bonded could be right now. Some of the masses had even taken to covering their own face as a fashion statement. It was considered very stylish and daring. Some adventurers thought it made their group look stronger.

Fools, the lot of them. It served her purpose, though.

As she waited on the arrival of her subordinate and her advisor, she was thankful that her surroundings were pleasant. The owner of the tea shop had been kind enough to let her entire party stay in the back rooms, rent free. They were provided with tea and basic food every day as well. Of course, the shop owner hadn't had much of a choice. If the foolish woman had refused, Liangyu would have killed her.

It was not her fault for being ruthless; Ludus had made her that way.

She'd come a long way from being a scared farmgirl deposited in the middle of nowhere by a peacock-dressed god. Dolos…she tapped the letter and smiled, the expression was not friendly.

Liangyu had missed her native China for the first 50 years she was on Ludus. She'd had a different name back then, too. That was also before she had begun to do what she had to, before she had begun to kill. She'd been naive in the past. It had taken a long time for her to realize that only the strong survived, only the cold-blooded prospered.

Now she had a very simple goal. She had family in Berber, several generations removed from her only child, long dead. Liangyu had massive amounts of blood on her hands already; what was a bit more in order to secure the future of her descendants? Of course, buying a noble house would be very expensive, especially for the several families she wanted to elevate, but she had time, and she had power.

Her musings were cut short as Ghinsja and Biivan arrived. High Priestess Biivan looked as haughty and frumpy as usual, her slight Areva frame draped in a shapeless, hooded jacket that covered her golden necklace. She walked in like she owned the place, secure in her power. Liangyu was glad she had a way to control the demigoddess, otherwise there would be a problem.

Her second-in-command, Ghinsja, was as fair as Biivan was dark. She dyed her light blonde hair into pink stripes and wore heavy pink eyeshadow. Liangyu thought it looked hideous, but she'd never say so. Ghinsja had also been in love with her for 20 years, and Liangyu pretended not to notice. She took care not to offend the other woman, nor let slip she was not interested in other women. Love was a very powerful tool…if used correctly.

Ghinsja also wore a veil, the grey of the fabric matching her dress. Liangyu thought it was overly dramatic for the woman to always dress in grey, but she was extremely competent. It was useful to humor her, despite Liangyu not being one to usually keep her opinions to herself.

Both powerful women came to a stop before Liangyu, who continued to calmly sip her tea. Ghinsja merely stood by patiently, but Biivan was not accustomed to waiting on a mere orb-Bonded. "What is this about? My time is my own. You will not waste it."

Ghinsja arched an eyebrow. "I will do as I please. Do not forget our relationship. Due to the rules you live under, you cannot procure your own...toys. As distasteful as it is, I will continue to provide you with what you so obviously desire as long as you continue to assist my team in every way you can."

Biivan scowled and growled, "You'd best watch yourself, orb-Bonded. You are just one of many that Dolos has blessed with a High Priestess overseer, but my patience will not last forever. I will live a long time, and my memory will not fade."

Liangyu took a sip of tea. Slowly. Biivan gritted her teeth and crossed her arms. Liangyu finally mused, "You have a long memory? So do I. So, are we going to continue sparring with words? A word spoken can never be taken back."

"No, get on with it, Death Witch. Why did you call us here?" Biivan huffed. Ghinsja remained silent. Liangyu approved; her second-in-command had learned some wisdom over the years.

Liangyu smiled lightly. "I called you because I got a message from Dolos." She tapped the letter.

"From Dolos? Are you sure?" Biivan's haughty manner had disappeared.

"Yes. I received a note from Dolos once before about two hundred ten years ago. I would immediately recognize another. This one was addressed directly to me."

Ghinsja's eyes were full of awe, her mouth open. Biivan merely snorted and asked, "Why didn't he send the communication through me?"

"I do not know. However, we have been gifted with a couple facts. As we all know, Dolos is encouraging orb-Bonded and Heroes to fight each other. In fact, we have been profiting from this very state of affairs." Liangyu briefly thought about the box that she kept in a safe place, holding spirit stones and Dolos orbs, each worth a fortune.

"This letter," she said, holding the note up for them to see, "describes a group of adventurers that will be heading this direction soon on the Mirana road. We can catch up to them and assess their strength outside Harmly if we spend some magic stones to buy a rail car."

"There is more to it, right, my lady?" Ghinsja's tone was respectful.

"Of course. We know for sure that one of their number is orb-Bonded, a young man named Aodh Antonni O'Breen. The letter is worded such that there could be other orb-Bonded with him as well. We will need to do surveillance before making a move.

"This is an opportune time for us to act on this information since we need to leave this city anyway. Coming from Berber to Tolstey to hunt weaker orb-Bonded was a great idea, but our time here is done.

"It's too dangerous to hunt in Taretha anymore. Plus, if this Aodh Antonni O'Breen has another orb-Bonded in his group, and we kill them both, we can head back to Berber once Dolos gives us our reward. We will have to be careful. I am guessing that Aodh is probably crafty and dangerous. I can't imagine why else Dolos would have specifically named him."

Biivan narrowed her eyes, thinking. She slowly said, "I can't fault your logic."

"That's great, but it wasn't your decision anyway. To be clear, I expect you to help as much as you can without breaking your rules."

The hooded demigoddess curled her lip. "Fine, but you will supply my payment."

"Yes, one more child for you to experiment on." Liangyu frowned; their arrangement was distasteful, even for her. She didn't understand what prevented the ancient woman from stealing her own children to butcher, but the deal benefited Liangyu…for the moment. As long as the twisted demigoddess desired her sacrifices, and as long as Liangyu could provide them as gifts, she maintained a powerful ally, even in such a diminished capacity.

"Are there any other questions?" The other women were staring off into the distance, probably mentally listing what they needed to do in order to get the group on the road again. Liangyu smiled and said, "Good. Please begin preparations at once. The sooner we arrive at the ambush point, the sooner I can prepare my tools."

Ghinsja shuddered slightly. She still did that whenever Liangyu mentioned her power, even after all these years.

The Death Witch smiled and poured more tea for herself. She smoothed her robes as she watched the other two women leave, intent on their tasks. It would feel good to hunt again, especially since another bounty orb or two meant she could go back to Berber. She might finally be able to give her surviving family a legacy, a chance she'd never had.

CHAPTER FOURTEEN

Necessary Input

Mareen was glad she had gotten to sleep in a real bed the night before, but she was still irritated with her hard-headed husband. The obstinate man refused to listen to reason about needing to protect his image. He wasn't famous yet, but he soon would be; either as an adventurer, or a noble. Well, actually he already was a noble, technically.

Even after Gonzo had officially sworn Henry and Jason into the Berber aristocracy, gave them deeds detailing the land they owned, maps of their holdings, and a quick rundown on etiquette, it still didn't feel real to Mareen. If Henry was a noble, she was a noble now too through marriage.

It wasn't something she could wrap her mind around yet.

Mareen was in a small park in the town of Pilk, practicing with the hammer Henry had made for her. She'd needed to get some air.

The rest of the group was resting or training outside of town.

Pilk was a large town, almost a city in its own right. The group hadn't really spent much time in the town proper, just laid low to rest while taking advantage of how spread out Pilk was. They'd been able to get rooms in an inn and resupply after parking the Battlewagons almost a half mile away.

Mareen had a lot on her mind, and she was still frustrated with Henry. The fact she knew she shouldn't be so irritated with him, and that it was her own discomfort around Thirsty that was causing problems in the first place, only increased her frustration. She savagely swung her heavy hammer down again, practicing the forms Henry had taught her.

She knew swinging around a hardened bronze hammer, so heavy a normal person could barely lift it, was probably not the best way to hide she was orb-Bonded, but she desperately needed to work out some frustration.

Suddenly, she spotted a glowing figure descending straight towards her and sighed. Ever since Henry and Jason had learned how to use MMBs, they'd started summoning them every time they needed to gather the group together. Magic messenger birds were paid in gold, and Henry could very easily find or produce gold from the land.

The MMB slowed and Mareen held her hand open in front of her. The creature gently alighted on her palm as Mareen waited patiently to hear its message. MMBs could carry notes, but most often, they just repeated simple messages.

The small, benign demon was bipedal, standing about ten inches tall with two sets of wings; one on its back, and one where its arms should have been. Its avian head was small, but its eyes were intelligent. This one was mostly blue with white trim.

It spoke, its voice strangely gravelly, "Seeking Mareen Jacobs."

Mareen sighed and responded, "That is me."

The little creature said, "Price has been paid. Message follows: Mareen, come to the inn we are staying at. We have business and need everyone here.

"From Henry."

Its message complete, the little creature shifted and said, "Please respond to indicate you have received the message."

"Yes, I got it," said Mareen irritably. The creature dipped its upper body and took off, accelerating almost instantly out of sight.

Mareen grumbled, her mood still sour. She squeezed her eyes shut tightly, barely avoided pouting, and began walking. Seriously, what had gotten into her lately? She knew her discomfort around homosexuals was only part of it. Henry had asked her why she was comfortable with homosexual women, but not with homosexual men.

She didn't know. She didn't have an answer. She felt like she had spent her entire life in study and self-reflection, but her aggravating husband was pointing out things she'd never even thought of before.

Mareen didn't hate anyone. She definitely didn't hate Thirsty, but she wished the man would hurry up and leave the group. She felt like he was taking advantage of her husband's good nature. On the other hand, she wanted to help people in need.

Deeply conflicted within herself, Mareen stomped into the inn and up the stairs to the private meeting room their group had booked. Once she entered the room, she saw the rest of the group sitting around the U-shaped table. Thirsty was working on enchanting something while softly chatting with Aodh and Bezzi-ibbi, as usual. Yanno-ibbi was discussing something with Gonzo, but the rest of the room was quiet and apparently waiting for her; she was the last person to arrive.

For some reason, this annoyed her too. Uluula caught her eye and smiled thinly. Mareen appreciated the support, but her friend had her own problems to deal with. Especially now that they were suddenly nobles, their fool husbands needed to take the task of growing their households seriously. Unfortunately, Uluula said that Jason still refused to even talk about it. Meanwhile, every time Mareen trying to bring up the matter with Henry, he just listed every type of woman he found attractive. Apparently he liked most types, and it was obvious he found her irritation with him to be hilarious. The fool man refused to take the subject seriously, and just ignored her when she told him the initial choice wasn't really his to make in the first place.

Mareen knew he was just teasing her, and normally she wouldn't mind, but it was driving her crazy that he either couldn't or wouldn't understand how serious family units were on Ludus. Finding a sister wife was about building the strength of their family, but Henry didn't get it. She kept trying to explain it to him, but she was starting to understand he had no cultural foundation to understand any of it at all.

Where he was from, small families were commonplace. There was very little danger where Henry came from, and people got married and divorced all the time. She kept trying to explain to him that divorce was extremely rare on Ludus, and family was a sign of a person's power and wealth, but he didn't get it. She had to concede it wasn't that he was trying to ignore her—he literally didn't understand. So when she got frustrated, she felt guilty about that too.

She felt she'd been constantly guilty or angry the past few days, and she hated it. She wanted to just cuddle with Henry and hear more about silly things from his childhood like "Gilligan's Island," but she was running out of ideas to describe Ludus culture to Henry in a way he could relate to. He didn't understand his role as the head of a family, much less a noble family.

Mareen wished she could be more eloquent, more patient. She could explain numbers, and she understood complicated matters in her heart, but it seemed whenever she tried to explain important things to Henry, she mixed up her words. Then when she got upset, she'd think of George, and how easy it had been for him to explain anything to anyone, and this would bring the crushing sorrow back. The fact Henry dealt with all of her mood swings and just…continued to love her made her feel like a terrible person.

When Jason cleared his throat and began to speak, Mareen shook her head slightly and focused on the matter at hand. A meeting wouldn't have been called unless there was something legitimately important to talk about. Mareen tried to settle herself. She wouldn't let anyone or anything control her, much less her own emotions.

Jason said, "Okay, we've actually needed to have this meeting for a while. A long time ago, Henry and I decided to be completely transparent with our plans and with gear distribution. As you all know, I went off with Keeja on the day we found Thirsty and acquired some loot. This was at the same place that Keeja found her music player that we've all been enjoying the last few days."

Mareen nodded slowly as she thought about the music player. Whenever Keeja actually traveled with them anymore and wasn't flying around somewhere, she hooked her music player up to a cone contraption Henry had made of thin bronze to amplify its sound. The group had been able to hear a large number of popular Areva and Terran songs.

It turned out the best singers in their party were Jason and Thirsty. Everyone in the group seemed to prefer Terran music, even the Mo'hali and Areva. Areva music was almost uniformly precise and martial.

Keeja was a big fan of Bonnie Tyler and some Indian artist whose name Mareen always forgot. She also liked something called "Disco," which upset Henry and Jason. Henry had started calling Keeja, "Grandma," but so far she just ignored him.

Mareen shook herself and focused on what her husband's friend was saying again. Jason continued, "We have some loot to divvy up." He paused and scratched his head. "So far, we have an unspoken rule within Delvers LLC that orbs or spirit stones found by individuals belong to those individuals." He gestured at Mareen to make his point, and a few pairs of eyes turned to her before focusing on Jason again.

"However, I recently came in possession of four spirit stones." There were a few gasps, but he kept talking over them. "The last few days, I've been talking to Henry about how we should handle this. We even asked Keeja's advice." He gestured to the demigoddess in the corner, who nodded before going back to listening to her music device.

"The spirit stones I found are technically mine to do with as I please. I really struggled with whether to give some of them to our first rank orb-Bonded like Mareen, or increase my own strength. No offense to Berber Intelligence, but giving Gonzo any spirit stones was never a consideration."

"No offense taken," said Gonzo.

Jason sighed and said, "My decision is to split the spirit stones between myself and Henry. Keeja told us this should be enough to bring us both to the next rank." Jason noisily inhaled and said, "I'm still not really happy about this, but it makes the most sense right now. Gonzo and Vitaliya can hold their own, Mareen is tough as nails, and we don't even know what Aodh can do yet.

"Anyway, that brings me to the other loot." Jason pulled a sheet off a side table to reveal what it had been covering. "We have two more health potions like the one Mareen has. I am going to claim one for myself and for Henry. The rest is up for grabs. There is even another magic flashlight like the one Mareen has, too."

Mareen narrowed her eyes and asked the first question that came to mind. "This is it? Didn't you say Yanbei had a full Battlewagon worth of stuff?"

"Well, I had to leave a few things behind, the bigger items," replied Jason. "However, I think the fact there were four spirit stones explains why there was a lot less loot in general. The amount of wealth was still roughly appropriate for a dungeon. Some of the gear I had to leave behind were full suits of armor. I can't exactly put that sort of thing in my pocket. I didn't see any weapons, but we can't go back to check."

"Why can't we go back?" asked Aodh.

Jason got a haunted look. "I'm not going anywhere near that place without Keeja to protect me. You guys wouldn't understand since you didn't see it. There are challenges out there that our group is not ready to handle yet."

The atmosphere in the room sobered. Jason smiled, obviously trying to lighten the mood. He patted the table with loot on it and said, "There are a few small magic devices here like fire starters, a pair of magic binoculars, and some other stuff. There are a few small, blessed steel folding knives, too. They're worth a lot of money, but since we use knives all the time, I figured this could be a bonus for our Delvers members."

Gonzo, Vitaliya, and Keeja stayed seated, but the rest of the group surged forward to check the table for anything they wanted. The situation seemed surreal to Mareen. Jason was casually giving away incredible wealth, and the rest of the group was just as casually accepting it.

She shook her head and moved forward. If she were being honest, she really could use another knife for mundane tasks.

Mareen couldn't find it in herself to use the blessed steel dagger at the small of her back as anything other than a backup weapon. The idea of using a blade that had almost ended her life to trim her nails or eat with was not…comfortable.

* * *

Jason regarded the spirit stones on his palm and sighed. Uluula was already asleep in the bed beside him, a testament to how long he'd been awake, thinking about upgrading his orb powers. He couldn't help but feel guilty for hogging the stones for himself and

Henry, but he really did think it was the right choice for the group.

He sighed again and finally swallowed the spirit stones before lying down. He was asleep almost as soon as his head hit the pillow.

The transition to sleep was so sudden, Jason felt like one moment he was in bed, and the next he was sitting in the Space Needle restaurant in Seattle. The city skyline out the window was gorgeous, the dawn light casting shadows over the trees and parking lots below. The restaurant was empty other than a familiar purple cartoon cat sitting across the table from him.

"You," he said.

"Yes, me," the cat responded.

"So, shall we get on with this?" Jason tapped the table with a finger in annoyance.

"With what? Upgrading? We can't do that right now."

"What?" Jason blinked. "But I just swallowed two spirit stones."

"True, and normally that would meet the requirements, but part of my job is to guide your evolution. Modular orbs like myself are a little different; we have some free will. Plus, the rate at which you are acquiring more spirit stones is very unusual. I can't allow you to rise in rank yet."

"What?" Jason blinked. The cat's answer was so unexpected, he wasn't sure what to say.

"Yes, see, you have been developing your power quite a bit. If

I were to force you into third rank now, you'd lose a lot of potential power. You need to continue to practice and grow your abilities organically before I take you to the next level. An analogy you might understand would be…you need to reach a higher RPM before switching to a higher gear."

"I am not an engine."

"Ah, but how do you know that? What are you actually? How does your power function? You are still ignorant of many things."

"Okay…fine. I guess I can live with this since it means I can still keep getting stronger on my own. So when am I going to level up, though?"

"I will start your expansion to the next rank as soon as you're ready." The cat settled back in his chair, eating candy from a bowl that appeared from nowhere.

Jason discovered he was beginning to get angry. "So what is all this, then?" He gestured around the restaurant.

"This place holds pleasant memories for you, the same reason I appear the way I do. As for why we're chatting, swallowing more spirit stones allowed me to communicate directly with you again. I figured you would want to hear about your situation instead of just waking up in the morning with no changes."

Jason narrowed his eyes. "You actually can talk to me whenever you want, can't you? You're under some sort of rules just like Keeja."

"You are a smart cookie!" said the cat. "It's not the same thing, but somewhat, yes. However, my limitations are less based on fairness or rules between competitors, and more because I don't want to melt your brain. Killing you would kind of mess up my mission after all!" The cat giggled.

"So talking to you puts strain on me?"

"Enormously so, yes."

Jason shook his head. The strangeness of such a silly cartoon character speaking to him about such important subjects really drove home the ridiculousness of the situation. Finally, he asked, "Well, since you're here anyway, can I ask you a question or two?"

"Actually, yes. I have some time left, and I can probably answer some more questions so long as they are related to your Dhu-based development."

"What about Henry? Does he get to advance and I don't?"

The purple cat cocked his head to the side for a moment before grinning. "I am allowed to tell you that he can't advance either. You two are both in the same circumstance for the time being. How exciting!"

Jason frowned and asked, "What else should I know about my orb that may be a pain in the butt later?"

"That is way too general of a question! Try again with something I tell you. It never hurts to help!"

"So you can't answer certain things unless I know to ask the questions in the first place, right?"

"That's right!"

"And this is why you didn't mention certain things to me when we talked earlier?"

"Yes, yes." The cat grinned.

"Okay," Jason said with a tight-lipped smile. His mind started spinning and he felt a little predatory. "I'd like to know about combining magic schools and how that would work with my advancement in the future."

"Ah, that is an excellent question!" said the cat. He held up one pudgy cartoon finger, extending a sharp claw. He began drawing a grid on the table and said, "It's quite simple, see…"

Jason paid rapt attention.

* * *

Liangyu sipped tea, relaxing in her room in Harmly. Things were going smoothly, perhaps even too smoothly. Her mercenaries had an ambush site scouted out about a day outside of town, and she was about to move her entire operation there to prepare for the ambush she had planned.

Aodh's group had moved faster than she'd allowed for, but they were staying on the outskirts of Pilk longer than she had thought they would. Luckily, the distance between Harmly and Pilk was barely within the range of Ghinsja's power, although reaching so far was exhausting the Areva orb-Bonded every night.

No matter, she can just rest during the day. Liangyu sipped her tea some more as Ghinsja stumbled into the room, fatigue written upon her face.

"I was able to see them again, but this will be a lot easier when we are closer," she said, dropping to the floor and guzzling a large cup of lukewarm tea that Liangyu had left out for her.

"Is that so?"

"Yes, but I was able to see a few things. First off, they definitely have more than one orb-Bonded in their group. The darker-skinned girl obviously has enhanced strength and hasn't demonstrated any magic that would account for it. I would guess she is a warrior type. There is an Asian man with the group who could be dangerous, too. I've seen him carrying heavy things without much effort."

"Good, that helps. So far, what do you think?"

"I think it will be difficult to get reliable information in the time we have even if I continue to watch them every night." Ghinsja swallowed another mouthful of tea. "They actually have a fairly large group, and they're using vehicles unlike any I've ever seen before."

"What about scrolling orb messages? Have you gotten a chance to look them in the eyes?" This was the question Liyangyu was most curious about. The fact Ghinsja hadn't said anything about it yet was interesting in itself. The woman was usually very thorough.

"Yes, I've looked in almost all their eyes and I have not seen any messages," Ghinsja said, her voice flat.

"I see, so Aodh, and perhaps a companion or two, are nobles, then. Only nobles or extremely rich people know the secret to hiding the messages." Liangyu tapped her chin with a dark nail. "This has suddenly become more personal for me."

"I thought you might say that."

"Yes, and I'd like to move out to our ambush point immediately so I can start creating my tools."

"I thought you'd say that, too," said Ghinsja. "I would urge more caution with such a large group, but I know you will take every chance you can to kill aristocrats. I've had the mercenaries start working on the ambush point for you since I knew what your order would be."

Liangyu smiled. She was lucky to have Ghinsja. Capable help was so hard to find these days. She agreed with Ghinsja's assessment that there would be a great deal of risk involved with attacking a group with so many unknowns. However, Liangyu's magic worked best if she could prepare for combat before it occurred. Knowing exactly where her prey was headed, and the route they'd take to get there, was a huge advantage.

Liangyu smiled. Getting enough orbs and spirit stones to justify heading back to Berber would be sweet, but the opportunity to kill more spoiled nobles would definitely make her team's efforts all the more worthwhile.

She'd never loved nor hated Dolos. However, she was thankful he'd sent her the note about Aodh's group. She was enjoying the challenge.

CHAPTER FIFTEEN

Approaching Storm

"Are you sure you can't tell us what it is?" Jason asked Keeja.

"Yes, like I told you yesterday, my legs are restrained with cables."

Well, that's another strange idiom, thought Jason. Their group had ended up staying near the town of Pilk a while longer, and they'd been on the road for two days heading towards Harmly, the next major town down the road. They were making really great time and monster encounters were low. The only problem was that Yanno-ibbi had reported a strange feeling of being watched since before they had left Pilk. After he'd said so, a few other members of the group admitted they'd been feeling uneasy too.

Jason and Henry had taken these concerns seriously and decided to start pulling watch shifts of their own. Two nights before, while on watch with Bezzi-ibbi, Jason had seen something.

More than anything, it had looked like a heat distortion in the fog, and he probably wouldn't have noticed anything in the first place if he hadn't been familiar with a certain cloaking, predatory alien from movies.

Jason had been going to attack it, but he'd decided to watch instead. Whatever it was had moved around the camp all night. Nobody knew if it was a monster or something worse, but the fact Keeja refused to discuss the matter was putting everyone on edge. Henry had already ordered the group to stay battle ready at all times, and Jason had been encouraging everyone to hide their powers.

After thinking about it for a while, Jason decided the apparition was most likely a scout of some sort. They could be under surveillance. The thought disturbed him.

Only a few members of the company could even see the entity, whatever it was, but the whole group felt watched at night. Hardly anyone spoke during the day anymore; they just listened to Keeja's music player, discovering new songs and requesting favorites in order to keep the worry at bay. Henry hadn't even been complaining about Keeja's disco music choices anymore.

Those that could see the figure in the mists did things occasionally to try interacting with it, but nothing overt. Jason had considered asking Vitaliya to try hitting it with flame, but he had thought better of it. He wasn't sure it'd actually do anything more than show off Vitaliya's power and tip off that they were aware it was there.

Henry had already told everyone that the best they could do for the moment was try to be prepared for anything. Towards that end, Jason and Henry were both training hard to improve their powers. Jason had even figured out several of the abilities Keeja showed him, including how to store items in what he was calling "sideways space," a small...pocket he created for himself.

It was an amazing ability, and he would have normally been extremely excited if not for the dread hanging over the group. He hadn't really even told anyone about his new abilities yet other than Henry, and that was only to explain why he was asking his friend to make him a couple dozen more throwing knives.

Jason had been able to put plenty of knives in his new storage, but it had used up most of the group's remaining stash of bronze. Henry wasn't happy about it, but he had agreed with Jason that it would be smart to prepare as best they could in case of unexpected danger.

Plus, if Henry needed to, he could just melt down some of the other tools he'd already made to craft new ones. Jason thought his friend just liked having lots of metal on hand and was being a bit of a drama queen. He couldn't pull bronze from the earth because it wasn't as common as gold, which was also why it wasn't effectively worthless like gold on Ludus.

Either way, he was happy with the decision to use up the bronze. Jason felt the comforting presence of his sideways space storage and the reassuring knowledge it now contained plenty of throwing knives to ruin someone's day.

His sword, *Breeze*, had gotten an upgrade, too. Actually, most of the group's weapons had gotten at least one enchantment courtesy of Thirsty. Jason had actually acted on a hunch based on his conversation with his orb and asked Thirsty to enchant *Breeze* with air and fire magic. So far, the sword just burned things and created tiny gusts, but Jason was hoping the two elements would somehow combine to create a new enchantment.

Keeja started speaking again and Jason snapped back to the present. The entire group was taking a rest from traveling. The demigoddess said, "Just the fact I can't say anything should speak volumes if you've been paying attention."

Jason nodded. He'd already figured out what was probably going on. He had even talked to Uluula, Henry, and Gonzo about it. It was time to tell the group, and it was a good time to call everyone together since they were all slowly heading back to the Battlewagon and magicycles.

"Okay, everyone, circle up! We need to have a chat!" Jason hollered.

"Can you please keep your voice down?" Henry called down irritably from the Battlewagon turret. "Do you want to let every fucking monster for miles around know we're here?"

Jason absently nodded. He had to concede that Henry had a point. Of course, he knew the real reason his friend was irritated was because he'd already had to gun down two flying monsters that day, and one had been a wizened owl demon. Henry hated them. Jason wasn't sure if Henry was more creeped out by how they looked, or outraged at what Ludans called them.

As soon as the everyone was present, Jason cleared his throat and reluctantly gave the news. "Okay, I know everyone is on edge. We all feel watched. Some of us can see the thing that comes with the mists at night, and some can't. Some of you think it's a spirit or a monster. Unfortunately, the reality is probably worse." Jason sighed and said, "Gonzo, please tell everyone about our best guess."

"Right," said Gonzo, stepping forward. "As you can probably guess, even if you haven't seen it, there is a lot of orb-Bonded violence all around the world right now. This is obviously a result of Dolos's planet-wide message. I have gotten reports suggesting that some groups are even attacking orb-Bonded and Mo'hali Heroes in a semi-professional manner. They look like adventuring parties at first glance, but they're actually focused on hunting Heroes and Bonded."

"So, basically we have a PVP situation on our hands," said Jason.

"PVP?" asked Vitaliya.

In English, Jason responded, "Player versus player, or person versus person." He switched back to Luda and said, "It's the first term that came to mind, and it's somewhat accurate for this situation."

"No it's not," scoffed Henry. "We're not talking about gamers. These are murderous assholes scoring some easy wealth by hunting other people. Also, I thought you hated acronyms."

Jason glared at Henry for a second, but didn't say anything. The smug SOB had a point. *Christ, I'm even thinking in acronyms. Did I always do that?* Jason shook his head and ignored Henry, saying, "Realistically, our feeling of being watched and the figure in the mist are all connected, and they're probably related to one of the PVP groups."

Henry snorted, and Jason briefly imagined teleporting his friend above a lake. He didn't have the ability to teleport other people, only himself, but he could dream. Trying to learn the ability was definitely on his to-do list. He wasn't sure if it was possible, but Henry made him want to keep trying.

"So what do we do?" Aodh asked, his voice trembling.

"Well, I figured we should ask the person in our group with the most experience with caravans. Yanno-ibbi, can you give us your suggestion?"

Yanno-ibbi took a step forward and made a curious gesture, dipping his head and eyes down. He said, "I must make it known I probably have far less experience with caravans than High Priestess Keeja."

"You are a nice boy, Yanno-ibbi." Keeja smiled. "Yes, I do know a thing or two about, well, pretty much everything—"

"Yeah, but she's useless," interrupted Henry. "Just let us know what you think, Yanno-ibbi."

"Useless?" Keeja raised an eyebrow.

"Yeah, we all know you can crack the land and boil the sea, whatever, who gives a shit? What you're actually going to do is sit on your ass and listen to more shitty disco music. The one time you actually did anything was to go blow up a mountain with Jason, and that was only so you could listen to the Bee Gees or whatever in the first place."

"Oh, I sit on my ass? Have you been gazing upon my figure? You know all you need to do is ask and you can come taste the forbidden fruit." Keeja hand her hand down the side of her body. Then she put a hand by her mouth and said in a stage whisper, "What about your little wife, though? Does she know you're propositioning me?"

Henry frowned and gave her the finger. Keeja smiled wildly and fanned the fabric of her frilly top. "You know what that gesture means, right? Are you asking? If you are, you might want to get some healing potions because I might break a few bones… of yours."

Mareen gasped and visibly restrained herself. She glared at Henry and Keeja.

Jason put a hand over his face and sighed. Everyone had been getting along just fine, but now that the group was facing an actual danger and needed to stick together, they were all acting like children. It didn't help that Thirsty Zha Zha was laughing and shouting, "You go, girl!"

Jason prayed for patience.

Uluula looked like she was about to say something, but Jason gave her a very small shake of his head. He glanced at the other members of the party. Aodh appeared ready to pass out from fright at any moment, and Vitaliya was slowly but surely making her way over to her cousin.

What a bunch of weirdos. Jason reached into his sideways space and pulled out a throwing knife. He used it to rap on the Battlewagon a few times. Everyone immediately stilled; Jason wasn't sure if it was because of the noise or because he had just pulled a knife from midair. Ultimately, he decided he didn't care.

"Look, let's just get this over with. I know everyone's on edge but just...chill, okay?"

"Be cold?" asked Bezzi-ibbi.

Jason groaned. He'd just pulled a Henry and hadn't thought carefully enough about what he was saying in Luda. He corrected in English, "I meant 'chill.' It's slang." He switched back to Luda and said, "Yanno-ibbi?"

"Yes, thank you, Jason-ibbi." Bezzi-ibbi's uncle scratched his head, partially unsheathing his claws as he did so. "We're already doing a lot of what we should be. Whether someone is watching your caravan with magic or from the top of a cliff, you should never show the length of your claws.

"That is to say, you hide your strength. Staying prepared for a fight is good. We've already been doing that, but we should increase it. Lastly, we should slow down. If we travel slower, there is a higher chance we won't walk as deep into an ambush before noticing one."

"Excuse me." Thirsty held up a hand. "Why don't you all just...go somewhere else? If you know someone is looking for you and they wanna throw down, why keep heading towards it?"

"That's actually a good question." Jason nodded. "Basically, we don't know where the enemy is or what they plan. It's the same reason we're not directly trying to do anything about the shadow in the mists. I've already talked to Gonzo about misinformation. Basically, we could try to appear as strong as possible and maybe whoever it is would leave us alone, but there is no guarantee of that.

"This is an entire planet of people and we are being hunted. If we appear strong, given enough time, someone could just get reinforcements or build a better trap.

"By trying to play dumb and hide our strength, we might force our watcher to play their hand and maintain our own advantage. Basically, since we're probably up against other orb-Bonded, there are a lot of dangerous unknowns."

Thirsty asked, "So why not just go back to that city you were in before? Mirana, right?"

"If we head back, we could be hit en route. Plus, being in a city might result in our enemies being stronger, or end up hurting innocent people. But most importantly, I don't think that's an option. I don't think we can stay in this country while refusing the orders of the queen."

"Correct," declared Gonzo. "For better or for worse, you've been given a mission. The only way to realistically get out of your task would be to find the deepest, most monster-infested forest you possibly could and live a dangerous, miserable existence. The fun thing about being orb-Bonded is that the rest of your life can be hundreds of years. This means you could really drag out the boredom and loneliness unless you get eaten. You'll probably need to eat a lot of the natural, edible plants in the forest to survive, too."

"Rad," muttered Henry.

"So let me get this straight," said Thirsty. "You could be getting hunted by like thirty people who can throw around magic and shit, and you're just gonna, what, keep doing what you've been doing? You are gonna put yourself, and by extension, my black ass in danger?"

"Basically, yes," said Henry. "Because we don't know if the danger will increase if we change something. If we keep trying to hide everyone's abilities, slow down the speed we're traveling, and stay ready for the shit to hit the fan at any time, we have a chance of giving anyone who attacks us a nasty fucking surprise. Plus, we have vehicles. It might be a matter of giving them a quick black eye and then getting away."

"So we're just screwed and trying to make the best of it with zero information? Well, y'all are making this decision, but it's putting me in danger too?"

"Yeah, we're pretty much fucked either way," said Henry. "And you'd be dead as hell by now if we hadn't found you anyway, so simmer down."

"Okay, that makes sense." Thirsty sniffed and looked at Jason. "Why didn't you say what Henry said in the first place? Stop making everything so complicated."

Jason clenched his teeth. He was about to answer when he noticed Aodh quickly move to the other side of Yanno-ibbi. Vitaliya was conspicuously close to where he'd just been standing, but the red-haired O'Breen woman maintained an attentive, innocent expression.

He still wasn't convinced that Vitaliya was as insane as Tony claimed, but he had to admit she'd been acting more…erratic as the days passed.

Jason answered Thirsty, "I will keep that in mind next time." He addressed the rest of the group. "Stay ready for a fight at all times from here on out. No displays of magic or power. Bezzi-ibbi, start wearing a glove or something in case whatever it is hasn't noticed your hand yet. That metal part of your body is a dead giveaway that you're a Hero.

"If we get ambushed, our first goal is to stay safe, whether that means trying to run away or fighting it out. Try to keep a positive attitude, do what you can to prepare for combat, but be sneaky about it.

"We're only a few days out from Harmly. After that, we're going to cut cross country and find the Stem River before heading north. Hopefully everything blows over."

"So we should continue to avoid directly interacting with the shadow?" asked Uluula.

"Yes. Right now, it would be better if they only suspect we know about them watching us than be certain about it." Jason clapped his hands. "Okay, everyone, let's get going again. Since we're slowing down our pace, start looking for nice campsites and we'll start quitting earlier each day when we find one."

Then Jason followed his own direction and hopped up into the driver's seat of the Battlewagon. He really needed to talk to Henry about some way to focus the group and keep morale from dropping further. It was possible they were all heading to a nasty fight, maybe even to the death, but it wasn't like this was exactly uncommon for adventurers on Ludus.

Maybe more music would help. He'd have to ask Henry if his friend could make Keeja's music player get any louder. If Jason were being honest with himself, he'd have to admit he wanted to hear more music, too. It was weird to hear popular music from home while driving an armored vehicle on a different planet, but it did make the experience more enjoyable.

He just hoped that Keeja actually stayed with the group like she had been for the last two days. When she took off, her music player went with her.

* * *

Liangyu crossed her legs, the motion stirring her red silk Hanfu. The expensive outfit's material was made from silk produced on Earth, not monster-created material. She absently tightened her black sash and adjusted the lethal little enchanted dagger she kept at her waist.

She was sitting in a rough-hewn chair on a military outpost. The furniture had belonged to one of the Tolstey soldiers manning the location until a few days ago. The outpost hadn't been very large, only around 10 soldiers, probably chosen for their uselessness. Liangyu's mercenaries had made short work of them.

Now that she thought about the mercenaries, she realized she needed to update them, too. She might as well have them attend when Ghinsja gave her report. She ordered one of her thralls over, this one some sort of feline creature with spider mandibles and spikes along its spine. She wrote a note for each of her three leaders, folded them all with the intended recipient's name printed on the outside, and stuck them on the creature's spines.

As the thrall scampered off to find Liangyu's leaders, she smiled. The expression didn't touch her eyes. She knew they hated when she used her creations to fetch them, but she didn't have time to spare their feelings. The note to Raquel had also instructed the mercenary captain to ensure her group attended the meeting.

Before long, Liangyu's subordinates arrived, each of them sporting different expressions. Biivan's eyes were narrowed. Her entire frame spoke of barely contained violence as usual, even under her baggy clothing. The High Priestess's dark eyes fixed on Liangyu as she entered.

Mourad was next into the room. The big, middle-aged mercenary wore her usual camouflage-patterned armor. The woman's huge, blessed steel flamberge rode in a sheath on her back.

The big mercenary had a few pieces of enchanted gear, as did most of her team, but Liangyu had never cared enough to find out more. All that mattered was their effectiveness and willingness to follow orders.

Mourad was frowning slightly, and her deep-set eyes nervously watched the two thralls Yiangyu still had in the room. The big woman was surprisingly light on her feet, and tentatively found an empty place to stand at attention.

Next to arrive was Matilda, by far the loveliest member of the mercenary team. Her blonde tresses fanned out behind her in a wave, her dark tunic embroidered in decorative patterns of orange. Her tights were orange and her boots dark. Liangyu thought the clothes looked gaudy, like a rotting squash. The woman was lucky she had a sweet face.

Matilda carried her enchanted bow over one shoulder, her

monster-wood rapier hung at one hip. Despite her attempts to take on airs and act the part of a mysterious ranger, the woman's roots as a slum rat were obvious. Her lip curled in disgust as she saw the thralls in the corners of the room. Her every emotion was always plain to see.

Raquel was next in the room, her face homely, her eyes dull and hair ratty. The fire mage didn't look like much, but she led her group with iron authority. Her clothing was just like the woman herself. She wore a thin coat with no decoration, but lined with so many knives it doubled as armor.

She carried a staff with silver ferrules. Liangyu had a suspicion that the staff was made of monster-wood just like Matilda's rapier. The mercenary captain's face was carefully schooled, her nod to Liangyu respectful. However, Liangyu's experienced eyes caught the hints of disgust and anger. It was interesting that such a remorseless mercenary could still hold such stigma against reanimation magic.

On Raquel's heels came Anz'wei. The big Adom was of some reptile race. Liangyu thought she looked a bit like a walking crocodile, but then again, she thought most reptilian Adom looked like walking crocodiles.

Anz'wei didn't need much gear; her body was a weapon. She wore some kind of flowing garment and a thick yucca leather vest with pouches. She had a strange, massive ring on her back, but she'd never done anything with it. The seven-foot-tall Adom took up so much space, Liangyu decided to send one of her thralls out of the room. The thrall was still wearing the armor he'd had on before he was killed; the crest on the back of his tabard was probably for the Tolstey guard outpost he'd been manning.

As he passed Anz'wei, the big Adom female's nostrils flared. Her expression was otherwise unreadable. Her slitted, reptilian eyes offered no clues of her thoughts. Liangyu really didn't like Adom much...well, living Adom. If Anz'wei were killed, she'd make an excellent thrall for a few weeks at least.

Last through the door was Ghinsja. The pale, Areva orb-Bonded looked wan. She'd been exercising her power almost constantly the last few days. She wore robes of blue and white, and now that they were actually on the hunt, she also wore a jacket made of yucca leather and plates of bronze. On her belt, she kept a hand crossbow and a sloshing water skin.

Her pale, pink-streaked hair was tied back in a ponytail, and her eyes tightened when she saw the thralls. Even after all this time, Liangyu's magic made her nervous.

Now that the whole group had gathered, Liangyu stood up. It was one thing to remind everyone of her position, but staying seated any longer would have been pushing it. She said, "Thank you for coming. It will save everyone time for the whole group to be here during this report. First, Raquel, how does the hunt for raw material go?"

The mercenary captain answered, "Very well. The device the

High Priestess 'dropped' and we 'found' has been very effective at attracting monsters from the surrounding area. Just today, we already killed six of them and laid them out for you to do your... magic thing, my lady."

"I see," said Liangyu. Then she said formally, "And Mistress Biivan, would you like us to return the device you dropped?"

Biivan raised her front lip in an approximation of a smile. "No, that is fine. I am much too busy with my experiments right now. I don't know where I'd put it. However, I could use another test subject. That would definitely keep me busy, much too busy to take the device back."

Liangyu smiled but inwardly she grimaced. The shameless creature was demanding another child. Well, there wasn't anything she could do about it. She felt disgusted, but one did what one had to; it was like a strand of cow hair amongst nine cows. She said, "Raquel can help with that later. Raquel, please continue your report."

Raquel lifted her nose in disgust, but realized Biivan was watching and quickly tried to school her expression. Biivan merely smiled. Raquel blanched, but spoke like nothing had happened. "We've already emptied out the nearby dungeon. We didn't find much treasure, only some magic stones and some random items from the Terran and Areva homeworlds. The dungeon was populated by a handful of those cat creatures with big pincers, like the one you delivered our notes on."

Liangyu absently nodded. "What are they actually called?"

"I think they're something like 'short-furred, spined beetle cat demons.'"

"That is correct," confirmed Biivan.

Liangyu waved a hand. "Very interesting. Now I'm sure the corpses you have procured are all lined up in the usual place, correct?" Raquel nodded. "Good. I will be out there later today to grow our little army. Speaking of which, Ghinsja, please report on our targets."

The Areva orb-bonded wearily stepped forward. "I have some conflicting news. Last night, my mist form was still able to roam around unmolested, but the members of Aodh O'Breen's group I've seen use magic are using it less now. Plus, the group has slowed down. I don't know if they can see my mist form or if something else tipped them off, but they appear to be acting more wary. However, they haven't changed direction."

"They're still heading down the road towards our ambush point?" Liangyu asked.

"Yes," replied Ghinsja.

"Excellent. If they changed directions, we would need to terminate the ambush and find a different target, or perhaps find this group later.

"So, what is the tally of powered individuals in the group now?"

Ghinsja replied, "As you know, I can't hear much while in my mist form. However, the closer they get to us, the more detail I can see and the more easily I can read lips.

"Aodh O'Breen still shows no evidence of any powers, although he keeps strange devices on his belt. It's very possible he is an enchanter, water mage, or some other orb type we haven't seen before. That said, he is fairly young and always looks nervous, so despite him being our primary target, he is likely not the primary threat.

"The dark-skinned girl named Mareen and the Asian man Henry both have power and they are probably orb-Bonded, especially the girl. The man usually wears armor that could be enchanted, but he uses Earth school magic, so he is at least a mage. Luckily, Earth school is weak.

"I have looked for Hero marks on the Mo'hali but haven't found any.

"The other man who leads the group with Henry—I believe his name is Jaceen, the tall one—I haven't seen him use any magic. He seems to get made fun of a lot, too. I have no idea whether he is orb-Bonded. He also usually wears armor and he carries a really pretty sword. He could be using enchanted equipment.

"In fact, you've heard my rundown of the entire group before. I still cannot see scrolling confirmation of any of them being orb-bonded. I don't see it with Aodh O'Breen, either. We know he is Bonded. This means at least Aodh is noble or well connected; others could be too. This is even more likely since the red-haired

Terran girl and the Hispanic Terran man remind me of Berber mercenaries." Ghinsja turned towards Raquel and her group, smiling apologetically. "No offense."

"None taken," said Raquel.

Liangyu produced a fan from a hidden pocket and tapped her chin while she pondered. There was a bit of a conundrum to think through. The fact the group was continuing despite apparently feeling impending danger was worrying, but at the same time, she needed them to head into the ambush point.

The likelihood that the group was an escort party for a noble or two was high since they were heading towards the Tolstey capital by road. The presence of nobles made the job personal for Liangyu, but she didn't want to make stupid decisions based on emotion. She asked, "What are your suggestions? First Ghinsja, then Raquel."

"I would actually suggest we avoid this target altogether," said Ghinsja. "However, I know this isn't really an option even if we hadn't gotten a note from Dolos. So that being said, I would suggest you use your thralls to stop the caravan immediately, and split the target group up before I cover the area in fog."

"Isn't that difficult for you to do, especially if we have to attack while it's still light outside?"

"Yes, but I can do it. There are small ponds and a lake. This is enough standing water to lessen the strain." Ghinsja patted her water skin. "I'll need to get full, uninterrupted rest while they're still a couple days out so I can regain my strength, though."

"That's fine." Liangyu pointed her fan at her second-in-command. "Anything else?"

Ghinsja nodded. "Yes. This probably goes without saying, but you should set some of your stealthiest thralls on the most problematic member of the group, taking care of them immediately."

"That is indeed what I am planning to do," Liangyu assured. "Raquel, what are your thoughts?"

"I agree with everything Ghinsja said, but there are a lot of unknowns here. It's unlikely, but what if all these rotting aristos are Bonded? The random Mo'hali are weird, too. These ones are apparently not slaves and not being used as porters. They could be merchants, but then why do they have the little boy there?

"I would suggest sending two of my group to target the Mo'hali and deal with them, whether they're Heroes or not. A Hero can cut the strings between you and your puppets." She gestured at a thrall in the corner. The undead thing used to be the commander of Tolstey guard post Liangyu had commandeered as a base of operations. The thrall still wore her armor and a simple bronze sword at her waist.

Liangyu tapped her chin and thought carefully. She didn't bother to ask Biivan's opinion. The woman would be restrained by her mysterious rules from offering any advice even if she were the type to help, which she wasn't. Liangyu thought carefully about how to phrase her next few words. She eventually said, "Without the object that Biivan dropped and we so luckily found, I'd be less likely to continue with this attack.

"However, I will have dozens of thralls when the time comes. Dozens upon dozens. We will also have Ghinsja obscuring vision and offering support as I control the thralls. She will be able to give you better vision in the fog than our enemies will have.

"There is also the fact that this is Tolstey. Even if there are other orb-Bonded in Aodh's group, they're probably first rank and have no idea what they're doing.

"The fact that Dolos's note specifically mentioned Aodh O'Breen, who is a boy and is not in charge of this group, lends further evidence that he is a noble. As you all know, I hate nobles, and many of you do too. The opportunity of a payout this large while exterminating nobles is not something we can ignore. However, we are going to go about this as intelligently as possible." She looked between her leaders.

"We can always run away if things go bad," Ghinsja said, nodding. "Plus, if we kill a few and escape, we will still be rewarded by Dolos for any Heroes or orb-Bonded slain."

Raquel snorted and said, "Just more reason to kill the animals right on the quick step. Just point us at things to kill. As long as you keep paying us, we'll fight."

The rest of the mercenaries nodded...except for Anz'wei. The big, reptilian Adom showed no sign she was even paying attention.

"Good, then that's settled." Liangyu snapped her fan shut and put it away in her hidden pocket. "You all know your remaining tasks for the day. Our targets are still several days away. Let's work to make sure we have every possible advantage we can get before they arrive. Realistically, there are probably at least three orb-Bonded in this group.

"This is probably going to make all of us very rich, girls." There were predatory smiles all around the room. "Dismissed," said Liangyu.

As all her subordinates filed out, Liangyu sat down again and thought back to a time when she wasn't so lonely. Her daughter had been the only good thing she'd ever had on Ludus. It seemed fitting that Liangyu would be working to elevate her descendants to the nobility with funds gathered by killing nobles, nobles just like the one that had killed her daughter over one hundred and fifty years ago.

The symmetry appealed to Liangyu, even if all the details didn't. Dealing with Biivan was absolutely intolerable. She really wished the woman hadn't been assigned as her overseeing High Priestess by Dolos.

Supplying children to suffer whatever it was Biivan did to them was another dark mark on Liangyu's soul. She was very honest with herself about this. She admitted she wasn't much better than the noble who'd killed her daughter.

But she didn't care. All that mattered was ensuring her sweet

Li Jing's family, and Liangyu's family by extension, were taken care of for the next few hundred years. Liangyu might not always be around to watch over them. The simplest solution was to make sure they had the resources and power to take care of themselves.

Liangyu narrowed her eyes as she felt the surety of her purpose again. She'd do anything to accomplish her goal. She would paint the world in blood and sow suffering like seeds. She already knew she was damned; the god Yan Wang would have much to say after she died. What was more sin on top of what she already was responsible for?

She calmed herself and willed a thrall to fetch her a fresh cup of tea. It was time to stop dwelling on the past, to think clearly on how best to kill her targets. It was a cruel world. The strong ruled the weak.

She would be strong, strong for her dead Li Jing. Liangyu waited for her tea and tried to ignore her loneliness. She'd run out of tears one hundred years ago.

CHAPTER SIXTEEN

Unraveled

Henry was starting to feel a little more comfortable with being on the road. The weird shadow thing hadn't been seen for a night or two, and overall, the morale of the group had improved. He'd rigged up a system of tubes from Keeja's MP3 player that enhanced the sound all over the Battlewagon. Even those riding magicycles in front and behind of the Battlewagon could hear it.

The caravan had spontaneously established a new rule that every member of the group could pick two songs to go on the playlist at a time. Henry was just glad Keeja had stopped playing like ten disco songs back to back anymore. He actually didn't mind if she played Indian pop or any of the other genres she liked from Earth, but her disco songs needed to die in a fire.

Currently, "Girls Just Want to Have Fun" was playing, probably requested by Mareen. It was one of her new favorite songs.

Henry narrowed his eyes and scanned the forest to either side of the road. Traveling slower made him feel vulnerable, even though they hadn't seen a monster for a couple days. He couldn't complain that freaky, dangerous creatures with stupid names hadn't tried to kill him for a while, but Henry's gut was telling him something was wrong.

The Battlewagon was entering a thin bank of mist, and Henry's instincts were damn near shouting at him. He tried to scan more aggressively, but he couldn't see much. Fog was a pain, but he'd been getting accustomed to it. Ludus seemed to have random fog banks from time to time. It was really weird.

Up ahead, water was spilling out over the road, so much that it actually appeared to be part of a small lake. Henry was getting a really bad feeling. About that time, Keeja buzzed right over him, taking off into the air until she could no longer be seen through the mist.

"What the fuck does she think she's doing?" Henry muttered. He irritably adjusted his rifle's sling before his brain started working again and facts clicked. Keeja had never buzzed over him like that before. On top of that, he could still hear Cyndi Lauper singing about what girls really wanted. *Keeja didn't take her music player.*

Henry thought about the last few days and also realized that, uncharacteristically, Keeja hadn't left the group once. They'd had the music player the whole time, and now she randomly took off without taking it with her…almost like she was trying to tell them something.

"Oh, fuck me…" Henry whispered. "Jason! Jason! Go the other direction. Turn around!"

"What?" Jason craned his head from the driver's seat to look back at Henry.

"Turn around now!" Henry pointed in front of them and hissed, "It's a trap!" Jason's eyes widened in sudden comprehension and he snapped his head forward, his hands on the controls.

While warning Jason, Henry had been hurriedly armoring his torso with steel skin. He had much better control over his abilities now, and he could deploy his steel skin with a thought.

As the Battlewagon approached the pond, an enormous, shambling creature rose out of the water directly in its path. Jason desperately tried stopping the vehicle, but its inertia caused it to slam into the monster, albeit slower than they otherwise would have. Most of the creature seemed to be made of mud, and Henry realized they'd seen something like it a couple months ago.

The fact the monster's type was familiar was the last thought he had before an arrow buzzed out of the tree line unnaturally fast, hitting him square in the chest. To his side, the water exploded and an ugly, mantis-looking monster the size of a person leaped onto the Battlewagon. One powerful, bladed forearm slammed into

Henry from behind so hard he flipped out of the Battlewagon's turret.

While in midair, time seemed to slow down like it had for him before in car crashes. Regardless of what anyone said, none of his crashes had ever been his fault. His thoughts were dreamy; everything was happening so fast. He absently wondered if he was going to die. He noticed the huge monster reach for Jason, who teleported away. Then the huge, shambling thing began to stomp out of the pond.

Rark-han had been riding behind Bezzi-ibbi, but he was down in the middle of the road. The big man was unmoving.

Bezzi-ibbi and Yanno-ibbi were both under attack. Yanno-ibbi was desperately trying to avoid a big woman with a huge sword. Bezzi-ibbi looked like he was running away from a giant lizard. A horde of monsters spilled out of the forest by the road. Mareen was screaming something. Something was attacking Gonzo and Vitaliya.

The mist was growing thicker; Henry couldn't see the sky anymore. Before he crashed into the ground with bone-jarring force, he thought, *Well, isn't this fucking lovely?*

* * *

Mourad paused to clean her giant flamberge's blade. The blessed steel shimmered again in the fading light after she wiped it clean of fresh blood. She gazed down at the fallen Mo'hali dispassionately. It wasn't personal. At least he would bleed out in relative peace. She'd taken two limbs, and the middle-aged jaguar race man was breathing shallowly, his body in a heap.

The wolf race Mo'hali man was down, too. Mourad was glad she hadn't had to fight him. He'd looked like a big, mean bastard.

The muscular woman spared a glance for Anz'wei chasing the Mo'hali boy into the forest. She sighed and thought, *Poor kid.* Nobody could run from Anz'wei. The big Adom was too fast and too good of a hunter. The boy was done.

The fog rolled in unnaturally quickly as Ghinsja flexed her power, obscuring the entire area. Mourad knew she had a respite, so it was time for her to finish her second mission she'd been tasked with. It'd be a shame if any of their enemies somehow escaped on one of the smaller vehicles.

One of the weird contraptions the Mo'hali had been riding had been broken in half by Anz'wei. Mourad sighed again and started pulling the second one towards the lake. The sooner she was done and the sooner all these poor bastards were dead, the sooner she could get paid and hopefully get the hell away from Liangyu, the Death Witch.

* * *

Uluula's mouth felt like parchment and her ears tingled. When the Battlewagon had crashed, she'd been thrown into boxes of supplies and came up bruised. However, any complaints she might have had died on her tongue. She really registered the huge, lumbering monster passing by the Battlewagon for the first time.

The thick mist was already obscuring her vision, but she could see a large group of monsters emerging from the forest.

Aodh, Thirsty, and Mareen were all with her in the back of the Battlewagon. Aodh was bleeding, not moving. Thirsty was crying and panicking, and Mareen was still dazed. Without thinking, Uluula grabbed Mareen and summoned desperate strength to pull her friend out of the Battlewagon.

They needed to protect their vehicle and the people in it. Their group was obviously caught in an ambush. Uluula's military training asserted itself and she began focusing on the problem. She needed Mareen awake to protect the others. The large, shambling creature that was heading for Gonzo and Vitaliya needed to be stopped. She briefly wondered why the monster wasn't attacking the Battlewagon, but realized that if it had chosen to do that, it would probably just be getting in the way of the swarm approaching from the tree line.

The thought chilled her.

The group of attacking monsters were almost on them; there was no time to be gentle. She cocked her arm back, made a fist, and socked Mareen in the nose.

* * *

Mareen had been in a daze until she got punched in the face. She clawed her way out of her stupor in a fury, preparing to lash out with the massive hammer that she'd somehow held on to. Uluula's eyes didn't even flicker as Mareen got a hold of herself, slowly lowering the hammer instead of trying to kill her friend.

The ground softly shook as the enormous, plodding monster that had stopped the Battlewagon walked off towards the rearmost magicycles. Before the fog obscured the last of her visibility, Mareen noticed that Vitaliya and Gonzo had somehow been thrown from their vehicles. They looked dazed.

Uluula pointed at the strangely quiet monsters trotting towards them from the nearby forest and ordered, "You need to protect the Battlewagon. I am going to help the spies."

In the next couple seconds, Mareen began to better understand why some races felt as uneasy about Areva as they did Fideli.

Uluula activated almost all of her enchanted equipment at once. Her cloak shimmered and she became harder to see, almost blending in with the fog surrounding them.

Uluula's faux *jaalba*, her plasma halberd, burst into life, the blade hissing with angry orange light. A shield of pale blue energy sprung up on her arm. The monsters were only a couple steps away when Uluula held up an arm, her enchanted bracer shooting a line out toward the massive mud monster, making a solid *thunk* when it embedded into the creature's back.

Uluula nodded once before shooting off into the fog, the flame of her halberd trailing her like a comet's trail. Most of the approaching monsters began chasing after Uluula's light, but several were literally almost on top of Mareen.

Mareen was eternally grateful that she was wearing her heavy, wooden armor. She dodged away from the closest monster, some sort of giant cat with insect parts. Her hammer flicked out and crushed its front leg.

The sheer desperation of the group's situation hadn't sunk in yet, and it wouldn't for a while. There was no time to think. The strangely quiet, slow-moving monsters crowded around her, and Mareen snarled as she whirled into them.

She would not be a burden to her group, to her friends. She refused to ever be useless again. The old Mareen, the cowering Mareen, was dead. She was orb-Bonded now and wearing armor that weighed more than she did. She thought again of Aodh, dazed on the floor of the Battlewagon, and realized the stakes were too high to fail.

She hated fighting, but she'd hate letting everyone down so very much more.

* * *

Thirsty had never been so scared in his life. He wasn't screaming anymore; he didn't want to attract anyone or anything's attention. The music was still playing from Keeja's device, but he was too terrified to turn it off.

The fog kept getting thicker, and he could barely see Aodh in front of him. The boy wasn't completely lucid yet; he'd taken a hard fall. Thirsty knew what was happening. They were under attack, it was actually happening. Before the fog had become too thick, he'd seen dozens of monsters moving directly towards them.

Mareen had been battling them. He could still hear her fighting for her life—for their lives.

Thirsty didn't like Mareen very much, mainly because it was obvious she didn't like him. But still, she was standing between him and danger, putting her life on the line to do so.

Suddenly, a monstrous head appeared over the side of the Battlewagon, its eyes milky white. It looked like a cross between a pig and a bird, beady eyes below a feathered crest. Its snout had tusks. Thirsty screamed, the sound ripping from of his throat with desperate intensity. He fumbled at his wrist and activated one of the shield bracelets he'd made.

A bubble of solid air formed over the back of the Battlewagon, pushing away the pig monster and the cloying fog. Thirsty collapsed near Aodh, holding his knees and sobbing. His diaphragm shook as he just reacted to the complete horror of the situation. He couldn't think straight through his terror. He didn't know what to do, and his helplessness was only making him more hysterical.

Thirsty's tall frame rocked back and forth in the fetal position. "Please, God, please, God," he whispered to himself. Outside the shield, the porcine monster began to probe the shield with its crude spear.

* * *

Bezzi-ibbi ran for his life. So far, the only thing keeping him alive was a lifetime of experience running through alleys from the

Mirana Guard and the strength training his Clan had introduced him to at a young age.

Dodging through the underbrush and the deadfall wasn't quite like his adventures in Mirana, but he was using a lot of the same muscles, and he was Jaguar Clan, after all.

The last few moments had been confusing, scary, and his heart still hurt, but he was suppressing the pain. He'd been riding on a magicycle when the caravan had been attacked. Yanno-ibbi had been riding the other vehicle, so Rark-han had been riding behind Bezzi-ibbi. Sometimes they doubled up so everyone in the back of the Battlewagon could have more breathing room.

At the same time the huge creature had appeared from the lake to stop the Battlewagon, a few other swift-moving, smaller monsters had attacked the Mo'hali on the magicycles. Bezzi-ibbi should have been dead. His vehicle had been hit, and he'd been thrown to the ground. A monster had reared up to finish him off with a wicked-looking clawed arm…and Rark-han had jumped in the way.

Bezzi-ibbi had watched in horror as the big wolf man had been impaled by the dead-eyed monster. Rark-han's mouth had moved, but nothing had come out but a bloody froth, dripping from his teeth. The big man had locked eyes with Bezzi-ibbi, trying desperately to communicate with the Jaguar Clan heir. His eyes had been at peace and before the light left his eyes, he'd simply given a Mo'hali grin before falling limply to the ground.

The creature had moved towards Bezzi-ibbi again, but before it could take another step, Yanno-ibbi had cracked a large, dry branch over its head. The unnatural thing had dropped like a stone.

The fast-moving, ambushing monsters had been deadly, but fragile. Yanno-ibbi had been able to unsheathe his claws and kill another one with his bare hands. Bezzi-ibbi had eventually gotten his wits together and killed another with a dagger he'd made from his metal arm. However, a large, armored Terran woman and a huge Adom had followed the monsters to attack. Bezzi-ibbi had immediately known they were much more dangerous than the initial attacking creature. Yanno-ibbi had yelled at him to run, and the Hero had obeyed his uncle.

Unfortunately, the huge, reptilian Adom was right on his heels. He could tell she was female, but didn't know what tribe she came from, not that it mattered. He could practically feel her hot breath as she barreled through the forest after him.

As he sprinted, he occasionally caught sight of the attacking monsters, their movements strangely sluggish, all focus entirely on the distant Battlewagon. Bezzi-ibbi tested a theory and manifested his Hero field while running near one of the creatures. His awareness moved outward and he could feel the ugly thing like a dark, prickly void.

Bezzi-ibbi reached out to the void and squeezed. It hurt, the feeling was like the pain from eating ice chips too fast. He could sense the void disappear and the lethargic monster fell to a heap like a puppet with cut strings.

Thralls. Bezzi-ibbi had heard of them. Mages or Bonded with extremely rare magic could create and control them. No wonder he and Yanno-ibbi had been specifically targeted. A proper Hero could destroy a lot of them before the pain became too great.

Suddenly, Bezzi-ibbi tripped. He almost panicked; falling would mean certain death. The Adom was only ten paces behind him. Luckily, he barely kept his head. He whipped his left arm out, willing the metal to change shape. He elongated the metal to form a tool, a new skill he'd been praticing.

He barely managed to snag a tree limb with his new arm hook, pulling himself up and preventing himself from falling. *That was close.*

Bezzi-ibbi's chest pumped, his breathing harsh. He needed to get back to his team. They needed his help and he needed their muscle. He didn't have any ideas yet. The Jaguar Clan heir thought furiously, willing himself to think through the problem. He tried to ignore the thundering steps of his pursuer slamming closer and closer.

Bezzi-ibbi loved the way he usually dressed, but for once he was willing to concede that wearing formal shoes all the time as an adventurer might not be very practical. As Henna-ibbi always said, "The wise hunter dresses for the hunt."

Bezzi-ibbi continued to run and wondered if he would ever see his family again.

* * *

Liangyu stood with her arms crossed, her eyes closed. Controlling so many thralls was difficult. She could choose to inhabit one at a time, but other than that she could only get a general idea of what they were doing. Orders could otherwise be given singly or in groups, but the thralls tended to be stupid.

The fog was helping less than she'd thought it would. True to her word, Ghinsja had covered a large area in her power and allowed the mercenaries to see better in it than their targets, but it was inhibiting the sight of Liangyu's thralls.

Matilda had only gotten off one good shot with her bow. Now she was on standby along with Raquel, waiting for further orders.

Liangyu turned to her second-in-command. "Report," she snapped.

Ghinsja's eyes lost focus for a moment before replying, "As you know, a few thralls are down. Two of the Mo'hali are down. The Areva woman with the flaming spear is attacking the bog shambler demon; they are both heading towards the two at the rear. They are completely surrounded.

"Anz'wei is chasing the Mo'hali boy, who is now confirmed to be a Hero. Most uncertainty is with the main vehicle, where a shield of some is pushing the fog back, and the girl with the big hammer is still alive and beating off your thralls. She doesn't seem to be putting many down for good, though."

Liangyu pursed her lips in thought. On one hand, the fact the target group wasn't all dead yet was worrying. On the other hand, they'd confirmed that there were at least two, probably three bounties to claim.

It was a high-risk, high-reward situation.

Liangyu tried to observe the operation from multiple angles as dispassionately as possible before making a decision. She nodded and said, "Relay a message. Tell Raquel to move towards the rear fight with the bog shamble. Tell Matilda to head towards the larger vehicle to support the thralls if she can. I will be directing most of the remaining thralls still in the forest towards the large vehicle. I want that area cleared."

She thought further and nodded, saying, "Let Matilda know to prepare the artifact weapon."

"But it only has one shot," stuttered Ghinsja.

"I know. It's worth throwing all we have into this fight. Let's fully commit. That means you and I are going to head there as well. You need to be closer to use your fog as a weapon, correct?"

Ghinsja mutely nodded.

"Okay, let's go. Also, I haven't heard about Mourad doing anything useful in the last minute. Tell her to head to the large vehicle, too. Let's finish this."

Liangyu smiled. It would all be over soon. She was a bit worried about the Mo'hali Hero, but he was just a little boy. The greatest wild cards right now were the enemy leaders. One had disappeared as soon as the attack had started—literally disappeared. The other had gotten shot by an arrow and clawed in the back by one of her thralls.

He should be dead, but Liangyu didn't believe in assumptions. It was time to personally ensure the job was done right.

She walked with Ghinsja into the thick fog, towards the screaming and other sounds of combat.

Delvers LLC: Obligations Incurred

CHAPTER SEVENTEEN

Parry

Jason stared down at the huge fog bank in frustration. He had to keep teleporting himself back to his starting position with an upward vector; he was yo-yoing in midair. It wasn't taking much power to do so, but his magic reserves were not unlimited.

He'd discovered a weakness of his signature power the hard way; he couldn't teleport to what he couldn't see through the magic fog. He still wasn't entirely sure how his power worked, but he got the overwhelming feeling it would be a bad idea to teleport into the fog bank. His current assumption was that teleporting through someone else's magic would end badly for him.

What's more, he could faintly hear the sounds of combat down below. Henry was down there. Uluula was down there. Bezzi-ibbi was down there.

When he'd been attacked, he'd teleported straight up before

the fog had started rolling in, and had quickly found himself with nowhere to go. Jason clenched his fists in frustration. For all his new power, he was helpless.

He teleported in place a few more times while clenching his jaw in thought. He mentally explored all his options and eventually settled on the only viable course of action. With a grunt, he began traveling as fast as he could to the edge of the unnatural fog. He was going to find the road at the closest point he could actually see it, and he was going to run back to his friends as fast as he could.

* * *

Henry woke up next to the Battlewagon, covered in mud. The surrounding mist was cold and his armor was covered in condensation. There was a scaly, nasty-smelling creature lying on top of him.

Henry listened carefully. He could get a general feeling of what was happening around him with his enhanced hearing, but sounds echoed strangely in the fog. He could hear his friends fighting for their lives and he knew he needed to help them, but it wouldn't do them much good if he ran off and immediately got killed.

First, he examined the creature. It looked sort of like a giant praying mantis with a fish face. It was missing half its head. Henry realized that he had reflexively killed it with an exogun after being attacked. The creature smelled horrible, like swamp and rot. Its skin was mottled grey and looked like it was about to decay.

So, so disgusting, Henry thought. It was going to take hours to get the smell out of his armor and his nose. He felt around his body and realized he still had almost all his gear, but he was missing his rifle.

He ran his hand over the chest and back of his armor. He had holes on both sides from the creature's attack and the arrow that had hit him. Both strikes had been enormously powerful. They'd actually made him bleed; the arrow in particular had penetrated a half inch into his chest before bouncing out.

That meant it had gone through his bronze armor, through his thick steelskin, and penetrated his natural toughness from his first level Durability skill. That arrow must have hit like a rocket. He didn't want to catch another one of those, that was for sure. He might not be so lucky next time.

The jagged holes of his ruined armor were easily fixed with a trickle of magic. Henry gritted his teeth, pushing the carcass of the creature off of himself. Almost immediately after he was free, the mist swirled to his right and another monster attacked him.

The creature swung a sword and Henry cursed, springing sideways in a spray of filthy mud and water. He drew his short sword in time to block another heavy strike. As Henry got his bearings, he got his first good look at his attacker and grunted in shock.

It was a zombie. Its undead condition was obvious. The

creature used to be a man, but now its eyes were milky white and its teeth showed through a cut in the side of its face. It also moved a little unnaturally. In retrospect, the creature that he just pushed off of himself had been a zombie, too.

Fuck this, thought Henry. He reloaded his exogun, took aim, and put a gold bullet through the zombie's head. The creature crumpled to the ground, somehow pitiful upon dying the second time. Henry absently loaded up all three of his exogun tubes and attached them to his metal forearm. Then he tried to find his rifle in the muck at his feet. Its sling had probably been cut when he was attacked.

I hate zombies, he thought as he tried to search for his weapon as quietly as possible. He could hear the unnatural zombie fuckers shuffling all over the place. The sounds coming from Mareen's battle weren't good, either.

He grunted with the reality of his situation. It could take forever to find his rifle, and his friends needed him now. Henry hissed through his teeth as he stood up and began walking forward with purpose-driven steps. He was extremely pissed. Zombies weren't smart enough to pull off an ambush. He needed to find out who was pulling the strings behind the scenes and deal with them.

As Henry strode toward the fighting he could hear, he wondered where the rest of the Delvers were. He could hear Uluula and the spies in the distance behind him, but even with his hearing cranked up all the way, he couldn't locate the rest.

* * *

Mareen was getting desperate. She felt like she'd been fighting nonstop for ages. Her lungs burned, and sweat ran freely under her thick, wooden armor.

The armor itself had saved her life multiple times. It was peppered with quills, barbs, cuts, and even a burn. Luckily, the heavy mist made everything wet, and an odd-looking beetle monster that ejected flames out its rear hadn't been able to catch Mareen on fire.

The strangely diverse horde of monsters she'd been fighting weren't particularly fast; in fact, their jerky movements made them look sick. They also seemed to have a hard time seeing. On the other hand, there was obviously some sort of foul magic at play. The creatures didn't bleed much, and they stood right back up after receiving mortal wounds. They didn't cry out when Mareen crushed limbs with her hammer.

The monsters were slow, but when they got close enough, they could put on a surprising burst of speed and almost act as they would if they weren't gripped by whatever dark magic held them. Right before one would start moving quickly, its milk-white eyes would take on a glow. Mareen's attention to detail was the only reason she was still alive. She'd been carefully conserving her energy and preparing for a flurry of attacks whenever she saw a shuffling monster's eyes change.

Still, she knew she was about to die. They were closing in

from all directions, and they got right back up after she shattered entire bodies with her hammer. One was even crawling towards her on the ground. It was hopeless.

Then she heard the familiar, *pop-hiss* of Henry's exogun through the fog. She didn't think he was too far away, but she couldn't be sure. She couldn't see very far and had no idea where she was. Just in case, she started humming "Girls Just Want to Have Fun" between her hacking, rattling breaths. With Henry's hearing, he should be able to find her. Hopefully.

The monsters moved in for the kill. One monster's eyes flashed. Then another. Mareen wasn't giving up, but there were just too many. She hefted her hammer and prepared for one last clash. She had no regrets. She hadn't been useless. She'd given her all to protect her friends.

She braced for an attack that never came. The mists swirled and Henry jumped through the throng of monsters, his blade flicking out and his arm-mounted exoguns spitting death. Four of the creatures went down and stayed down, giving Mareen a brief respite.

Henry slid to a stop in front of her, breathing deeply. He loudly exhaled and asked, "What's up, hottie?"

Mareen's eyes blazed and she fiercely kissed her husband. The infuriating man acted like he had been expecting it, but she didn't care. She was so tired and relieved she began chuckling into his lips as she leaned against him. She heard Henry fire an exogun over her shoulder and she didn't even look. She knew he probably had destroyed another monster that got too close.

Being useful was great and she was proud of herself. She felt like a real adventurer. Mareen knew she was truly powerful now... but damn it was nice to have her husband at her side again.

* * *

Vitaliya dodged another lethal strike. She concentrated for a moment and her flame flexed, twisting and charring the attacking creature's clawed limb. She cursed when the unnatural thing just switched to its other arm.

The twisted, rotting monsters seemed endless and they felt no pain. Vitaliya had been in a number of battles, most of them through her training. When she wreathed herself in flames, other living creatures usually shied away or at least took pause. Not these things.

She'd never felt so helpless. Her flames didn't even faze the huge group of monsters converging on her position.

And she could feel the ground thumping beneath her feet as something huge got closer.

Gonzo was holding his own. He was strong and fast, his ice attacks were debilitating, and he could even heal himself. He didn't advertise his abilities, but Vitaliya had seen him heal a deep cut on his arm before.

The man was currently standing in a ring of ice spikes facing outwards from the ground at chest height, keeping the monsters off of himself as he tried to thin them out. He calmly fashioned magic spears one after another and threw them into the horde.

Gonzo and Vitaliya had both realized that hitting the diseased monsters in the head put them down for good, but Vitaliya had a hard time using her magic with that much precision. Her short sword wasn't exactly the best weapon to be taking heads with, either.

At least Gonzo was effective, but he was still slowly, surely getting overrun. The monsters were impaling themselves on his spikes and starting to climb over each other. Whatever huge thing was approaching their location was almost on top of them, judging by how the ground shook. The situation was looking grim.

Suddenly, the footsteps stopped and a huge crash rattled the ground. Vitaliya spared a glance and saw Uluula rocketing out of the mists, her halberd trailing fire.

Vitaliya was mildly surprised. Uluula had never impressed her very much. She'd just assumed the Areva woman was a calculating aristocrat, working towards a cushy life through her association with Jason. Uluula practiced combatives and wore weapons, but Vitaliya had never taken the smaller woman very seriously.

Vitaliya's blood chilled a bit when she saw Uluula almost casually cut a couple creatures in half. Uluula held an arm pointed behind her, her bracer throwing out a line. She let the line pull her back, zipping away from a couple attacking monsters.

The woman was fast and extremely skilled. Vitaliya immediately adjusted her assessment. One aspect of her training for Berber Intelligence was to never let personal pride interfere with analyzing facts.

"Hit them in the brain or cut off their heads," she yelled.

Uluula nodded and called back, "That makes sense. I couldn't bring the big one down until I put a mist spear through its eye." Uluula's polearm spun in her hands. She began hacking and slashing through the surrounding monsters. The halberd's magic-fueled plasma blade charred putrid flesh and bones; the stink was overwhelming. Vitaliya gagged but she still preferred the smell to being dead.

Perhaps she'd have to buy Uluula a gift. Staying alive was a priority. If she were to die, she wouldn't be able to see her precious Aodh again. Actually, where was Aodh?

She felt a flash of a panic and ruthlessly suppressed it, but her attacks on the surrounding creatures redoubled and her eyes hardened. She lashed out with her flames again and again, the attacks hitting with all of her desperation behind them. Where was her cousin? What if he died?

Vitaliya gritted her teeth and created a powerful jet of flame, burning a dog monster's head until it stopped moving. She was going to figure out who had attacked them, and there would be hell to pay.

She didn't even want to think of what she'd do if Aodh wasn't safe.

* * *

Bezzi-ibbi gasped in exhaustion and fear. He was still keeping ahead of the big Adom that chased him, but just barely. The gap was getting closer and closer.

The huge, reptilian female was like a force of nature. Logs, branches, and small trees that Bezzi-ibbi had to go around, the big Adom just went through. If she ever got a hold of him, Bezzi-ibbi would be done.

He needed to loop back and get some help to deal with his enormous, scaled problem, but he'd gotten turned around and he wasn't sure where he was anymore.

He didn't even know what general direction the Battlewagon was in. For the first time in his life, Bezzi-ibbi felt like circumstances were entirely beyond his control. He still fought to maintain his calm, his focus, but he wasn't sure how much good it would do.

He wondered if he would ever see Henry-ibbi and Jason-ibbi again. Even if he died, he was glad he had met his brothers. They'd given him the courage to be who he truly was, to become the best male he could be.

Still, even though the situation looked grim, he would not give up easily. Bezzi-ibbi smiled savagely, his eyes flashing as he pumped his arms and legs. He began looking for rock outcroppings and thicker trees to duck around, obstacles the Adom would not be able to smash through.

The Jaguar Clan heir chuckled, ducking around yet another tree. He heard a rock whiz past where he'd just been running. The big Adom had started throwing things at him.

If he somehow survived this test, Bezzi-ibbi would have excellent material for his first Troubadour song.

* * *

Jason hit the ground running. The fog bank covered more ground than he would have hoped. He could barely hear the sounds of combat anymore. Once his long legs began to eat up the ground, he focused on getting a good breathing rhythm.

One advantage of his Endurance skill was that he could run faster and farther than he ever could before in his life.

He focused on his task with single-minded determination…just one foot in front of the other. The rhythm of his pounding feet became his world.

He tried not to think about anything else. He didn't remember how Henry had been attacked. He didn't wonder if Uluula was still alive. He couldn't afford to give in to despair.

He had to help his family, the only sense of home and belonging he had on Ludus. He would not let this world take them from him.

Jason ran faster and felt his rage growing, waiting to be unleashed.

CHAPTER EIGHTEEN

Fighting with the Past

Thirsty couldn't move. His fear was like a physical weight crushing him to the back of the Batttlewagon. Every time the porcine creature outside the barrier jabbed with its spear, Thirsty flinched and felt the strength of his air shield fading. The bracelet on his wrist that sustained the protective shield was developing cracks.

Nobody had come back for him. They could all be dead. He was on his own.

Thirsty knew the barrier wouldn't last that much longer. It was true he had more shields he could generate with the bracelets on his wrist, but he couldn't move, couldn't even think. It felt like he'd gone back in time. He wasn't Thirsty anymore, he wasn't anyone's friend. He wasn't chatting every day with crazy Mo'hali or hot, armored men in a fantasy world. No, he was just Dashawn

Givens again; a skinny, awkward, black queer kid with no friends.

Every time the monster outside the barrier thrust with a spear, it was like he was 12 years old again, being beaten by his stepfather with an extension cord. Ron had never been able to "beat the faggot" out of him, but he sure had tried.

He was fourteen again. He relived being slapped in the face by bullies "because bitches get slapped" while walking to the lunchroom. He heard kids call him a fairy, a butt pirate, and an ugly faggot when they thought the other kids or the adults wouldn't hear. He remembered what it was like to fear his peers.

He was fifteen years old again and his best friend Gregory was denying their friendship in order to avoid being bullied. He watched himself spend a miserable year in a new school where he was shunned for being black, or gay, or both…Or maybe he'd just been depressed and angry. Maybe he'd done it to himself; wouldn't that be ironic? But the end result was the same: he had been alone.

He was sixteen again, and the boy he had kissed at summer camp was pretending to be straight at school, pretending that nothing had ever happened between them. The boy he'd thought he loved over the summer, Jeremy, told other students some of the embarrassing secrets that Dashawn had confided. That year was a living hell.

He was seventeen again, hating himself for secretly dating Jeremy.

He was eighteen, staying home alone on prom night. He was looking at himself in a mirror with his dress on, knowing he had to hide it before his mom saw. She thought he was going to be a nice, normal boy. She didn't understand. She asked why he hadn't asked a girl to prom like his best friend Jeremy had.

He was nineteen again, broke with no job, no prospects. He was couch surfing and stressing already thin, strained relationships.

He was twenty and being beaten by the older man he dated.

He was twenty-one, the year his mom disowned him. He was wondering how he was going to feed himself.

The years rolled by and Dashawn drowned in the past. Yet still, with all the terrible memories he cycled through, his current situation was the worst he'd ever experienced. If he could just give up, just let it all be over and done with…if he could surrender, it would be fine.

But he couldn't.

A tiny speck of stubborn pride remaining within him, the core of who he wanted to be, the part of him that was inspired by his idols on Earth, by Bezzi-ibbi and Henry…That part was whispering, "No." He wanted to live. He wanted a chance to see his drag momma again, dammit. He missed his entire drag family.

Tears of frustration ran down his cheeks and he gasped deep, racking sobs. He was letting down his new friends. He was a failure. He was nothing. His stepfather Ron had been right. If the man had not died in an alcohol-fueled accident, he would have been vindicated for sure.

Dashawn curled his hands into fists. He clenched his jaw, wishing the terrible creatures outside the shield would just get it over with.

The tall, thin man was continuing to wallow in depression and helplessness when he heard Aodh groan. Aodh, the young man who had befriended Dashawn, was also trapped. Aodh, who had so much in common with him despite being a different race, age, and even coming from a different world.

If Dashawn did nothing, he wouldn't just be letting down everyone in the group, he'd be directly betraying his half-conscious young friend. The thought hurt him somewhere he wasn't even sure he could hurt anymore.

Dashawn hadn't prayed in over a decade, not since a woman had told him that God hated him, had said that he was spitting in God's eye for being gay. But in that moment, in his darkest hour, he whispered, "Please, God, help me." His prayer wasn't for himself, but for all the people in the fog.

His heart ached for his companions, the people he'd come to care about in such a short amount of time. He prayed for his friends who were no doubt fighting for their own lives…and for his.

Suddenly, Dashawn noticed that Keeja's music player was still on. It was louder than usual, too. "White Wedding," another of

Mareen's song picks, was playing at full volume.

He frowned, the distraction barely overcoming his fear enough to make him crack his eyes open. Through tears, he stared at the monster outside in horrified fascination. It was hitting the Battlewagon with its spear.

Dashawn could feel the vibrations...but he couldn't hear anything.

In a flash, he understood. His barrier was blocking sound, keeping it from entering or leaving. He looked out into the dense, swirling fog and realized he had probably been further dooming his friends. They had no way to even tell where the Battlewagon was.

Dashawn was about to curl up again and just wait for death when everything changed. Billy Idol's song came to an end, and a new song began playing.

The next song was "Champion," by RuPaul, the goddess herself. Dashawn listened to for a few seconds and his eyes widened. Despite his fear, he began lip syncing the words. "Champion" was the first of the songs he'd queued up on Keeja's music player. His eyes widened as the words of the song seemed to pierce his heart, hit him right at the core of who he was as a person.

He gritted his teeth. He might not feel strong enough to do anything as Dashawn, but anything was possible as Thirsty. When he was Thirsty, he felt strong and beautiful. He realized his feeling about the transformation made no sense, since Thirsty was a part of him, but there were freaky-ass monsters less than 10 feet away. It wasn't time to have an existential crisis. Logic could get fucked.

Dashawn took a deep breath and forced his hands to uncurl. He crawled on hands and knees to his backpack.

With shaking hands, he got his heels and his wig out of the backpack. Every movement was slow and deliberate. He'd never had a harder time putting on a wig in his life. Each bobby pin seemed to take an eternity to fasten.

When the wig and heels were both on, Dashawn squeezed his eyes shut tightly, cleared his mind...and became Thirsty Zha Zha. The situation sucked, but she could do this...even in an old-ass pair of dirty man clothes. There was no time to tuck or put on a dress, much less any makeup...Even just the bare essentials in her backpack would take too long. Fuck it. She would be gorgeous in a straightjacket.

First things first, she had to wake up Tony. After that, she was going to drop her shield to let the music out. Then everyone would know where the Battlewagon was.

She was gonna serve up some magical powers realness. Fuck all this crying and moaning bullshit. *It's time to buckle down, bitch. Do yo' thang.*

Thirsty gave one last sniffle, rubbed her eyes clear of tears, pursed her lips, and got the fuck to work. It was time to beat some monster ass and look fabulous doing it.

* * *

Aodh woke up fully with a splitting headache. Someone was shaking him. He groaned to make the shaking go away, but it wouldn't stop. He opened his eyes.

Thirsty was standing above him, wearing the shirt and skinny jeans he'd brought from Earth. However, he was also wearing high-heeled shoes and his drag queen wig. He looked like he'd been crying.

Aodh blinked and glanced around, hissing through his teeth when he saw the monster outside the barrier. As he watched, another creature joined it. The new monster looked like it might have been a man once, but now existed as a decaying corpse in armor. Its dead eyes were disturbing and its cloudy pupils focused on him.

"What, what is going…" Aodh muttered. "There's fog and monsters and—"

"That's right, honey. We're in a world of shit." Thirsty was holding his wand made from bronze cones and his bare arm sported all his enchanted bracelets. He stood tall and looked more confident than Aodh could remember. The wig and women's shoes coupled with his face full of stubble seemed a little odd, but Aodh thought everything about Thirsty was odd. He was just glad his friend had woken him up and had apparently been protecting them. He realized the barrier had to be Thirsty's.

The roiling fog outside looked ominous. Thirsty breathed

deeply and said, "Okay, Tony, we need to help everyone. They're all out there fighting. You've been unconscious for a while and I was feeling sorry for myself, but it's time to work. It's time to be a fierce bitch, you know what I mean?"

Tony had no idea what Thirsty meant, but he nodded anyway.

Thirsty sighed and said, "Right now, my shield is blocking sound. Everyone else is fighting out there. I think I can change my shield to let sound out, but if I do, I have a feeling that more of these freaky things might come and start attacking. We might as well just drop the whole thing and try to clear an area for everyone. Are you ready?"

Aodh gulped and found his quarterstaff. He unpacked one heavy claymore mine and held it under his arm. He understood the situation and also understood that without Thirsty protecting him, he might already have been dead. Aodh swallowed and decided he had to speak what was on his mind, or he'd be more of a coward than he already knew he was. "Thank you," he said, "for everything. You saved my life, didn't you?"

Thirsty smiled. "I'm Thirsty Zha Zha, kid! Being amazing is my job. Plus, what are friends for?"

Aodh absently noted that Keeja's music player had started playing a new song. Aodh recognized it as one of Thirsty's favorites. He thought it was called "Glamazon" or something, but he didn't understand most of the lyrics.

Thirsty's eyes got huge and he smiled. "This is the perfect

song to make my Ludus debut. The show is about to start, honey. I think these things are zombies, so aim for their heads."

Suddenly, the barrier protecting the Battlewagon fell and the fog slowly moved in. The two monsters stood still for a moment, slow to react. Thirsty pointed at one of them and discharged his wand. With a loud pop, one small piece of bronze zipped through the pig-looking creature's head. The back of the creature's head blew outwards and it collapsed in a heap.

Thirsty crowed, "Say hello to Thirsty Zha Zha, bitches!" The drag queen stood tall and made a pose. Aodh had no idea what the hell his friend was doing. Why wasn't his friend just dealing with the monsters? Why make poses?

Thirsty yelled, "I'm like a drag magic girl. Call me Sailor Dragalicious." Thirsty pointed his wand and the second monster went down, its head splattered all over the ground.

Aodh was terrified. He was glad Thirsty was with him, even if his friend was doing a lot of unnecessary things. He didn't understand half of what the man in high heels was saying, but he grasped they were going to help everyone. It was time to make a stand. He gripped his staff tightly and set his jaw. He wished he could be brave and powerful like Thirsty.

He'd just have to do the best he could.

* * *

Liangyu walked through the fog, carefully choosing her steps to avoid stumbling. Ghinsja and Matilda were matching her pace,

301

and it would not be proper to show any weakness. Her three most powerful thralls trailed behind.

Matilda carried an enormous, boxy weapon. She'd met Liangyu and Ghinsja on the way back from fetching the artifact weapon as Liangyu had ordered.

The artifact weapon looked menacing and alien as it balanced on the blonde woman's shoulder. It had been expensive to procure and it only had one shot left. Liangyu hoped they wouldn't need to use it, but she wanted a contingency plan in place in case the operation went bad. If she had to cut her losses, she still wanted to walk away with a reward.

Suddenly, she heard faint music in the distance, the sound warbling strangely in the fog. Liangyu stopped walking and her subordinates fell in beside her. Her eyes snapped to Ghinsja and she barked, "Report!"

The pale Areva woman nodded and closed her eyes. After a few silent moments, she said, "Quite a few thralls are down. The bog shambler is down. The two Mo'hali men are still the only downed enemies.

"The large vehicle is no longer shielded but is being guarded by two enemies. One of them is Aodh O'Breen. Our initial target, the Asian Terran man, is alive and heading towards the large vehicle. All other enemies are heading towards this point too; I assume the music is guiding them.

"The group of three to the rear of the enemy caravan is making steady progress towards the large vehicle. Raquel is shadowing them.

"The enemy Mo'hali Hero boy is attempting to circle back, but Anz'wei is preventing him from doing so.

"The taller man that disappeared before my fog covered the battlefield is on foot, running towards us. He is still far enough away that there are no thralls near him.

"To the best of my knowledge, Biivan and the enemy High Priestess are holding position in the sky. Every time a bit of fog touches them, I can confirm they are still there.

"Mourad is done dragging one of the smaller vehicles into the water—"

"She's been wasting time," Liangyu said quietly.

Ghinsja licked her lips nervously and said, "Mourad is moving slowly to the fight in front of the large vehicle. She seems to be looking for a good time to strike."

"Is that it?"

"Yes, my lady."

Liangyu tapped her lip with a finger while she thought. She asked, "Are the surviving targets currently wounded? What is their status?"

"They are all tired with superficial damage, but no serious injuries. The Hero boy is slowing down and may be eliminated soon."

Liangyu nodded. "Anz'wei is utterly dependable. I am not

worried about the boy." She thought further and instructed, "Tell Mourad and Raquel to meet up near the large vehicle. Tell them to look for an opportune time to strike together or to just wait for us. Ghinsja, can you start using the fog as a weapon yet? Are we close enough?"

"We are to the large vehicle, yes. I won't be able to move very fast while concentrating, though."

"Okay, fine. We will begin moving slower." Liangyu turned to regard Matilda. The silly woman had wisely stayed quiet and even more wisely looked nervous. She kept glancing back at Liangyu's most powerful thralls.

Liangyu ordered, "Matilda, watch for the Asian orb-Bonded man that you attacked before. He is trouble. If he is still alive when we get to the main battle and you have a clear shot with the artifact weapon, take it."

Matilda mutely nodded. *Perhaps she isn't as foolish as I thought,* Liangyu mused.

* * *

Mourad's attention was completely focused on the sounds of combat ahead of her. Her enhanced vision in the fog allowed her to see fuzzy shapes moving around. Suddenly, a whispered voice hissed directly in her ear and she clamped a hand over her mouth to keep from screaming. She turned enough to see the half-corporeal mist person that had formed next to her.

She calmed her heart and slowed her breathing as she listened to Ghinsja's new directions from Liangyu. She wished the Death Witch had just ordered their entire force to form up and attack at once, but she knew Liangyu thought of herself as a tactician. She rolled her eyes.

The big mercenary hoped the evil woman would get herself killed. That would make escaping even easier. She sighed and began moving towards her rendezvous with Raquel. She had to admit it made sense to pair up with the mercenary captain.

Deep down, she had to concede she wanted the mage to back her up, too. From what she'd seen so far, the thralls were not doing so well against their targets.

* * *

Henry ran towards the sound of music, Mareen's feet pounding the ground right behind him. Her heavy armor made a hundred hollow thunking sounds as the wooden plates jostled together. He hadn't even needed to discuss his course of action with his wife. Suddenly hearing the music after fighting in relative silence not only meant someone from their group was still alive, it also meant they had a rally point. They'd just looked at each other and run towards the sound.

A zombie loomed out of the fog and Henry didn't even pause running. He snapped off a shot with an exogun and the unnatural thing went down. He was almost out of bullets. Why was he always out of fucking bullets? How many of these damn things were there?

Suddenly, he saw the fog thickening out the corner of his eye and he reacted on pure instinct. He shoved Mareen away, knocking her to the ground, and sprang away before a claw made of fog slashed the space where they'd both been standing.

"Well, that isn't creepy or anything," he muttered. Mareen just grunted as she got to her feet and began running again. They both kept an eye out for more fog claws.

Henry was amazed how far from the Battlewagon he and Mareen had been fighting. They were both exhausted, but he was happy she wasn't too badly hurt. It sucked he was almost out of ammo, but it'd been worth it to keep the nasty, diseased creatures off of them both.

A group of zombies in their path were slow to react; Henry and Mareen split the undead things' heads open from behind. Henry had been aghast earlier that Mareen hadn't known to hit zombies in the head. Then he remembered that people didn't grow up on zombie horror movies on Ludus.

Henry took a few more steps forward and stopped in his tracks, his mouth open. To the background beat of Men at Work's "Down Under," Thirsty Zha Zha was in her element. She blocked a weapon wielded by an undead soldier with a blast of air, then used two remaining bronze cones of her wand to destroy its brain and take another zombie down with it.

A tentacle materialized out of the fog, and Thirsty summoned a shield of air from her hand, stopping it cold until it dissipated.

The drag queen's long wig whipped around in the violent air currents from the battle, threatening to come off at any moment. Blood from a dozen cuts and scratches covered her, and she was limping, but she stood proud in heels. She snarled as another group of zombies rushed her position. Thirsty held out a hand and bowled them over with a wall of air. As Henry watched, one of the bronze bracelets on her wrist crumbled to dust.

"Toss one now, Tony!" she yelled.

Aodh threw one of his grenades towards the group of zombies and Thirsty helped it with a small gust of air. As soon as it landed among them, Aodh clenched his fist and the grenade exploded, destroying the pile of undead. Aodh looked terrified, but he stood firm.

Henry shook his head. "Badass," he whispered. He heard pounding footsteps out in the fog and cursed. He couldn't use his enhanced senses very well in the obviously magical fog that covered their entire location. He prepared for another nasty surprise, but thankfully Vitaliya and Gonzo burst out of the fog, Uluula right behind them with her flaming polearm.

The entire group met up and Henry shouted, "Everyone behind Thirsty. She can block all the claws and shit coming out of the fog!" Nobody argued or even acknowledged the command, they just moved. Henry took it as a sign of how exhausted the entire group was.

"How many of these damned things are there?" growled

Gonzo.

Henry just shrugged. Another couple zombies lunged out of the fog and were put down in seconds by Vitaliya's fire followed by an ice spike thrown by Gonzo. The Asian orb-Bonded man glanced around and frowned. *Where are Jason, Rark-han, Yanno-ibbi, and Bezzi-ibbi?*

Henry scowled. In all the chaos, he'd forgotten to use his earth sense ability. He concentrated, trusting his team to watch his back for a moment, and laid his awareness out over the earth. He'd developed the ability to such a degree that it was many times more powerful than the paltry power he'd started with.

His rifle was stupidly easy to locate with his magic, and he felt it lying in a deep puddle a surprising distance the Battlewagon. Henry shook his head ruefully. Of course, the damn thing was deep in the fog and past a line of zombies. He stretched his senses out further.

He located Jason, his footsteps pounding toward them in the distance. Henry had no idea what his friend was doing, but he seemed okay. Bezzi-ibbi…

He gasped. "Mareen, I have to go!" he hollered.

"What, what are you—"

"I have to help Bezzi-ibbi! Stay with the fucking group!" Henry didn't allow her to answer. He knew she was better at arguing than him, and he didn't have time to discuss it anyway. Sometimes Mareen could be sort of fuzzy on the chain of command if she was upset.

Women. Henry shook his head as he tore off by himself into the fog. As he ran, he dodged the rapidly decreasing number of undead and kept slowly drawing more strength from the earth.

* * *

Bezzi-ibbi had hit the end of his tracks. He knew it was his last hunt, his last walk in the day. He was exhausted and there was nowhere left to run, but he was tired of acting as prey anyway. He stood with his back to the cliff that had blocked his flight, watching the big Adom cautiously approach.

Bezzi-ibbi snarled. He drew a sword from his metallic arm and coughed phlegm onto the ground. He absently noted the flecks of blood. He'd really run hard, harder than he ever had in his life. It hadn't been good enough, though.

He slowly chuckled under his breath. He knew he was about to die, but he had no regrets. He'd followed his true spirit, his path as a Jaguar Troubadour. He could sink his claws into that as the long night took him.

Plus, the irony that his situation would have made an incredible song made him proud down to his marrow.

The huge, reptilian Adom was almost on him, and Bezzi-ibbi readied himself to make one last stand. He knew he was no slouch with a sword, but he was also realistic. He wasn't fully grown yet, and the Adom would have outclassed him in every possible way even if he'd been an adult.

He held up his sword, his spine straight. He would meet death head on with an unwavering gaze. If he had to die, he would die like a true Jaguar Clan hunter. He bared his teeth and snarled a challenge.

Suddenly, the Adom female looked puzzled and turned her head. Bezzi-ibbi watched closely, waiting for her to attack. He had been so intent on his enemy, he'd missed the sound of rapidly approaching footsteps. Bezzi-ibbi registered the sound through his exhaustion and turned his head in time to see what was making all the noise. Henry burst from the fog, moving as fast as a galloping zebra. From the flashes Bezzi-ibbi could see, almost his entire body was covered in steel.

The Adom's eyes widened and she tried to spring back, but Henry was moving too fast. With no hesitation, he swung at her with his short sword. The big Adom parried the flat of the blade with a scaled arm, bending the sword.

Henry responded by channeling all his momentum into his other hand, delivering an open-palmed strike with the full power of his body, twisting his hips and shoulders. He skidded forward with the force of his momentum, every ounce of muscle and weight put into the strike, slamming into the Adom's center of mass.

Bezzi-ibbi watched in astonishment as the huge, heavy Adom flew back ten feet from the power of the attack before rolling. She crashed through a few small trees before springing to her feet with a roar of rage.

Bezzi-ibbi felt a new fire of hope and a strange, giddy feeling take root within his hunter's spirit. He was living in legendary times. He slowly, painfully took off his shoes before flexing his toes. As the Jaguar Clan heir, he had to meet his enemies head on. He would not be prey.

He would rather die than let his Clan brother take all the danger for him. He would meet the threat together with his Clan in the gaze of the day.

Bezzi-ibbi had never been so tired, nor so excited in his life. This was a true test of his right to live as a Jaguar Troubadour. He snarled with joy and flexed his claws. To meet such a challenge at such a young age and find true battle kin…

It was a rare thing indeed. Bezzi-ibbi's eyes lit up as he bared his fangs and summoned the energy to dart forward. This had turned out to be a very full day! Despite the sadness, despite the struggle, he felt joy to be alive. The Jaguar Clan heir hissed in pleasure as he looked for ways to support his Clan brother.

Delvers LLC: Obligations Incurred

CHAPTER NINETEEN

Out From the Fog

For the first time since he'd fought Thod the bandit leader, Henry truly feared he might die. Sure, the monsters he had fought before, the zombies he'd been battling against with Mareen, might have killed him through weight of numbers. However, ever since he had become Bonded, he hadn't met many individuals he'd thought could end him all by themselves.

Meanwhile, the lizard person he was fighting had already almost killed him twice.

The creature was incredibly fast, strong, and tough. It had dark green scales and wore a vest with pouches over what looked like a strange kimono. Ropes covered its chest and wrapped around its torso. It was huge, towering over Henry, but what was really terrifying was its obvious intellect and skill. Henry had never had a fight quite like this one before.

What's more, for reasons that completely eluded him, Bezzi-ibbi hadn't run away. The kid was circling, obviously intending to fight, and Henry simply couldn't pay him any attention.

He sort of had his hands full.

He had been surprised to realize that the lizard creature was slightly stronger than he was. Henry had already lost his bronze short sword. The metal had been bent up and the weapon wasn't very effective anymore, so Henry had thrown it away.

As they circled each other, the giant lizard had untied a massive bronze ring with sharp edges from behind its back, obviously a weapon. It looked a lot like an oversized chakram, but probably weighed over thirty pounds.

From that moment on, Henry really understood how much danger he was in. The first time he'd blocked the bronze disc with his steel-clad forearm, his entire arm had gone numb and actually started to bleed. He'd been shocked. Without his Self Healing skill, he probably would have lost the use of his limb for the rest of the fight. Henry sprang back and absently patted his leg while he considered what to do.

Unfortunately, the lizard warrior didn't give him any respite. Henry bobbed and weaved, keeping right out of the warrior's range. Eventually, he decided that covering most of his body in steel wasn't all that helpful if his opponent was strong enough to penetrate the armor.

Henry grabbed a stone from the ground as he dodged the next

attack. He snarled as he flexed his magic, throwing the rock at the lizard person's face. His aim was terrible as usual, but at point-blank range, he still managed to nick its shoulder. The power of the stone's kinetic energy flung the creature back a few feet, but it managed to continue tracking Henry with its eyes.

Suddenly, with a sound like the biggest, angriest cat Henry had ever heard, Bezzi-ibbi jumped onto the creature's back. He slashed downwards with his quicksilver sword before jumping away to avoid the huge reptile's claws. While his opponent was turned, Henry saw that its scales were so thick, Bezzi-ibbi had barely managed to do any damage at all.

Henry used the short reprieve to concentrate. He commanded the steel covering his body to move in a new way. In the space of a couple heartbeats, he had thick bracers covering his hands and arms all the way to right above the elbow. A pair of long blades arced gracefully from the outside of his forearms to a couple feet in front of his fists. The rear of each blade extended a bit past his arms.

The big reptile cocked its head and spoke. In a strangely accent voice, it said, "I have never seen anything like that before. You move the steel around your body like water. I am impressed."

 Henry was barely fazed that the giant lizard thing was talking, or that its voice sounded fairly normal other than the accent. Ludus had completely, forever changed his sense of surprise. Talking to a giant, murderous, intelligent lizard thing? All in a day's work.

He responded, "I'm surprised too. You're the first enemy I've had a tough time with in a while. Actually, how can you even talk? You look like a giant alligator…but with more teeth."

The big lizard creature responded by showing all the teeth Henry had just mentioned. He wasn't sure if the gesture meant it was angry or amused. It said, "Ah, yes, traditional battle taunts. I will return the gesture. You look like a primitive primate with intestinal parasites."

Henry wasn't quite sure how to take that. He coughed and slowly replied, "Ah, yeah, sick burn. That definitely got under my skin. Uh…I'm all riled up to fight!"

The lizard slowly blinked, its slitted pupils focused on Henry. "Let us have a short truce. I wish to know the name of the one that can fight me claw to claw without tricks. I admire this. Despite being orb-Bonded or a powerful mage, you have not attempted to kill me through ranged attacks or magic—nothing underhanded.

"Even when you made room for yourself before with the stone, you only hit my shoulder. You are a very honorable opponent."

"Uhhh…yeah," Henry muttered. He figured this would be a bad time to tell the giant lizard-crocodile-thing that he just didn't want to use his very last exogun bullet unless he absolutely had to. Also, he wondered why the universe seemed to somehow illustrate his crappy throwing aim on such a regular basis.

"Yes," the creature continued, "the ground is littered with

stones. The power you can throw with means this fight would be in your favor if you were less honorable. I have eyes to see."

Henry coughed into his fist. The conversation was not making him feel better about his aim. "So…what now? I really need to get going."

"And my mission is to destroy the Hero you are with. I suggest we agree to an honorable duel with no distractions."

"Okay, that sounds good and all, but, well, what even are you?"

Bezzi-ibbi grinned and growled, "Female Adom. Reptile. Powerful warrior. Tracked me down and was about to kill!" He hit his palm with a closed fist. "Very impressive!"

The giant lizard person blinked, the membrane nictitating from the bottom of her eyes. "Yes, I am female Adom."

"So Adom are giant lizards?"

"No, I am part of the reptile tribes. You are surprisingly ignorant."

"Yeah, well, people tell me that a lot," Henry grumbled.

"What is your name? I would know that name of a worthy adversary."

"My name is Henry Sato. What about you?"

"I am known as Anz'wei."

The entire time they talked, Henry did his best to draw even more strength from the earth. He felt good about his new arm weapons. The feel of the blades on his outer arms reminded him of tonfas he'd learned to use in karate school as a teen.

"Okay, buddy," Henry said to Bezzi-ibbi out the side of his mouth. "You need to stay out of this one, alright?"

The Mo'hali boy hissed, but after a moment, he slightly bowed his head and backed away.

"More bravery than sense, that one," Henry muttered. Still, at least now he had one less problem. He knew he'd be wasting his breath if he told Bezzi-ibbi to run, but at least he wouldn't have to watch the kid die now. The boy would still be toast if Henry failed, though.

He would just have to not fail.

Soon he was squaring off against the big Adom again. Anz'wei gripped her giant disc weapon with one hand, her other hand held chambered at her hip. Her tail thrashed behind her.

Henry knew that this time, with Anz'wei prepared and focused, the fight would probably not last long. He narrowed his eyes and focused without focusing, and the technique came to him after years of practice.

The worst problem he had with his opponent was that she had weapons all over her body—the disk, the claws, the tail. She hadn't tried to bite him yet, but he knew it was possible.

Anz'wei moved first. With a roar, she attacked overhand with her huge bronze weapon. Her speed was even more startling this time. In a detached sort of way, Henry noted that she was using her tail as a counterbalance. He also knew intuitively that if he dodged the big, linear attack, Anz'wei would be able to get her claws on him.

That would be bad.

Henry gritted his teeth and braced himself, crossing his blades as he blocked. The impact rattled his whole body; his arm went numb, and Henry's steel forearm blade bit deeply into the Adom's bronze weapon.

Henry grunted with effort, his legs screaming as his shoved his opponent away. He blocked her weak return strike with one arm and opened a wicked cut on her other arm as she tried to go for his face with her claws.

The reptile warrior's eyes widened and her slitted pupils focused on her damaged weapon after springing away. She hissed, and it took Henry a second to realize she was laughing. "It is real steel after all? I am further impressed."

Henry didn't reply. He knew the next exchange would probably determine the outcome of the fight. He was stronger than the lizard woman now, but not by much. She also had a few hundred pounds on him, greater reach, and probably faster reflexes, too. He'd have to think his way out of this fight.

He really didn't want to use his last exogun bullet, but he definitely wasn't going to die and let Anz'wei get Bezzi-ibbi, either. He knew if he had to, he could attach his exogun and fire in a split second, and he was considering doing so. Suddenly, an idea occurred to him and he narrowed his eyes.

Henry watched his opponent carefully; he'd have to time his move perfectly. Anz'wei tensed, ready to spring forward.

When the huge reptile person finally attacked, Henry moved, diving forward and low. The big Adom roared in surprise as Henry passed right beneath her, taking advantage of his smaller size. He used his wickedly sharp forearm blades to gore the side of her body.

Henry hit the ground hard and immediately rolled away. Anz'wei's huge, taloned foot barely missed his head as she hissed with rage and pain. Henry jumped to his feet, covered in dirt and dodged Anz'wei's backswing. He sliced her other arm, his enhanced strength providing enough power to overcome her thick, scaled defense. Her arm went limp and he slammed both of his blades on top of her bronze weapon, knocking it to the ground. He spun and smoothly placed the tip of a forearm blade against the reptilian warrior's throat.

Anz'wei grew very still. Henry and the Adom warrior looked into each other's eyes for several heartbeats, breathing heavily. "What are you waiting for?" Anz'wei asked. "This was an honorable duel. I have no regrets."

Henry was conflicted. He ignored Bezzi-ibbi hissing in delight behind him and tried to think. His lungs were pumping like bellows; adrenaline suffused his body. He wasn't sure why he hadn't already gone for the killing blow in the first place. He looked in Anz'wei's eyes and thought, *Why did I hold back?*

He realized that his gut was telling him not to go for the kill. He wasn't sure why he got that feeling, but he thought back to the bush he'd avoided right after arriving on Ludus. Ignoring his gut was dumb.

Henry slowly lowered his wrist blade. Anz'wei made her strange, hissing chuckle again. "I almost killed your young Mo'hali friend, you cut me up, and then show mercy? What a strange monkey man."

Henry somewhat stiffly retrieved the giant bronze ring weapon that Anz'wei had been carrying, watching her warily the whole time. "I'm keeping this," he said. "I'm not sure why I'm letting you go, but that's what my gut is telling me to do. Of course, you should probably start walking the other direction and never come back, or I'll have no choice but to punch your ticket."

Henry ruefully realized that Anz'wei might not understand the expression, but she nodded, a strangely human gesture. "I understand, Monkey Warrior. Truth told, I hated this job. This has been the most dishonorable work I have ever done. Now I have an excuse to leave my position without violating pride or contract. Farewell."

With a stiff back, the reptilian Adom limped away, her mighty body trailing blood. Henry watched her go until he couldn't see or hear her anymore.

He shook his head. That had been one of the most dangerous fights he'd ever had in his life, and one of the strangest. Bezzi-ibbi walked up behind him and patted him on the shoulder. The boy chucked and said, "Not sure if smart, but definitely interesting, Henry-ibbi."

"Yeah, people tell me that sometimes," growled Henry. He absentmindedly rubbed his scarred leg and sighed, hefting the giant bronze ring weapon. "Let's head back. Everyone still needs us."

Henry wasn't sure if he'd made the right decision, but deep down, he knew that a part of himself was glad he'd chosen mercy. It made him feel more human. He wasn't sure what he was anymore. Calling himself a vanilla human these days simply wouldn't have been accurate. The little choices he made, showing compassion and empathy sometimes, helped him feel better about whatever he was becoming.

*   *   *

Mareen strained to see past the fog. Thirsty kept trying to expand her shield, but the byproduct of pushing the fog back was that it was especially thick right outside the barrier.

The tawny-skinned farmer turned adventurer hefted her hammer and clenched her jaw in worry. She knew it was part of who he was, but she hated when Henry went tearing off after something on his own. Sometimes she thought he forgot that he wasn't invincible.

She laid awake at night sometimes wondering if her husband was going to get himself killed and leave her all alone. Lately, the feeling had been getting stronger. Sometimes she woke up next to Henry in a panic and had to reach over to touch him, to make sure he was still there.

He was the last family she had left. Even in the middle of a battle, the hurt and anger from her grandfather's death rose out of nowhere, but she suppressed it. She could examine her feelings later.

Out in the thick fog, an occasional animated corpse was able to push through the thin barrier, but every time one did, it was easily dispatched.

Mareen held her hammer tightly and continued to look for movement or any sign of her missing husband.

* * *

Mourad frowned, her shoulders tense. She held her flamberge in sweaty hands, the huge sword's blessed steel blade was beaded with perspiration from the fog. She hated this. She wasn't opposed to violence, or even murder, but working for Liangyu made her skin crawl.

Luckily, it would all be over soon.

The full attacking group was gathered together, far enough away from the bubble of air their enemies had created that they couldn't be seen. Mourad found the entire situation ironic. The big woman paused to spit. They should have all grouped up to attack to begin with.

Now their position had been weakened. Most of the thralls had been destroyed and the enemy was no longer surprised. *I bet Liangyu still thinks she's some dark, evil genius, though.*

The plan now was simple. On Raquel's signal, they'd all began to move forward and Raquel herself would take down the barrier with magic. At that point, the entire group would follow the last of the thralls in to kill their enemies. Liangyu and Ghinsja would be supporting from the rear.

Mourad breathed deeply, trying to dispel her jitters. She was forty-one years old, she'd been a mercenary for over a decade, and she still got the shakes. It was ridiculous.

The big woman settled in to wait. Raquel would be giving the signal any second now.

* * *

Mareen was startled when one side of Thirsty's protective dome suddenly became wreathed in flames. Behind her, the music device on the Battlewagon was playing some song she didn't recognize, a "rock" song. The song's beat seemed to match the waves of fire outside the barrier.

Thirsty called out a warning, "My bracelets are breaking! They're breaking fast!" Mareen glanced over and noticed that tall drag queen was only down to three bracelets. As she watched, another crumbled, leaving Thirsty with only two more. Mareen wasn't sure what was happening.

Luckily, Uluula kept her head and seemed to understand what Thirsty meant. She shouted, "Drop the barrier! Save what you have!"

"Okay," yelled Thirsty. "Get ready!"

The barrier faded away. The fog started rolling in again, and with it came a flurry of motion. Dark shapes hurled themselves out of the grey wall, and it was all Mareen could do to figure out what was even going on.

In the next few moments, everyone would have died if not for Vitaliya and Gonzo. Balls of fire came flying out of the wall of fog, but Gonzo met each one with a thick burst of snow. Steam began to create open patches in the grey, suffocating blanket.

Vitaliya and Uluula destroyed the walking dead as they appeared. Vitaliya's fire withered their legs and Uluula took their heads. Mareen sprinted forward to deal with an undead soldier, but spun as an arrow bounced off the back of her armor. The arrow had hit with so much power that even at an angle, it still ripped several wooden plates off of her lamellar.

"Watch out, honey!" yelled Thirsty. Another arrow buzzed out of the thick fog, but bounced off a shield Thirsty had erected around Mareen.

Mareen tried to nod in sincere thanks, but she was almost thrown off her feet by an explosion of steam as Gonzo stopped yet another fireball. It was madness. Mareen didn't know if the moisture covering her skin was perspiration, or water, or blood, or all three. It didn't matter. She continued to fight for her life.

* * *

Liangyu dispassionately watched the battle before her and made a decision. Their enemies were surprisingly powerful and resourceful, but the thralls had worn them down. It was a good thing, too, as she was almost out of them.

"Ghinsja, start attacking with the fog again before the steam makes it impossible to do so anymore. I think they're softened up enough now."

She glanced over at Matilda. The pretty archer was drawing another arrow. Liangyu ordered, "Target the tall, dark pervert. He is the one creating the barriers."

"But the barriers will stop my arrows," Matilda said, frowning.

"Just do as I say, you fool girl," Liangyu hissed, and the other woman blanched. It seemed she was stupid after all. It was good she was at least pretty, but Matilda needed to learn to play to her strengths. Anyone with a brain would have found it obvious that keeping the shield mage busy was necessary for Ghinsja to do damage with the fog.

Liangyu wanted a report of what else was going on around them on the battlefield. Anz'wei should have been back by now. However, she knew that Ghinsja didn't have an unlimited amount of power and a lot was going on. She decided not to bother her second-in-command for the time being.

Liangyu glanced around and noticed that not all of her mercenaries were engaged yet. "Mourad," she snarled. "What are you waiting for? Get out there and do your job."

Mourad's face held no expression at all as she answered, "Yes, Lady Liangyu."

Liangyu watched the large, cow-like woman jog forward. It was hard to hire good help these days.

* * *

When Uluula saw the hands made of fog begin to attack again, she knew what might come next. She smoothly cut the head off a dead, rotting monster with her blazing *jaalba* and located Thirsty. Then she flicked her arm out, activating her enchanted bracer. A line shot out and pulled Uluula through the air, much faster than she could run.

She barely got there in time, interposing her enchanted shield between Thirsty and the vicious arrow that whizzed out from the fog. Thirsty's eyes widened and he said, "What the—"

"Silence, degenerate. I do not agree with anything you do. However, you are part of my team, and my husband will be angry at me if I let you die."

Thirsty sputtered. "Bitch, please. You—"

Uluula ignored Thirsty and yelled, "Gonzo, come protect Thirsty! Thirsty, deal with the fog hands! Vitaliya, start working with Gonzo to create more steam and clear up this fog! Mareen, you're with me. Let's take out the dead things."

Her orders given, Uluula shot out towards one of the remaining animated corpses. She heard Thirsty grumbling behind her and secretly grinned.

Her situation was dangerous, she very well may die, but damn the Maker did she feel alive!

* * *

Mareen heard Uluula's orders, but she already had her hands full fighting the undead abominations. In fact, she was so focused on her task, she nearly missed a big woman coming out of the fog with a huge sword. She barely saw the sword swinging at her head out the corner of her eye.

Mareen got her hammer up in the nick of time to block. The two weapons met with great force, the sound making Mareen's ears ring. The other woman narrowed her eyes in surprise. If Mareen had been a normal Terran, the middle-aged woman's strength coupled with the inertia of the large, wavy sword would have ended the fight right there.

Mareen had no idea who the other woman with close-cropped hair was, nor where she'd come from. All she knew was she was trying to take her life.

In the next few moments, nothing existed in Mareen's world other than the big woman in camouflage armor. She was deeply thankful for all the drills and training that Henry had put her through. She was stronger than her opponent, but far less skilled. As orb-Bonded, she was tougher than any human had a right to be, but she knew without a doubt that the warrior she faced would be able to end her.

All that saved her was her training. However, the other

woman's blessed steel sword still opened nasty wounds on her arms and legs. Mareen blocked a quick strike at her head, using the hook on the back of her hammer to lever the blade to the side before striking with the flat of her weapon.

The woman just danced to the side and Mareen growled in frustration. Despite all her orb-given strength, there was a huge gap in experience between her and her opponent.

Mareen wasn't sure she could live through this duel. She might survive a clean strike to the body due to her natural armor, but she wasn't in a hurry to test the theory. She narrowed her eyes and growled. She wasn't going down without a fight.

However, luckily for Mareen, there were other people on the battlefield. A wave of fire flashed past her head and impacted the camouflage-armored fighter. The woman screamed and, without thinking, Mareen kicked forward, delivering a glancing blow with all her augmented strength.

The big woman flew out into the fog, her large, wavy sword clattering to the ground in front of Mareen. She blinked and glanced behind her. Vitaliya waved briefly before shooting another tongue of flame into the fog.

Mareen quickly glanced around but couldn't see any more walking dead.

Suddenly, the fog began to clear. Mareen looked around in confusion until she realized what was really happening. All the nearby fog was flowing down to the ground, creating a thick, roiling blanket close to the earth.

She panicked and jumped back, trying to get closer to the other members of her group. In horror, she felt a fog hand reach up and grab her ankle, tripping her.

In that moment, with the grey blanket concentrated along the ground and the surrounding fog thinning, Mareen saw her real enemies in the distance.

A woman held a bow, another held a staff, and two other women stood behind them. Of the two women standing in the rear, one was Areva. She wore blue and white, her hair dyed in pink stripes. The other was Terran and looked Asian. Her robe was dark and beautiful, with intricate needlework up the sides.

Mareen heard two dings in her head. Text began scrolling over her left eye:

Do'Birnwi Mo Ghinsja, Exile Born Areva, Berban

Dolos Orb, Specialist Type, Generation 1

Third Rank

and

"Death Witch" Liangyu, Terran, Chinese

Dolos Orb, Specialist Type, Generation 1

Fourth Rank

"Oh no," whispered Mareen.

CHAPTER TWENTY

Brilliance

Checkmate, thought Liangyu. She watched in satisfaction as all her enemies were brought down by the grasping fog hands, pinned to the ground, and rendered helpless. The darker-skinned woman in wood armor struggled mightily, but even her obviously enhanced strength couldn't break the bonds that held her.

"Good job, Ghinsja," praised Liangyu. The other woman nodded, her brow furrowed in concentration, trying to hide her beaming at the compliment. Liangyu grinned inwardly. Her subordinates were easy to manipulate.

The Death Witch was in a great mood. She was about to be objectively wealthy. She would be able to save her descendants from drudgery, make them safe, and disappear into the mists of the future. Liangyu pointed at the dark man on the ground, the pervert wearing strange clothing. "Kill that one first," she ordered Raquel.

"Understood," the homely merc responded. She held out a hand and a ball of fire appeared on her palm, spinning while growing brighter.

Raquel released her fire magic and the bolt of energy struck the dark man in the leg. Each enemy had a fog hand over their mouths, preventing them from crying out, but Liangyu could hear the pervert scream past it. "What are you doing?" she demanded. "I said to kill him."

"Yes, but this group cost me some of my people. Don't you think we should make them suffer a bit?" Raquel's expression was neutral, but Liangyu could see the spite burning in her eyes as she began forming another fire attack.

Liangyu wondered if she should let the mercenary leader have her way. On the other hand, insubordination just created more insubordination. She was opening her mouth, about to answer, when the red-haired woman's head abruptly flew off. A heavy spray of blood arced through the air and splashed Liangyu across the face. The huge bronze circle blade that had decapitated the mercenary leader flew past the body into the distance.

She was so shocked, it took Liangyu a moment to process what was happening. An Asian man, the enemy Ghinsja had identified as probably being orb-Bonded, had appeared out of the fog at a dead run. He had the well-dressed Mo'hali boy at his heels. The man snarled and spun around. "Bezzi-ibbi!" he shouted. "Help the others!"

The Asian man with the goatee turned and Liangyu felt the gaze of impending death. After spending centuries molding and controlling the antithesis of life, she recognized when it touched her. She was truly about to die.

She didn't want to attack directly, but she didn't have a choice. Everything was happening too fast and her three remaining thralls were still behind her. Even if they had been closer, she didn't trust them to keep her safe from this man.

She exhaled, the breath carrying much of her power with it. Her body immediately grew weak. The cost was great, but her breath formed a dark cloud like living smoke, shooting towards the muscular Asian man and melting into his chest. He fell to his knees with an anguished grunt, glaring at her, struggling to move. The dark magic Liangyu had just cast began immediately bleeding into his eyes.

"Matilda, use the artifact weapon! Now! Ghinsja, keep the rest of them pinned!" she yelled, her energy fading so fast the volume of her voice noticeably dropped.

Everything was going to hell! She had to stay strong, but she was feeling woozy. The direct magic attack had taken its toll. With iron resolve, Liangyu gritted her teeth and focused on maintaining consciousness.

Her attack would definitely kill the man, but not right away, not if he was orb-Bonded. She needed him gone before he could do any more damage.

* * *

Bezzi-ibbi ran forward, skidding to a stop next to Thirsty and using a cloth to smother the flames on his friend's pants leg. The Jaguar Clan boy growled when he heard Henry cry out, but didn't look back. He needed to focus.

When the fog hands from the ground latched on to him with an iron grip, he released his Hero power, pushing it outward. He flexed his brain and extended his ability to Mareen's location, too. The invisible bubble he created was enough to suppress Thirsty and Mareen's power, but he merely focused on dissipating the fog. He hoped his intent would allow his friends to regain their power sooner, but either way, now at least they were safe from the grasping grey hands.

Mareen gasped and thrashed, undoing the releases on her armor and climbing to her knees. She yelled, "Henry! The Areva in the grey dress with the veil, Do Bir Mo Ghinsja or whatever. She's the one controlling the fog! The one with pink streaks in her hair!"

Bezzi-ibbi turned in time to see Henry cry out and lift a shaking arm. He wheezed as he aimed his exogun at Do'Birnwi Mo Ghinsja, the Areva orb-Bonded woman. A couple of the enemies began to shout, but before they could move, there was a sharp, hypersonic crack of Henry firing his last remaining bullet. The Areva woman fell back, a look of shock plastered across the half of her face that still remained.

* * *

"Matilda, use the weapon!" Liangyu's screamed as loud as she could, her eyes wild.

Ghinsja was dead. She was really dead. It was unreal.

Everything was ruined. Liangyu wasn't even sure if she'd be able to escape alive. Staying awake was taking most of her concentration, but she'd be damned if she didn't make the man that had killed her people pay. He was going to die anyway, but she wanted to watch his existence come to an end, even if it was her last act on Ludus.

* * *

When the fog began to lift, Aodh had shakily gotten to his feet. Time seemed to stand still for him when he saw Henry on his knees, obviously in great pain. Two enemies were still standing. The orb-Bonded woman—the text that scrolled over his left eye named her Liangyu—was swaying on her feet. She had a group of three large undead creatures behind her, but they weren't moving. However, the other woman had a huge, boxy contraption on her shoulder and she was manipulating levers on it in a near-panic. It had an opening that was pointed directly at Henry.

In that moment, Aodh's mind grew still and calm. He had no more worries, no doubts. He knew what he had to do. Henry was his friend and an important man. Aodh didn't matter. He was just a weak fire mage from a farming community nobody had ever heard of.

Aodh got up despite his fatigue and bruises, then sprinted forward as fast as he could. His determination was so great, he didn't even feel the familiar flash of fear as the bronze grenades on his belt jostled against each other.

He slid in front of Henry right before the blonde woman's unfamiliar weapon began to glow. Aodh stood between his friend and destruction, his arms spread wide. He had found his certainty. He could not stand by and passively watch the people he cared about get hurt. He might be a coward, but he'd protect those important to him with his last breath, with his life if necessary.

As the light enveloped him, Aodh felt at peace with his decision. He might be a coward, but now he knew he wouldn't live a life full of regret. With the burst of light came pain, pain that seemed to last an eternity in the space of a split second.

Aodh still felt no regrets as the brilliance took him.

* * *

Uluula got to her feet and moved as fast as she could, but the fog hands had wrenched her limbs around savagely while she'd been held down. She was sore in places she wasn't even aware she could be sore in. She tried to join the fight again as quickly as she could, but she'd been too late.

She'd seen when one of the two remaining enemy women lifted some kind of boxy contraption to her shoulder, and she'd watched in horror as it fired a beam that passed through Aodh and hit Henry. Two unearthly shrieks shattered the scene—Mareen and

Vitaliya's raw, vocal emotion overlaid each other, seeming to make the air vibrate.

Uluula felt her heart drop. The horrible tableau seemed to freeze until, a heartbeat later, Aodh and Henry disappeared. Not a trace of them remained.

She snarled, and before she knew it, despite her aching body, she was rocketing over the ground, her blazing halberd leaving a fiery tail. She noted the look of surprise on the blonde woman's face, feeling savage satisfaction as she slammed the blade of her weapon through the woman's chest. Uluula dimly noted angry tongues of flame flying past her shoulder towards the other woman, but one of the three remaining undead had intervened, soaking up the flames.

Vitaliya screamed incoherently as she threw her magic at Liangyu, the last remaining enemy. The Death Witch. The undead creature blocking all the attacks looked like a giant birdman with huge claws where its fingers should have been. Its dead eyes showed no intellect, but it held out a hand, generating a shield that stopped all of Vitaliya's attacks.

A huge spear of ice slammed into the barrier a moment later, Gonzo having recovered. Uluula wrenched her halberd out of the body of the blonde woman she'd just killed and turned in time to see Mareen throwing herself at the undead thing, tears streaming down her face. Her hammer hit with such force, the barrier shattered and she pulped half the bird creature's body in one swing.

Another undead monster stepped forward and backhanded Mareen. Her body flew across the ground to land in a sobbing heap.

Uluula felt anger rising to give company to her shame. She'd allowed Jason's best friend to be killed. How could she even look him in the eye again? However, she'd just watched her own best friend get attacked. Mareen could have been killed or crippled.

Uluula hissed and began stalking toward the dazed, orb-Bonded woman, Liangyu. The white-haired Areva woman was furious. She and her friends hadn't even chosen this fight! These *hravam* had attacked them first!

Lost in murderous thoughts, Uluula was shocked when she ran face first into an invisible shield. She blinked in surprise and confusion. Then she heard a voice that somehow chilled her soul. The voice stated, "That's enough of that. Go no further." Uluula felt her heart sink when Keeja and another woman descended from the sky.

Keeja looked distinctly unhappy, but the other woman, a dark Areva in a robe far too large for her, was grinning nastily.

* * *

Thirsty felt numb as she watched the two women slowly drift down to stand on the ground. Keeja alighted near Vitaliya, but the unfamiliar, dark Areva woman stood between Uluula and Liangyu. Thirsty heard a distant pop; the sound was familiar, but she dismissed it. Her eyes were transfixed on the new arrival. For some reason, she felt terrible dread.

Vitaliya sobbed and threw another stream of fire, but the new woman lazily waved her hand and the fire vanished. She tugged the neck of her oversized robe down, revealing a gold necklace like Keeja's. Even Thirsty knew what that meant.

The woman said, "Unfortunately, I cannot hold that attack against you since I had not announced myself yet. I am Biivan, High Priestess of Dolos. Please attack me again." She smiled.

Keeja growled, "I protest this, Biivan. We are not supposed to use our free actions like this. You are meddling in the affairs of orb-Bonded."

"I can do whatever I want within the rules. I am a High Priestess! For one of your supposed power, you act too timid for your station."

Keeja snarled, "Yes, I know your stance. I just had to spend this entire battle observing in the air with you, per our code, but I know your reputation. I would have accompanied you anyway to ensure you wouldn't bend the rules—exactly as you are now."

Biivan smirked. "My reputation? Is it because I experiment on children? Who cares? They are only mortals. How is my indulgence in my studies any different than giving orbs to mortals of different worlds on Ludus? How is it any different than supplying the Mo'hali with rings so they can kill themselves? How is it any different than those experiments you did a couple hundred years ago?"

"The difference," Keeja snarled, "is that you offer no choice. You just take, you do as you please. You act like you are a god."

"Am I not a god, at least to these small creatures?" Biivan gestured toward the Delvers. "You are a High Priestess. You should have more pride."

Thirsty sucked in a breath when she noticed Uluula take a step forward. The pale Areva woman set her shoulders and calmly said, "Please move. I have business with the orb-Bonded woman behind you."

"Oh, I don't think so, little toy. In fact, white hair? Are you of the Blue? Some things never change in the Quadrant, do they?" Biivan laughed. The sound was dark, ominous, and made Thirsty feel dirty. "No, I think I will stay right here and intervene until Liangyu is ready to move again. I have to salvage this disaster somehow, even if it means only saving my mortal business partner. We have an understanding. It's hard to find tools with the... malleable morality necessary to pursue my research."

Thirsty glanced around and was disheartened by the state of the team. Gonzo was barely conscious. Mareen was hugging herself and sobbing so deeply that she produced vibrations more than sound. Vitaliya was dazed, probably from overexerting her power. The red-haired woman's eyes were dull, almost lifeless, but her tears fell to the ground in a steady rain of despair.

Thirsty wanted to help, but she was down to a single

enchanted bracelet left. Without her magic, she was just a fierce bitch with great fashion sense. Unfortunately, none of that would be of much use against a High Priestess. She couldn't even attack with words. If she tried to read this new, evil wannabe munchkin Biivan bitch, it'd probably just get her killed for no reason.

She glanced at Keeja, hoping the other High Priestess would do something, but the demigoddess just stood there with her hands on her hips, a look of open disgust on her face.

Uluula seemed to read Thirsty's mind. She asked, "Keeja, a little help? We need to at least find out where Henry and Aodh went. If I have to, I'm going to cut that Liangyu woman's fingers off until she tells us what we want to know."

Thirsty swallowed. The way Uluula spoke made it clear she had been entirely serious.

Biivan snorted, the sound ugly and condescending. "Keeja, you let these tiny beings talk to you like this? And you keep company with mortals stupid enough to even suggest torturing the Death Witch?" The creepy High Priestess laughed for a while, holding her sides, but suddenly stopped, growing still. She glared glaring at Uluula and in a different tone she hissed, "Perhaps I should dissect you while you're living? You dare even hold a weapon in my presence?"

"Keeja," Thirsty wailed, "help her! Please!" The entire world was falling apart. The wounded drag queen was watching her friends all fall and fail. It couldn't all be for nothing!

"I'm sorry, my legs are restrained with cable." Keeja's sounded miserable. "Biivan is bending the rules, but she's using a free action like I did when I went to the dungeon with Jason. If you attack her, she has the right to kill you even though you are under my protection."

"Yes, white-haired child of the Blue, strike me," Biivan purred at Uluula. "Perhaps I can send you to where the artifact weapon sent your friends—oblivion. Would you like to follow them?"

Behind the evil High Priestess, Liangyu swayed, one of her zombie creatures holding her upright. Thirsty thought she heard the Death Witch whisper something.

Uluula gripped her weapon tightly and slowly began moving to an attack stance when a voice rang out that shocked Thirsty to the bone. "Uluula, stop, come back."

Thirsty turned her head and felt tears of relief when she saw something entirely unexpected. Jason strode out of the dying mists, his bronze armor covered in condensation. The tall man had his sword in his hand. He was slightly panting, and his expression was set in a snarl.

Thirsty felt a sense of hope chased by a chill. It was great to see Jason after he'd been gone for so long, but the man didn't have the look of someone who was in control.

Thirsty twisted her last remaining bracelet and sincerely hoped she wouldn't have to use it.

CHAPTER TWENTY-ONE

Silver Eyes

Mourad was alive. In excruciating pain, but alive. She was aware her situation could be a lot worse, and felt grateful for her continued existence. However, since her present was accounted for, now it was time to secure her future.

After fighting with the freakishly strong, dark-skinned woman wielding an enormous hammer, Mourad had forsaken the battle, eventually leaving behind all the sounds entirely. Nobody from her team had checked on her after she'd been knocked into the fog. She knew the lack of loyalty was usually just part of being a mercenary, but it still rankled. Still, she'd hated working for Liangyu, and with everyone distracted, she knew she might be able to make some of her own luck.

She'd been spending the last few days watching carefully for opportunities to exploit, opportunities exactly like the one she currently found herself in. The big, armored woman limped along, nursing her side and cursing softly. The burn she'd suffered hadn't been too bad, just surprising. Meanwhile, the dark-skinned girl had hurt her badly, and it hadn't even been a solid blow!

The world wasn't fair. Even as skilled as Mourad was, against an orb-Bonded opponent, she'd only roughly been on the same level. Maybe she could fix that soon. The warrior woman smiled grimly. She fought through the pain and made her way back to the military outpost that Liangyu had been using as a base.

Mourad wasn't sure, but she had a strong suspicion that Liangyu hid all the team's valuables and treasure, probably because she wanted to only wear her sheer, fancy robes to maintain the dark, mysterious look. Mourad snorted. Vanity was for fools.

The building Mourad headed towards was a small, locked outbuilding behind the cabin that Liangyu had been sleeping it. Mourad had observed that some of Liangyu's thralls had always managed to be loitering nearby.

Liangyu probably thought that by keeping her treasures in a different place than she slept, they'd be safe. Mourad rolled her eyes. The Death Witch had fallen victim to a common trap for the intelligent and powerful—she'd begun to believe her own hype. Especially being so long lived, she'd had a long time to develop glaring blind spots.

Mourad slowed her pace and crept around the side of the cabin near her target. The rough, splintered logs scraped her exposed arms as she hugged the side of the building. She was trying to be as stealthy as possible, but she was badly hurt. She'd lost her sword, too. That stung; it had been worth a fortune. The only option now was to hopefully find another, larger fortune. There was sure no way in hell she was going back to the battlefield.

She crept up to the corner of the building, peeking out and darting back, smiling broadly. One of Liangyu's thralls was standing in front of the outbuilding, more of a shed. The undead creature was strangely still and staring into space. Mourad shrugged. The undead creature's immobility just meant her job would be easier.

She pulled her trusty throwing spike from the rear of her belt. The weapon had cost her a great deal of money in the distant past, but it'd been one of the best investments she had ever made. The low-level enchantments on the spike made it weigh more after it left her hand, and maintain speed better in the air. It had taken her a long time to master throwing it, but after she had, it was the best concealable, ranged weapon she had ever owned.

She breathed deeply, concentrating on the target she knew was only about thirty feet away. She had to attack as fast as possible so that, hopefully, Liangyu wouldn't notice the loss. The big merc had no desire to tangle directly with the Death Witch. That path led to certain death.

Mourad kissed her throwing spike for good luck, cocked her

arm back, stepped from concealment, and threw. As soon as the spike left her hand, she relaxed—she could tell the throw had been true. The spike took the thrall—some sort of arachnid monster—directly in the head and dropped it without any fuss.

A second later, Mourad's entire body lit up with screaming nerve endings. She bent over in anguish, hissing as she waited for the pain to pass. She'd forgotten for a moment that she had been so badly injured.

After she could walk again, the muscular woman crept forward, retrieved her spike, and forced open the door to the outbuilding. It didn't take her long to find the loose board on the floor and she shook her head. *This is child's play*, she thought.

Her eyes lit up as she regarded the crushed velvet bag full of Dolos orbs, spirit stones, and magic jewelry that Liangyu had taken from their victims. She quickly tied the bulging sack to her belt and limped away as fast as she could.

She desperately hoped Liangyu got herself killed, but that was probably wishful thinking. Barring that, she wanted to be long gone by the time the Death Witch realized she'd been burglarized.

* * *

Jason felt tired, frustrated, shocked, but above all, utterly furious. On top of his group having been attacked without provocation, he had never felt so useless and powerless in his life. He hadn't been able to use his magic in the fog, and he'd been forced to physically run back to his friends. Then, finally, the fog began to clear.

He'd teleported forward a few times, tired from running so hard, even with his Endurance skill. As he flashed forward, he'd learned some terrible things.

He passed by Yanno-ibbi and Rark-han, lying in pools of their own blood. He hadn't stopped to check on the Mo'hali men. He felt guilty, but he didn't know how critical the timing of his arrival could be.

When he'd gotten closer to the main group, he'd felt his heart drop and he'd feared the worst. Everyone was down or wounded. The entire situation looked terrible. Jason had stood still in the dying fog, and nobody had seen him. Instead of rushing in, he'd watched events unfold with a growing sense of shock and emptiness.

He'd seen the scrolling information over his left eye about Liangyu. He'd listened to the terse exchange between Biivan and members of his group. He'd learned that Aodh and Henry were gone.

Henry, his best friend, the person who'd had guarded his back and kept him sane from his first day on Ludus…was gone. Jason hadn't been there for him. He hadn't been there for his best friend in his time of need.

All his other friends were hurt and bloodied. Some might be dead, for all he knew.

Jason had failed. He had catastrophically dropped the ball. His reflexive teleport up into the sky when the ambush started had prevented him from fighting alongside his team. His absence might have cost his friends' lives. The way he'd let his mother down as a kid paled in comparison. He'd told himself he'd never fail anyone he cared about again, but here he was. Henry was gone.

His friend was gone. It was hard to form coherent thoughts past that fact.

Also, someone was threatening Uluula, his wife. Someone. Was. Threatening. His. Wife. She was in danger. The sweet, white-haired Areva woman who'd questioned her own culture to be with Jason. The brave, honest, loyal, beautiful person that he had been lucky enough to meet on a hostile planet. A woman he had rescued from a lonely cell, who'd become the most important person in his life, the woman he wanted to spend the rest of his life with.

They were threatening his wife.

No.

Jason had heard enough. "Uluula, stop, come back." He called Uluula away from the last remaining enemies and began stomping forward, feeling the rage overtaking him again. He only cared slightly that he was heading towards a High Priestess.

She had been threatening his wife.

Uluula fell back, stopping near Jason and looking conflicted. She looked like she wanted to hug him, flee, and fight at his side all at once. She looked between Biivan and Jason. "My love, I—"

Jason shook his head. "No, go with Keeja. I'm sorry. I'm sorry I let you all down. I won't do it again. Never again."

"But you—"

Jason stalked forward, his thoughts turning red. His heart burned like a volcano, magma flowing through his veins at a quickening pace. Jason fed the rage. He gave it everything he had. All of his other emotions went into the fire. All of his rational thought fed the blaze. When he ran out of things to shove into the growing inferno of his terrible anger, he began feeding it magic, dumping raw power into himself, into his soul.

He thought he could hear voices at the edge of his mind. He ignored them, focusing on his sword, *Breeze*. His grip tightened.

When his muscles cramped, he just kept feeding magic to the growing wildfire inside of him. When racking pain came, he welcomed it. When he felt his soul grow dark, he embraced the change.

…Threatening his wife! His WIFE.

Decades of shame, years of tormenting himself for allowing those closest to him to be harmed, came crashing back. All the powerlessness, frustration, and regret felt over an entire lifetime assaulted him all at once, amplified by his magic.

NOT ANYMORE.

He would never stand by again and let someone threaten the health or life of a loved one. He'd never endure standing on the sidelines and observing someone important to him be hurt again, especially and most importantly his wife.

He didn't care if he destroyed himself in the process; he was going to eradicate anyone or anything that threatened those dear to him.

Jason's eyes narrowed and gave in to his darkest emotions. He gave in to the power thrumming through his body and became something new, something dangerous.

* * *

Uluula had conflicting emotions as she watched Jason glide past. Overall, and it shamed her a bit to admit, she felt overwhelming relief. At least she wasn't alone anymore, the last standing member of the group. A part of her knew that her husband might be walking into danger, but she'd been willing to risk her life just moments before, too. Fair was fair.

Still, she didn't know what Jason was going to do and it was making her nervous. She trusted Jason's judgment, but although it rankled, they really couldn't afford to provoke a High Priestess.

Despite the danger, deep down, Uluula held on to hope. Henry and Jason had somehow managed to keep themselves and the rest of Delvers LLC alive since they'd arrived to Ludus. Uluula desperately wanted to believe in her husband. *He surely wouldn't be foolish enough to attack a High Priestess...right?*

However, as Jason continued forward, she could feel his anger coming off of him in waves, almost like a physical thing. She wanted to support her husband, but she didn't know what to do. Jason was their only hope of surviving the situation with any kind of answers about where Aodh and Henry had gone.

Deep in the pit of her stomach, she suddenly felt dread. Uluula's eyes few open. *Henry.* Jason's best friend...was gone. Missing. *Oh no!* She silently screamed in her mind. Jason probably knew!

She reached out to her husband, opening her mouth to call him. She took a step forward, her heart lurching in her chest, her entire being overcome with a mixture of love and fear.

She was too late.

Jason exploded.

His form burst out like a living cloud. Inky darkness with pinpoints of light provided a mesmerizing kaleidoscope of moving patterns. It looked like a window to the starry heavens hung in the air for a couple moments before snapping back to where Jason had been standing. Uluula gasped.

Where her husband had been standing before now stood a shadow person with silver eyes. Jason's dark silhouette roiled, flashes of light randomly zigzagging from one side to the other. The only way Uluula could have known the new figure was even Jason anymore was his grip on his sword, *Breeze.*

However, even *Breeze* had changed. The low-level enchantments Thirsty had put on the weapon in the past had never been visible before, but now Breeze crackled with energy, arcs of electricity leaping off the blade to Jason's shadow form with no obvious effect.

But most disconcerting at all, Uluula heard music. Just like when Keeja had used her power in the past, Uluula…experienced music when she focused on Jason. It was a song she recognized, "I Stand Alone" by a Terran band with a ridiculous name, Godsmack. The song was one of her husband's favorites.

Uluula immediately knew what she was experiencing—she was somehow hearing Jason's soul song. *How is this possible?* Only Holders like Keeja could manifest a soul song…Uluula put a hand to her mouth, tears in her eyes. *What is happening?*

Biivan's haughty expression under her cowl dropped. She took a half step back. Uncertainty had replaced all the venom she'd had in her voice before. "What is this—"

The demigoddess didn't get a chance to complete the thought. Jason, or whatever Jason had become, darted forward, *Breeze* descending in a glittering, sparking arc.

* * *

Jason was dimly aware that whatever was happening to him was not normal. However, he was too angry to actually form any thoughts or questions about it. In the back of his mind, he dimly heard a Godsmack song stuck in his head. He thought it was appropriate.

He knew he was going to do his best to kill a High Priestess now. He was past lying to himself at this point. He was going to fucking destroy her.

She had been threatening his wife. *Unforgivable.* His thoughts were heavy and dark, their edges as sharp as razor blades.

He would destroy anyone who threatened his family. He felt this truth in his bones. Jason dimly recognized the electricity arcing off his blade but paid it no mind. *Limitbreak,* a corner of his mind murmured. The whispers around his spirit grew louder and Jason listened.

He was going to destroy anyone who hurt his friends, those who THREATENED HIS WIFE!

He flickered forward, closing with his enemy. Every cell of his body resonated with his rage and indignation. He slowed his perception of time as he moved, noting every flicker of emotion that crossed Biivan's face. The number of expression changes he saw in her face in the span of a moment allowed the rational part of his mind to deduce that Biivan had enhanced senses too.

Jason delivered a devastating cut from a modified *vom tag* stance. He felt grim satisfaction as the blade descended. Biivan was not a woman to him anymore, she was not even a person. She was an obstacle to crush. However, somehow Biivan's hand came up with lightning speed and materialized a glowing sword, blocking Jason's blow. Her eyes widened as the two weapons met and stopped, the null-time layer on *Breeze*'s blade countering Biivan's obvious strength.

The High Priestess snarled and batted Jason's sword away

from the side, flat to flat, and changed her motion to strike impossibly fast at his throat. Jason was dimly aware that he could hear a thrumming melody now from Biivan, sounding something like old Earth opera music but with more percussion.

Jason's heightened awareness warned him of the glittering, curved blade on a collision course for his neck. He flexed his magic and teleported away. The corner of his mind that still retained rational thought knew to move the fight away from his friends and his wife.

He snarled, teleporting above the shore of the nearby lake. Biivan made a beeline for him, flying at a breakneck speed, the air around her growing hazy from the power rolling off of her body.

Jason dispassionately waited for her to come, noting that he was effortlessly flying in place, manipulating time and space. It was as natural as breathing for him now. He lifted a hand, his fingers pointed forward, and unleashed hell. Wicked needles of null-time shot out at Biivan, who avoided them at the last second, flinging her body to the side.

The shadow man darted forward, his silver eyes wild as he followed up with a few swift, brutal cuts, chasing Biivan toward the ground. The woman snarled, a corona of energy erupting from her body to incinerate Jason, but he'd already teleported away.

Jason felt deep, suffocating rage as he darted in, aiming a thrust at Biivan's back from a floating *ochs* stance. Somehow, Biivan spun in time to block the attack with her scintillating blade.

The small corner of Jason's mind that could still think clearly noted the sword looked like a shotel from back on Earth.

He bared his teeth and threw a null-time needles blast into Biivan's face, but she somehow generated a marigold-colored shield that stopped the attack cold. The next couple seconds, Jason's glowing eyes narrowed as he traded blows with Biivan. He had a longer reach with *Breeze*, but they were flying, his opponent was more skilled, and Biivan was also faster and stronger than he was. By a lot.

Before Biivan managed to cleave Jason's head from his shoulders, he had teleported away. After he had some space, he slashed forward with *Breeze* and unleashed a dark arc of destructive energy at the distant High Priestess. This time, the demigoddess couldn't create a shield in time, crossing her arms as the attack struck.

Jason felt savage glee, hoping he'd destroyed his enemy, but Biivan uncrossed her arms and glared at him. She hadn't suffered any damage at all other than her destroyed robe fluttering to the ground. She'd been wearing some sort of metallic singlet underneath, revealed now along with her dark, sharp-featured appearance.

"I don't know what you are, or what—" Biivan began, chewing her words. Jason didn't care what she had to say. He wanted her to die.

He teleported behind the Areva woman, too close to use his

sword, but smashed *Breeze*'s null-time-enhanced pommel on the back of her head. The High Priestess yowled like a startled cat, falling out of the sky.

Jason didn't relent. He followed up with another slashing arc of energy. Biivan blocked the attack, waving her hand and shielding herself with yellow energy. Jason teleported next to her and slashed with *Breeze*, the sword's blade alive with spitting electricity. Biivan blocked with her shotel and the dark-skinned High Priestess snarled. Her eyes were crazed as she thrust a hand at Jason, generating a brilliant golden orb of energy.

The enraged orb-Bonded flexed his mind, willing a field of time to surround the attack, slowing it. He flew past the energy orb, putting his closed fists together before violently separating them towards Biivan. The attack ripped apart time and space itself. Biivan crossed her arms, defending herself again.

Bass from "I Stand Alone" thumped in his head as he teleported away, simultaneously releasing the time dilation he'd placed on Biivan's energy orb. The projectile zipped off into the distance, generating a bone-jarring, golden explosion on the horizon.

Jason's heavy attack hadn't noticeably damaged Biivan, but it ripped apart a swath of trees on the ground below, made the water of the lake explode into mist, and violently dismantled a rock outcropping.

He teleported again, but this time Biivan had been waiting for it. As soon as he was back in regular space, he barely had time to react to another explosive energy orb flung towards him. Jason managed to slash with *Breeze*, generating another arc of destructive energy that met the orb in midair.

Both attacks exploded together in a violent crash of destructive energy. Jason willed himself to fly away from the blast, and the wave of pressure and heat that actually reached him didn't have any real effect on his shadow body.

Biivan screeched, her movements and attacks growing wilder, but no less powerful as the battle raged in the sky. She rushed at Jason several times, and the air around her actually seemed hazy with power. The tiny, analytical portion of Jason's mind that remained knew that continuing to trade blows with her was just waiting for death. She was too fast, too strong, and too skilled.

Without warning, Jason teleported straight up into the air as high as he dared, holding his breath. He needed more time!

The pinpricks of starlight in Jason's shadow form began spinning wildly as he fed more power to *Breeze*, causing the blade to throw off thick, angry arms of electricity. He only spent a couple moments charging his blade, but his instincts warned him of coming danger and he teleported. After his hop, a golden orb of explosive energy sped through the space he'd just been hovering in. The attack shot up into the sky, out of sight.

Jason teleported back down towards the lake below and barely had time to block as Biivan came screaming in out of nowhere, slashing with her glowing, curved sword. As *Breeze* met the High Priestess's shotel, Jason pushed as hard as he could, engaging in a corps-à-corps, sword against sword. Then he pushed with magic as hard as he could through his sword.

Angry tree branches of lightning leapt from the blade, slamming into Biivan. The demigoddess screamed in rage and pain, momentarily falling back as her exposed skin smoked. However, as Jason watched, the dark patches where she'd been burned rapidly healed, leaving her skin flawless again.

Biivan shrieked, the sound slicing through the sky, spreading tremors of hate and madness. The High Priestess redoubled her attacks, sending waves of golden energy at Jason, her attacks growing even more erratic than before.

Jason bared his teeth, listening to the voices muttering around his soul. He needed more power. He needed more weapons. He ignored his growing headache and the pains shooting through his body from his neck and shoulders.

His fury ran through his body like an electric current and he embraced it. He wanted to rip his enemy apart. He just needed more power!

CHAPTER TWENTY-TWO

The Ravager

Bezzi-ibbi watched in awe as his brother, Jason-ibbi, fought a High Priestess to a standstill in the sky. Such a thing, only heard of in ancient songs and history books, was actually taking place before his eyes. The hair on the back of his neck stood on end and his tail bristled.

It was common knowledge that High Priestesses were the most powerful beings on Ludus. To challenge them was death, yet Jason-ibbi was fighting Child Thief Biivan paw to paw. Bezzi-ibbi felt deep pride as he watched his Clan brother duel one of the most evil High Priestesses on the planet. Jason-ibbi brought incredible honor to the Jaguar Clan through his actions.

Even if Bezzi-ibbi died this day, despite all the hardship he'd been through, he could not have been more proud of himself and his family. And if he lived to see another dayrise, he would have the foundation to become a great Jaguar Troubadour!

Nearby, Bezzi-ibbi heard Gonzo whistle in disbelief. He glanced over and saw Uluula with a hand over her mouth, her eyes wide as she witnessed her husband fight in a duel to the death in midair. The rest of the group was watching with rapt attention too, the only exception being Mareen, who lay in a fetal position, softly sobbing as she held herself.

Bezzi-ibbi hissed as he realized the last enemy, Liangyu, had disappeared with her last two undead minions. He had no idea where she'd gone, and there was just enough fog left to hide her passage. Bezzi-ibbi couldn't do anything about it now, but it bothered him that such a powerful enemy was unaccounted for. She'd also escaped with any answers about what had happened to Henry-ibbi, too.

The Jaguar Clan heir shook himself. He needed to move. He passed Mareen and gently placed a hand on her shoulder. He understood. Henry had been her heart song. Bezzi-ibbi chose to believe that such a great warrior would somehow find his way back to them. If not, he would merely be hunting with the ancestors before Bezzi-ibbi saw him again. It was only a matter of time either way.

He had to find Yanno-ibbi and check on Rark-han. He did not know if his uncle was hunting with the ancestors yet. He had a feeling he already knew Rark-han's fate, but he didn't want to risk a storm while hunting.

Bezzi-ibbi padded towards the Battlewagon, figuring it was the best place to start looking for his kin. He feared the worst, but would not give in to his worries. He kept an eye out for any remaining undead creatures and also warily watched the sky to witness Jason's fight.

He found Rark-han in exactly the same spot where he's saved Bezzi-ibbi's life. The boy bit his lip with enough pressure that his fangs drew blood. There would be time for mourning later, time for honor. There was nothing he could do for the wolf Mo'hali man, but his uncle might still be of this world.

He smelled the blood before he actually found Yanno-ibbi. Bezzi-ibbi rushed forward and checked the older Mo'hali man's pulse before sighing in relief. His uncle was somehow still alive. He was terribly cut in several places, but the resourceful man had crafted tourniquets out of strips of cloth to stop the worst of the bleeding. He was unconscious and his breathing was shallow, but he was still alive.

Bezzi-ibbi gritted his teeth and blinked away a handful of tears. He didn't have time for that. He had to get to work. He wasn't big enough yet to carry his uncle, so he hissed an apology before dragging him. Mareen wasn't at her best, but she was still probably Yanno-ibbi's best hope to survive.

Bezzi-ibbi struggled, his tired muscles screaming in agony as he pulled his wounded uncle by the man's undamaged leg. When he finally reached the rest of the team, he rested on his haunches in exhaustion. It was eerie how quiet everyone was other than Mareen's soft sobs and Vitaliya's occasional sniff. Every gaze was fixed on the sky.

Jason suddenly flashed into view, followed by Biivan hot in pursuit. The Areva High Priestess snarled, savagely hacking at Jason with her curved sword.

Bezzi-ibbi crossed his arms in worry. Jason seemed to be teleporting more often and his soul song was not as loud as it had been. Meanwhile, Biivan didn't seem to be tiring at all. The evil demigoddess had Jason on the run.

She began pumping her arms, launching multiple exploding orbs at Jason, catching him off guard right after he teleported again. He slipped away, but not before creating a shimmering shield at an angle to deflect an exploding orb. The energy blast rocketed into the lake where it detonated, launching water and debris high up into the air.

Bezzi-ibbi focused on maintaining his balance as the ground shook, a wave of pressure washing over him. *Jason-ibbi is creating entire shields of null-time?* He shook his head in amazement. His brothers were already becoming living legends.

However, his earlier assessment that Jason was tiring had unfortunately been correct. The combatants were close enough in the sky now for Bezzi-ibbi to watch everything. He was mildly worried that they were getting too close, but no place nearby was truly safe with Biivan throwing explosive energy around. This fact was probably why nobody else was taking cover, either.

The Jaguar Clan boy's ears pricked forward as he watched one particularly furious exchange. The strikes and parries were so fast, Bezzi-ibbi doubted the Terran Delvers could see each individual blow.

Suddenly, Jason managed to get a solid cut on Biivan and Bezzi-ibbi's grinned in triumph! However, his heart fell again when Biivan snarled, backed off, and her body healed itself. Even her silver singlet mended, looking completely whole again.

It wasn't fair. Jason's intimidating dark form flickered; his glowing silver eyes narrowed. He began launching some sort of null-time attacks at Biivan, but Bezzi-ibbi had tracked the truth. Jason was being worn down.

About a minute later, Jason slashed his blade in the air, creating one last crescent of energy racing toward Biivan, but she crossed her arms over her body, generating a pale yellow shield. After the wave passed, she stood proud in the sky again, openly sneering. Steam rose from her skin, but she ignored it.

Suddenly, Jason's shadow form wavered. His silver eyes faded away, the twinkling shadow that covered his body drifted off like smoke, and his limp body began to fall.

Bezzi-ibbi gasped and Uluula shouted, "Jason, no!" The entire group could do nothing but watch helplessly as he fell, though. There was no way any of them could make it in time to try catching him. Uluula fell to her knees, landing bonelessly as she witnessed her husband's defeat.

Bezzi-ibbi watched grimly as Biivan grinned, the evil woman beginning to follow Jason to the ground. This was the end. She'd probably kill all of them. Bezzi-ibbi was resigned to his fate. He was honored he was able to have known such amazing people on his journey through the Day.

He slowly twisted his palms backwards in resignation, sure of his fate. However, he was still looking upwards when Keeja suddenly blurred forward and caught Jason in the sky. Bezzi-ibbi gasped in surprise. He'd forgotten Keeja was even with them!

"What are you doing, Keeja?" screeched Biivan. "You're breaking the rules! Dolos will have your head for this!"

"I do not fear Dolos," replied Keeja with a sneer. She floated over to Uluula and gently set Jason down on the ground. "Give him room, he'll be fine. Just let him rest," she ordered the white-haired Areva woman. Uluula nodded, spastically dashing the tears from her eyes. Then slowly, stoically, she sat on the ground near Jason's head, resting a hand on his chest.

Standing in midair, Biivan shouted, "You can't do this, Keeja! You are breaking the rules! I'm going to kill every one of those pet mortals of yours and you are powerless to stop me!"

"So you admit you were trying to kill this man?" Keeja asked, pointing at the unconscious Jason.

"Of course I was, you *bvantisti hrando*! I'm going to finish the job, too, him and all your other little mortals!" Spittle flew from

Biivan's mouth as she screeched, "There is nothing you can do! You always follow the rules, like a good little pet! All those stories, all the other High Priestesses being afraid of you. It's all a ruse! You are nothing, a deceiver! Who are you to judge me? How dare you let this puking mortal attack me? They'll all die! I'll make them suffer!"

"I think not," replied Keeja, unruffled. She pointed at Jason and snapped her fingers. His sleeve fluttered down to the ground, revealing the mark Dolos had placed on him. "You just admitted to using lethal force on a priest of Dolos, personally chosen by his hand, no less."

"Wait, what?" Biivan's expression went from cruel to confused to frightened in an instant. "All Priestesses are female, and—"

In a blink, Keeja was simply gone. Wind billowed out in every direction, kicking up dust, dirt, and rocks from where she'd been standing. Her movement was so sudden, so fast, there was no warning before Keeja appeared before Biivan in the sky. Her hand effortlessly immobilized the evil High Priestess by the wrist above her sword hand.

Keeja's expression was devoid of emotion, cold. Bezzi-ibbi swallowed. *Keeja the Ravager*, he remembered her ancient title. The Jaguar Clan boy had secretly wondered how Keeja had such a dangerous reputation after observing her lazy, silly behavior the last few months, but the name didn't seem so farfetched after witnessing her new bearing.

Biivan struggled, trying to kick Keeja to get away. The taller High Priestess just smiled, effortlessly blocking each attack with her free hand. When Biivan tried forming an energy blast at point-blank range, Keeja casually punched the other woman in the jaw. The wet crack from Biivan's jaw snapping followed by the snap from Keeja breaking the wrist she was holding was sickening, and somehow loud enough to reach everyone on the ground.

The dark Arcva woman's glowing, curved blade fell from her nerveless fingers, twisting end over end before hitting the ground near the Battlewagon. Biivan gasped in pain and fear, the sound sharp enough to reach Bezzi-ibbi's ears. He watched the unfolding spectacle with wide eyes.

Keeja's voice was cold as she said, "You were not tricked. You were careless. You didn't scan. You made assumptions. I am truly not sorry for you. You are vermin with a power complex. If I were to claim I didn't get any satisfaction from doing my duty in this situation, I would be lying."

"No, wait, I didn't mean to say that—"

Keeja held Biivan steady, her iron grip on the other woman's broken arm preventing her from escaping. With a detached calm, Keeja brought her other hand up, pointer finger extended.

"No, please, you have—" Biivan's last words remained forever unfinished as Keeja's finger erupted in an eye-searing viridian energy beam. Bezzi-ibbi had to look away.

When he glanced up again, the afterimage of the attack was

still burned into his vision, but Biivan had been reduced to a headless corpse. Keeja dropped the body, letting it fall to the earth near the discarded sword.

Keeja shook her head and became her normal self again. The change was immediate. She called down, "Don't touch that body. It might still be dangerous, and I want to see if I can crack her n-space storage." Bezzi-ibbi found Keeja's sudden change in personality slightly disturbing. Henna-ibbi had always said, "Beware a hunter whose garb changes too often."

Which personality was the real Keeja?

The High Priestess's clothing billowed in the wind as she hovered in the air, putting her hand to her chin in thought. After a moment, she looked up at the sky and shouted, "I give this kill to Jason James Booth! He was instrumental in the death of Biivan, a High Priestess of Dolos!"

Bezzi-ibbi cocked his head after the announcement, alert for any new developments. However, nothing obvious happened. He shrugged and moved over to the rest of his group, most of whom almost seemed to almost be coming out of a trance with the battle in the sky being resolved.

The Jaguar Clan heir had always been told he was a brave boy, but Keeja was terrifying. He'd prefer to be standing with his friends when the demigoddess floated back down to them.

* * *

After the battle was over, Vitaliya suppressed her raging

emotions out of necessity. Only a couple more undead creatures were discovered wandering around. They'd seemed to have no more direction, and were immediately put down. The Death Witch had fled. One other attacker, the big, armored woman that Mareen had fought against, was missing too.

Vitaliya was irritated. Leaving enemies behind was unfortunate, especially enemies who had taken her Aodh from her. Her cousin was delicate and special...She ruthlessly suppressed her thoughts. She couldn't cry. There would be time to figure out how she was going to find little Aodh once the group got moving again. Aodh being sent away, being lost, was the only possibility she was willing to entertain.

He couldn't be dead.

She couldn't bear thinking about what that horrible woman had said before. Vitaliya rejected it. She was glad the bitch was dead.

Mareen was the most shaken and the least emotionally stable of the group. She'd still somehow managed to pull herself together to stabilize Yanno-ibbi's injuries and heal a few other wounds the group had sustained, but after that, she'd climbed into the back of the Battlewagon by herself.

Everyone left her alone to her grief.

The mood among the group was grim. They'd all survived, but Henry and Aodh were missing, and everyone had been bloodied and bruised. They could all very easily have died.

Eventually, everything that could be salvaged had been. Only three magicycles still worked, and one was sluggish now.

The group stood in a loose semicircle around Keeja. Jason was lying on the ground, still unconscious, Uluula cradling his head in her lap. When Vitaliya had first met the white-haired Areva women, she hadn't liked her much. Now she had to concede that Uluula was a fierce warrior and had a backbone made of bronze. She'd earned her respect.

"Why won't Jason wake up?" Uluula asked.

"Because he's dying," Keeja replied offhandedly, rummaging around in a sack she'd placed on the ground.

"What?" Uluula still sounded calm, but only just. Her voice rose slightly in volume, her eyes narrowed dangerously. "You said he'd be fine."

"I lied. He's dying. But luckily, we can fix him."

Uluula gritted her teeth and restrained herself with obvious effort, all while holding Jason's head protectively. "Please do what you can, if you can find the time, of course."

Keeja ignored the sarcasm. "I can definitely find time to help Jason after he displayed so much potential. He also allowed me to kill someone I have deeply despised for several hundred years." She looked up at the sky, muttering, "That was so, so incredibly satisfying."

Keeja suddenly turned, holding a hand out to Jason, and her vision grew unfocused for a moment. Before Uluula could even say anything, Keeja grumbled, "Yes, I'm fairly sure I'm right..."

From the sack she'd been searching, she produced a box. At first glance, it looked like the boxes that appeared after an orb-Bonded person was killed, the boxes that held an orb or a spirit stone. However, this one was several times larger. It had Jason's name on the lid. "I found this by Biivan's corpse," Keeja said offhandedly. "It's Jason's reward for killing Biivan."

"But you killed Biivan," Vitaliya stated, confused.

"Yes, we all saw it," said Gonzo. Thirsty just nodded. He'd been quiet, withdrawn ever since the battle ended.

"No, I had enough reason to give the win to Jason, and even though killing a High Priestess was not part of Dolos's game, Jason has been rewarded." Keeja opened the lid to the box and Vitaliya gasped. She couldn't even count how many spirit stones were in it at first glance. Keeja handed a spirit stone to Uluula. "Get him to swallow that and he should recover."

Uluula eyed the demigoddess out the corner of her eye, but eventually complied, rubbing Jason's throat so he'd swallow the spirit stone. As soon as he did, color almost immediately returned to his cheeks and he began breathing easier.

"There. Now we wait," pronounced Keeja.

"Why don't we just leave now? I want to quit this place," announced Vitaliya. The sooner they began to move, the quicker she could begin formulating a plan to look for little Aodh.

"No!" They all turned to see Mareen standing up in the back of the Battlewagon, her face wan. "We can't leave Henry behind!"

Saw some of the group looked down awkwardly. Vitaliya pressed her lips together tightly when she noticed they pointedly weren't looking at her, either. *Aodh is not dead! I'll show them,* she thought.

Keeja looked Mareen in the eye and said, "Henry is not anywhere nearby. I would sense it if he was." Mareen seemed to deflate a bit and settled back into the rear of the Battlewagon, ignoring the rest of the conversation.

Gonzo spoke up, patting Vitaliya on the shoulder. "We should wait for Jason to wake up since High Priestess Keeja said he will. None of us are still any good at driving the Battlewagon, anyway."

Vitaliya nodded. Her trainer was right, and more importantly, he knew about Aodh. Gonzo knew her secret. He would help her look for him, she was sure of it. Not for the first time, she was grateful that Gonzo had been the trainer assigned to her. It eased some of the burden she felt.

"Okay, fine, let's wait," said Bezzi-ibbi, shrugging. With that, the Jaguar Clan heir levered himself up from where he'd been sitting on the ground and began to walk away. He was obviously done with the conversation.

Vitaliya envied the boy. She wished she could care so little too. It must be nice to have no responsibilities. Meanwhile, she felt the weight of an entire country crushing down on her. The responsibility, the duty she had possibly failed at—she couldn't think about it. She couldn't dwell on it or she'd have trouble breathing. She had to focus on solutions to her problems.

She wished Jason would hurry and wake up.

CHAPTER TWENTY-THREE

Respect for the Fallen

Jason found himself sitting on his butt in the middle of a baseball field. With a start, he realized it was the baseball diamond where he used to play little league when he was a kid. From behind him, he heard a very distinctive voice say, "I thought a change of scenery was in order, again."

Jason sighed and turned to regard the purple cartoon cat.

His orb's cartoon avatar was lounging in a chair, sipping a drink of some kind. The drink and its glass also looked animated. The scene was a bit bizarre.

Jason sighed and rolled his eyes. He asked, "Can I have a chair?"

"Oh, of course!" said the purple cat. He waved a hand, and a cartoon chair rose out of the field near Jason's feet. Jason eyed it warily before he shrugged and sat down.

"You know, this isn't really real. You won't really feel any different if you're sitting or standing." The cat took a sip of his drink. The cartoon umbrella coming out the top was bright yellow with little pink hearts.

"Yes, the thought has occurred to me," Jason replied. He was weary already. Talking to his orb's avatar always gave him a great deal of useful information, but the more he did so, the stranger he found the entire experience. "So why are we talking today?"

"Ah, straight to the point! I like that!" The purple cat's crooked whiskers quivered as he smiled. He threw his drink behind him and it vanished before it hit the ground. "You were just dying! It was very interesting. I wasn't even aware that you could do what you did before you started to kick the bucket. I'm glad you're still alive, though. I really don't want to die with you."

"Wait...what?"

"Don't you remember? You're still only a second rank orb-Bonded, but you drastically increased your power to fight against a High Priestess! Granted, she was one of the weakest High Priestesses, but that was still quite a feat!"

Jason put a hand to his temple, closing his eyes. Everything was fuzzy for a moment, but then it all came back to in one confused lump of emotion and memory. If he hadn't been talking to some sort of alien computer in his unconscious mind, all of the blood would have run from his face. "How did that happen?"

The cartoon cat looked embarrassed for a moment. "Gee, I

don't super know, Jason. See, I don't have any knowledge about what you did, but routines were built into me to let it happen. It still almost killed you. If I had to guess, and my guesses are good, you probably shouldn't have survived your limitbreak at your rank. It you were higher rank, it probably would have put less of a strain on your body and soul." The cat grinned, showing off big, blocky white teeth.

"Limitbreak?" asked Jason.

"That's what you called it, remember?"

Jason slowly nodded. "So how did I survive, then?"

"Kumbaya, you almost didn't!" the cat exclaimed. "I've been monitoring your surroundings and High Priestess Keeja made a very smart decision! She told your wife to give you a spirit stone. That stabilized you. But it seems you were dying because you used up all your extra spirit stones and started consuming your own Dhu...or something. I'm still not super sure."

"What?"

"You were dying because you didn't have enough Dhu feeding you power anymore! It's all quite fascinating. I still don't know what happened, so it would be great if you could ask Dolos or Keeja about it!"

Jason scratched his head, the action strangely calming despite his body being a figment of his subconscious. "So, you're telling me that I managed to use up the spirit stones I swallowed earlier, the ones I hadn't actually used yet because you didn't want me to level up right away, and I just needed another one to stabilize back to normal levels?"

"That's correct!" The purple cat seemed excited that Jason understood.

"So to get to third rank, I need to find more spirit stones again?"

"Correct again!" The cat was out of his seat and dancing now. The display was ridiculous. Jason closed his eyes shut tightly before opening them again. He needed to ask a few more questions, and then he needed to think.

* * *

Bezzi-ibbi had just gotten done burying Rark-han's body. Once he'd left the little meeting earlier, he'd immediately gotten to work with the grim task he could never entrust to anyone else. Once he was done, on the way back, he saw most of the group milling around the Battlewagon. Uluula had suddenly shrieked and began crying happily. Jason had woken up.

The Jaguar Clan heir was glad that his Clan brother was awake, but the events of the last few hours had left him feeling numb. Mareen was still not talking to anyone, either.

He knew if he'd asked, others in the group would have offered to help him bury Rark-han, but Bezzi-ibbi had needed to do it for himself. Henna-ibbi always said, "The wise hunter owns her own mistakes, she is not owned by them." Bezzi-ibbi's *rekke* was wise, truly the best female to lead the Clan in Mirana.

When he was laying Rark-han to rest, he'd taken off the man's bronze arm that Henry had crafted for him, and the reality of the situation had hit him. Rark-han was dead. Yanno-ibbi was alive, but crippled. Aodh was missing. And Henry, the man who had made the bronze replacement arm for Rark-han, was missing too.

He'd only cried once when he'd looked at the dead Mo'hali man in the face and seen he still wore a slight, satisfied smile. Bezzi-ibbi was glad nobody had been nearby to see his tears.

Rark-han had been a big man. It had taken Bezzi-ibbi a long time to dig a suitable grave. He'd crossed the wolf man's arms across his chest and buried him Jaguar Clan style. As he did, he'd prayed to the Maker of the Day, absolving Rark-han of any more responsibility. The man had paid his debt in full with his life.

While laying the body to rest, Bezzi-ibbi had found a letter in the big, lupine man's pocket. It had been addressed to him. With dull eyes and a heavy heart, he'd pocketed the letter and vowed to read it later. He was exhausted, and keeping his shadow proud in the Day was becoming increasingly difficult. He felt shame for feeling satisfaction earlier about his beginning as a Jaguar Troubadour.

His dream was already being built on bodies.

After Jason had woken up in Uluula's lap, he'd stumbled around, mumbling about purple cats for a time. The entire group was exhausted, but they had all managed to pile into the Battlewagon. The one damaged magicycle was scrapped, sliced apart by Jason, the parts stored for transport. The two undamaged magicycles belonged to the Berber spies. Bezzi-ibbi would ride in the Battlewagon for the remainder of the trip.

Mareen had wordlessly climbed into Henry's turret before they'd left, her eyes puffy, her expression haunted. Nobody had stopped her.

Even Keeja was quiet, her expression withdrawn and introspective.

Bezzi-ibbi wasn't sure how long it took to get to Harmly. The trip was a blur. He sat the whole time by his unconscious uncle, resting a hand on his shoulder. He couldn't stop thinking about Henry, Aodh, and Rark-han.

He wasn't completely unobservant while traveling. He noticed that the Delvers had acquired a decent amount of loot, including a monster-wood staff, a monster-wood rapier, a powerful enchanted bow, a blessed steel sword, and a few other things. The device that had hit Aodh and Henry with a beam of light was an enigma. Nobody could figure out what it was, not even Keeja. Either that or she wasn't telling.

Normally, most of the loot would have been doled out, or everyone would have at least been more excited about obtaining it. However, the pall over the company just got worse over time. There had been so much blood, death, and senseless violence. Fighting monsters was something Bezzi-ibbi had been prepared for. He'd been involved in the battle with the bandits months ago, and in hindsight, he felt naive for not considering that they could be attacked.

The Jaguar Clan heir had always known it was a possibility, but he hadn't really believed it in his hunter's heart. In the midst of all the fighting, while his heart pumped and he fought for his life, he'd felt a hunter's glee. However, now that the cost of survival was counted, he felt empty, numb.

Once the group got to Harmly, Bezzi-ibbi just sat and watched the world move around him. He'd never before experienced anything quite like what he was going through. He just felt heavy, heavy and powerless. He'd witnessed amazing events, he'd been involved in a glorious battle, a fight to his life, but all he could keep thinking about was Rark-han.

Bezzi-ibbi had been responsible for the man. He'd ordered Rark-han to atone for his crimes by serving. The problem was, the man had served, and done so well, even without a tongue most of the time. Bezzi-ibbi was almost starting to consider him Clan-trusted.

And now he was dead.

Bezzi-ibbi had killed before. He'd killed his first man a couple years before, a man condemned by the Clan council. As the heir, he had been required to end the man in order to prove he was coming of age.

He hadn't enjoyed it, but it'd been necessary. Bezzi-ibbi was no stranger to grim realities, but he was not accustomed to feeling like he'd failed. He'd never felt his heart hurt before this way, like he had lost something.

The next day passed almost like Bezzi-ibbi was watching someone else live his life. Uluula had gotten them all rooms in a decent inn. Bezzi-ibbi was distantly aware of Jason talking to the town guard and possibly the military. He was probably giving them an account of everything that had happened. There would definitely be an investigation.

Bezzi-ibbi couldn't bring himself to care.

If Rark-han were still around, the big wolf man would have looked at Bezzi-ibbi and rolled his eyes while flicking his ears sideways, communicating his impatience without words. Bezzi-ibbi smiled, tears running down his face as he traced his metal Hero arm with his flesh-and-blood hand. His power was effectively useless.

Without warning, Bezzi-ibbi felt a hand on his shoulder. He blearily glanced over and noticed Yanno-ibbi sitting next to him. His uncle's new crutch was leaning against the bed they were sitting on.

Bezzi-ibbi felt a sudden, hot flash of guilt. His uncle was still alive, and had been maimed. Yanno-ibbi had lost a hand and a leg, his mobility hampered for the rest of his life. Bezzi-ibbi had barely checked on him.

He tried to hold the tears in, but his renewed guilt made it impossible. He looked at the ground in shame, biting his lower lip with sharp teeth.

Yanno-ibbi began to speak. "You know, not many spoke in support for you to leave the Clan house in Mirana. However, I was one of them. I have known your father since he was born. Not many know that I am actually the eldest. However, it is the duty of the Jaguar Clan to face the truth and not show our backs, to never run from facts like cowardly prey.

"The reality is, your father is a better leader than I am. I am more friendly, I am smarter, I am better at most things, but your father learned one thing that I never could."

Yanno-ibbi paused. Bezzi-ibbi continued to stare at the ground and listen. Yanno-ibbi continued, "Your father learned how to kill his own people. We have both fought in skirmishes, you see. A good commander tries to keep their people alive. But the mark of a great commander is one who spends the lives of soldiers dearly, but is willing to spend them all the same.

"Henna-ibbi is a strong woman, but she still defers to your father on the hardest decisions in private. Most don't know that, nor should they, or it would weaken her position. But your father actually has a kinder heart than me. He is just willing to take the burden, to cry about it and claw himself later, but focus on the larger mission.

"This is not something I can do."

Yanno-ibbi gestured at himself. "My life has just been completely changed. I knew when I woke to a new dawn, greeted the light of the Day and saw my changed form, I had a choice. I could move on, or I could live in the past. Regret is an enemy that stalks in memories and dreams, Bezzi-ibbi. Great hunters never become prey, even to themselves.

"You left at a young age, risked your life to become a Hero so you can become a great Clan chief. I believe in your quest, Bezzi-ibbi. Unfortunately, now you know how difficult that journey will truly be, and why so many who love you were against you going. One of the things we love most about you is your pure heart. However, by the time you come back to the Clan, you will bear many scars, and some of them will be inside of you, on your spirit."

After that, Yanno-ibbi stood and hobbled out of the room with the help of his crutch.

Bezzi-ibbi loved and respected his uncle. He was not as wise as his father, or as smart as Henna-ibbi, or as observant as Bezzi-ibbi's mother, or as powerful as Kinwe-na-ibbi, but he usually growled truth. Yanno-ibbi was worthy of great respect.

It took some time, some reflection, but eventually Bezzi-ibbi stood, slapped his face, and took a deep breath.

He was not going to be healed inside for some time, but he would meet his enemies head on, even, no, *especially* if his enemy was himself.

He walked from the room, noticing Uluula with her arm around a sobbing Mareen in a room down the hall. Bezzi-ibbi's ears drooped. Mareen would have to face herself too. There was nothing he could do for her.

The Jaguar Clan boy glanced down at his disgusting, soiled clothes and winced. The first thing he was going to do now that he was walking again was obtain a new set of clothes and clean himself up. By the Day, if he truly wanted to be a Jaguar Troubadour, he needed to look like one!

* * *

The next day, the entire group had breakfast in a private dining room that the luxurious inn had accommodated them with. Knowing Uluula, she'd probably gotten it at half price.

Not long after he'd started eating, Bezzi-ibbi was shocked when Yanno-ibbi stood and made a surprise announcement. His uncle rapped on the table with tin spork and said, "Jason-ibbi, Bezzi-ibbi, all, I must leave this morning. You will be leaving from Harmly to travel north to the Stem River soon, but I will not be coming with you. I feel I have no place among your company anymore. I will just be a liability. I have already spoken to a few members of this group, and Thirsty will be coming with me."

"Wait, what?" asked Jason, scratching his head. "You're leaving, and Thirsty too? Thirsty, from what I hear, you were a huge help during the battle, and most if not all of us owe you our lives. I thought you'd be staying with us."

Thirsty shook his head. "Jason, sweetie, I love you, I love all of you. You all saved my life. But, how do I put this?" The tall, black man held up a hand dramatically before saying, "Uh, not only no, but hell no. Hell to the fuck no. Fuck all of this ratchet, medieval-ass fighting bullshit."

Thirsty pulled his wig out of his backpack and held it up. "Drag used to be my escape. It used to be a hobby, a way to make a little extra money and deal with stress. Do you know what I see now when I look at my wig and my heels?" He paused a moment and said, "Armor. I see armor. And during my dreams now, I see fucking zombie hands grabbing for me. I see my friends dying. I didn't sign on for this shit."

Thirsty quietly put the wig back in his backpack. "Actually, I didn't sign up for any of this. I feel like I'm lost, Jason. I just...need to find where I belong. I really do care about all of you, but...Aodh is gone." Thirsty's eyes began to tear up. He softly continued, "I just don't think I can do what I need to do in this group, I don't think I can be who you want me to be."

The entire room was quiet for a while after that.

Finally, Jason responded, "I respect your decision. It's not like I can keep you from going, but we've been through a lot together. Dashawn Givens, Thirsty Zha Zha, you will always be a member of Delvers LLC." Jason turned to Yanno-ibbi and asked, "And what will you do?"

Yanno-ibbi flicked his ears forward, displaying genuine affection for Jason. "I have contingency plans with the Clan. I will be heading to the capital of Tolstey to the west and working with a branch of the Clan to increase our strength. I believe Thirsty wants to work with me to see if I can help him open a clothing shop."

"Damn right," sniffed Thirsty. "I didn't ask for none of this orb-Bonded bullshit, but now that I can make real magic stuff, I just need someone to turn me loose. Maybe I can find my calling after all. I always knew I'd be a fierce-ass fashion designer."

Jason considered a moment before nodding. "Okay, but you are still our extended family. I am not going to leave you emptyhanded. We picked up a few things that should help with seed money. I want to give you the blessed steel flamberge—"

"The what?" asked Uluula.

"The big, blessed steel sword," replied Jason with just a hint of exasperation.

"I thought that would be going to Mareen." Uluula patted her Terran friend sitting next to her. The dusky-skinned woman showed no reaction, just stared at the table.

Jason shook his head, "No, it's not well suited to someone with her body style. Her hammer is still a much better weapon for her, especially with her enhanced strength, plus Henr—" Jason paused mid-word, and there was an awkward silence around the table for a moment.

Jason cleared his throat and continued, "Uh, so, uh, I want to give you the monster-wood rapier we found—not that I knew what monster-wood was before—and also the monster-wood staff—"

"No," Mareen said softly, but slammed her hand on the table.

Bezzi-ibbi winced. There had been enough strength in that slap to break a normal person's bones. "No," Mareen repeated. "Aodh should get the staff when he and Henry come back." With that, she settled back into her chair and looked at the table again.

Uluula pursed her lips, staring at Mareen in concern before turning to Jason and shrugging. Jason wetted his lips with his tongue and said, "Ah, I meant to say, the monster-wood rapier and the enchanted bow we found. The only archer among us is Mareen, and the bow is not meant for someone with enhanced strength."

Yanno-ibbi nodded, saying, "That is very generous, but the Jaguar Clan—"

Thirsty spoke over him, "We'll take it." Yanno-ibbi laid back his ear in surprise, but Thirsty continued, "I'm not taking it as a gift, though. I've worked for every damn thing I've ever had. No, this is a loan, you sexy teleporting bastard."

Jason blinked. "Ah—"

Thirsty held up a hand. "Yeah, this is a loan. I'm gonna get rich, and I'm gonna get more powerful, and I'm gonna give all you badass pimps and pimpettes the most fierce fucking outfits and accessories on this whole ratchet-ass planet." Then Thirsty snapped, ending the conversation.

Jason blinked while the rest of the table just stared at Thirsty. Finally, he said, "Okay, sounds like a plan! We'll do that, then."

Bezzi-ibbi wrestled with himself briefly. He didn't want to

make a scene, but he felt like he had achieved some small amount of wisdom over the last couple days. Finally, he steeled his resolve to do the right thing, the honorable thing, and the brave thing. He would show respect to his loved ones. He would be true to his heart and never take life for granted again.

Bezzi-ibbi stood, walked around the table and hugged Thirsty in the Terran fashion. The tall, strange Terran man stared, but Bezzi-ibbi just hugged him tighter before letting go. He said in English, "You are a pervert, but I don't care. I love you, Thirsty, my friend. You are a near-brother to me. I hope to see you again under the light of the Day."

Then he moved to Yanno-ibbi. His uncle already had his hands out, and Bezzi-ibbi put his on top of them. Then Yanno-ibbi reared his hand back and smacked Bezzi-ibbi across the face. Bezzi-ibbi immediately dropped back, snarling, showing no weakness while his Family member gave him respect. After a heartbeat, Yanno-ibbi settled back, satisfied with Bezzi-ibbi's response.

The young Jaguar Clan heir took a step forward, placing his forehead against Yanno-ibbi's and softly said, "Thank you for everything, Uncle. I will remember your words until the day I die. I hope to see you under the light of the Day again. If not, we will hunt together with the ancestors. You will always be welcome on my hunting land."

"And you on mine," said Yanno-ibbi, his voice thick with emotion.

Bezzi-ibbi jerkily squared his shoulders, then returned to his seat. He glanced around in confusion, wondering why everyone was crying. Why were the others emotional? The farewell had been a good one. He didn't understand Terrans at all sometimes.

Jason cleared his throat. "Delvers LLC and friends, now that we're all together, we—"

Suddenly, Uluula elbowed him in the ribs, stopping him in his tracks. "Where's Keeja?" she asked.

"I didn't see her at all last night," said Gonzo.

"You're right," muttered Vitaliya. Mareen just nodded.

"When was the last time anyone saw Keeja?" asked Uluula. "We still have a ton of questions, especially about that boxy weapon. We need to figure out where Henry went." Mareen nodded again, harder this time.

Bezzi-ibbi watched the scene and silently hoped Henry and Aodh were not dead. He knew everyone else in the group was secretly hoping the same.

"Where the hell did that irresponsible High Priestess go this time?" asked Jason, irritation coloring his voice. The rest of the table looked somewhat uncomfortable, still aware of Keeja's recent display of enormous power. Bezzi-ibbi just smiled. It was good to know his brother had not had his spirit bent or broken in any way.

If anyone could find Henry, it would be Jason. If anyone could survive just about anything, it would be Henry.

His brothers were worthy of respect. Bezzi-ibbi believed in them.

CHAPTER TWENTY-FOUR

Different Burdens

Jason wished he were still back in Harmly. Sleeping in a real bed for a few days had been nice, even if he hadn't gotten to see Uluula much. His wife had been spending a lot of time with Mareen, helping her deal with Henry's disappearance.

Missing. It'd been over two weeks since the group had left Harmly. The whole party felt the absence of everyone who wasn't with them anymore. In particular, Thirsty was sorely missed by almost everyone. The strange, flamboyant man had been subtly improving morale the whole time he'd been with them, and Jason had never even noticed. He felt like an idiot.

On top of Thirsty not being with them anymore to talk about random things from Earth, or remark on everything they passed, or sing along to songs on Keeja's music player...they didn't even have the music player itself anymore. Keeja had taken it with her when she'd vanished over two weeks before.

Jason drove the Battlewagon slowly; the land between Harmly and the Stem River had been rough, and now that they had found the river, it wasn't much easier to navigate. Plus, nobody was manning the turret anymore. Henry was the only one who could use it, and he was gone.

Gone. Henry and Aodh being missing was one of the many things he had been avoiding thinking about.

Jason glanced back at Mareen. As usual now, she was riding in the turret where Henry used to be. She'd been getting much better with her bow, and while she wasn't as effective as Henry used to be on the Battlewagon's guns, her efforts had made the trip a little smoother. Not having to slow down for every random flying monster they ran into helped a lot.

The group was still fairly quiet, but beginning to come around. Bezzi-ibbi in particular seemed to have grown up a lot over the last few weeks. Jason had a hard time thinking of the boy as a kid anymore, despite the fact he was probably still middle school aged. His eyes just had a depth of wisdom, insight, and personal pain that the programmer-turned-adventurer found disconcerting sometimes.

Jason had decided to honor Mareen's request and save the monster-wood staff for Aodh if he returned. Hopefully he would return. Quite frankly, the weapon freaked Jason out. He couldn't wait to get rid of it.

Monster-wood, he'd learned, was a fairly rare material that only grew on the northern tip of Halal, the largest island on Ludus. Apparently, the Areva nations of Hilil and Hanana controlled all access and trade to the island. The material was harvested and weapons were made from it. It was even stronger than steel.

Unfortunately, it was alive. He looked at the staff and shuddered. It had bonded with him. Monster-wood weapons bonded with one person and reverted to a natural state when the bond was broken. Vitaliya had found the staff while it was slowly crawling off like an inchworm after the big battle two weeks before.

Monster-wood weapons were expensive, but they needed to be fed. In fact, after learning about them, he'd had been informed they were popular with people who did a lot of killing, like hunters and active soldiers. Meanwhile, Jason had to just throw a cup of blood at the staff every few days and hope for the best. Gonzo had told him that if a monster-wood staff got too hungry, it might bite the hand holding it.

The plain, bumpy, reddish-looking wood staff didn't look like much next to Jason, but he'd seen the thing moving before. The fact a solid, rigid weapon could move was something out of a nightmare. Deep down, Jason feared the damn thing would get hungry and just reach over to take a bit out of his arm.

He'd never seen a mouth. He wasn't even sure how it ate, but he didn't want to find out.

Jason shook his head and stopped thinking about the disturbing staff. He had other, more important things to ponder.

He glanced at the box full of spirit stones by his feet and swallowed. The amount of wealth he had just sitting around in a wooden box was staggering. Minus the one spirit stone that Uluula had used to save his life, he still had ten left. It was insane.

Deep down, Jason knew he was hoping Henry would get back before he had to make a decision about what to do with all the stones, but he couldn't afford to wait much longer. The most recent battle had been an eye opener. Now the entire team knew they had to get much stronger.

Jason had to be honest with himself. He was a little scared. He had a feeling that if he swallowed enough spirit stones again to go up a rank, he would. But he wondered what he was becoming. His transformation when he'd fought Biivan was terrifying in retrospect. He'd essentially been burning up his own life to maintain that level of power, and he hadn't fully been in control of himself, either.

He eyed the box warily, realizing that spirit stones were no longer only a means for him to advance as an orb-Bonded. Now they were also fuel for his limitbreak. However, even if the purple cartoon cat hadn't warned him against swallowing too many spirit stones at once, Jason wouldn't have done so.

The spirit stones held so much raw power, the fact he was swallowing them in the first place was completely insane. He shook his head. He more or less knew how he'd spend his points when he ranked up next. He had advancement points already saved up, too. He'd been dragging his feet, but he knew he was putting the group in danger by not leveling up.

Still, he appreciated that everyone was giving him time. Losing Henry and Aodh had hit him, Mareen, and Vitaliya hardest. Mareen was beginning to become more animated, but Jason saw a brittleness, a sharpness about her now that made him worry. Mareen was Henry's wife, but she was Jason's friend.

He worried for her mental health.

Jason hoped she wasn't tearing herself up. He knew all too well how poisonous that could be, but he didn't know how to broach the subject with her.

He sighed and shrugged. What would be, would be. He was glad he wasn't a control freak, or he'd have been having a fit.

That said, he found Keeja's disappearance completely aggravating. More than anything, he needed answers, but the fucking eons-old demigoddess riding shotgun with his little group had decided to take off without telling anyone.

Jason huffed and began steering the Battlewagon to a handy clearing in order to make camp. After a few moments, Vitaliya and Gonzo zoomed past him, riding the last two remaining magicycles. They'd obviously understood what he intended, probably not too difficult since the sun was beginning to set in the east. The Berban spies usually followed behind the Battlewagon in case a large monster popped out of the Stem River. It didn't happen often, but it was worth taking precautions.

Luckily, Jason had truly been mastering his null-time-enhanced throwing knives. So far, he'd been able to kill almost any monster they encountered with very little effort. He wondered again what he was becoming. Was he even really human anymore? The thought was sobering, and he couldn't help but remember how it'd felt to battle Biivan across the sky.

The raw energy that had coursed through his body…it'd been like a drug. Jason could almost remember how he'd achieved the limitbreak state, too. He knew if he really had to, he could probably do it again, and the realization scared the hell out of him. He didn't think he was meant to have such power, not yet, anyway.

In the last couple weeks, he'd tried replicating some of the abilities he remembered using while in his limitbreak state, but he had no luck. It was like his memories were him riding in his head, controlling his body like a video game. His memories almost didn't feel real. He could recall what he had done, but not how. Jason wondered if he even had the power to do the things he'd done in his normal state.

Probably not. The thought strangely comforted him a bit. Remembering he had limitations made him feel a little bit grounded, a bit more human. Having superpowers and magic was cool at first, but Ludus was a dangerous world, and he was beginning to really feel the added danger of having a target painted on his back by Dolos.

Dolos, that dickhead. Jason frowned. Other members of the Delvers LLC company had been nervous around Keeja after she'd killed Biivan, but Jason had been largely unaffected. He'd not only already suspected how powerful she really was, but he'd seen Dolos casually exert enough power to obliterate a forest while only slightly annoyed.

The world was insane, or at least Ludus was.

After stopping the Battlewagon, Jason disembarked and ran his hand over the bronze exterior. He'd built this thing with Henry. It had Henry's touch all over it, even down to the stupid name. For a guy who constantly bitched about stupid names on Ludus, Henry sure hadn't had any problems coming up with his own. Jason chuckled at the thought.

Speaking of stupid names, Jason spotted a flash of light in the sky, probably a magic messenger bird, or MMB as the group was all calling them now. He smiled crookedly, but the expression changed to surprise when he saw the light had indeed been an MMB, and it was descending to his group.

He watched in astonishment as the MMB slowly came to a stop before Mareen, hovering expectantly. Mareen said something but Jason couldn't hear it. Then she hesitantly held her hand out, letting the creature deposit a note before zooming off into the sky.

With trembling hands, Mareen unfolded the note. Jason quickly glanced around and noticed that the beautiful, dark-skinned woman had the attention of every member of the group. Bezzi-ibbi in particular watched with interest, his eyes bright, nose twitching.

Mareen took a deep breath with her eyes closed, and then she began to read. After a few moments, she slowly put the note down, took another deep breath, and said softly but clearly, "Henry is alive. He's really alive." She shed a single, slow tear, before collapsing against the side of the Battlewagon's turret.

Uluula raced past Jason, nimbly climbing to the top of the Battlewagon to check on her friend. Jason's mind went blank. Henry was really alive? A great weight he'd been carrying on his shoulders and hadn't even been aware of seemed to vanish.

Jason wasn't sure how he ended up in on the ground, but the next thing he knew, he was sitting on his butt, his hands spread wide behind him. He closed his eyes, looking up at the sky, thinking, *Thank you, God, thank you for not taking my friend. Thank you…thank you.*

Jason began to cry and didn't care who saw it. It was like part of him that had died had been reborn. He didn't even have a word for the emotion he was feeling, but the closest would have been gratitude.

While he sat on the ground of a dangerous, alien planet, a grown man wearing a sword, crying, Jason decided to swallow two more spirit stones that night and become a rank three orb-Bonded.

He had to move forward. As long as he was on Ludus, he had to move forward. He was like a shark—if he stopped swimming, he'd die. Jason has been through a lot and he bore a lot of wounds from it, but he was still whole.

The tall, sandy-haired man felt deep, profound relief. He hadn't lost Uluula, and Henry was still alive. All the spirit stones in his box paled in comparison to the wealth he felt knowing that his only family on the entire God-forsaken planet were still among the land of the living.

Jason wept.

CHAPTER TWENTY-FIVE

Politically Expedient

Yelm tapped his foot impatiently. He let his magic creep through his body, manifesting on his fingertips in a subtle warning. He growled a question. "Why haven't you found them yet?"

The woman he spoke to, a Ludus-born Terran, a Ludan, merely smiled. She was obviously not intimidated in the slightest.

With an effort of will, Yelm reined in his temper. He was aware of all the other eyes on him. There would always be time to properly deal with Celina; the smug bitch was not as untouchable as she thought she was.

He grimaced as he swallowed his frustration. He was in too deep now to throw a fit. Too many plans were in motion, and too many sacrifices had been made.

He glanced at the symbol of Asag on the wall in distaste. The dark altar still sported wet blood pooling around its base. One good thing about living on a planet with so many more women than men was how easy it made virgin sacrifice. Asag was an old-school god, apparently. He wanted the sacrifice of pure girls, even if finding them wasn't particularly difficult on Ludus.

Yelm steeled himself. Originally, he'd just been out to get revenge for Jeth, but eventually his contact in the Berban seditionists had convinced him to work with the Asag cultists. He found the entire assignment extremely distasteful, but he couldn't argue with the results.

He also couldn't deny that the cultists somehow had a very impressive intelligence network. He didn't know how, but they'd known about Henry and Jason heading to Berber before his own contacts had.

As he always did, Yelm had ingratiated himself with his fellows and attained a lofty rank in a relatively short amount of time. Being orb-Bonded hadn't hurt. Still, now it seemed he just sat around and watched the dark-robed zealots murder girl-children.

Celina, the priestess of this cell of cultists, said, "Ludus may be smaller than Earth, Yelm, but it's still a large place. Besides, we know where they're going. In point of fact, they're coming here, to this city. It makes more sense to set up resources to find them when they get here than try to patrol an eighth of the world looking for them. You should feel lucky. Your personal vendetta seems to align with our purpose.

"I am not sure why the Terrible Lord wants your enemies dead, this Jason and Henry, but we listen to his law, not to your threats."

Yelm clenched his teeth, holding back a retort. The bitch was telling the truth. Every cultist he was surrounded with in the subterranean hideout would gladly give their life for the demon god and cared little about the Berber sedition.

Yelm had seen terrible things. He'd done terrible things. He'd looked the other way when his...troubled son had done terrible things. However, the Asag cultists were on another level, one that even made him feel uncomfortable.

He'd accepted that his soul was probably going no place good long ago. He'd briefly thought he might be able to find redemption among George's scruffy little band of farmers, indulging in Jeth's obsession over that pretty girl Mareen. But no more. The powers that ran Ludus were corrupt, and he would bring them down, even if it meant damning himself to do so.

"So you have your...people looking for Henry and Jason near the capital?"

"Yes, and a couple other cities. We will find them."

"They're orb-Bonded. They're dangerous."

"We've already discussed this," Celina replied, rolling her eyes. "We have powerful allies. You think your faction is strong. Yes, we know about the noblewoman you have in your pocket. However, you should forget what you think you know. Terrible

Asag has a firm grip on Ludus. This planet will belong to our dark Lord!

"Our reach is far indeed, backed by the power of Terrible Asag! Yes, we have many favors to call on. Anywhere the enemies of Asag tread, we will pull purses, or hearts, or debts to uncover their souls, ripe for the picking."

Celina's eyes closed in some sort of religious ecstasy. Yelm took a half step back before he could stop himself. He carefully managed his expression. He knew he was watched at all times. It was fine if the cultists knew he reviled them. However, they could never know he didn't fear them.

He hadn't stepped back out of fear; he'd stepped back in disgust. In retrospect, it had probably been the right thing to do. Plus, the cultists would see what they wanted to see.

He couldn't wait to be done with these people. They made his skin crawl, and that was when they weren't parading around Asag's twisted minions the demon god had somehow sent to this world. Yelm knew he was truly trying to fight evil with evil, but he'd made his choice. Plus, if he could get revenge for his murdered son along the way, it would all be worth it.

He would see the world burn, and he'd dance a jig before the flames consumed him too.

"So what is plan B?" he asked. "You shouldn't underestimate these men. Thod did, and he is nothing but dirt by now."

"Yes, well, Thod was a thug working for your organization.

We serve a higher calling, a higher power. Plus, Thod was only second rank orb-Bonded. Need I say more?"

"No, I understand." Yelm swallowed everything else he wanted to say. There was no denying that Celina was powerful. Third rank for a mere low-level priestess—he had to admit her boasts about the cultists' strength might not be entirely inaccurate. Plus, he couldn't exactly be too picky after getting in bed with devils.

All of this was true, but Celina didn't know what else he knew. If she had, she would have immediately killed him and fled for the hills. Yelm kept his face blank but smiled inwardly. There would be a reckoning. Yes, he would see the whole world burn. He'd burn it all for Jeth.

* * *

Keeja crossed her arms. The building she stood in was magnificent. Its beauty was unparalleled on the entire planet. The continent she stood on was entirely off limits for mortals. She was surrounded by power and wealth the likes of which most souls on Ludus would never even knew existed, but all she could feel was disgust.

Dolos sat on his throne and smiled down at her. The throne itself was enormous, and Dolos had changed his size to fill it. He towered over the diminutive High Priestess.

The huge man's expression was subtly mocking in a way that made Keeja's hackles stand on end. She wanted to lash out, to attack her de facto employer, but she knew from experience how utterly useless the gesture would be. Worse, she knew it would amuse him.

In the end, it would just also create more work for her and all the other High Priestesses, as well as their servants. Plus, she hated to admit that as much as she despised Dolos and his methods, the universe would probably be better off if he could accomplish his goals…even if he was only in it for selfish reasons.

"Okay, I'm here," she snarled. "What was so Host-bound important that it couldn't wait even a few minutes?"

"You know I don't like that oath," said Dolos, lazily waving a hand, causing a memory cube to float into his hand from a nearby table.

"Too fucking bad, buttercup. If I don't get right to the point, I'll be here longer than I should already be. You gave me a job. I didn't want it. Now I do. I want to see it through. In fact, it benefits your purposes if I do."

"Ugh, Areva. Just a step up from animals. Terrans are worse, but Areva have discovered a little bit of technology and no longer see themselves as the stupid primates they still are." Dolos sighed theatrically and Keeja clenched her jaw.

Dolos put the back of his hand to his forehead and theatrically looked at the ceiling. "Just little pointy-eared animals, scurrying around, piloting little spaceships, steeped in their own hubris. And then one in particular that I've cared for and trained talks to me this way? What is the Terran expression? 'Biting the hand that feeds'? Perhaps I should ask this little High Priestess. She has been to Terra, after all. Actually, who sent her there? That's right, I did!"

Dolos chuckled, pretending to examine the data cube. "It's almost like some of these mortals forget their place, believe that they actually have some wisdom after only a few thousand years. It's a travesty. A true travesty."

"Listen, asshole, you avoided me before, and now you want my attention so bad you forced me to drop everything and come here. I am not in the mood to be talked down to. If you want to impress someone, go show up to a random fishmonger or a sewer cleaner and impress her or something."

With no warning, Keeja's shoulders hit the wall, pinning her there. The impact rattled her entire body and would have turned a normal woman into pulp. The pressure was intense. Even with all her power, it was all she could do not to pass out. With an effort of will, she continued glaring at Dolos.

The huge man pretended to not even be paying attention. He continued to fiddle with the data cube. Eventually he adjusted his stone crown, set the data cube down, and looked up. Keeja gulped. Dolos's eyes were narrowed.

Uh oh, she thought.

"Sometimes silly mortals mistake kindness for weakness," Dolos said conversationally. "Sometimes, a good servant who has distinguished herself among her peers can forget her place, forget who it is that made her.

"I am beginning to get tired of such small beings showing such disrespect to one such as I. My tool has been tainted by associating with a few filthy Terrans, bad influences on my loyal servant.

"The matter at hand is bigger than you, little High Priestess. It's bigger than me."

Now Dolos had Keeja's undivided attention. He very, very rarely acted this way. "Fine," she grated. "I'm listening."

In a snap, Dolos was back to his usual self, lounging on his throne and not even looking directly at Keeja again. However, he'd made his point. Despite her disdain, Keeja would have to be fool not to listen. Dolos seemed to actually have something serious to discuss. Plus, she was a valuable resource, but he really was capable of killing her any time he wanted.

For a few minutes, Dolos examined his fingernails and muttered about broken tools and Areva arrogance. Keeja took calming breaths, biding her time and releasing a trickle of power to repair her body. Eventually, Dolos sighed and turned, saying, "First, the obvious. Jason James Booth, despite his repulsive Terran heritage, has managed to exceed all expectations and ascend after a fashion. He has somehow managed to go from expendable to not as expendable.

"You killed Biivan fairly. You abided by every rule, every

guideline. However, this inconvenienced me. I am passing the inconvenience on to you." The huge man smiled. "I have elevated Philana to High Priestess."

Keeja was horrified. "Little Lana? You made Philana a High Priestess!?"

"Ah, yes, she has been your research assistant for three hundred years, right? You should work well together, which is good. You will be training her. Due to Jason James Booth's increased importance, I will assign a High Priestess individually to both nasty little Terrans you were assigned to up until now. Which one do you want to preside over?"

Keeja's mind was spinning, but she still answered, "Henry," without even needing a pause. If she was going to spend the next few hundred years babysitting either man, she wanted to take the cute one she could tease for at least the next few decades. It really didn't require much thought.

"Fine, then Philana will be assigned to Jason James Booth. She will be heading out with you immediately and—"

"Wait, she's leaving now?" interrupted Keeja. "She's a nymph who hasn't seen a single man in over three hundred years, and you want her to come with me to the mainland?" Keeja's voice became louder and shrill, but she couldn't control herself. Her assignment was turning into a nightmare again.

Dolos's smile was nasty. "I'm sure you will think of something. She idolizes you, after all. Plus, it's only fair that you help out since you killed another High Priestess. Then again, you did give me an excuse to send Jason James Booth a box full of spirit stones. What he does with them is a matter of heavy betting among all the Research Priestesses in the divine palace."

Keeja hissed. This was terrible news, and Dolos was enjoying every second of it.

"The other information I called you here to relay, information that I couldn't risk transmitting directly to you, is that the struggle among my brethren has escalated. It seems that a few other gods have finally taken notice of my paradise planet and desire to lay claim to it." Dolos's eyes flashed. "They have overstepped themselves enough that I now have more tools at my disposal."

"What do you mean?" asked Keeja.

"I have activated the portways again."

Keeja gasped. "Those haven't been working in almost five hundred years!"

"Just so! But my foolish brothers and sisters have given me the justification I needed to power them again! The change should yield great results and increase strife on Ludus. We will get wonderful data! Of course, should your little orb-Bonded Terrans find them, they could make use of them, too.

"The rules are the same as before. If a mortal finds a portway shrine, they may travel to any other portway shrine they've already found and imprinted. After using a portway, there must be at least two days between another is used by the same person."

"I don't understand why such a useful travel tool requires such arbitrary rules and wait times," muttered Keeja.

Dolos sighed. "Areva are always looking for meanings in things that their small minds cannot understand. The entire species would be far less odious if they would just accept the limitations of their kind and cease looking for patterns they can't grasp."

Keeja narrowed her eyes, but otherwise stayed silent. She knew there was probably something else Dolos was going to tell her.

The huge, strangely clothed man continued, "Lastly, because of my siblings' overreach, I had a choice to exercise some amount of godly power! You can't give your orb-Bonded charges valuable information because of the rules. However, there are a few low mortal priestesses in my ranks who have divined universal truths that Henry and Jason would greatly benefit from knowing."

Keeja heart pounded. She immediately knew where Dolos was headed with his murky statements. She had to give him grudging respect for being so sneaky.

"A total of four priestesses have been given pieces of a key to unlock the restrictions we are all under from sharing information with low mortals. Plus, it will free up the holder a bit from the other rules we abide by, too."

"Fragments of a soul shroud..." breathed Keeja, reverent despite herself.

"Yes. I have been able to locate pieces of a complete artifact.

If you found it, you or any High Priestess who wore it would be exempt from the rules and guidelines. I could not use it, of course."

"But, this is huge. This is—why are you telling me?"

Dolos grimaced. "There are two reasons. One is that despite their lowly heritage and distinct lack of manners or intellect, the newest group of Terrans to Ludus are actually giving us good data. They may actually allow me to accomplish what I set out to do eons ago. Second, and most important, there are whispers that the Enemy has returned."

Keeja gasped, a chill running down her spine.

"Yes," said Dolos, suddenly uncharacteristically direct and serious again. "The hypothetical situation I have been fearing since before Ludus even existed isn't as hypothetical anymore.

"If the rumors among my brethren are true, we might not have much time left."

Keeja had not peed herself in over a thousand years, but in that moment, she almost lost control of her bladder. In her mind, everything had changed. Everything.

She clicked her heels together and swallowed her pride. This truly was greater than herself. It was greater than all of Ludus. She hated Dolos, but unfortunately, his goal was even more important now. Keeja touched her open palm to her throat in salute. "I will go now."

"Yes, see that you do," replied Dolos, shrugging. He adjusted his seat on his throne and began fidgeting with his data cube again. "The fate of the universe may depend on the combined efforts of filthy Terrans, uppity Areva, and a horny nymph." Dolos laughed, the sound ugly and mocking. The self-proclaimed god's mirth followed Keeja out of the room.

She would have been furious if she hadn't been so terrified. Everything had changed.

Delvers LLC: Obligations Incurred

End of Delvers LLC: Obligations Incurred,
---Book Two of Delvers LLC
Please read on for a note by the author.
…And don't forget to review this novel!

School--::--Subschool:
Earth-:-Metal
Air-:-Void
Water-:-Life
Fire-:-Matter
Consciousness-:-Time
Light-:-Darkness
Force-:-Attraction

About the Author:

Blaise Corvin served in the US Army in several roles. He has seen the best and the worst that humanity has to offer. He is a sucker for any hobby involving weapons, art, or improv.

He currently lives in Texas with some silly animals, and enough geeky memorabilia to start a museum.

He likes talking about himself in third person within author biographies.

It's all very eccentric.

Cheers!

Continue reading for ways to connect with Blaise Corvin, and a sample of *Secret of the Old Ones, Luck Stat Strategy!*

Delvers LLC: Obligations Incurred

To Readers,

PLEASE, PLEASE LEAVE A REVIEW! You are wonderful, and reviews are amazing for all authors, but especially indie authors like me.

I really hope you enjoyed this book!

Ludus is a part of something huge, a universe I've been working on for 10 years and can probably explore for the rest of my life.

Please make sure to connect with me on my mailing list or on social media!

1. **My website**

If you're interested in checking out my website, the URL is http://blaise-corvin.com/. You can find news, Delvers artwork, and advanced (rough draft) chapters of what I'm working on.

2. **These is my social media accounts where you can connect with me!**

Twitter - @Blaise_Corvin

https://twitter.com/Blaise_Corvin

Facebook - Leave me a like on facebook!

https://www.facebook.com/BlaiseCorvinWriter/

LitRPG Society Facebook Group

https://www.facebook.com/groups/LitRPGsociety/

3. **Recommendations:**

If you liked this book, you may like other LitRPG stories too! Some authors I interact with often and can recommend are:

I want to recommend a great series Realm of Arkon by a friend, G. Akella (Georgy Smorodinsky). At the present, he is the most popular and best-selling LitRPG author in Russia.

https://www.amazon.com/G.-Akella/e/B01BJ7HJVK/

Check out a great LitRPG series Fayroll by Andrey Vasilyev, a pioneer and one of the top LitRPG authors in Russia. Fayroll has been one of the longest and most popular series there since 2014.

https://www.amazon.com/Andrey-Vasilyev/e/B06WGQ54SX/

The Lion's Quest series by Michale-Scott Earle:

https://www.amazon.com/Michael-Scott-Earle/e/B019QSNVA2/

4. **My email**

If you want to drop me a line for any reason, you can email me at:

Blaise.Corvin.Art@gmail.com

5. **Until next time (and please leave a review!)**

Thank you for joining me on this adventure! I couldn't do it without all the knowledge and encouragement I get on a daily basis from everyone in this wonderful community.

I can't wait to spend time with you again in the third Delvers book, *Delvers LLC: Adventure Capital*.

:)

-BC

Continue reading for an exciting sample of *Secret Of the Old Ones, Luck Stat Strategy*!

I have another LitRPG series I am currently writing, **Secret of the Old Ones**.

SOO is a hard LitRPG novella series, which is to say there are stat tables, XP earned from kills, and linear character advancement.

I really wanted to write something different, and I think SOO fits the bill! It takes place in the near future and follows a hard core gamer of dubious moral character. The story is set in a world where gaming streams are the primary form of entertainment, and most of the action take place in a Virtual Reality (VR) game.

The game itself is a mash-up of a Victorian, Lovecraft, and Steampunk flavors. There are gun battles, sword fights, and freaky monsters galore!

The book's blurb reads:

Secret of the Old Ones is a deep dive VR game the likes of which the world had never seen.

Trent Noguero, a hardcore gamer, has been playing for a year and is about to get his big break. He is about to catapult himself into the ranks of the most powerful players in the world.

However, power comes with a price, and celebrity creates enemies. Trent has the keys to massive success, but he also accidentally painted a target on his back...both in, and out of the game.

Continue reading for a sample!

CHAPTER ONE

The World Tree

The character sheet read:

Name: Vale dePardon

Class: Occultist

Subclass: Explorer

Level: 10

Experience: 536542

XP to next level: 123468

Stamina: 49/49

HP 49/49

Mana: 70/70

Stats: (Total/Original/Level Ups/Bonuses)

Strength: 3/2/1/0

Agility: 7/3/4/0

Stamina: 5/4/1/0

Intelligence: 7/7/0/0

Willpower: 6/6/0/0

Luck: 15/8/4/3

Class Skills: Fencing, Ancient Body Magic, Paranoia, Ancient
Occult Lore, Map Reading/Cartography

Permanent Bonus Source: Mystic Clover (Luck +3)

Trent Noguero smiled in satisfaction. It had been a long, hard
road to hit level ten, but now his character, Vale dePardon, finally
had a subclass!

He'd been playing as Vale dePardon in Secret of the Old Ones
for a year and had just hit level ten a week ago. It was quite an
accomplishment. Of the millions of people who were playing the
game around the world, less than a couple thousand players had
made it to level ten so far.

Level ten was a huge milestone and allowed a player to choose
a subclass. He'd chosen Explorer, which allowed him to choose
his fifth skill, [Cartography].

Now he only had a few more steps before he could start his
grand, mystical experiment. He carefully tiptoed around the ornate
sigils he'd drawn in powder on the floor. He was trying to find one
of the reagents he'd taken out of his inventory earlier.

Where is it...where is it? Ah, there it is! He found the glass
tube of glowing blue liquid and grinned. He didn't have many
more preparations to make. Vale carefully moved to the most

concentrated area of the designs and symbols on the ground, some of which were glowing.

He took a deep breath. He only had enough *Distilled Azure Essence* for one try. He was about to make or break his complex magic gate spell. He uncorked the blue liquid and mumbled a few spells. The liquid began to bubble, and Vale threw it up in the air in a circular motion. In less than a second, the entire vial of liquid had turned to smoke. The sparkles in the air left over from the mystical reaction slowly settled to the designs on the floor.

Vale smiled and tilted his head back for a moment in triumph. *Finally,* he thought. He squatted down and carefully regarded the center of the spell network. The old, cracked parchment had probably been the luckiest thing he'd found in the game so far...if it actually was what he thought it was.

It was a big "if."

It had taken him a month to figure out what the map might do, and after he knew, his mouth had gone dry from excitement. However, preparing to discover if he was right had been very expensive and time-consuming. He'd spent every coin he had to buy all the materials for the arcane accelerators and intricate symbols drawn on the floor. All his wealth had been used to cover his hidden cellar in ancient hoodoo.

At least the cellar had been free. He was just hiding in an obscure, out-of-the-way area and would leave when he was done. He wasn't sure if the cellar actually belonged to someone, and he didn't care. Their building was helping further science—or magic, whatever.

He traced a finger along the mystic sigils rimming the map's edges and smiled. He'd been waiting a long time to test his theory. Now that he was so close, he felt anxiety building, the pressure crawling up his spine.

His subclass and his new [Cartography] skill were all part of a plan that he'd been working on for half a year. Secret of the Old Ones deviated from other games with unique bonuses, skills, even rumored one-of-a-kind classes. In a game with 30 starting stat points, a level cap of 30, and only one additional stat point every level for a possible total of 60 stat points at max level...

It was obvious that bonus stats would be a huge advantage.

When Vale had heard about these design decisions prior to playing SOO, he'd decided on his strategy before even creating a character. He'd put as many points into the Luck stat as he could. In a game where stats were so important, where his character sheet even showed his original, level one choices, finding anything that could give him permanent bonuses would be amazing.

Luckily, two months in, his gamble had paid off. What's more, he was able to find an amazing item that conferred a permanent attribute bonus of +3 Luck. Unfortunately, finding the Mystic Clover had been part of a long, involved adventure that had gained him a full-blown enemy.

Suddenly, he got a flashing system notice:

DANGER!

Unlike other notices, this one popped up and faded away on its own. Vale's stomach dropped and he whispered, "Oh no."

His [Paranoia] skill was currently letting him know an enemy was nearby, and he knew it had to be Brutus Vann, his nemesis, his enemy from the expedition where he'd found the Mystic Clover. Vale crossed his arms and tried to decide what to do. It would be a few minutes before Brutus found him…just like he always did.

They had shared history, after all.

In the past, he'd always fled from Brutus, managing to escape through luck and guile. Combat in SOO was a strange combination of in-game skills and real-life abilities. A character couldn't do things in the game very well unless they had a skill or class for it. On the flip side, if a character had a skill, they performed actions better if they had real-life skill and experience. The game's system helped for skills that players were unfamiliar with, but there was no substitute for real training…

The strange combat and skill system had actually motivated players to learn how to make antique crafts, pursue knowledge, and practice martial arts outside the game—presumably, as the mysterious designers of Yggdrasil Entertainment had intended.

Unfortunately, Vale was almost certain that Brutus had at least three skills devoted entirely to combat. He was also a skilled fighter, almost unnaturally so. Brutus's player had to have real skill in ancient weapons and armor. Sometimes Vale wondered who Brutus could be in real life.

Who the hell trained to use a longsword, anyway?

In a game where player deaths forced a mandatory one-week lockout from the game, Brutus was notorious. He'd been challenged by full adventuring parties in the past and still came out as the victor, helping himself to all their gear and becoming an even more formidable player.

Normally if Brutus showed up, Vale would run; he'd have no choice. Unfortunately, the whole reason he was so eager to get his tenth level, his subclass, and the [Cartography] skill was currently filling his laboratory. Six months of work was glowing on the floor.

His back was against the wall. If he fled, he'd lose half a year of progress. He couldn't let Brutus just have it. Eventually, he made the only decision he really could. His spine steeled, he ascended the stairs out of his borrowed cellar.

He reflected on his chances as he walked out into the moonlight. Luckily, Vale wasn't a terrible fighter himself. His high-quality Rapier of Twilight was an excellent weapon. Plus, his [Fencing] skill, 3 years of Fencing Club in college, and a year of hands-on combat experience in SOO had made him fairly dangerous in his own right.

Unfortunately, Brutus was a superior fighter in every way, except for one—Vale had magic. He usually avoided using it because of the risks, but the only way he was going to win this fight would be to cheat.

Sure enough, Brutus was standing outside. The shadows on his craggy, brutish face moved as he grinned. His heavy armor shimmered with enchantments, and his enormous sword glowed with fiery runes.

As amazing as the hulking man's gear was, it was common knowledge he had an even better set stashed away somewhere. The last time someone actually managed to kill Brutus, they'd taken his gear. They'd believed him brought down for good, or at least for a long time. The community had celebrated. However, a week later when Brutus had logged back into the game, he'd hunted down those who killed him. He'd killed them, taken out their friends, and even slaughtered the players who'd planned the celebration of his death.

He was ruthless.

Brutus stood a few inches taller than Vale and outweighed him by at least fifty pounds. It was a jagged pill to swallow, but Vale had to admit that the man was incredibly intimidating. Brutus wore full armor while Vale was dressed as an Occultist adventurer. He was wearing the game's latest adventuring fashion. He had to admit he liked how it looked.

As Vale drew his rapier, Brutus smiled and crowed, "So, we finally meet again and at last—"

Vale wasn't interested in talking. He sprinted forward, using his [Ancient Body Magic] skill to cast <Arm Speed>, <Leg

Speed>, <Superior Aim>, <Enhanced Reflexes>, and <Explosive Strength>. The combination of spells exhausted a great deal of his mana, and he felt the mental strain pushing against his paltry six Willpower.

He fought to stay conscious. If he went under, he would pass out and no doubt Brutus would kill him. He'd be locked out for a week. It was unacceptable to go down now, to lose everything. Vale fought through the pain.

As he closed, he focused on his target and his strategy. SOO supported massive criticals for killing blows. Hitting someone normally took away their health, but particularly deadly attacks could usually kill a player in one shot.

It was obvious that Brutus had not even expected Vale to defend himself. *Arrogant bastard,* Vale thought, and he snarled. Even just standing there with his sword sheathed, Brutus still almost managed to recover.

He pulled just enough steel and turned his body to block Vale's first attack. Then Vale dodged Brutus's hasty, surprised punch and sunk his rapier up to the hilt in the brutish man's eye socket.

The big man fell; the fight was over amazingly fast. Vale panted and wrenched his sword out of Brutus' skull. He had been awarded with the kill. The feeling was surreal. Vale closed a window that popped up without looking at the XP he'd earned.

He was a little shocked he was still alive. In any other circumstance, he was sure he would have lost. Only the full combination of all five spells had let him win, but it had been an enormous risk, one that most players, including himself, would usually not have been willing to take. He had come close to passing out just from the spell backlash, and he wasn't sure if he'd be able to replicate the feat ever again.

Ancient magic, the magic Occultists used in SOO was no joke. Each spell cast in quick succession got increasingly difficult to control.

Vale didn't pause to gloat. He didn't even stop to loot. He just dragged Brutus's corpse into his cellar laboratory and locked the door. He couldn't know who else might have been watching, and he had to move forward with his plans immediately. All the reagents, the careful planning, everything had to be used now.

The proper stars were even in alignment. There would be no better time, and he didn't want to further risk losing all his hard work.

Vale moved to his carefully inscribed circles and realized he was bleeding from somewhere. Oh well, it could wait. All his spells from the fight before were still active, so he was riding a high of magic. He paused for a second, breathed deeply, and called up his [Ancient Occult Lore] activation menu.

Do you want to activate your arcane portal?

Vale chose YES.

Are you sure?

The map tethered to this arcane portal is demanding a

permanent loss of -5 Intelligence to proceed.

Vale paused and thought for a while. The map was asking for an insane loss of Intelligence. It hadn't even occurred to him that he could lose any stats, that it might cost him more than he'd already given up to use the map.

He should have known there'd be more to it. He'd been a fool. It even made sense that he would have to give up Intelligence, the one stat necessary to have deciphered the map in the first place. It was the core stat for his primary class, too.

He stared at the prompt a long time, but finally gritted his teeth and chose YES. This was going to hurt. He had the bare minimum Intelligence necessary to use the map in the first place, but he had to know where this map led. He had to know if he'd been right.

Suddenly, he felt nothing but pressure, like the entire world was pushing in on him. Flashes of lights and color bombarded him, even with his eyes closed. He felt the brush of catastrophe a number of times. He wasn't quite sure what was going on, but he knew he was barely avoiding death. He hoped his Luck stat would be enough.

The map had been meant for the transport of a player twice his level, after all.

Eventually, the colors stopped spinning and Vale opened his eyes. He was greeted with the sight of an enormous, ethereal tree.

"Yes, I was right!" He whooped with joy.

He stood on a walkway leading directly into the World Tree.

To his left was the aspect of Autumn, the surrounding forest, all shades of honey gold and red. To his right was the aspect of Spring, trees dripping with lush vegetation and radiating the vibrant glow of life. Majestic mountains loomed in the distance, framing the World Tree like supplicants.

He slowly walked forward, giddy from his success. He had no idea what to expect. Over the last year, players had heard rumors of the World Tree, but nobody had found it. Vale was the first.

He stepped into the tree and got a flashing prompt:

Congratulations!

You have found the fabled World Tree!

You have a choice...of Power!

The World Tree is ancient and must gift some of its power!

Choose between:

Fire – +Strength +Intelligence

Air – +Agility +Intelligence

Water – +Willpower +Intelligence

Earth – +Stamina +Intelligence

Upon your choice you will receive:

-A Legendary class

-A legendary, elemental magic skill (required, takes one skill slot)

*Please note that this magic skill can be used without affecting player sanity.

*(Does not require a Willpower check)

-Additional awarded XP

-Additional stat points allocated

Do you wish to accept this power?

Vale chose YES.

Choose your Element

Each element can be chosen once by one person

The World Tree's energy only grows to this level every 1000 years

Vale thought carefully. He'd been working on his character being something of a gentleman scholar with a magical flair, and he decided to stick with that. He also didn't like the idea of choosing Water, although it would have been a good element for him too.

He chose AIR and all hell broke loose.

Stat points awarded

400,000 XP earned

Level Up!

Level Up!

New title earned: Legendary Air Adept

New legendary class earned: Air Adept

System Alert! Vale dePardon has found the World Tree. Vale dePardon is the Legendary Air Adept of Secret of the Old Ones!

Mandatory skill awarded

It was all a little overwhelming at first, but Vale quickly grasped what was happening. He grinned as he allocated his two stat points from gaining two levels and examined his new character sheet. All his health, mana, and stamina were maxed out again. He'd gotten lucky too. His new attribute points from his new class were applied before he leveled up so he'd gained more mana per level.

Name: Vale dePardon

Class: Occultist

Subclass: Explorer

Hero Class: *At level 20*

Legendary Class: Air Adept

Level: 12

Experience: 940542

XP to next level: 69458

Stamina: 59/59

HP 59/59

Mana: 90/90

Stats: (Total/Original/Level Ups/Bonuses)

Strength: 4/2/2/0

Agility: 10/3/4/3

Stamina: 5/4/1/0

Intelligence: 10/7/0/3

Willpower: 6/6/0/0

Luck: 16/8/5/3

Class Skills: Fencing, Ancient Body Magic, Paranoia, Ancient Occult Lore, Map Reading/Cartography, **Elemental Magic: Air**

Permanent Bonus Source: Mystic Clover (Luck +3), World Tree Tithe

(Int -5), World Tree Boon (Int +8, Agi +3)

Smiling from ear to ear, he called up his [Ancient Occult Lore] activation menu.

Do you wish to return?

Vale chose YES, and the World Tree instantly teleported him back to his dank cellar. His eyes glowed as he mentally went through the list of all his new abilities. It was all amazing, completely amazing. He'd made back the Intelligence he'd sacrificed and then some.

Giving up that five Intelligence hadn't been easy. In retrospect, he figured it'd been a test to determine if he was a real Explorer or something. If he'd been wrong about where the map took him, he would have been screwed.

He immediately folded the precious map and decided he needed to hide it as soon as possible. There were three more elements that the World Tree could give. He had to decide whether to gift them to friends or sell the knowledge. Each element would probably be worth over a million US dollars, but he'd have to sell them all at once. After someone else got an element, he would no longer be the only player that knew how to get to the World Tree.

He was tired, but he got moving. First things first, he had to loot Brutus's body. After being stalked for so long by the huge psycho, it was going to be super satisfying to sell all his gear. He'd have to find an NPC with decent rates, though. No players would touch it.

Brutus was scary even while he was dead.

Vale knew he was one of the most powerful players in the entire game now. Unfortunately, because of the system alert, the rest of the world knew it too.

Let them come.

Delvers LLC: Obligations Incurred

CHAPTER TWO

Wanted

Trent tried to pay attention in class, but ultimately gave up. He couldn't fight the inevitable; he had way too much on his mind.

His virtual university classroom didn't have the same level of realism as *Secret of the Old Ones*, but it was still fairly immersive. Everyone in the class looked as they did in real life. Avatars and cosmetic alterations were not allowed.

The professor droned on, displaying incredible skill. The man could somehow even make Astronomy boring, a subject Trent cared about deeply.

Trent secretly smiled as he overheard one of the other students whispering about Vale dePardon. SOO was such a popular game, important news was even more highly regarded internationally than the largest e-sports.

The whole world knew the name of Trent's in-game avatar. It was a strange feeling knowing that his virtual self was so famous.

Trent still had to figure out what he was going to do with his hard-won knowledge, though. Should he procure real-world money, or in-game favors?

The decision was even more complicated due to how so many players actually made money by selling items in-game. The line between wealth in the virtual world and wealth in the real world was a bit fuzzy.

Part of the problem was that Trent wasn't sure how he could sell such expensive information at once, nor even what path to take. There were websites dedicated to trading things in-game for real money, but they were all third party and relied heavily on trust. One player sent money, the other player met the paying party in-game to give them what they paid for.

This worked fine for most items, but for information worth a fortune, it would be risky.

Trent tapped his finger on his virtual desk while he thought. The feeling wasn't quite as satisfying as tapping a real desk. Still, if any of his classmates looked at him, he knew they'd see him exactly as he looked in real life; just shy of tall, dark hair, dark eyes, lean face, an air of wariness.

The virtual classroom perfectly captured the clothing he was wearing, too. He had on jeans, a t-shirt, and his Bluetooth-connected sneakers. Nothing fancy. He wasn't sure how his persocomp told the VR classroom what he was wearing, but it was hard to hide from something in your own head. He really wasn't sure why he needed to wear any clothes at all in the real world.

Whoever had built the VR infrastructure for private and public education had obviously not liked the idea of students hanging out at home naked while virtually attending class…or something.

Of course, students without persocomps, usually for religious reasons, and students who just wanted some social, face-to-face interaction went to the public pod facilities, but Trent usually couldn't be bothered. He wanted to log into SOO as soon as he was done with class.

He also hated public restrooms.

After class was done, Trent logged out. He glanced around his little dorm room before sitting up in bed and rubbing his eyes. He knew some people liked to Dive while sitting, but Trent preferred to lie down.

He knew some people thought colleges should do away with dorm rooms since classes were virtual, but Trent actually enjoyed staying in a dorm. If he wasn't living in student housing, he probably wouldn't have any in-person friends at all. The birth rate for the world was down enough, too. He agreed with the politicians who said that young people should still actually interact with other—Trent just didn't like to do so too often.

He got up and poured himself a drink while he thought about what he should do in-game. He needed to hydrate before Diving anyway, so he sipped his sports drink while thinking about the game itself.

Secret of the Old Ones, the second global deep dive VR game (DDVRG) was a multiplayer RPG with some very distinct differences from other games.

One of its greatest strengths was its realism. Players could not differentiate between *Secret of the Old Ones* and reality other than the in-game mechanics. It was even more immersive than *Strength and Magic Online* had been.

The first DDVRG, *Strength and Magic Online,* had been a revolutionary experience. For almost forty years before SMO was created, various companies had tinkered with deep dive VR tech. The gaming industry had always been huge, and it didn't take a genius to understand how much money truly immersive gaming could make.

One of the greatest hurdles developers had to overcome was hardware constraints. VR headsets and haptic suits had become incredibly advanced, but still couldn't offer a full deep dive experience. It wasn't until the invention of the persocomp, a personal computer link implanted in the brain, that true deep dive VR was possible. Plus, the United World Council's decision that a persocomp was a human right was a godsend for gamers.

Strength and Magic Online had been revolutionary, the greatest game made for its time. However, *Secret of the Old Ones*, or SOO had surpassed it in every way.

The design decision by Yggdrasil Entertainment to build its new game in an HP Lovecraft-style horror universe had made some early industry pundits scratch their heads. That was before the game came out. The emphasis on personal skills and learning, the difficulty in leveling, the compelling world and quests…it was all amazing.

Trent personally loved the game's setting. It was the perfect mix of fantasy, horror, and the familiar. Players who didn't like the combat aspect could play a largely social game in towns and cities. Meanwhile, power gamers like Trent could explore ancient ruins, poking around for buried treasure.

Trent suddenly realized he'd killed his sports drink. He knew he'd have to pee eventually, but luckily, his persocomp slowed most of his body's processes to a crawl after Diving.

He reclined on his bed and decided to visit a market while Diving. He still had all of Brutus's shit to sell.

***

Like always, Diving was a riot of colors and sensations. It almost felt like an out-of-body experience, like being connected to the universe. Trent tried to keep his mind as calm as possible. He didn't want to be one of those people who acted high their first 30 minutes in-game after Diving.

***

Trent found himself back in his body as Vale dePardon. He'd logged out before on the outskirts of one of his favorite towns, so he only had a short trip to the market. He'd already stashed his precious map. The map itself acted as a mystical anchor in the game. He couldn't just get away with memorizing the information it held.

He couldn't chance it being stolen if he was killed. Hiding things was always a risk in SOO because anything hidden could be found, but more experienced players like Vale all had special stash spots.

Vale smiled grimly. Anyone who went after his stash spot would get a very nasty surprise.

He trudged forward, his loot sack so full it actually felt heavy. Compressed packs were one way the creatures of SOO had bent reality that Vale was deeply thankful for. Lugging gear and loot around in wheelbarrows would not have been very immersive or dignified.

Eventually, Vale cut across one last field and found himself on the main road into Gabenz, a coastal town, and one of his favorite places to trade. In-game, it was near sunset, and the town's buildings made an interesting backdrop against the multicolored sky.

He made his way through familiar back alleys, dodging other players and troublesome NPCs alike. He didn't feel like dealing with an encounter or learning of a new quest. He was here to make money.

Gabenz was a coastal town, and most of the markets, the best markets known to adventurers, were near the docks. Trent continued to keep a close eye out, warily watching shifty men in top hats and ladies in bustles go about their business.

Vale ruefully thought about how easy it was to tell female players from NPCs. Most modern women hated bustles and petticoats. There were some hardcore role-players or female gamers who liked how they looked enough to put up with the inconveniences, though. The thought sobered Vale. There were plenty of female assassins.

His head was on a swivel as he grew even more paranoid. It wasn't too much longer until he got to the docks and the fringe of the commercial district.

Vale cautiously passed couples arm in arm, nearing the location of one of his favorite NPC fences. However, as he turned a corner, a piece of paper caught his eye. It said, "WANTED!" and it had a picture of his face.

Oh fuck.

Vale jumped as he heard a voice behind him say, "Just keep walking. Don't turn around or things will get really bad, really fast."

Vale didn't move at first until he felt the barrel of a pistol pressed into his back. "Go straight, right up into that alley up ahead. We wouldn't want to involve the town constables in any unpleasantness, right?" Vale heard laughter from at least a couple other people.

How had he missed them? He took a mental step back. His face was probably plastered all over town. If groups were actively looking for him, they could be sneakier than he was being vigilant, or they could be using special skills.

Vale was not in a good position, not at all.

Oh fuck, indeed.

CHAPTER THREE

Slaughter Alley

Vale slowly plodded forward, his mind racing. He wasn't sure if his ambushers were after the World Tree map, or whether they were just trying to score a bounty. Their motivations were important. If they were just after a bounty, they wouldn't expect him to risk a week of logout time by resisting. Most players were very cautious about dying after the first time they got locked out for a week and had all their gear stolen.

On the other hand, if the bastards behind Vale were just after a bounty, using his new magic to escape would spread like wildfire in the rumor mill—if any saw it and lived to tell about it. Getting locked out would prevent that, though. The only hope he had was to kill every single person who saw him use his new abilities.

Players could not post from verified accounts while locked out. The TOS of SOO forbade players from talking about events leading to their death while they were still dead too. Yggdrasil

449

Entertainment enforced their rules with an iron fist. Most players were smart enough not to risk being banned.

Vale's mind raced. Every possible thing his attackers could be planning ran through his head, checklist style. They could be planning to restrain him, or run a trace to find out who he really was, or try torturing him for information.

Torture of a kind did work in SOO. Of course, a player could always choose to log out, to stop Diving, to Surface. However, if a player Surfaced while in the middle of combat or conflict, they had 20 minutes to return or they would automatically die.

Most players thought the system was fair. Players who didn't want to engage in dangerous situations usually stayed away from them, and if a player didn't want to play anymore, they could log off. The penalty kept it from being abused.

The possibility that most worried Vale was the trace. He was just a poor college kid. He wasn't completely naïve. He knew that there were some people in the world who would be willing track him down in real life to get his secrets. There were quite a few individuals and several businesses that made a very lucrative profit off SOO, after all.

In fact, Vale had even been thinking about exploring ways to monetize his own play time in the next couple days. Of course, that might not happen for at least a week if he ended up dying.

As he walked into the alley ahead of his captors, Vale's heart sunk and his hand itched. He desperately wished he had room to draw his rapier. At the other end of the alley was another set of seedy characters. There were three of them in all, each of them grinning nastily.

Vale's pulse quickened. The rope held by one of the men in the alley meant the group was probably trying to collect on his bounty. He wasn't sure if the bounty had been created by someone who wanted to know about the World Tree, or by Brutus himself; maybe both. The man was locked out of the game for a week, but he obviously had connections.

Time seemed to slow down as Vale examined his options. He had his Rapier of Twilight, a decent enchanted weapon, two fire-enchanted throwing darts, and a crossbow in his pack that would not do him much good.

He had Ancient Body Magic, which would be helpful, but also taxed his Willpower. However, now he had his [Elemental Magic: Air] skill. He wasn't sure how much mana its spells would eat up, but like all magic in SOO, he could dump more mana into abilities in order to make them stronger.

He carefully examined his spell list and began to inwardly smile. He had a plan.

He walked forward a few more paces with his hands up, appearing to go peacefully to his capture. He figured there were at least three behind him, so he was facing six enemies at once, at a minimum. He needed to free himself from his enemies at the rear, especially if there were more than three.

When he was about halfway down the alley, he shrugged off his loot sack and used [Elemental Magic: Air] to cast <Gust> on himself from behind. He only put one mana point into the spell, as much to test the strength of his magic as to give himself some space from his attackers.

His eyes widened as the spell shoved him forward almost ten feet, practically into the second group. All his attackers began yelling. He spared a glance behind him, laying eyes on the three scruffy people who'd gotten the drop on him earlier. He snarled and cast <Gust> again, this time cranking up the power to seven mana.

The three thugs were bowled over like nine-pins, the powerful spell almost throwing them out of the alley. He barely turned in time to draw his rapier and block an attack by the first goon to reach him. Vale grinned, the expression showing all his teeth. He shoved with his free hand, casting <Gust> again for three mana.

As the second group tumbled back onto their butts, he checked his mana.

Mana: 79/90

He had used up eleven mana. Vale took a gamble and used [Ancient Body Magic] to cast <Arm Speed>, <Leg Speed>, and <Enhanced Reflexes>. He only used two points of mana for each spell, effectively raising his stats by three points in agility and his [Fencing] skill by an amount that was too difficult to calculate.

Natural stats were king, and Vale was already running a natural ten in Agility. His spell brought him up to around thirteen points in Agility, plus several combat bonuses that he couldn't see on his stat sheet, but he knew were there.

The first man to get up in front of him was a big, burly guy with a beard. He held a practical short sword and parrying dagger. Unfortunately for him, his dagger hand was on the ground as he pushed himself up. Vale lunged forward, the tip of his rapier punching through the man's mouth and out the back of his head, killing him instantly.

Vale's eyes narrowed in satisfaction. This was why he built towards speed and precision. Strength fighters like Brutus were terrifying, but there was something to be said for expert precision in SOO, just like real life.

Another man was up and rushed Vale with a couple nasty-looking hooked weapons. They were probably some sort of nautical drops. One glittered with enchantment.

Vale dodged one slash. He caught the man's second attack on the forte of his blade, riposting with a thrust to the chest. The Rapier of Twilight's keen tip punched through the ruffian's light leather armor with almost no resistance at all, destroying his heart and exiting out his back.

He kicked the stunned, dying man off his sword into the wall and stalked past him. *Two down*, he thought.

The last bandit before him was female, little more than a girl. Vale's thoughts turned cold and dispassionate. *She should not have fucked with a Legendary Class scholar having a bad day.*

The girl drew a couple throwing daggers, but her movements were glacially slow to Vale. He almost casually whipped his rapier in a glittering arc, the last two inches neatly severing the girl's carotid artery. Her hands reflexively went to her throat, dropping her daggers. To be thorough, Vale lowered his center of gravity and stabbed her through the diaphragm at an upward angle.

The girl died, her eyes clouding over, but her last expression was one of defiance and anger. *She died well. Probably a serious PVP gamer.* Vale respected that.

He turned towards the last three threats and sprinted towards the closest to him, a man with a mustache. The man's pale skin was heavily tattooed; his bare scalp sported some sort of occult sigils. The man growled, "You must think you're really hot shit but—"

I wonder why so many of these predatory types want to waste time talking? Vale danced to the side and tried to get a clean, killing thrust, but the man was too experienced. With a start, Vale realized he was the person who had demanded he march to the alley. He was probably their leader.

The bandit muttered something before holding a hand out that began glowing red. *Shit.* Vale dove to the side and barely had room in the alley to dodge the fire-ball. The thug leader obviously had some skill in magic, probably [Ancient Thermal Magic]. It was a popular type of magic for mercenaries, fighters, and other feisty players.

Vale didn't want to give the man a chance to get off another spell. He tucked a hand into his vest, and threw one of his darts in one smooth motion. The mustachioed, tattooed man had his long dagger's blade up, but he had no time to react. The dart took him right through the bridge of the mouth, the heavy steel spraying broken bits of teeth.

The man stumbled backward, snorting in anguish. Vale put him out of his misery with a precise thrust through the heart.

The last two bandits, a tall, older man and a middle-aged woman, both gaped in fear. The woman held up a percussion lock pistol in a shaking hand. Vale could actually see the hammer falling as she pulled the trigger. He dodged to the side, hoping he correctly judged where the bullet would fly. A cloud of gun smoke filled the alley, and Vale didn't feel a gaping hole in his body. Either he'd been right, or he'd gotten lucky. Either way, he'd take it.

Through the smoke, he saw the tall man with pinched features begin running away. The woman with the pistol still had it extended; the now empty gun kept shaking until she dropped it.

Vale whipped his hand forward with his last enchanted throwing dart while running forward. The dart nailed the woman in the sternum and she burst into flames. *Must have been a critical,* thought Vale.

The woman was thrashing around, dying as the fire ticked

away her remaining hit points. Vale kicked her down to the ground and stabbed her through the chest to put her out of her misery.

"Don't shoot at me again," he muttered as he ran past.

The tall man was almost to the end of the alley and relative safety, but Vale was too fast. He was easily three times faster than the last would-be bounty hunter. When the man was only a few feet from the mouth of the alley, Vale crippled his legs with an economical flick of his rapier. The man slammed to the ground and Vale stomped down on the man's back—hard.

The man tried to scream, but he had no air in his lungs. It didn't stop him from trying to draw a pistol, though. Vale snarled and thought, *What is it with these people and pistols? They're actually hard to use...*

He cocked his arm back and slammed his blade into the back of the man's skull. The tall man's body stiffened and grew limp beneath Vale's foot. He snarled in disgust. He really didn't like PVP. Why couldn't other players leave him the fuck alone?

He looked up and down the alley at the carnage and the strewn bodies. He checked his mana again.

Mana: 73/90

He had just killed six other players in decent gear, probably between level seven to nine. He had only used up seventeen mana, and he hadn't even gotten a scratch. He'd probably overspent a lot of mana. He needed to learn to optimize his [Elemental Magic: Air] skill better.

He whistled soundlessly at all the gear just asking to be taken. "Well, if it's just lying around…" he grumbled. He wasn't going to enjoy carrying everything in his loot sack, but at least it was only a short distance to his favorite fence.

***

"2,142 gold! Holy crap!" Vale exclaimed. He'd had a good haul indeed. The shady merchant just smiled. Vale had no doubt the unctuous man would make a killing reselling all the gear. Well, he would have if he wasn't an NPC. The NPC's name was Vernon Carlsmit, a name Vale always thought was a bit over the top.

Suddenly the shady merchant Vernon leaned forward and winked conspiratorially. "You've been a good customer to me, and I always see you wearing that pig sticker," he said, gesturing to Vale's rapier. "I actually heard about a weapon like that lost in some ruins some time back. A powerful one, too. It was probably nothing, but I can still tell you about it, though." The man guffawed.

In Vale's vision, a window popped up:

You have been offered a unique quest by an NPC due to your relationship with the shopkeep and your status as a Legendary class.

Do you accept the quest?

Well, that's a no-brainer. Vale chose YES.

Congratulations! You have started a quest for a legendary weapon!

Listen to the shopkeep's tale and watch for other opportunities to further this quest line!

Vale smiled as the sweating merchant began telling his story.

***

Trent was in the great mood when he logged out and Surfaced. His mood lasted right up until he checked his messages on his persocomp and saw several missed calls from his best friend Steve. The latest just said, <Seriously, watch the news.>

Vale was confused. Steve knew that Trent played as Vale, but he'd already seen almost everything the media was saying about him; most of it was just speculation.

However, after Vale used his persocomp to generate a telescreen in his field of vision and turned to a news station, he cursed.

Most stations were playing in-game footage from two hours ago. The FPR, first-person-recorded, video had caught a very pissed off looking Vale dePardon utterly dismantling the criminal bounty hunters in an alley.

"Well…shit."

This is the end of the sample.

Thank you for spending time with me!

-BC

73927035R00261

Made in the USA
Middletown, DE
18 May 2018